POPULARMMOs

Popular MMOS (aka Pat) is one of the most popular YouTubers in the world. Pat and Jen (aka Gaming With Jen) created their *Minecraft*–inspired channel, PopularMMOs, in 2012. Since then, they have entertained millions of fans around the world with their gaming videos and original characters.

Pat and Jen live in Florida with their cat, Cloud. *PopularMMOS Presents: Zombies' Day Off* is their third book.

For Aunt Kim—D.J.

ZOMBIE PARK

TICKETS

A special thanks to Joe Caramagna
for all his creative help!

Popular MMOs Presents Zombies' Day Off Copyright © 2020 by Popular MMOs, LLC.
All rights reserved. Manufactured in Italy. No part of this book may be used or reproduced
in any manner whatsoever without written permission except in the case of brief
quotations embodied in critical articles and reviews. For information address
HarperCollins Children's Books, a division of HarperCollins Publishers,
195 Broadway, New York, NY 10007.
www.harpercollinschildrens.com

Library of Congress Control Number: 2020941016
ISBN 978-0-06-300651-5 (trade bdg.) — ISBN 978-0-06-304210-0 (special edition)
ISBN 978-0-06-304777-8 (special edition) — ISBN 978-0-06-307162-9 (special edition) — ISBN 978-0-06-300652-2 (pbk.)

The artist used an iPad Pro and the app Procreate to create the digital illustrations for this book.
Typography by Erica De Chavez 21 22 23 24 25 RTLO 10 9 8 7 6 5 4 3 2 1 ❖ First Edition

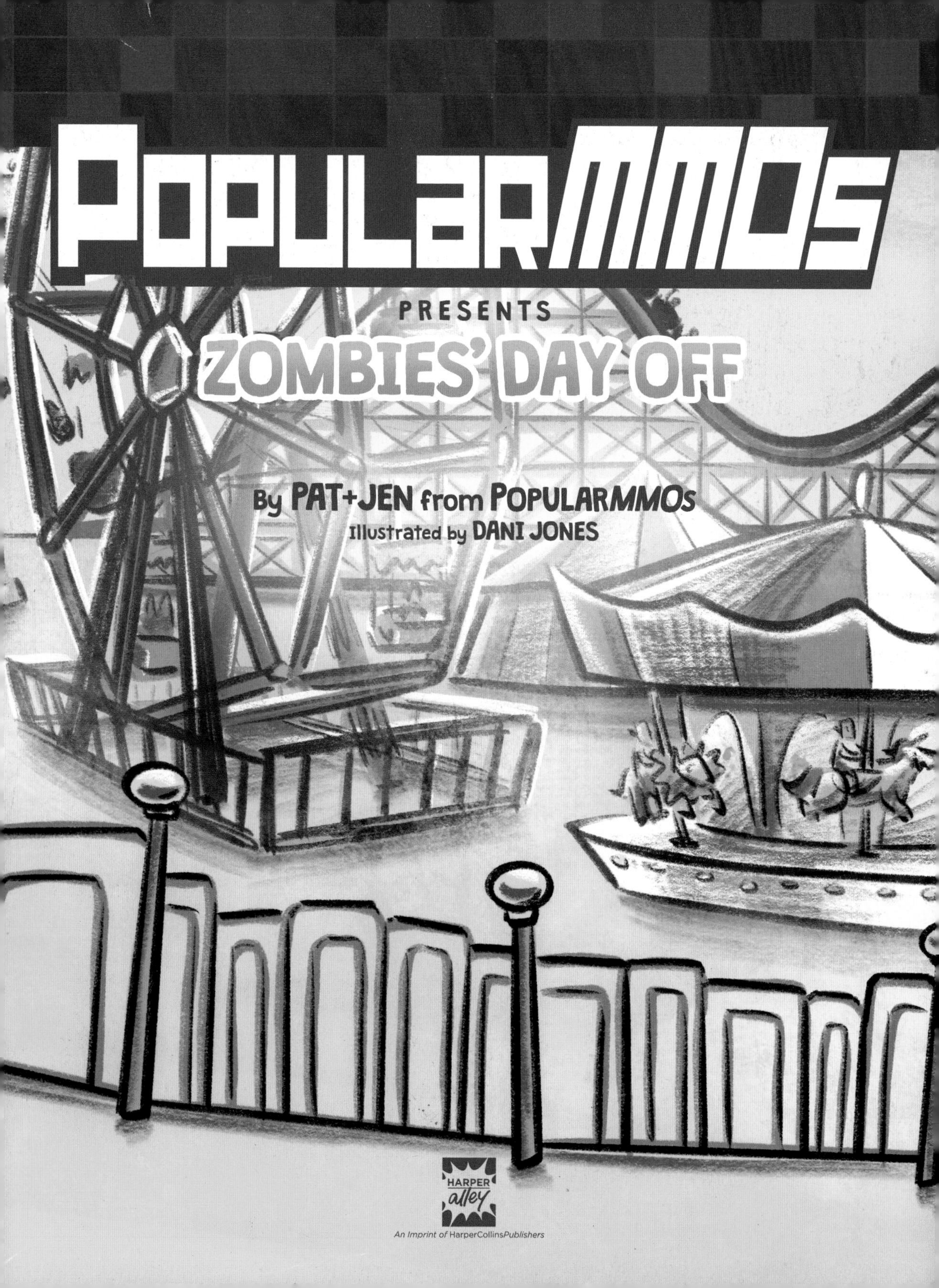

PopularMMOs

PRESENTS

ZOMBIES' DAY OFF

By PAT+JEN from POPULARMMOs

Illustrated by DANI JONES

HARPER alley

An Imprint of HarperCollinsPublishers

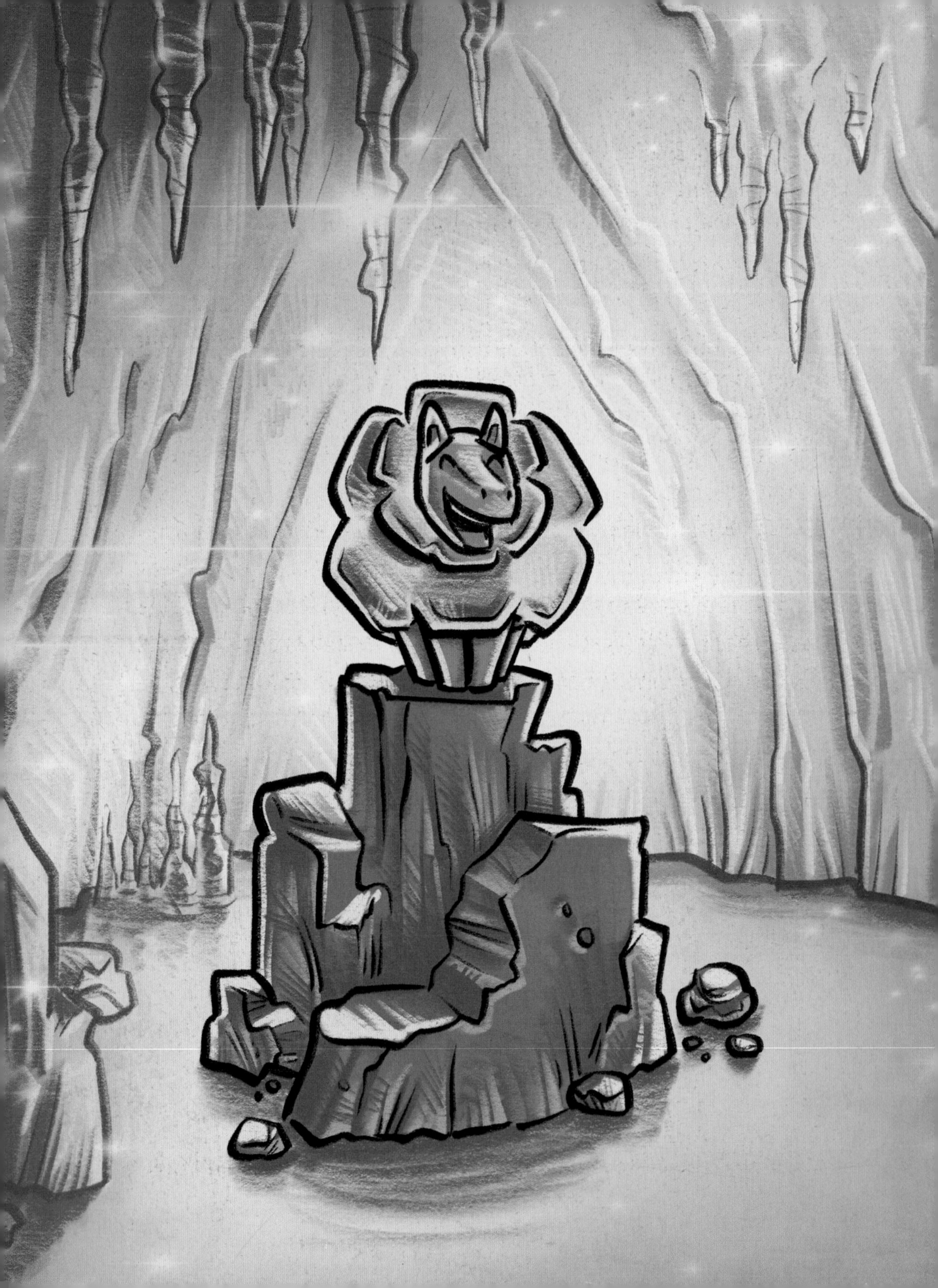

Welcome back, guys!

We can't believe it's our third book! We've already fallen into bottomless holes, battled vicious zombies, and blown up mountains, but we're back now for what might be our greatest adventure yet—to find out the truth about Jen's family. Of course, to do that, we'll have to visit a zombie amusement park, battle Herobrine, and use more TNT than we've ever done before. It's a story unlike any we've ever told, and we're so thrilled that you've decided to come along for the adventure. (And we do love adventure!)

Anyway, we hope you enjoy the book. We made sure it was filled with all your favorite characters from our videos—plus a few new stars that you might not have seen before. What we love most about the world of PopularMMOs is that on YouTube and in our books, Jen and I get to go anywhere, do anything, be anyone—all we have to do is let ourselves imagine it for it to happen. We hope this book encourages you to do the same, to tell your own stories, dream up your own worlds. It's fun, and it's actually pretty easy—and it doesn't have to be perfect. It just has to be yours. Actually, honestly, that's the best part—it's all yours.

And with that, we welcome you to *Zombies' Day Off*. Enjoy!

—Pat & Jen

PAT & JEN

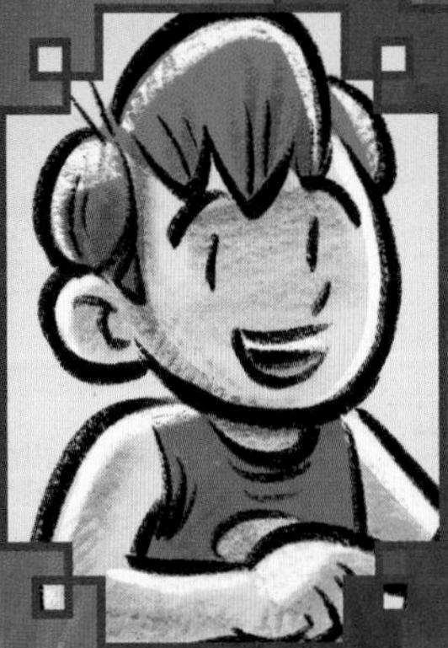

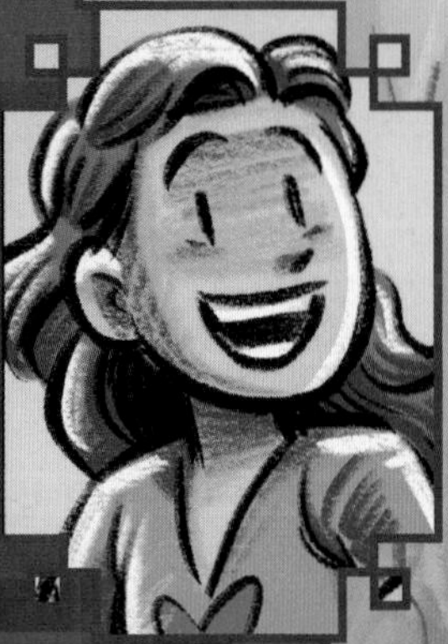

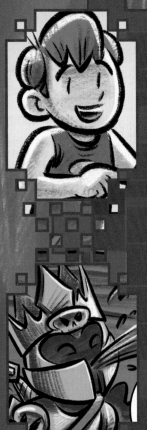

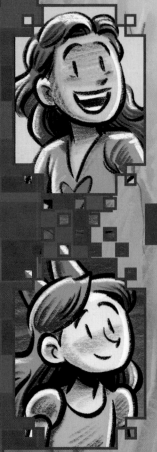

Pat is an awesome dude who's always looking for an epic adventure with his partner, the Super Girly Gamer Jen. Pat loves to have fun with his friends and take control of every situation with his cool weapons and can-do attitude. Jen is the sweetest person in the world and loves to laugh, but don't let her cheeriness fool you—she's also fierce. In fact, she could be an even greater adventurer than Pat . . . if she weren't so clumsy. Together, along with their cat, Cloud, they have a bond that can never be broken.

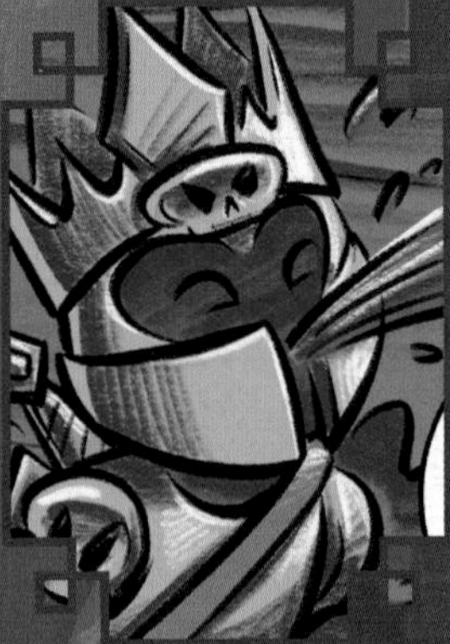

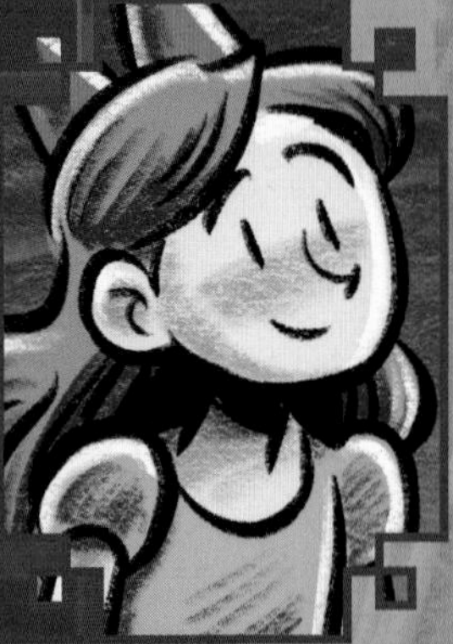

CARTER

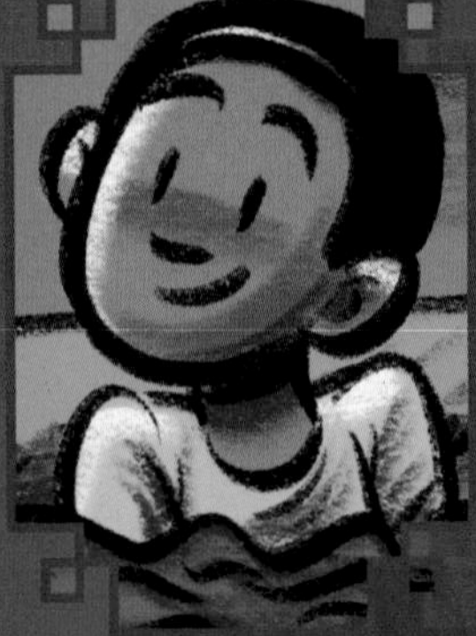

Carter is Jen's best friend and biggest fan, but he doesn't seem to like Pat very much at all. Carter is also not very smart and sometimes carries a pickle that he thinks is a green sword!

CAPTAIN COOKIE

No one is quite sure if Captain Cookie is a real sea captain or if he just dresses the part. He doesn't seem to be very good at anything, but that doesn't stop him from bragging about how great he is! He's rude to everyone he meets but always in a funny way.

EVIL JEN

Evil Jen's favorite thing is chaos. She lives for wreaking havoc on the world. What makes her truly evil, however, is that she would take someone as sweet as Jen and become an evil version of her. She even looks *exactly* like her (just don't tell Jen we said that!).

HEROBRINE

Herobrine longs to be the king of all realms. He's as evil as evil gets, and he'll stop at nothing to get what he wants. But Herobrine also has a secret that will change everything for Pat and Jen.

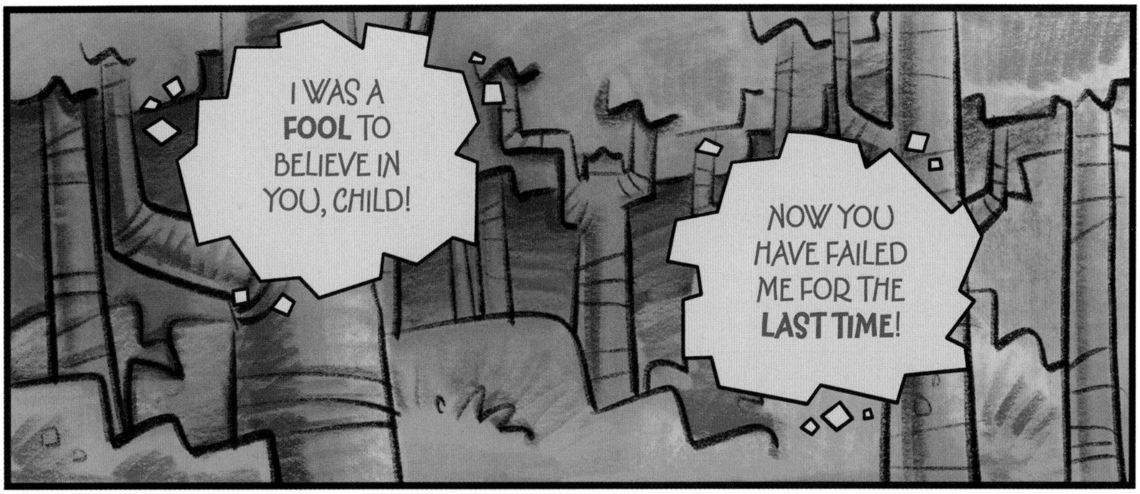
I WAS A FOOL TO BELIEVE IN YOU, CHILD!
NOW YOU HAVE FAILED ME FOR THE LAST TIME!

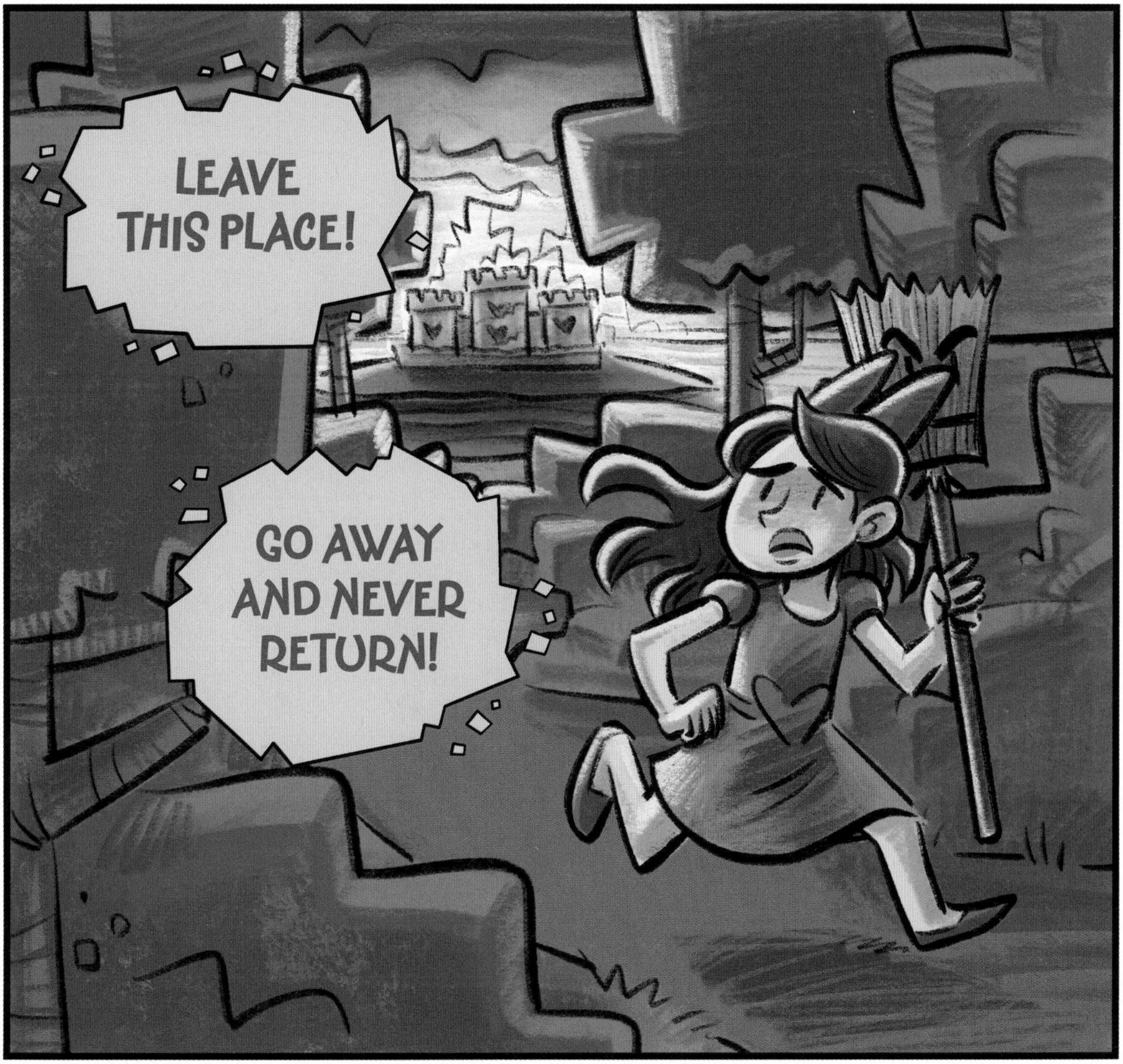
LEAVE THIS PLACE!
GO AWAY AND NEVER RETURN!

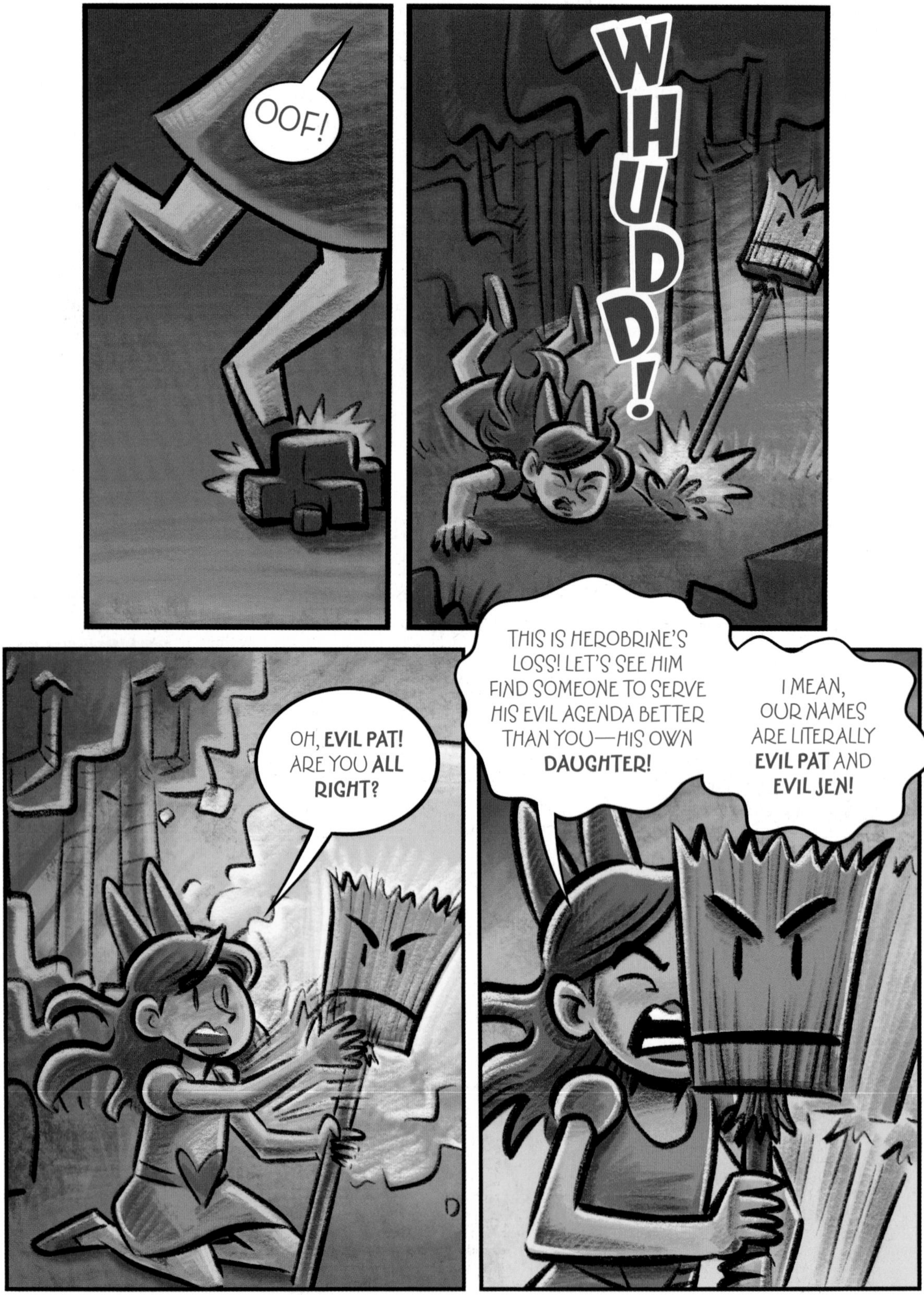
OOF!
WHUDD!
OH, **EVIL PAT!** ARE YOU **ALL RIGHT**?
THIS IS HEROBRINE'S LOSS! LET'S SEE HIM FIND SOMEONE TO SERVE HIS EVIL AGENDA BETTER THAN YOU—HIS OWN **DAUGHTER!**
I MEAN, OUR NAMES ARE LITERALLY **EVIL PAT** AND **EVIL JEN!**

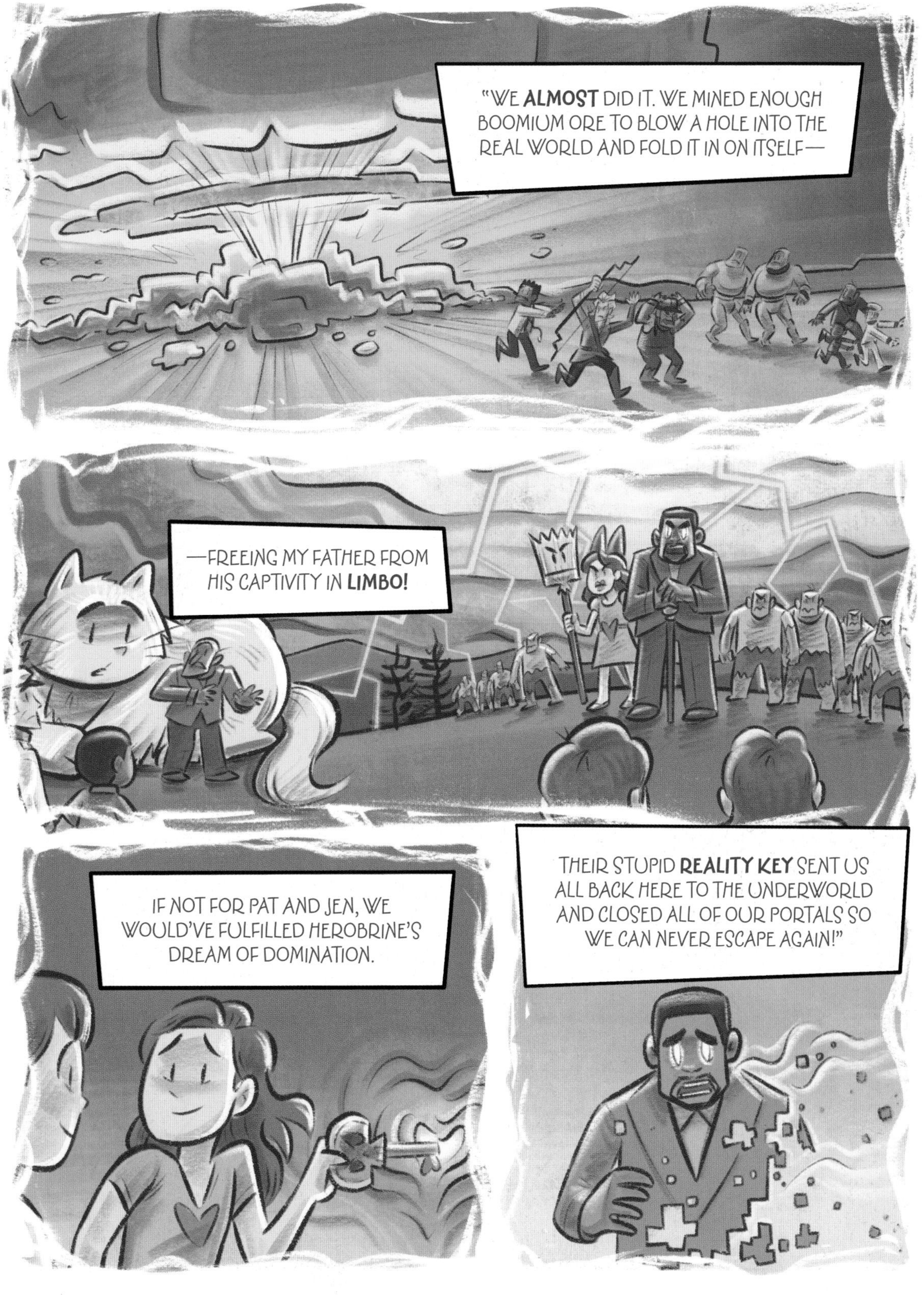
"WE ALMOST DID IT. WE MINED ENOUGH BOOMIUM ORE TO BLOW A HOLE INTO THE REAL WORLD AND FOLD IT IN ON ITSELF—
—FREEING MY FATHER FROM HIS CAPTIVITY IN LIMBO!
IF NOT FOR PAT AND JEN, WE WOULD'VE FULFILLED HEROBRINE'S DREAM OF DOMINATION.
THEIR STUPID REALITY KEY SENT US ALL BACK HERE TO THE UNDERWORLD AND CLOSED ALL OF OUR PORTALS SO WE CAN NEVER ESCAPE AGAIN!"

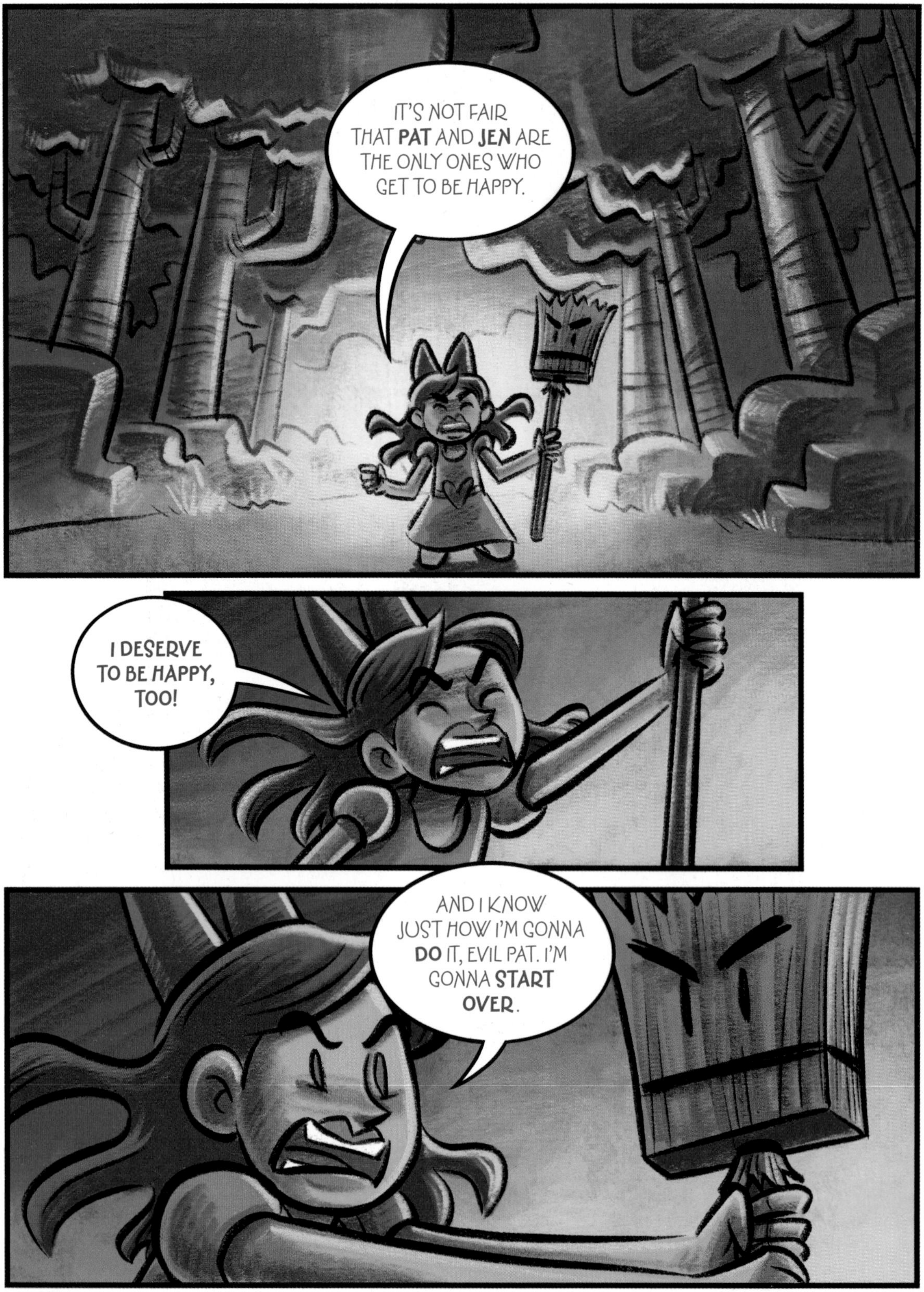
IT'S NOT FAIR THAT PAT AND JEN ARE THE ONLY ONES WHO GET TO BE HAPPY.
I DESERVE TO BE HAPPY, TOO!
AND I KNOW JUST HOW I'M GONNA DO IT, EVIL PAT. I'M GONNA START OVER.

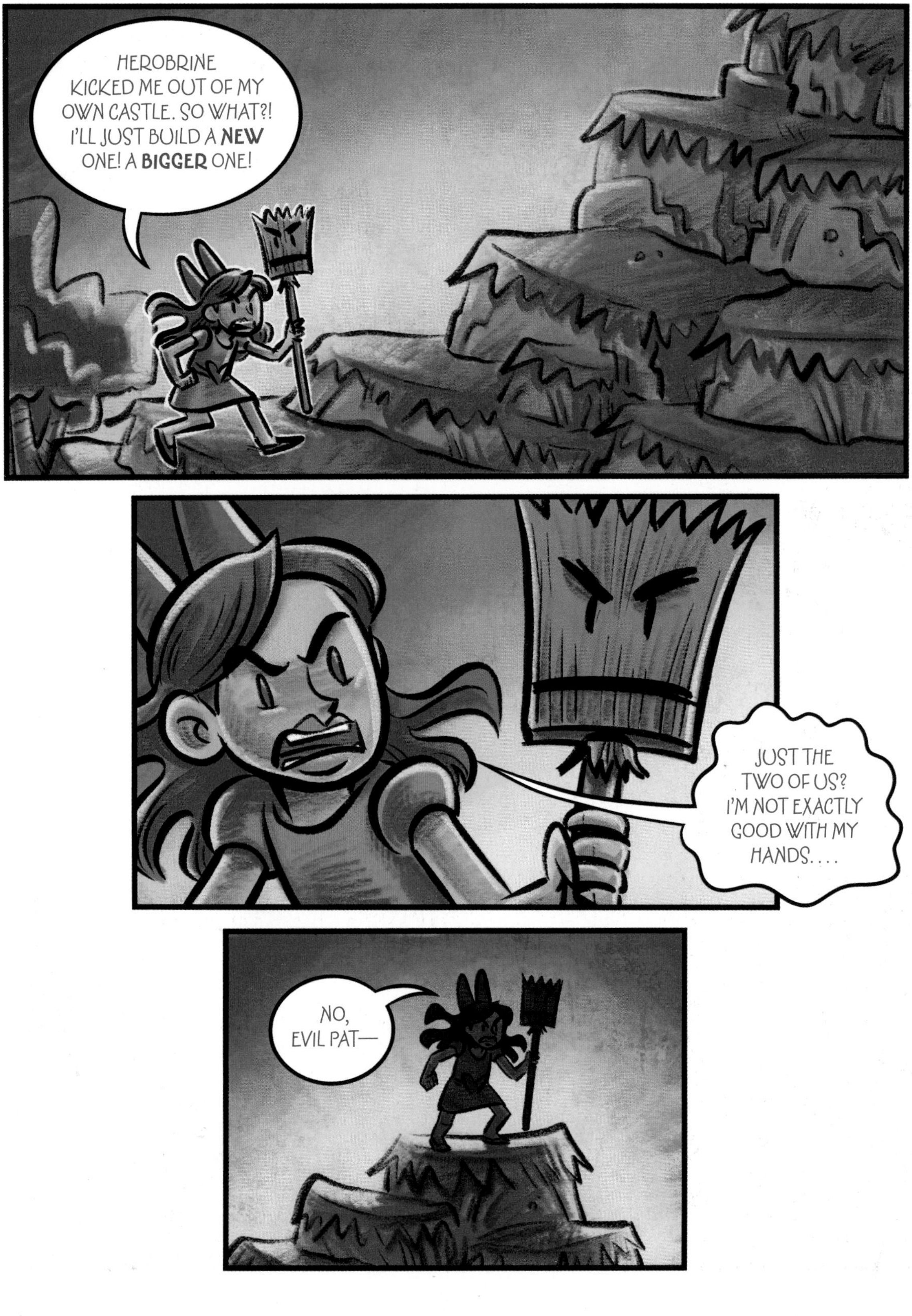
HEROBRINE KICKED ME OUT OF MY OWN CASTLE. SO WHAT?! I'LL JUST BUILD A **NEW** ONE! A **BIGGER** ONE!
JUST THE TWO OF US? I'M NOT EXACTLY GOOD WITH MY HANDS. . . .
NO, EVIL PAT—

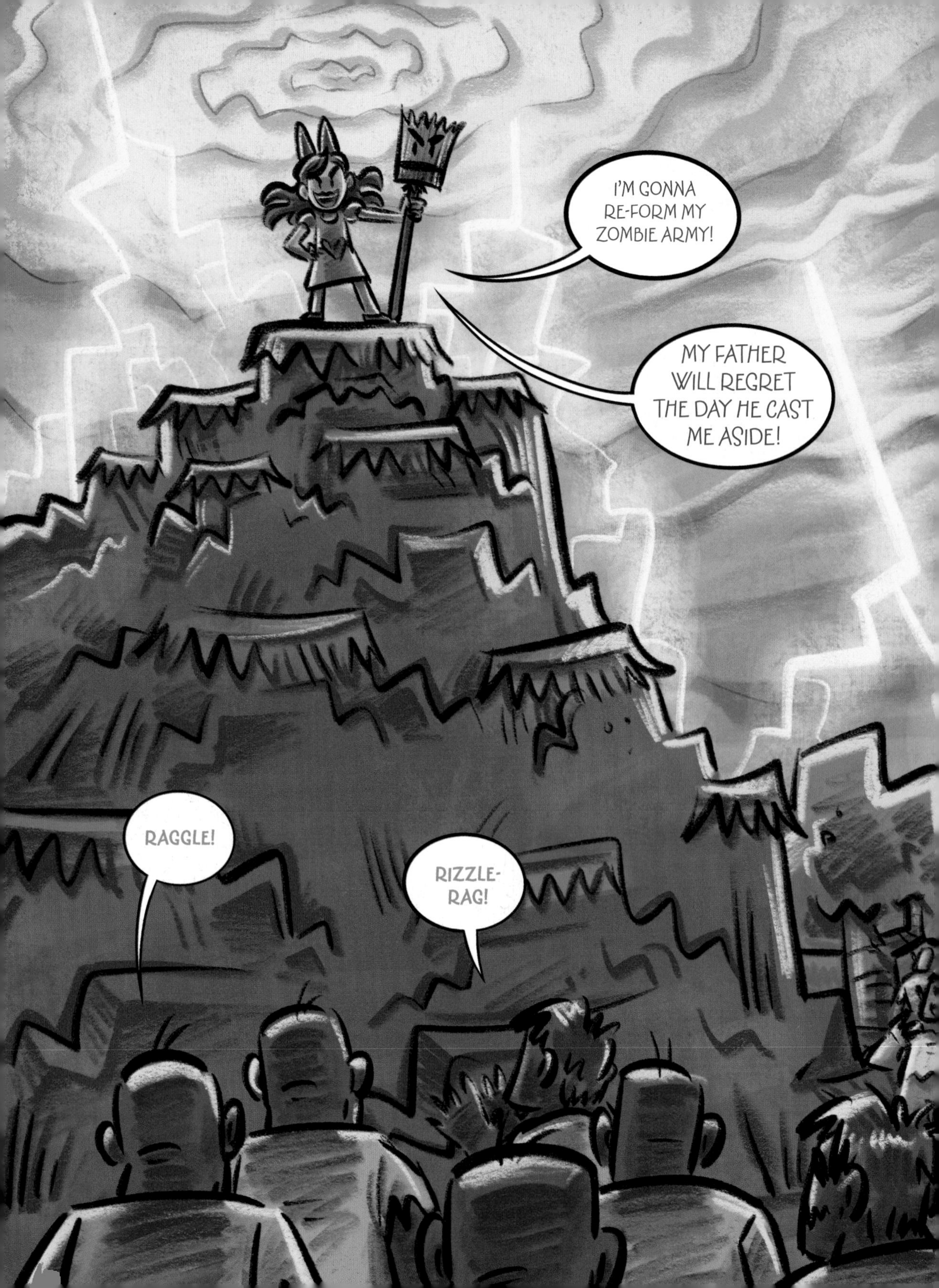
I'M GONNA RE-FORM MY ZOMBIE ARMY!
MY FATHER WILL REGRET THE DAY HE CAST ME ASIDE!
RAGGLE!
RIZZLE-RAG!

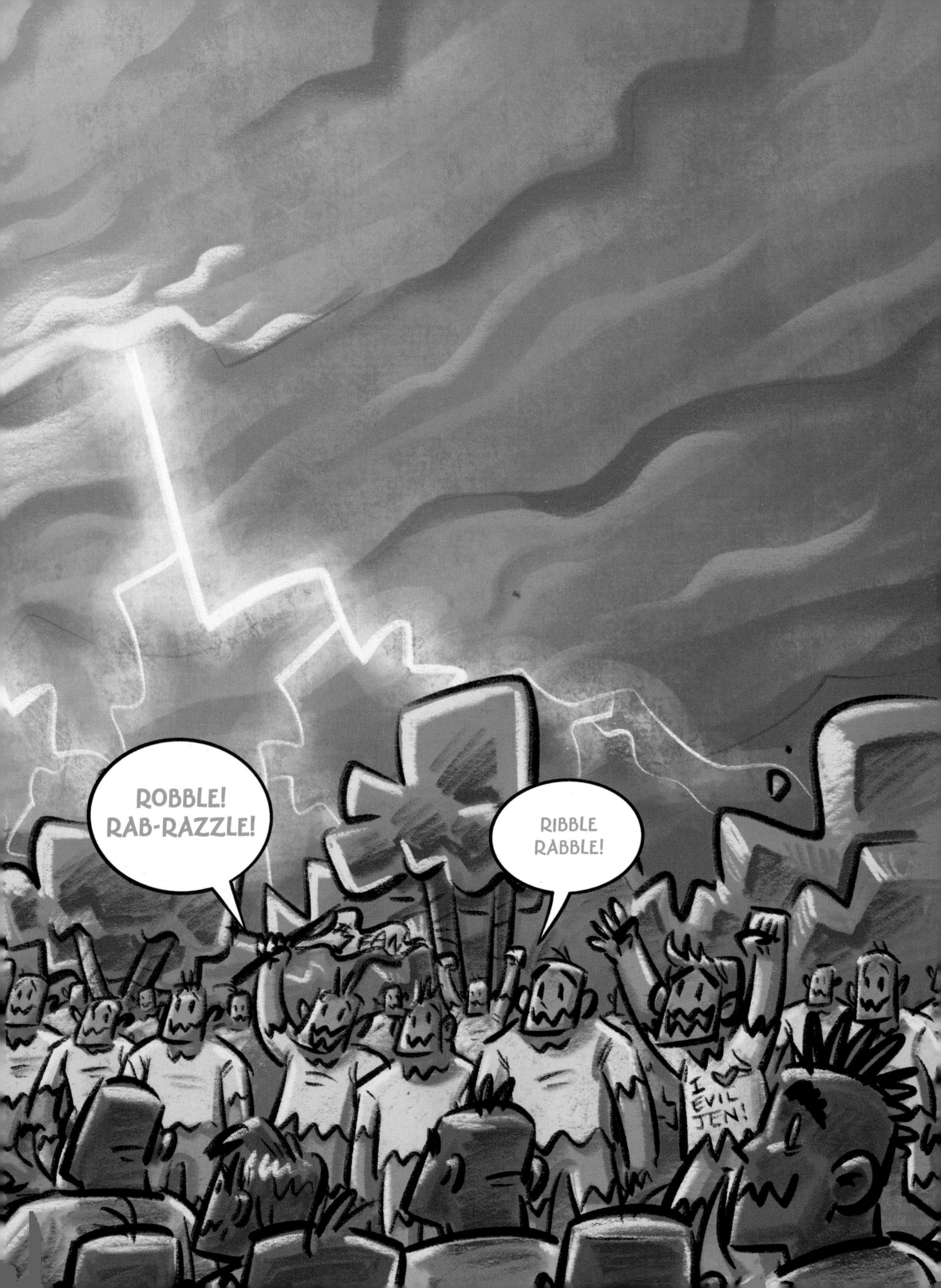
ROBBLE! RAB-RAZZLE!
RIBBLE RABBLE!
I ♥ EVIL JEN!

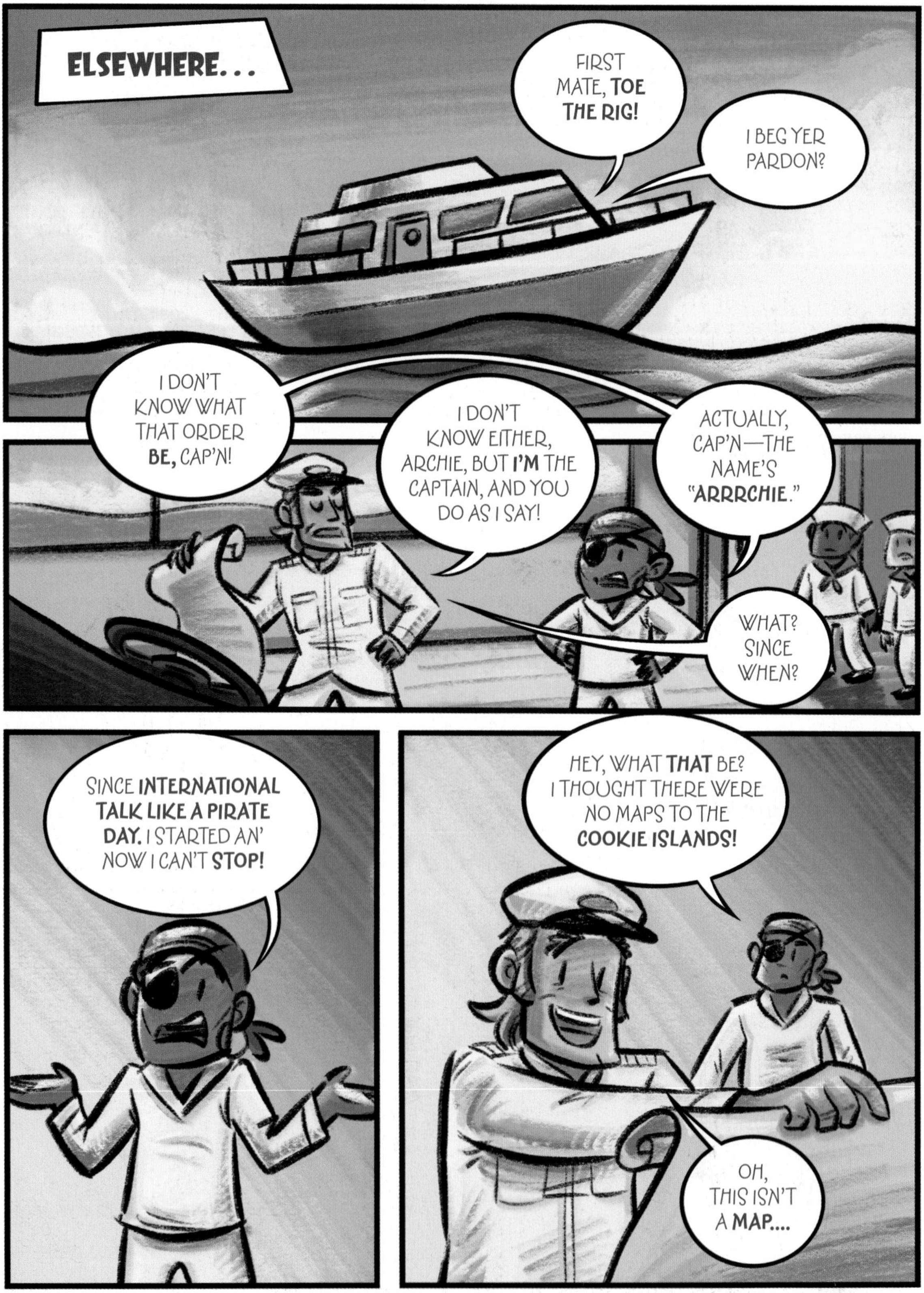
ELSEWHERE. . .
FIRST MATE, TOE THE RIG!
I BEG YER PARDON?
I DON'T KNOW WHAT THAT ORDER BE, CAP'N!
I DON'T KNOW EITHER, ARCHIE, BUT I'M THE CAPTAIN, AND YOU DO AS I SAY!
ACTUALLY, CAP'N—THE NAME'S "ARRRCHIE."
WHAT? SINCE WHEN?
SINCE INTERNATIONAL TALK LIKE A PIRATE DAY. I STARTED AN' NOW I CAN'T STOP!
HEY, WHAT THAT BE? I THOUGHT THERE WERE NO MAPS TO THE COOKIE ISLANDS!
OH, THIS ISN'T A MAP....

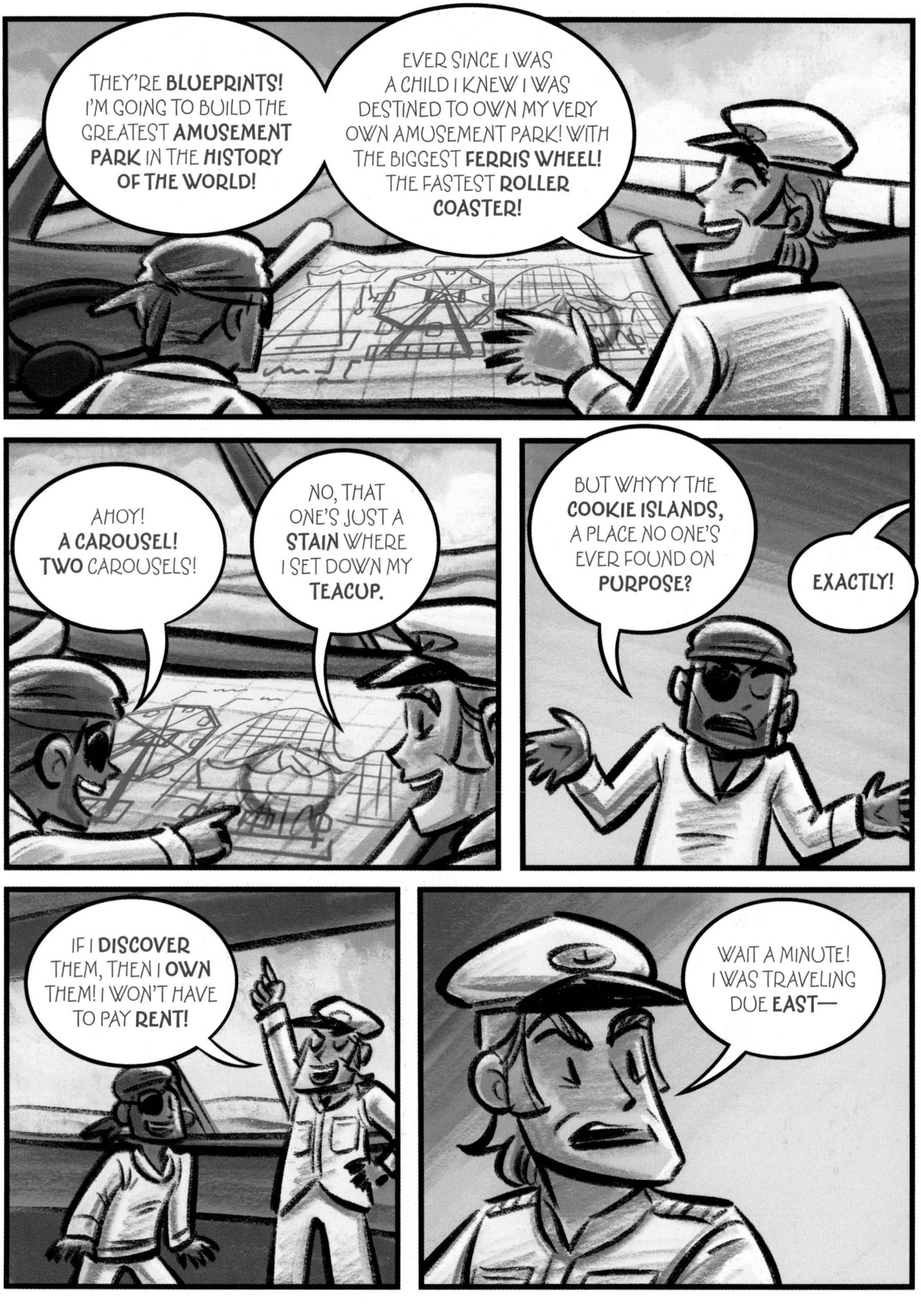
THEY'RE BLUEPRINTS! I'M GOING TO BUILD THE GREATEST AMUSEMENT PARK IN THE HISTORY OF THE WORLD!
EVER SINCE I WAS A CHILD I KNEW I WAS DESTINED TO OWN MY VERY OWN AMUSEMENT PARK! WITH THE BIGGEST FERRIS WHEEL! THE FASTEST ROLLER COASTER!
AHOY! A CAROUSEL! TWO CAROUSELS!
NO, THAT ONE'S JUST A STAIN WHERE I SET DOWN MY TEACUP.
BUT WHYYY THE COOKIE ISLANDS, A PLACE NO ONE'S EVER FOUND ON PURPOSE?
EXACTLY!
IF I DISCOVER THEM, THEN I OWN THEM! I WON'T HAVE TO PAY RENT!
WAIT A MINUTE! I WAS TRAVELING DUE EAST—

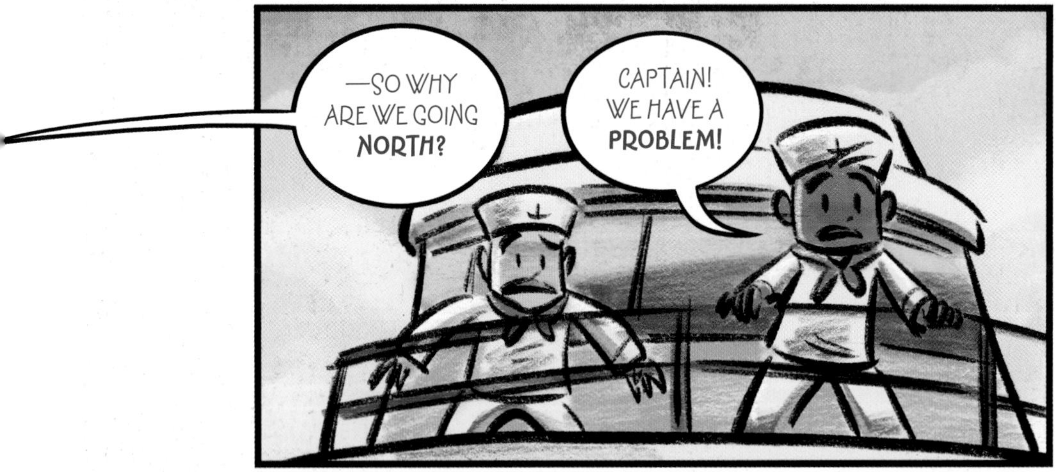
—SO WHY ARE WE GOING NORTH?
CAPTAIN! WE HAVE A PROBLEM!

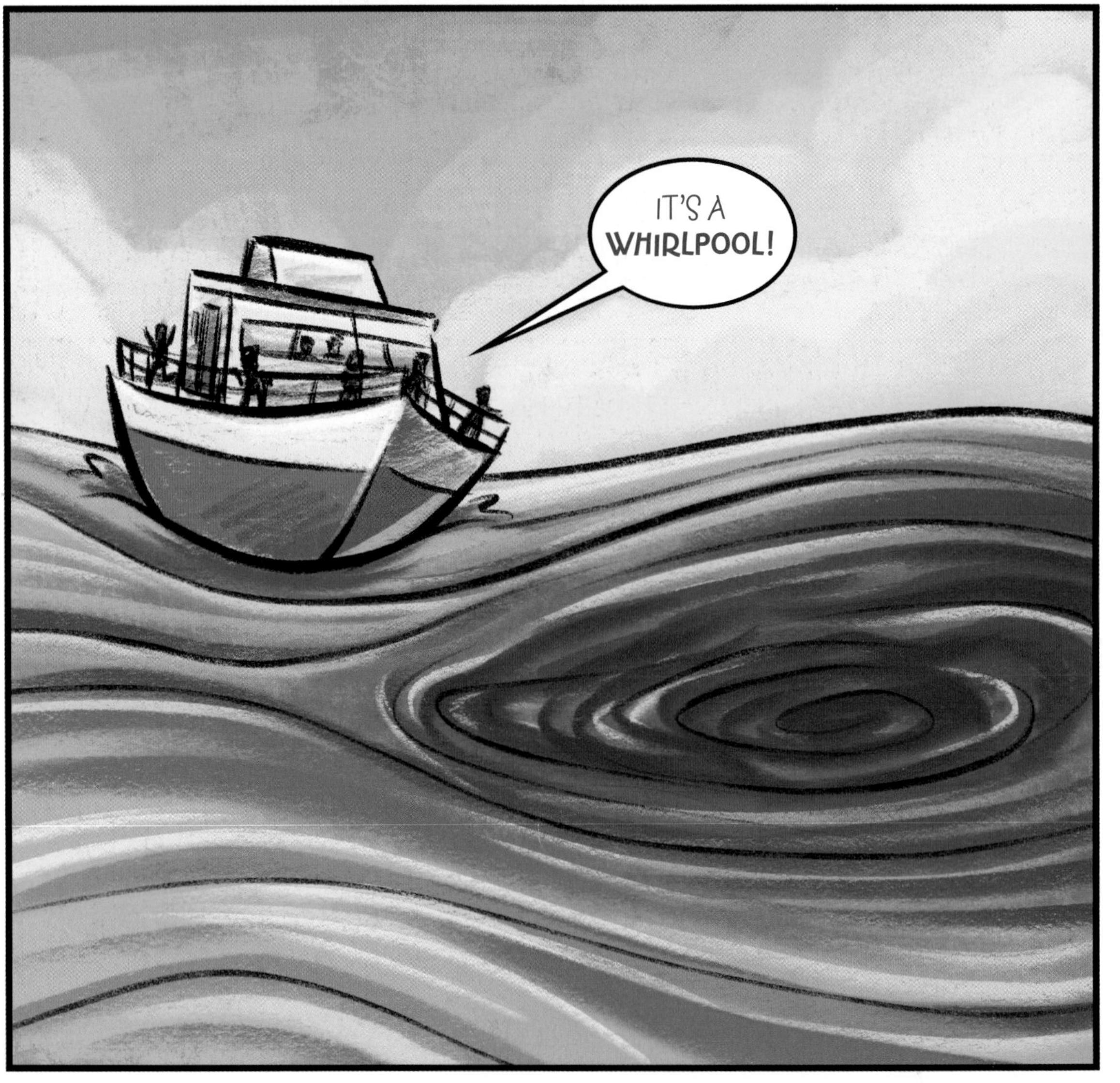
IT'S A WHIRLPOOL!

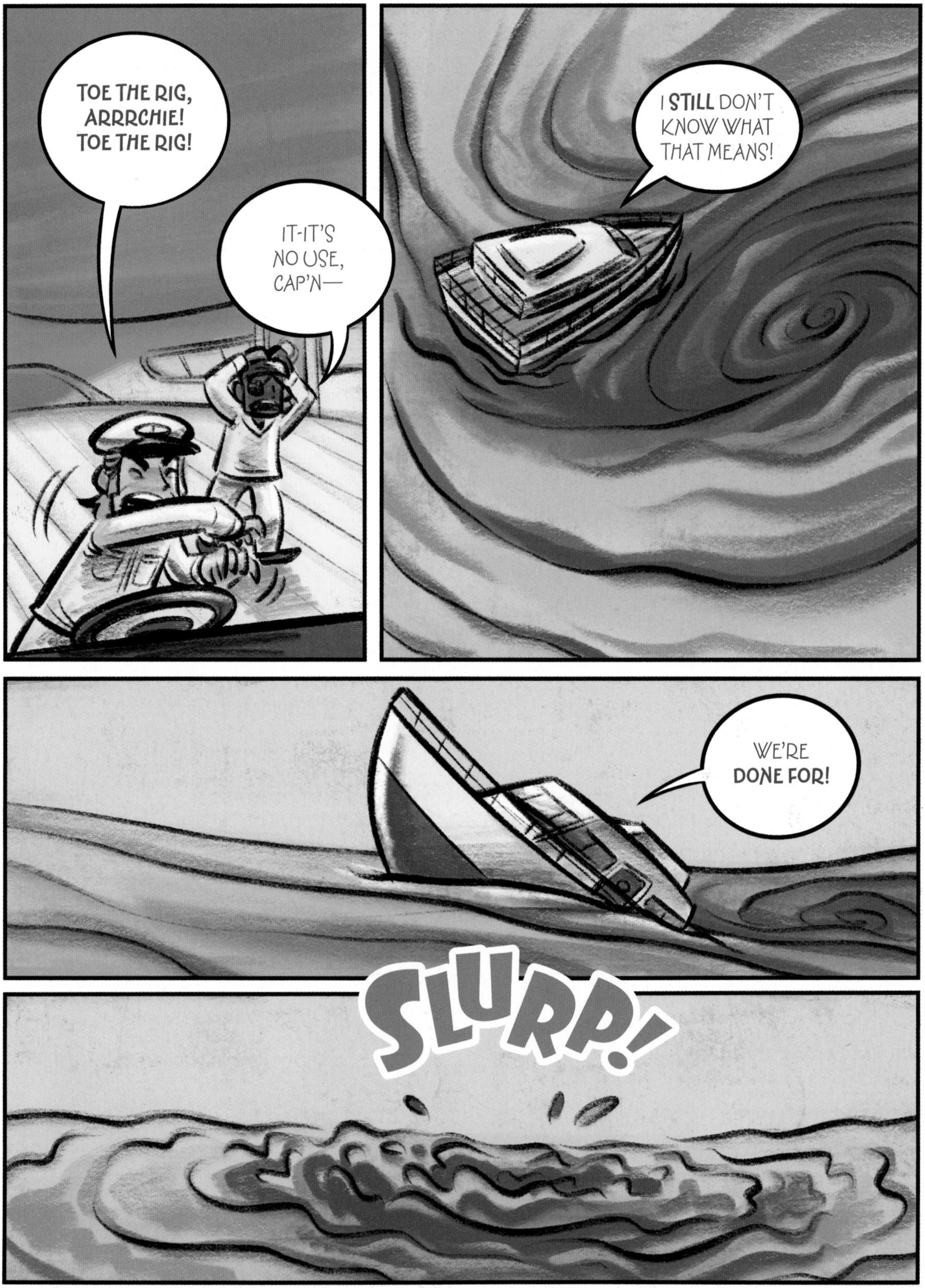
TOE THE RIG, ARRRCHIE! TOE THE RIG!
IT-IT'S NO USE, CAP'N—
I STILL DON'T KNOW WHAT THAT MEANS!
WE'RE DONE FOR!
SLURP!

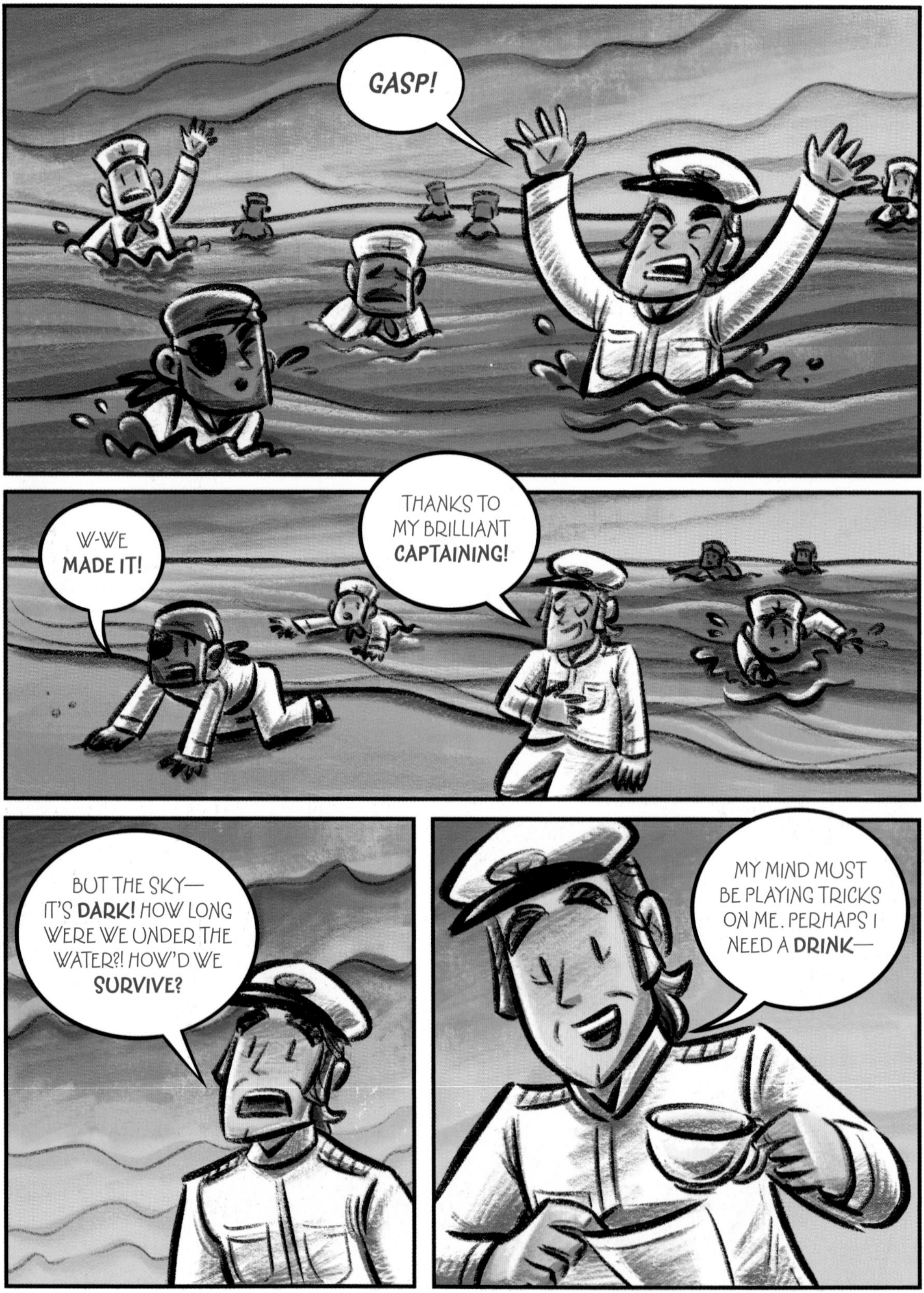
GASP!
W-WE MADE IT!
THANKS TO MY BRILLIANT CAPTAINING!
BUT THE SKY— IT'S DARK! HOW LONG WERE WE UNDER THE WATER?! HOW'D WE SURVIVE?
MY MIND MUST BE PLAYING TRICKS ON ME. PERHAPS I NEED A DRINK—

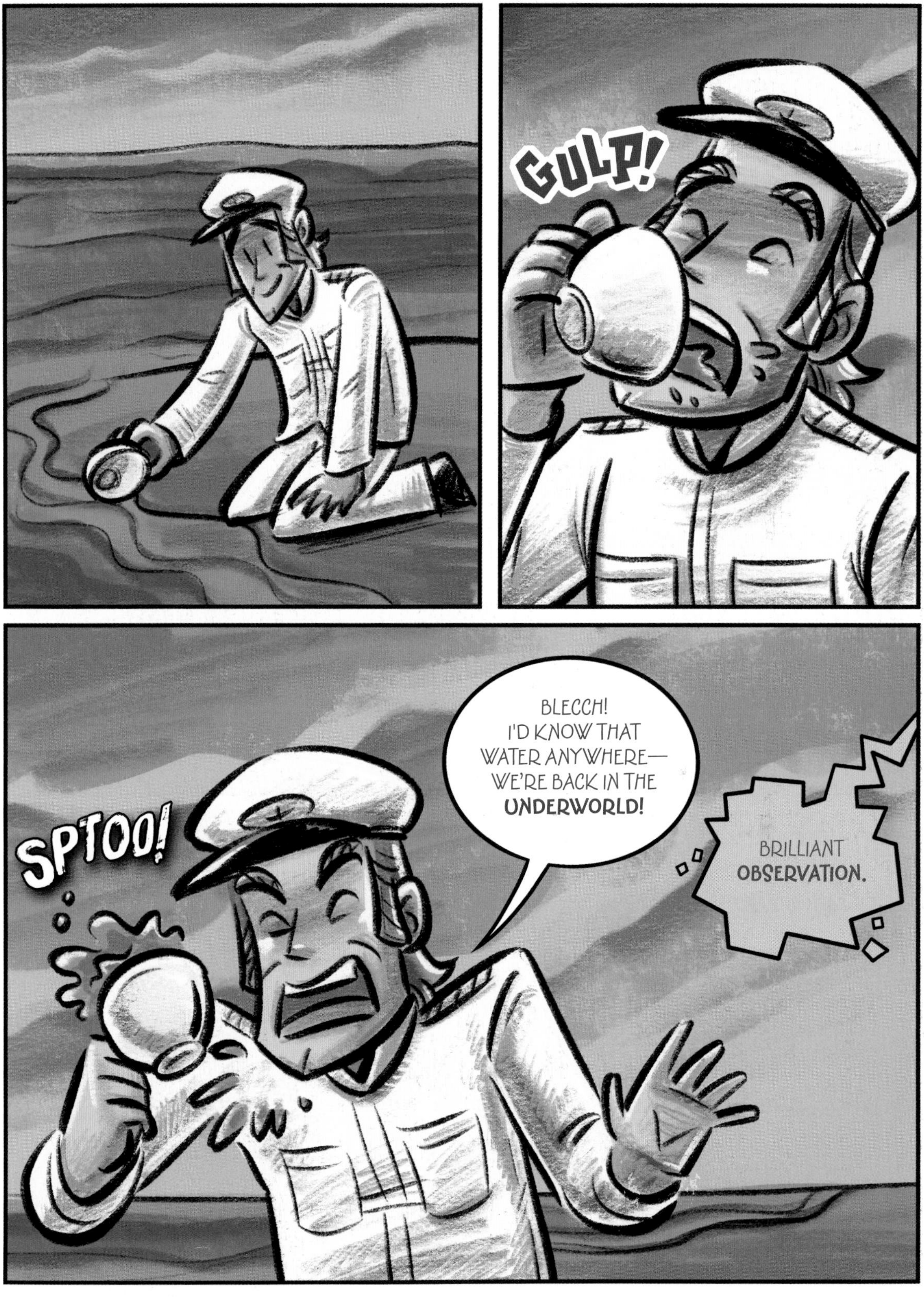
GULP!
SPTOO!
BLECCH! I'D KNOW THAT WATER ANYWHERE—WE'RE BACK IN THE **UNDERWORLD!**
BRILLIANT **OBSERVATION.**

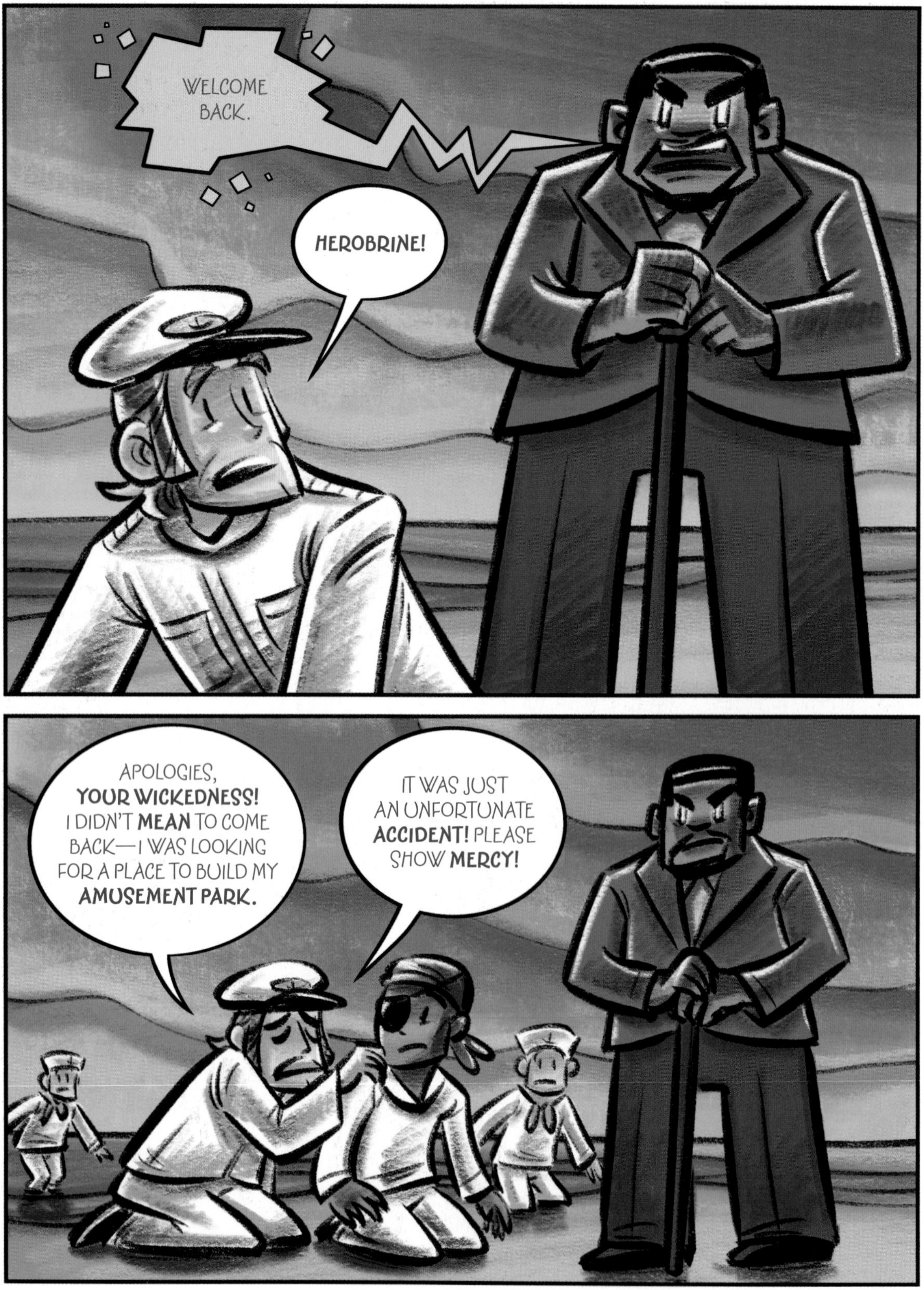
WELCOME BACK.
HEROBRINE!
APOLOGIES, YOUR WICKEDNESS! I DIDN'T MEAN TO COME BACK—I WAS LOOKING FOR A PLACE TO BUILD MY AMUSEMENT PARK.
IT WAS JUST AN UNFORTUNATE ACCIDENT! PLEASE SHOW MERCY!

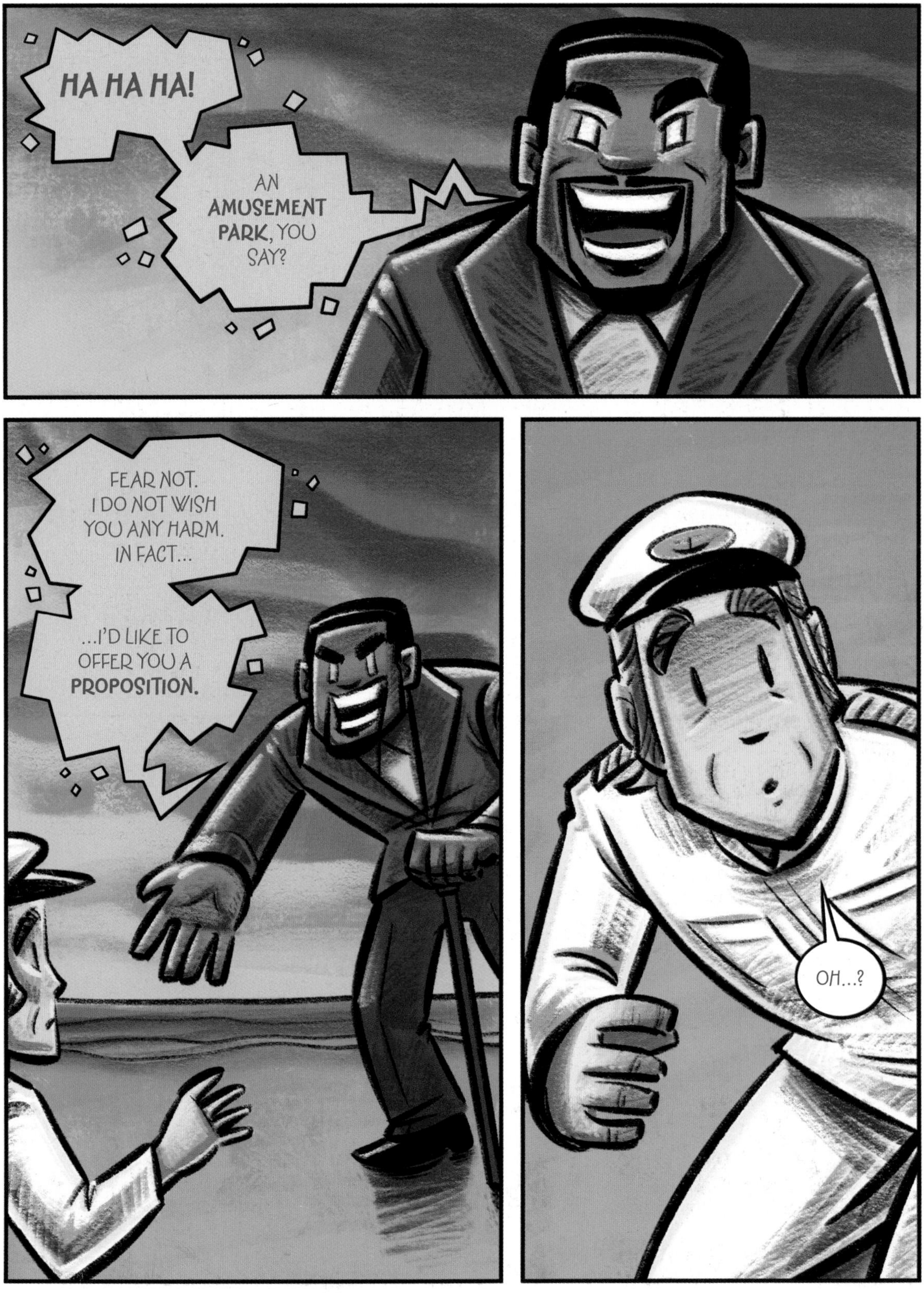
HA HA HA!
AN AMUSEMENT PARK, YOU SAY?
FEAR NOT. I DO NOT WISH YOU ANY HARM. IN FACT...
...I'D LIKE TO OFFER YOU A PROPOSITION.
OH...?

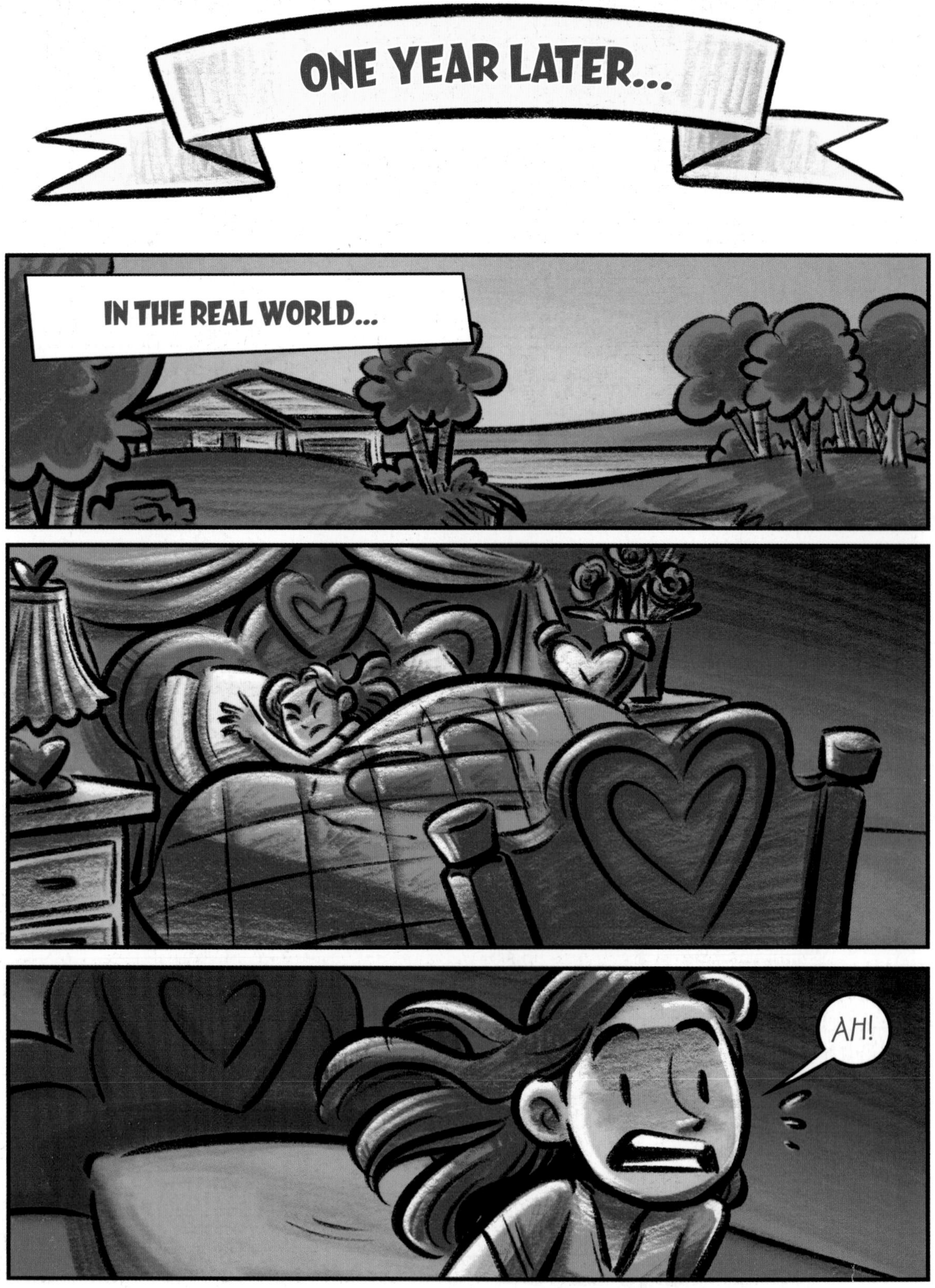
ONE YEAR LATER...
IN THE REAL WORLD...
AH!

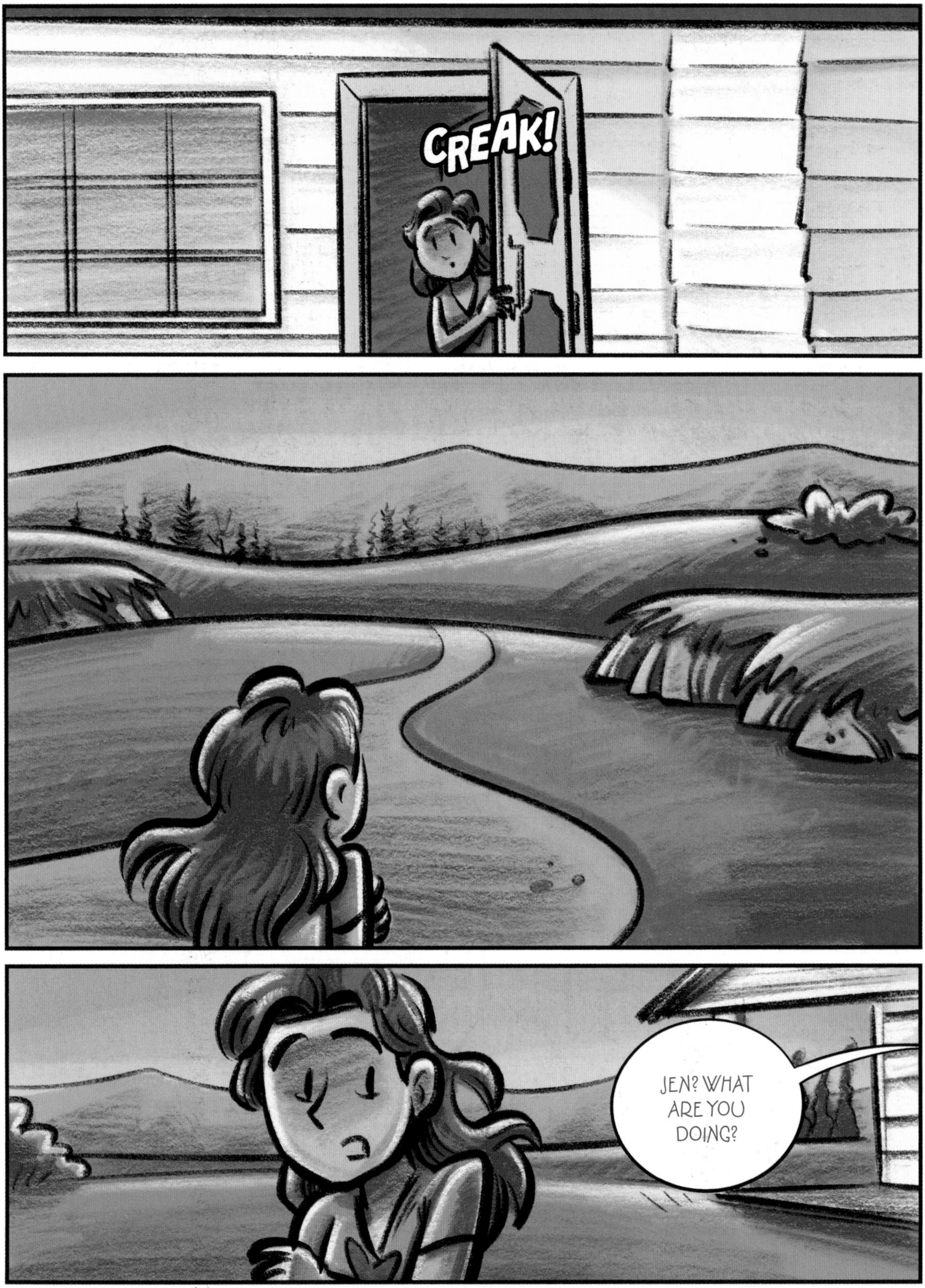
CREAK!
JEN? WHAT ARE YOU DOING?

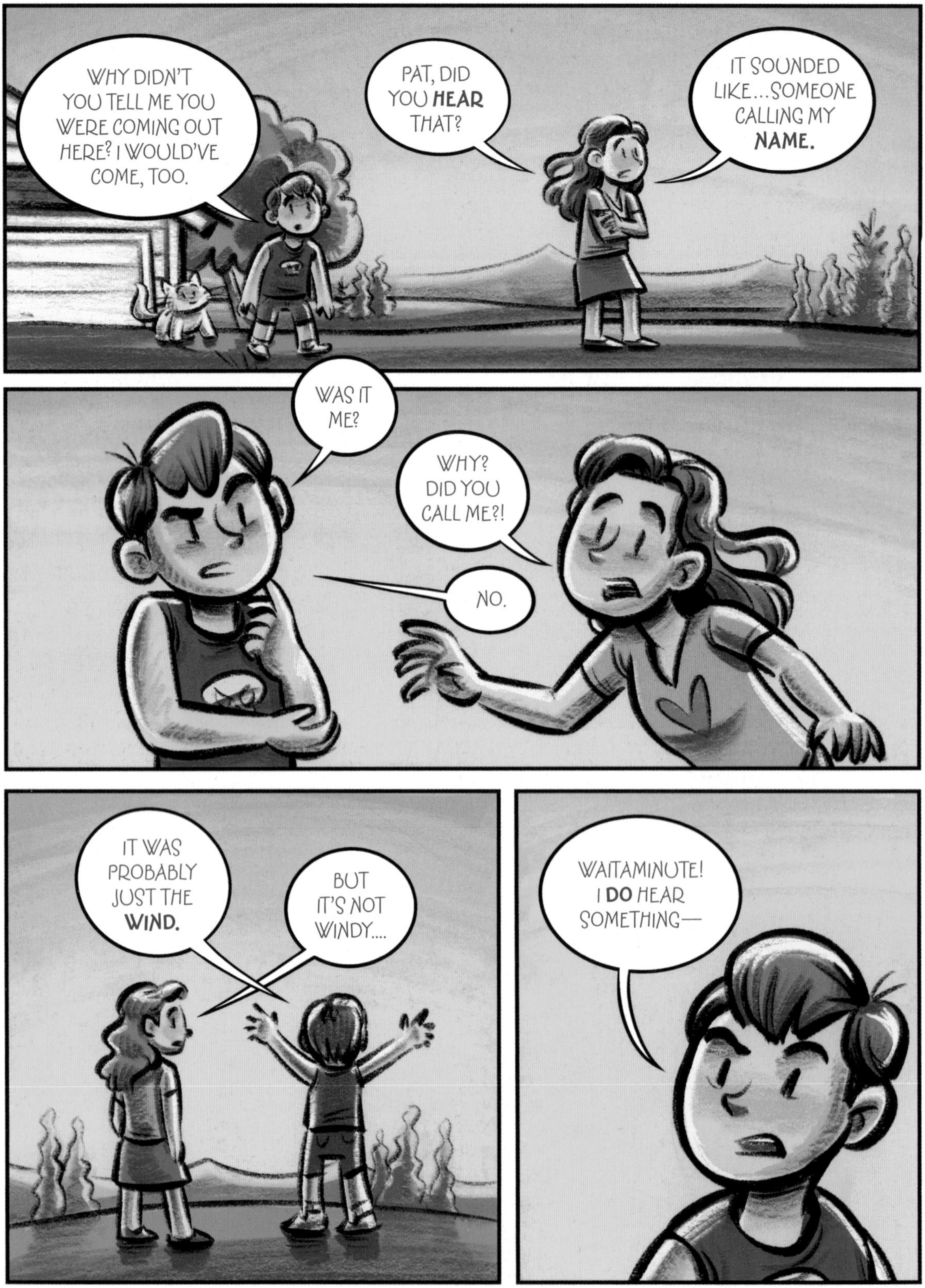
WHY DIDN'T YOU TELL ME YOU WERE COMING OUT HERE? I WOULD'VE COME, TOO.
PAT, DID YOU **HEAR** THAT?
IT SOUNDED LIKE...SOMEONE CALLING MY **NAME.**
WAS IT ME?
WHY? DID YOU CALL ME?!
NO.
IT WAS PROBABLY JUST THE **WIND.**
BUT IT'S NOT WINDY....
WAITAMINUTE! I **DO** HEAR SOMETHING—

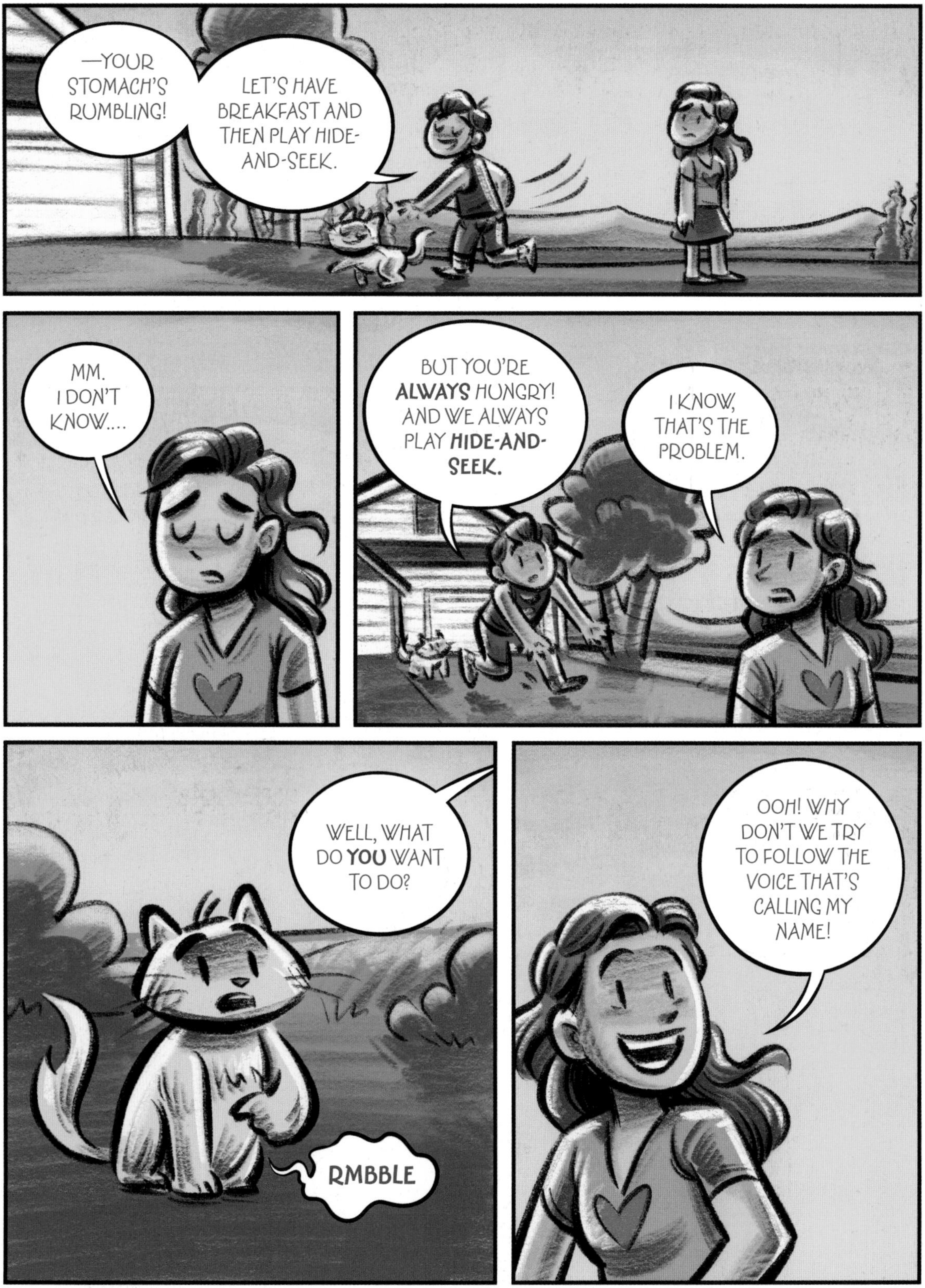
—YOUR STOMACH'S RUMBLING!
LET'S HAVE BREAKFAST AND THEN PLAY HIDE-AND-SEEK.
MM. I DON'T KNOW....
BUT YOU'RE **ALWAYS** HUNGRY! AND WE ALWAYS PLAY **HIDE-AND-SEEK.**
I KNOW, THAT'S THE PROBLEM.
WELL, WHAT DO **YOU** WANT TO DO?
RMBBLE
OOH! WHY DON'T WE TRY TO FOLLOW THE VOICE THAT'S CALLING MY NAME!

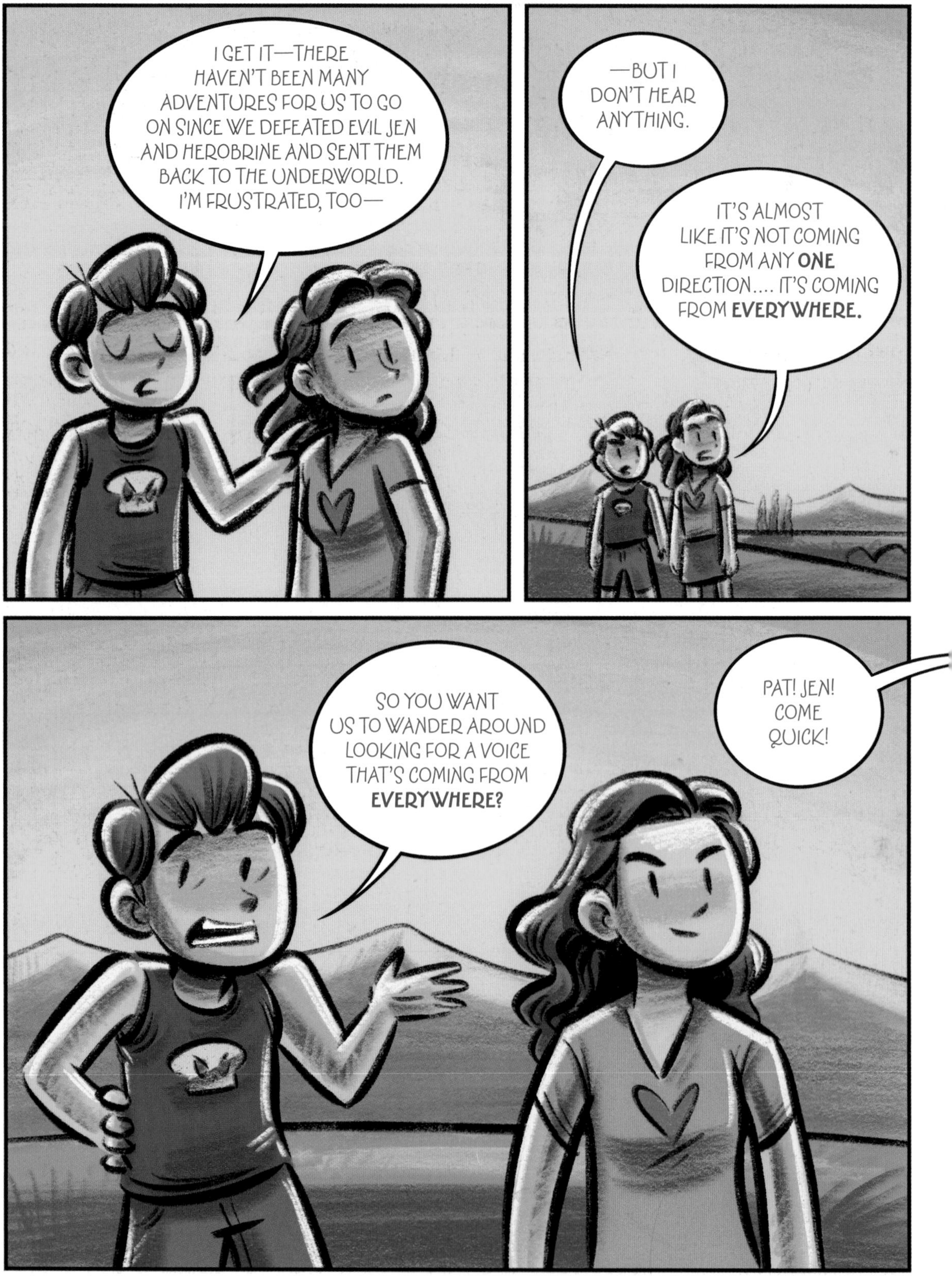
I GET IT—THERE HAVEN'T BEEN MANY ADVENTURES FOR US TO GO ON SINCE WE DEFEATED EVIL JEN AND HEROBRINE AND SENT THEM BACK TO THE UNDERWORLD. I'M FRUSTRATED, TOO—
—BUT I DON'T HEAR ANYTHING.
IT'S ALMOST LIKE IT'S NOT COMING FROM ANY **ONE** DIRECTION.... IT'S COMING FROM **EVERYWHERE.**
SO YOU WANT US TO WANDER AROUND LOOKING FOR A VOICE THAT'S COMING FROM **EVERYWHERE?**
PAT! JEN! COME QUICK!

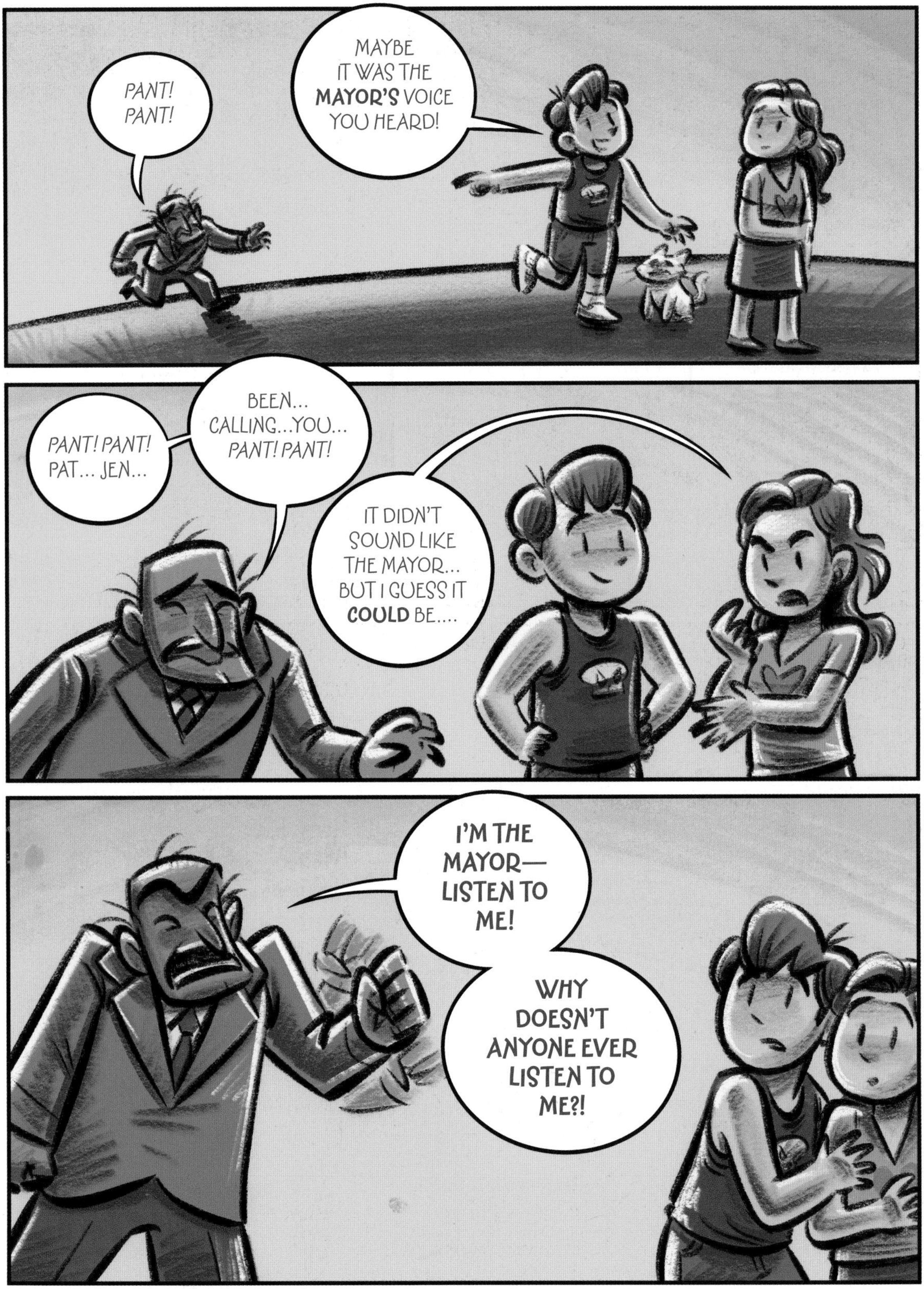
PANT! PANT!
MAYBE IT WAS THE MAYOR'S VOICE YOU HEARD!
PANT! PANT! PAT... JEN...
BEEN... CALLING...YOU... PANT! PANT!
IT DIDN'T SOUND LIKE THE MAYOR... BUT I GUESS IT COULD BE....
I'M THE MAYOR— LISTEN TO ME!
WHY DOESN'T ANYONE EVER LISTEN TO ME?!

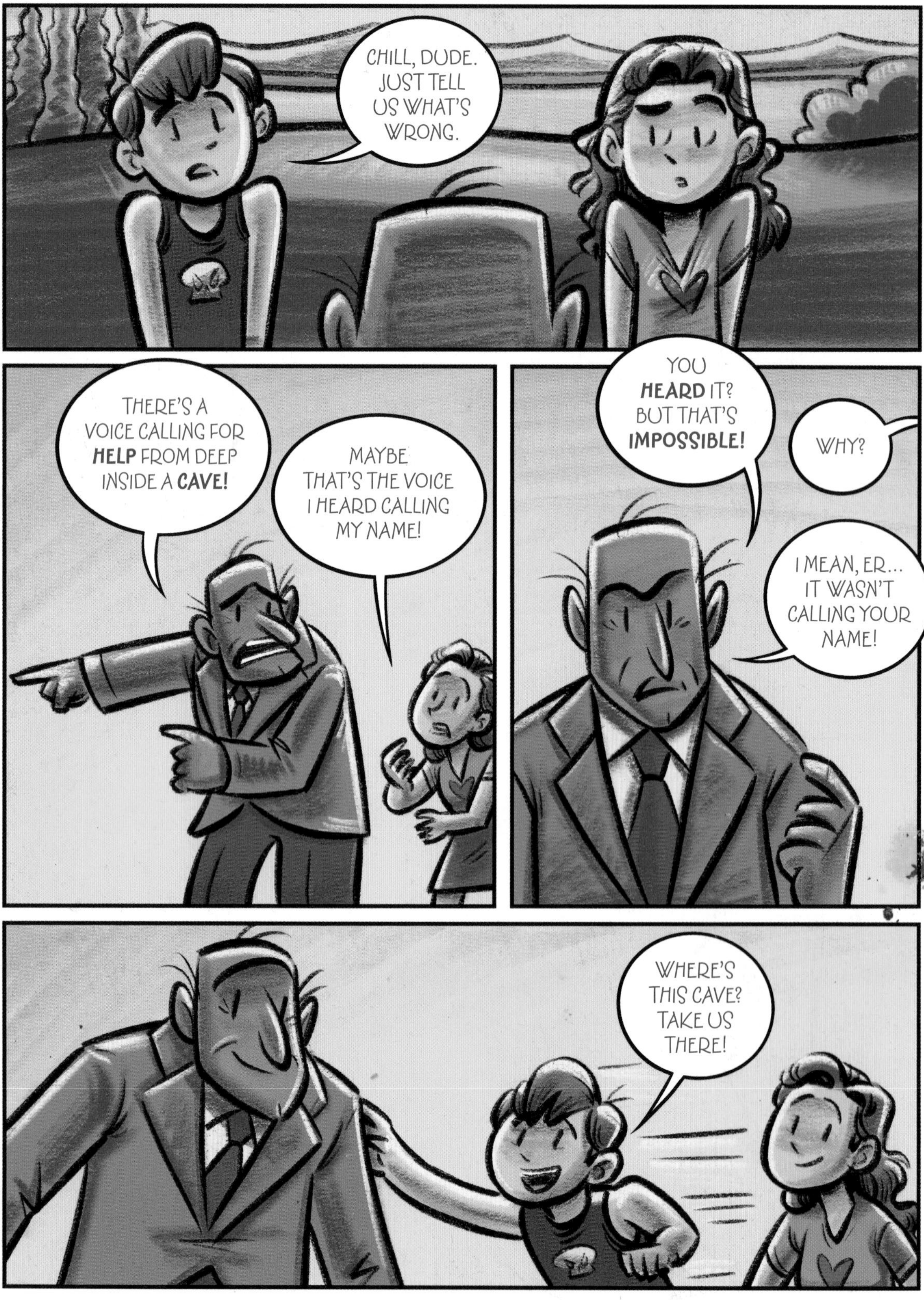
CHILL, DUDE. JUST TELL US WHAT'S WRONG.
THERE'S A VOICE CALLING FOR **HELP** FROM DEEP INSIDE A **CAVE!**
MAYBE THAT'S THE VOICE I HEARD CALLING MY NAME!
YOU **HEARD** IT? BUT THAT'S **IMPOSSIBLE!**
WHY?
I MEAN, ER... IT WASN'T CALLING YOUR NAME!
WHERE'S THIS CAVE? TAKE US THERE!

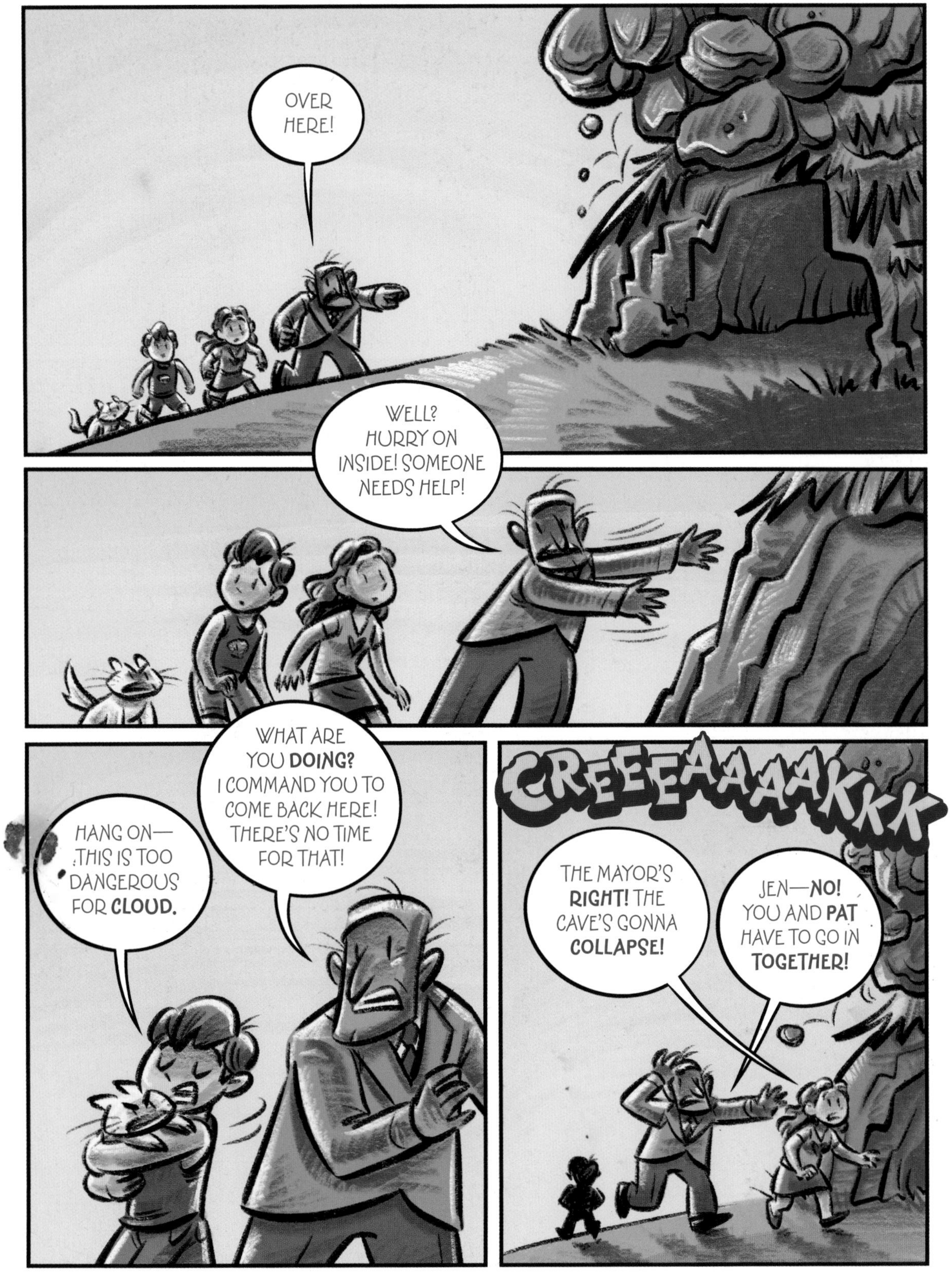
OVER HERE!
WELL? HURRY ON INSIDE! SOMEONE NEEDS HELP!
HANG ON— THIS IS TOO DANGEROUS FOR **CLOUD.**
WHAT ARE YOU **DOING?** I COMMAND YOU TO COME BACK HERE! THERE'S NO TIME FOR THAT!
CREEEAAAAKKK
THE MAYOR'S **RIGHT!** THE CAVE'S GONNA **COLLAPSE!**
JEN—**NO!** YOU AND **PAT** HAVE TO GO IN **TOGETHER!**

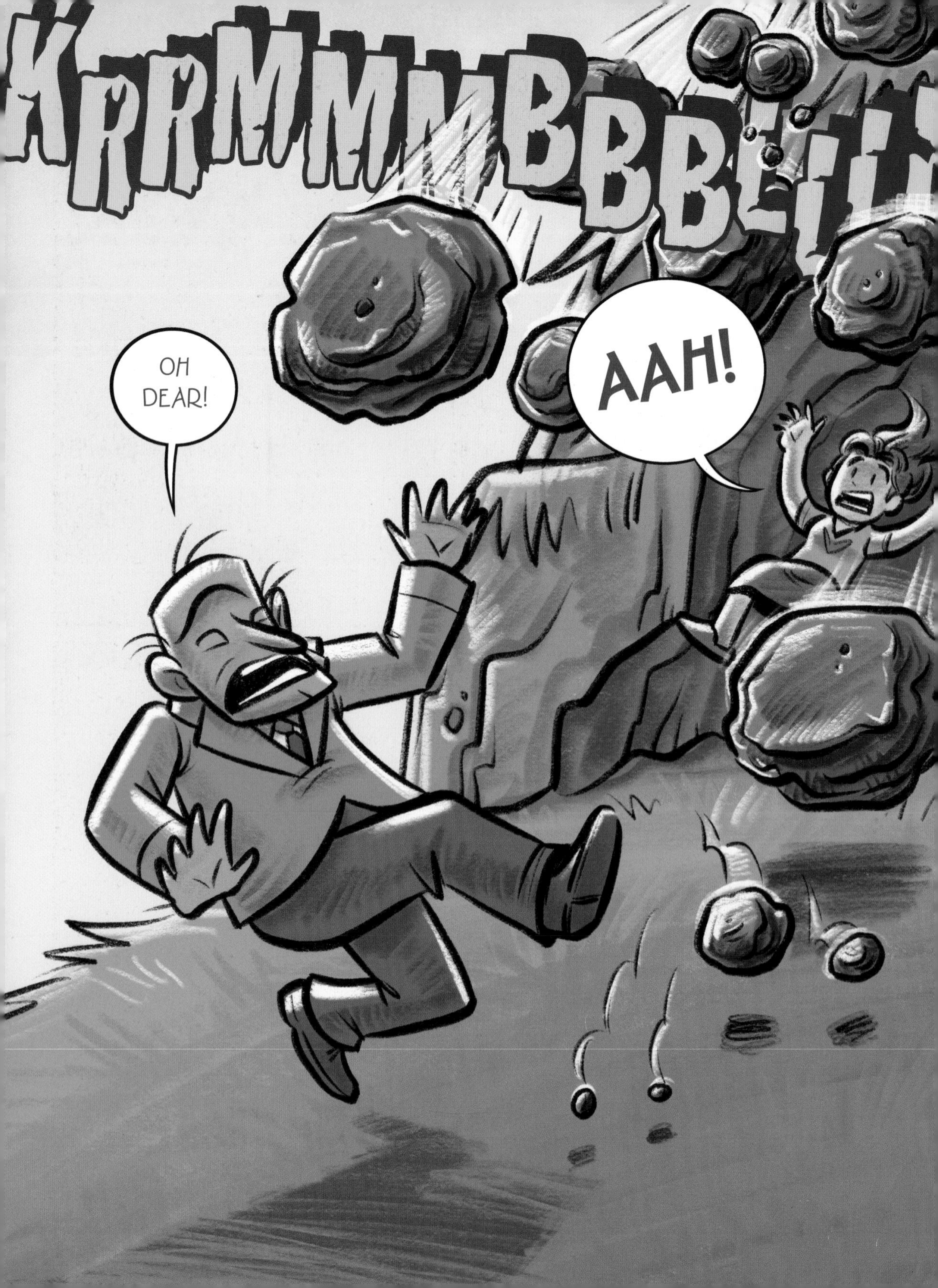
KRRMMMMBBBL!!
OH DEAR!
AAH!

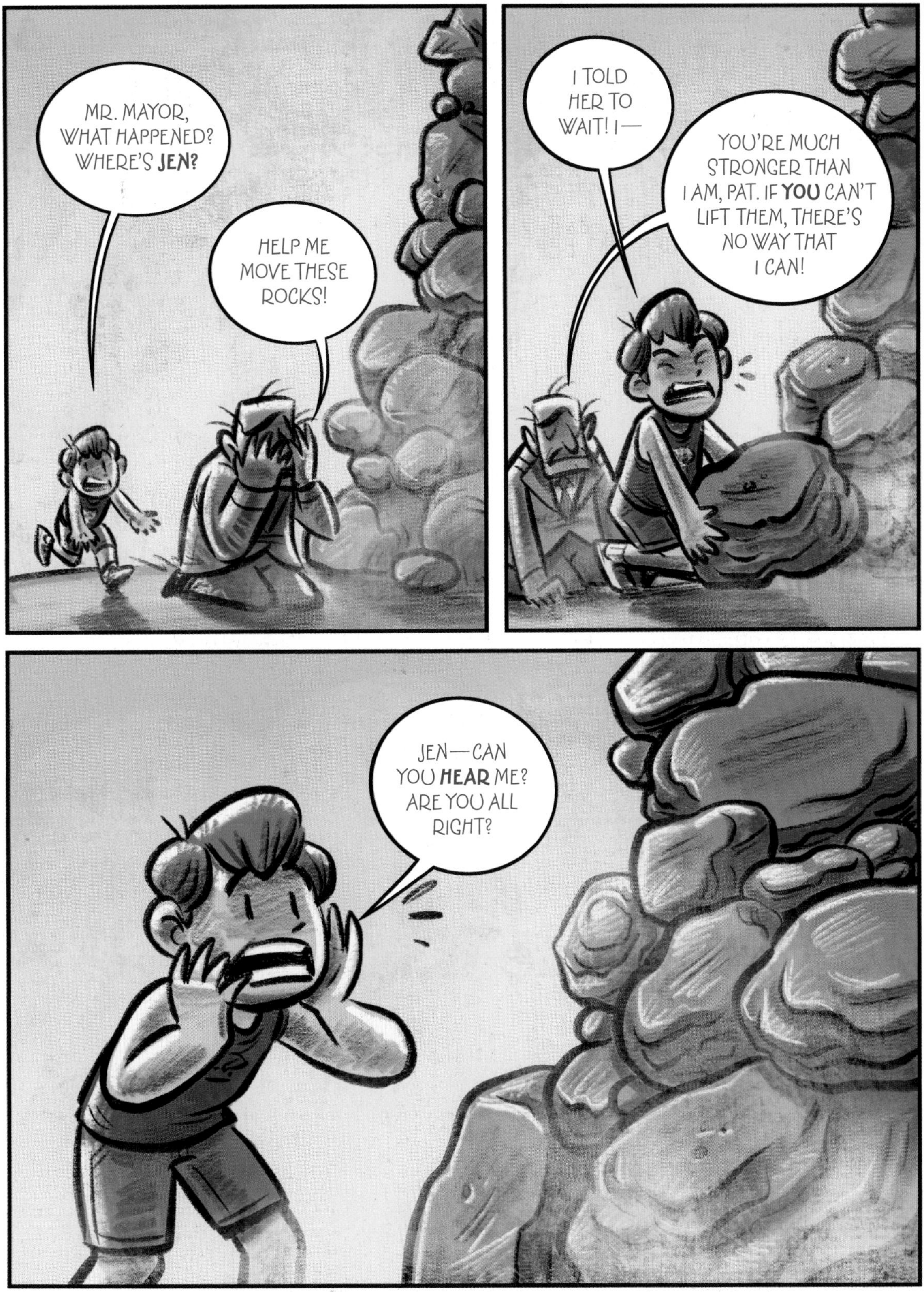
MR. MAYOR, WHAT HAPPENED? WHERE'S **JEN?**
HELP ME MOVE THESE ROCKS!
I TOLD HER TO WAIT! I—
YOU'RE MUCH STRONGER THAN I AM, PAT. IF **YOU** CAN'T LIFT THEM, THERE'S NO WAY THAT I CAN!
JEN—CAN YOU **HEAR** ME? ARE YOU ALL RIGHT?

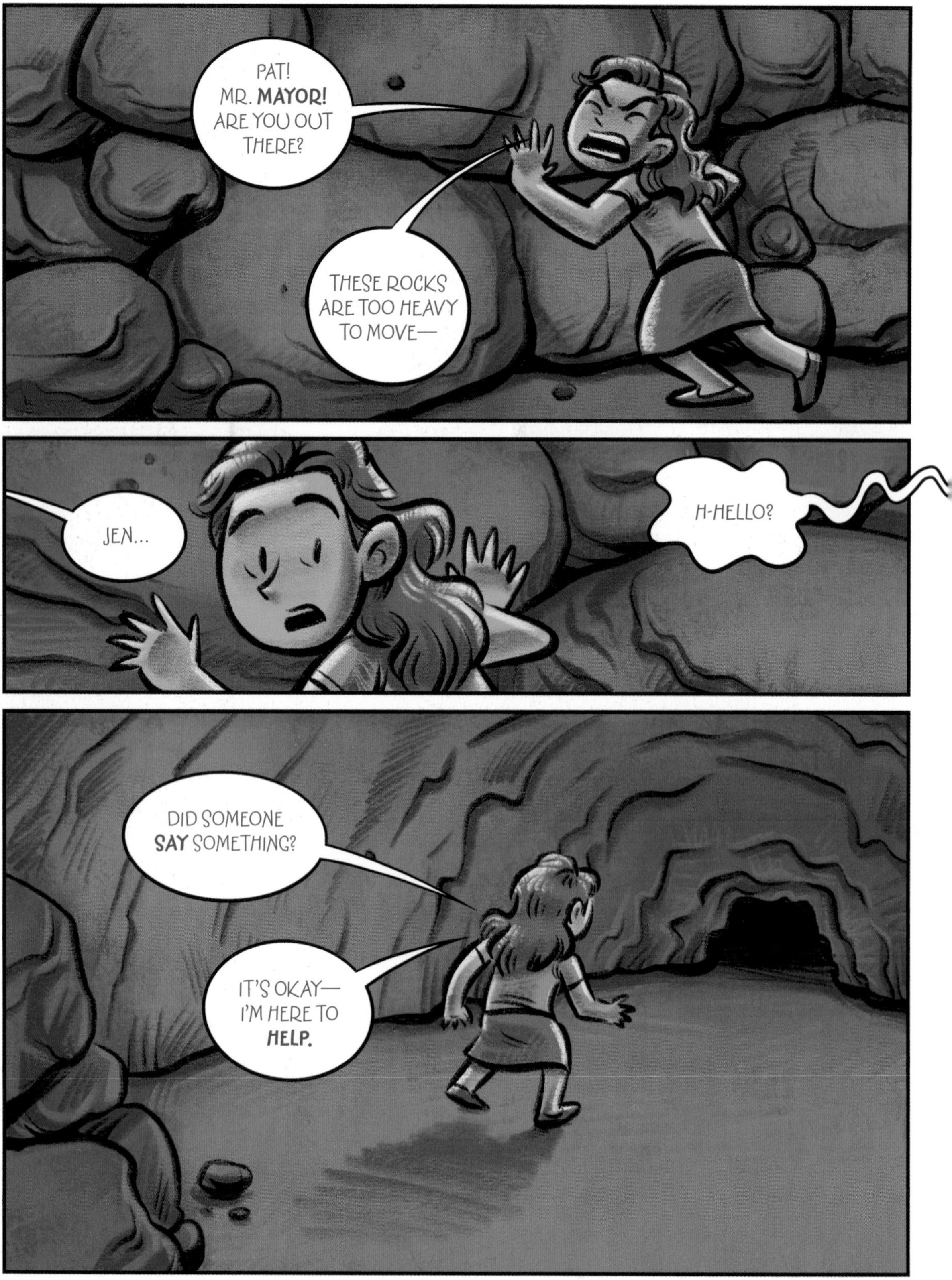

PAT! MR. **MAYOR!** ARE YOU OUT THERE?
THESE ROCKS ARE TOO HEAVY TO MOVE—
JEN...
H-HELLO?
DID SOMEONE **SAY** SOMETHING?
IT'S OKAY— I'M HERE TO **HELP.**

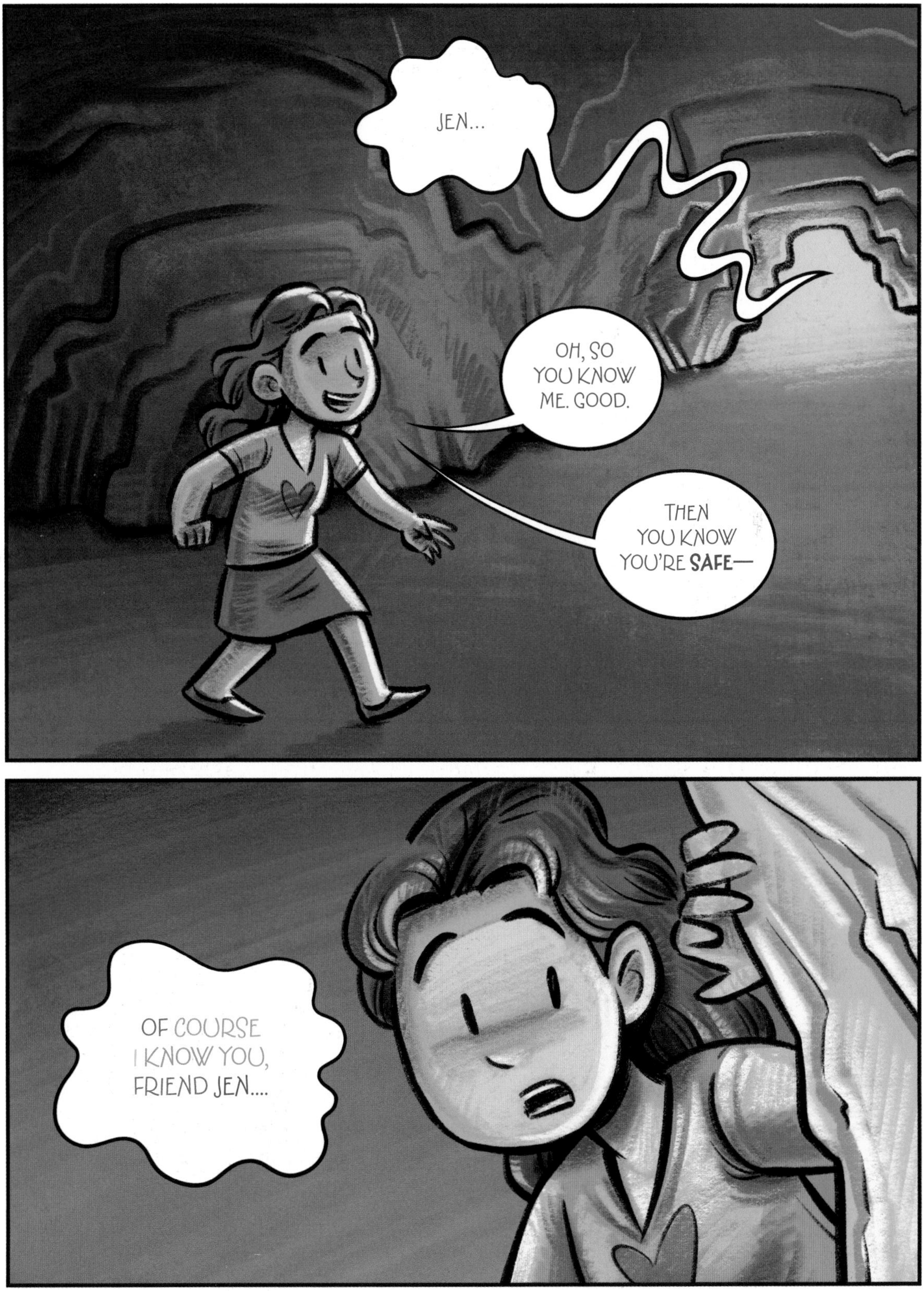
JEN...
OH, SO YOU KNOW ME. GOOD.
THEN YOU KNOW YOU'RE **SAFE**—
OF COURSE I KNOW YOU, FRIEND JEN....

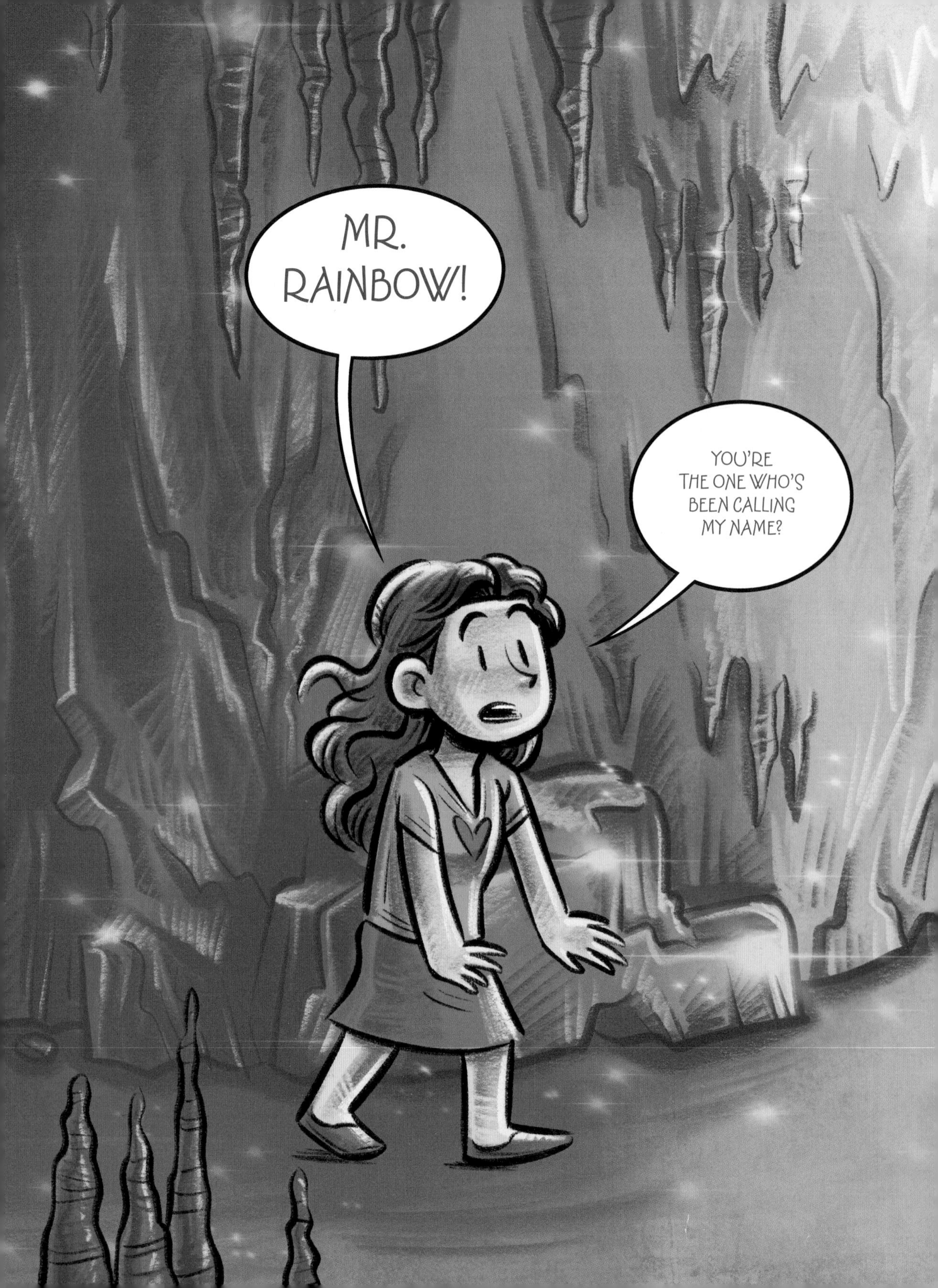
MR. RAINBOW!
YOU'RE THE ONE WHO'S BEEN CALLING MY NAME?

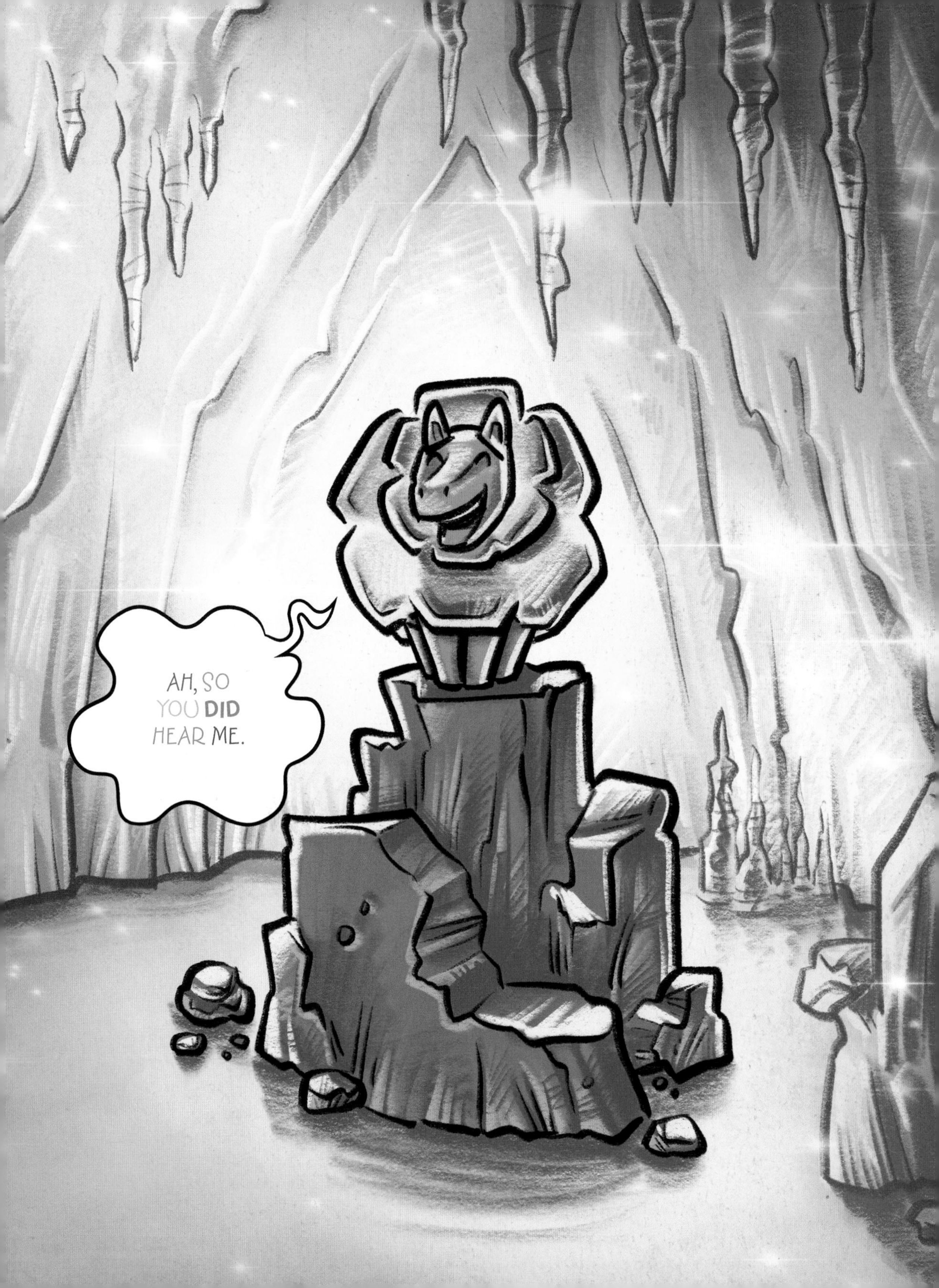
AH, SO YOU **DID** HEAR ME.

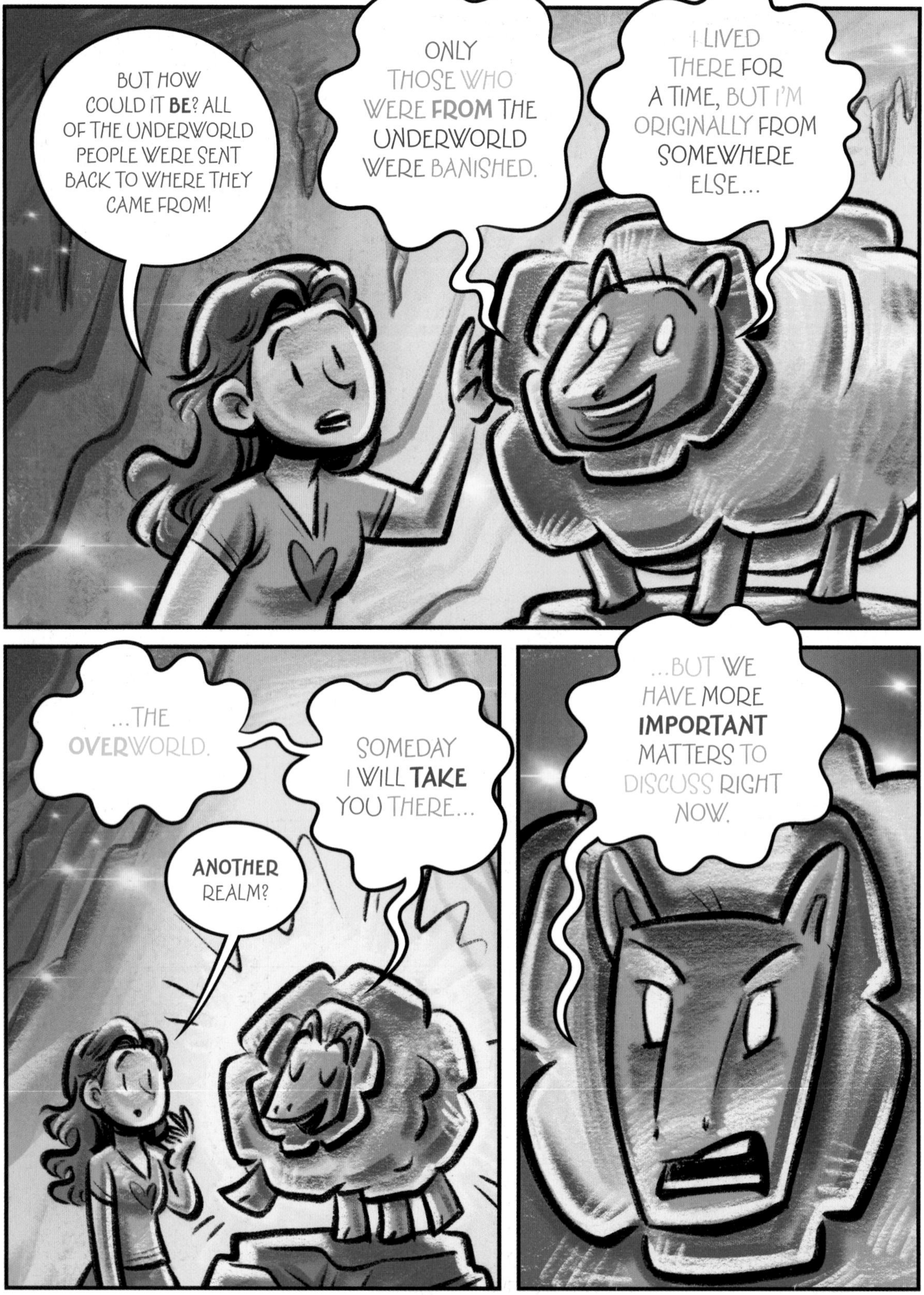
BUT HOW COULD IT BE? ALL OF THE UNDERWORLD PEOPLE WERE SENT BACK TO WHERE THEY CAME FROM!
ONLY THOSE WHO WERE FROM THE UNDERWORLD WERE BANISHED.
I LIVED THERE FOR A TIME, BUT I'M ORIGINALLY FROM SOMEWHERE ELSE...
...THE OVERWORLD.
ANOTHER REALM?
SOMEDAY I WILL TAKE YOU THERE...
...BUT WE HAVE MORE IMPORTANT MATTERS TO DISCUSS RIGHT NOW.

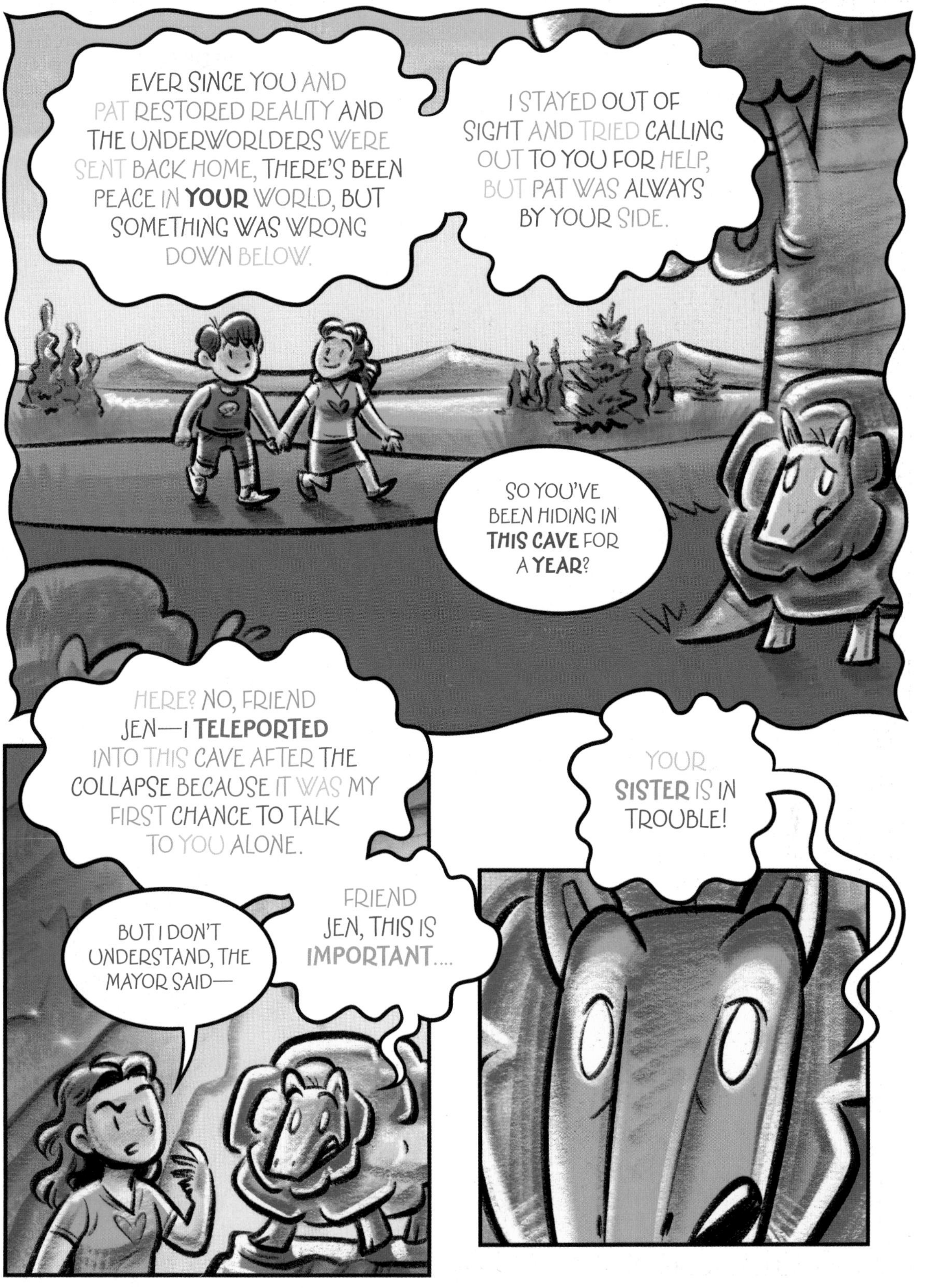
EVER SINCE YOU AND PAT RESTORED REALITY AND THE UNDERWORLDERS WERE SENT BACK HOME, THERE'S BEEN PEACE IN YOUR WORLD, BUT SOMETHING WAS WRONG DOWN BELOW.
I STAYED OUT OF SIGHT AND TRIED CALLING OUT TO YOU FOR HELP, BUT PAT WAS ALWAYS BY YOUR SIDE.
SO YOU'VE BEEN HIDING IN THIS CAVE FOR A YEAR?
HERE? NO, FRIEND JEN—I TELEPORTED INTO THIS CAVE AFTER THE COLLAPSE BECAUSE IT WAS MY FIRST CHANCE TO TALK TO YOU ALONE.
BUT I DON'T UNDERSTAND, THE MAYOR SAID—
FRIEND JEN, THIS IS IMPORTANT....
YOUR SISTER IS IN TROUBLE!

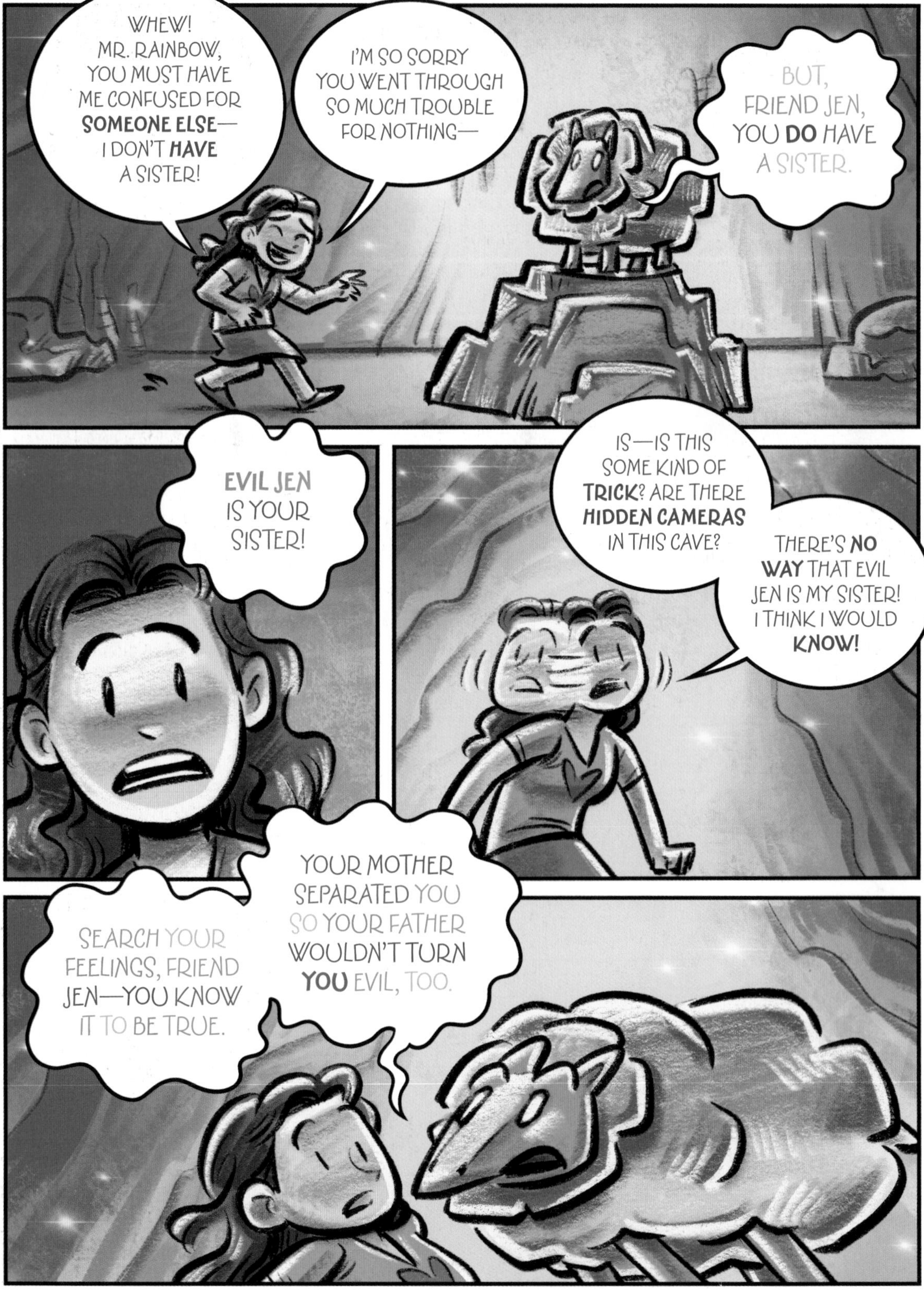
WHEW! MR. RAINBOW, YOU MUST HAVE ME CONFUSED FOR **SOMEONE ELSE**— I DON'T **HAVE** A SISTER!
I'M SO SORRY YOU WENT THROUGH SO MUCH TROUBLE FOR NOTHING—
BUT, FRIEND JEN, YOU **DO** HAVE A SISTER.
EVIL JEN IS YOUR SISTER!
IS—IS THIS SOME KIND OF **TRICK**? ARE THERE **HIDDEN CAMERAS** IN THIS CAVE?
THERE'S **NO WAY** THAT EVIL JEN IS MY SISTER! I THINK I WOULD **KNOW!**
SEARCH YOUR FEELINGS, FRIEND JEN—YOU KNOW IT TO BE TRUE.
YOUR MOTHER SEPARATED YOU SO YOUR FATHER WOULDN'T TURN **YOU** EVIL, TOO.

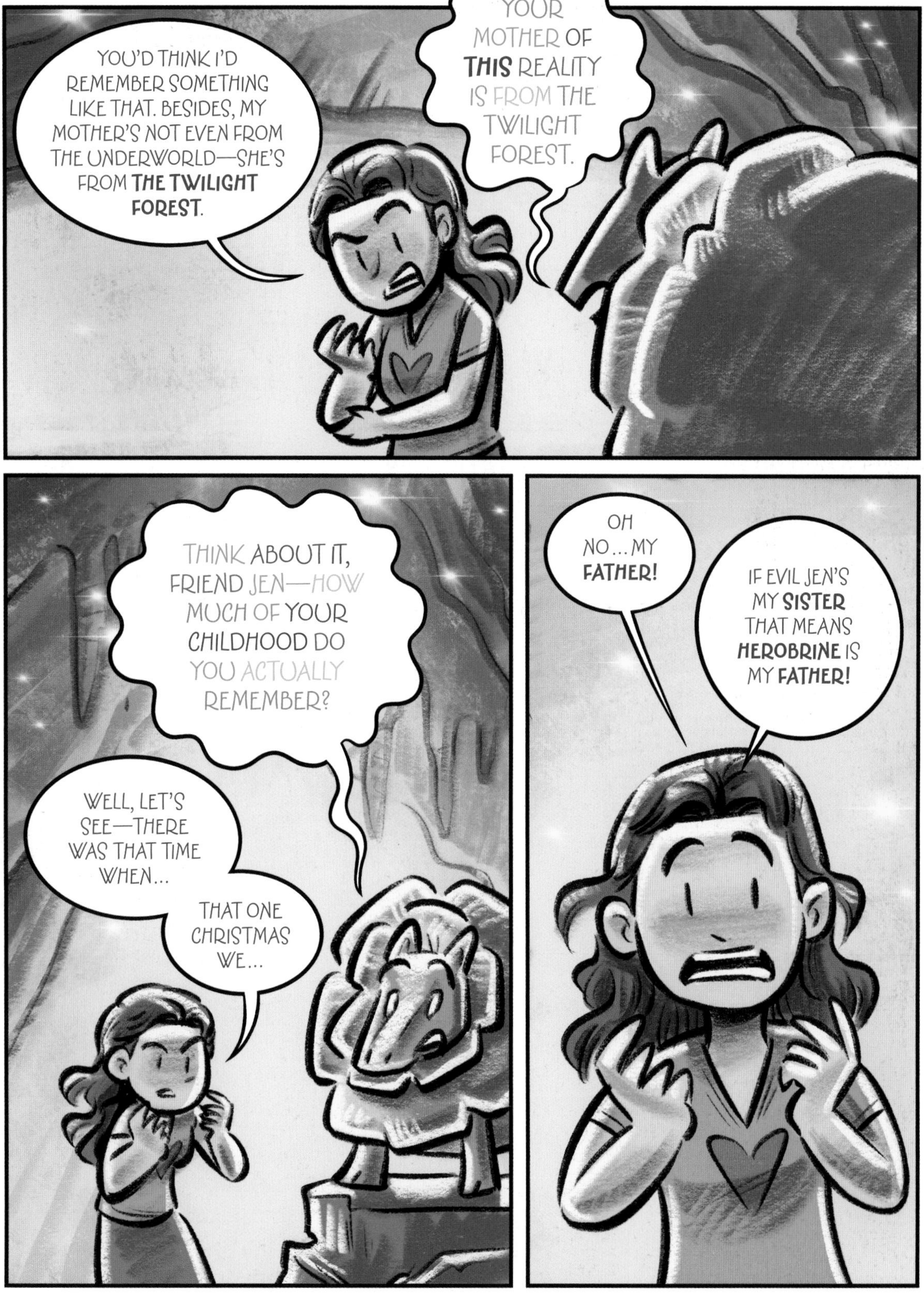
YOU'D THINK I'D REMEMBER SOMETHING LIKE THAT. BESIDES, MY MOTHER'S NOT EVEN FROM THE UNDERWORLD—SHE'S FROM THE TWILIGHT FOREST.
YOUR MOTHER OF THIS REALITY IS FROM THE TWILIGHT FOREST.
THINK ABOUT IT, FRIEND JEN—HOW MUCH OF YOUR CHILDHOOD DO YOU ACTUALLY REMEMBER?
WELL, LET'S SEE—THERE WAS THAT TIME WHEN...
THAT ONE CHRISTMAS WE...
OH NO... MY FATHER!
IF EVIL JEN'S MY SISTER THAT MEANS HEROBRINE IS MY FATHER!

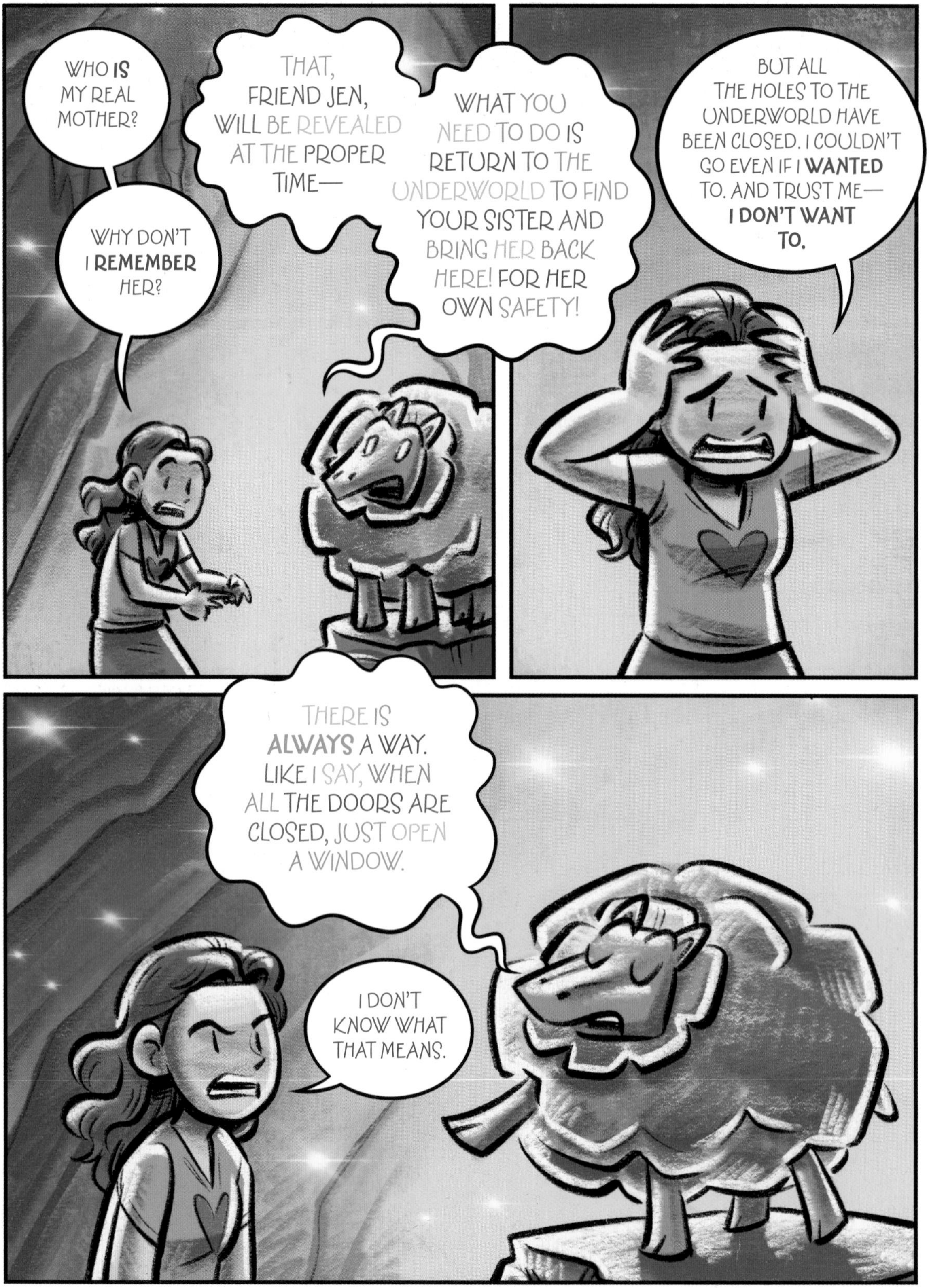
WHO IS MY REAL MOTHER?
WHY DON'T I REMEMBER HER?
THAT, FRIEND JEN, WILL BE REVEALED AT THE PROPER TIME—
WHAT YOU NEED TO DO IS RETURN TO THE UNDERWORLD TO FIND YOUR SISTER AND BRING HER BACK HERE! FOR HER OWN SAFETY!
BUT ALL THE HOLES TO THE UNDERWORLD HAVE BEEN CLOSED. I COULDN'T GO EVEN IF I WANTED TO. AND TRUST ME— I DON'T WANT TO.
THERE IS ALWAYS A WAY. LIKE I SAY, WHEN ALL THE DOORS ARE CLOSED, JUST OPEN A WINDOW.
I DON'T KNOW WHAT THAT MEANS.

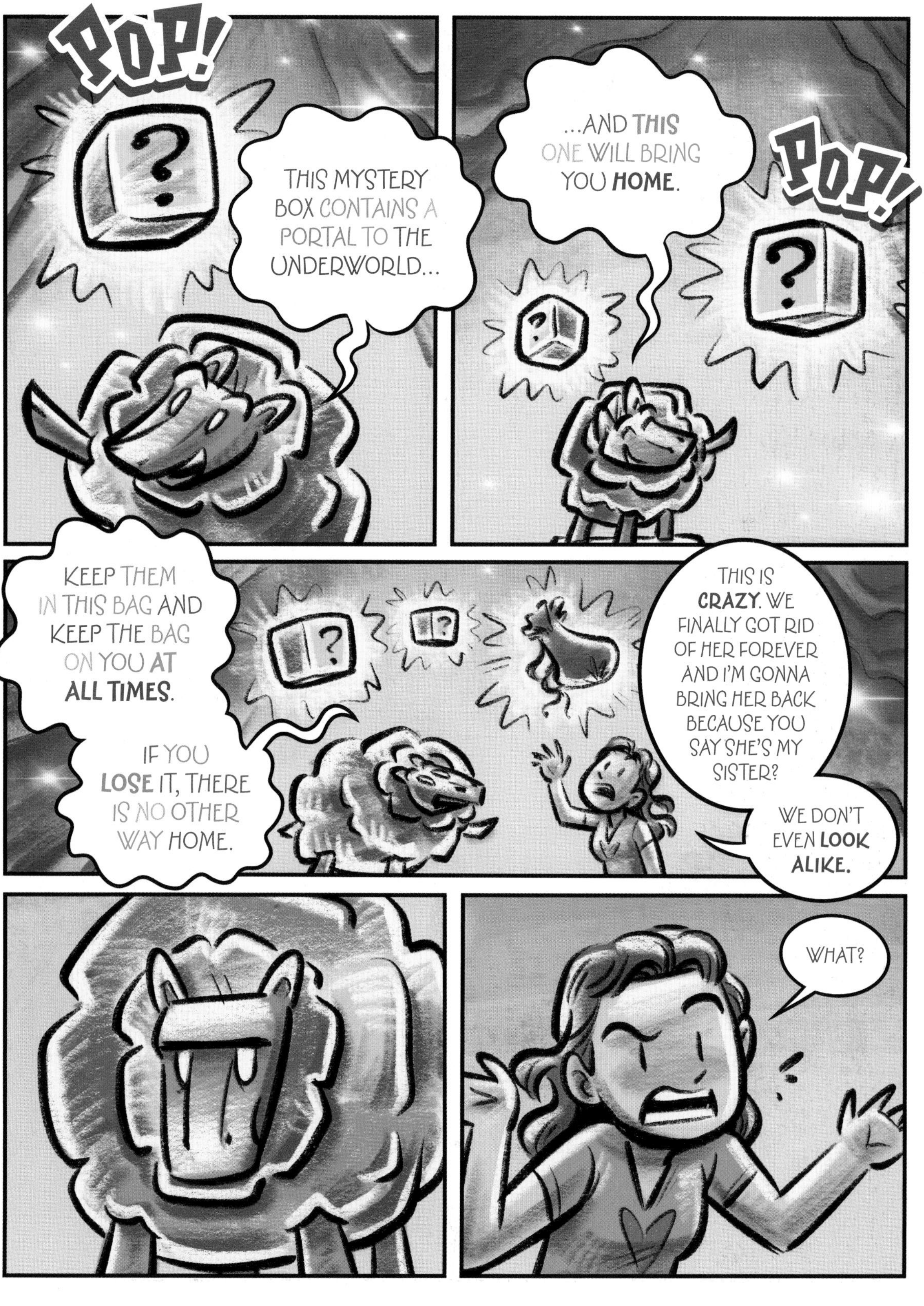
POP!
THIS MYSTERY BOX CONTAINS A PORTAL TO THE UNDERWORLD...
...AND THIS ONE WILL BRING YOU HOME.
POP!
KEEP THEM IN THIS BAG AND KEEP THE BAG ON YOU AT ALL TIMES.
IF YOU LOSE IT, THERE IS NO OTHER WAY HOME.
THIS IS CRAZY. WE FINALLY GOT RID OF HER FOREVER AND I'M GONNA BRING HER BACK BECAUSE YOU SAY SHE'S MY SISTER?
WE DON'T EVEN LOOK ALIKE.
WHAT?

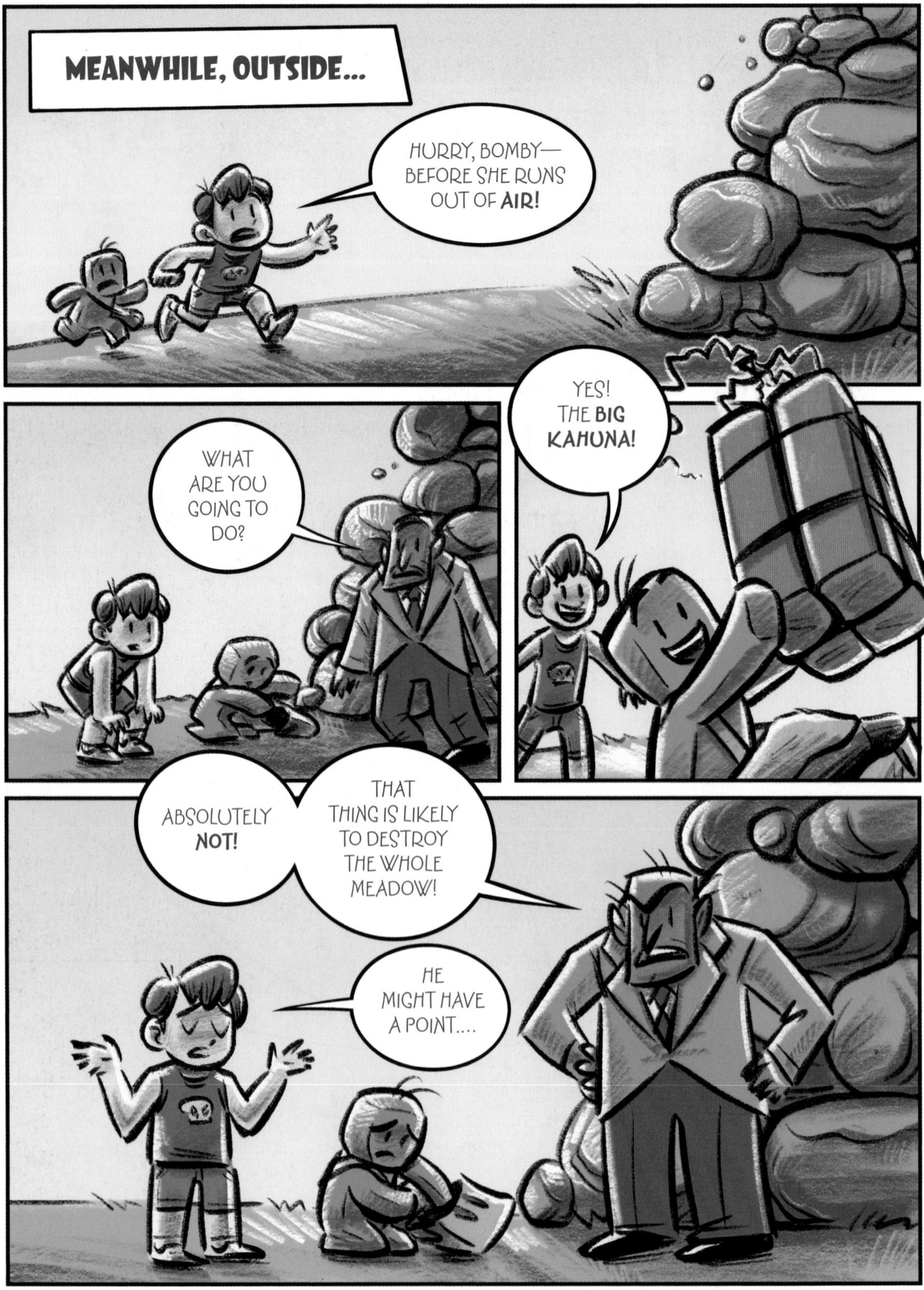
MEANWHILE, OUTSIDE...
HURRY, BOMBY— BEFORE SHE RUNS OUT OF AIR!
WHAT ARE YOU GOING TO DO?
YES! THE BIG KAHUNA!
ABSOLUTELY NOT!
THAT THING IS LIKELY TO DESTROY THE WHOLE MEADOW!
HE MIGHT HAVE A POINT....

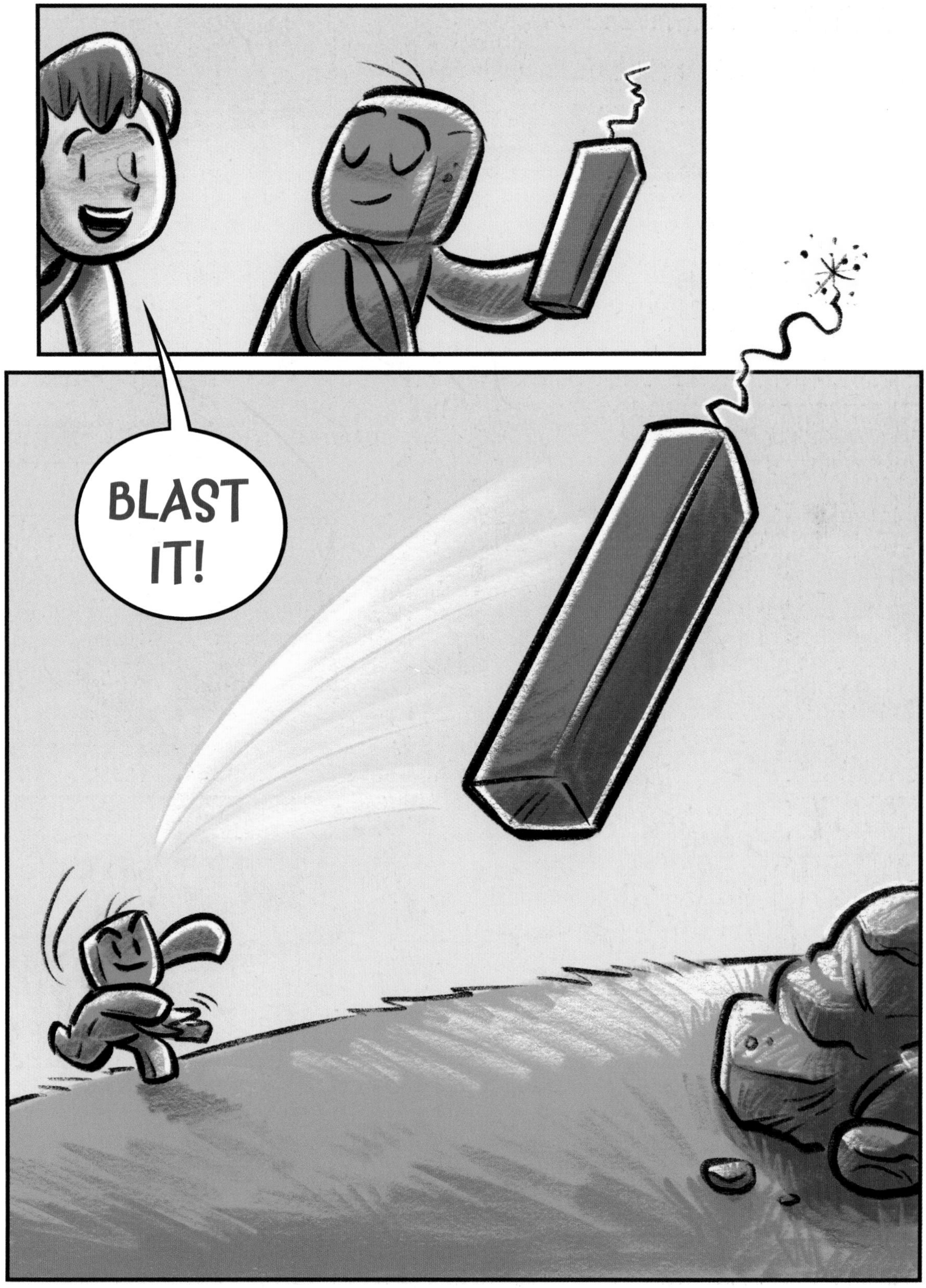
BLAST IT!

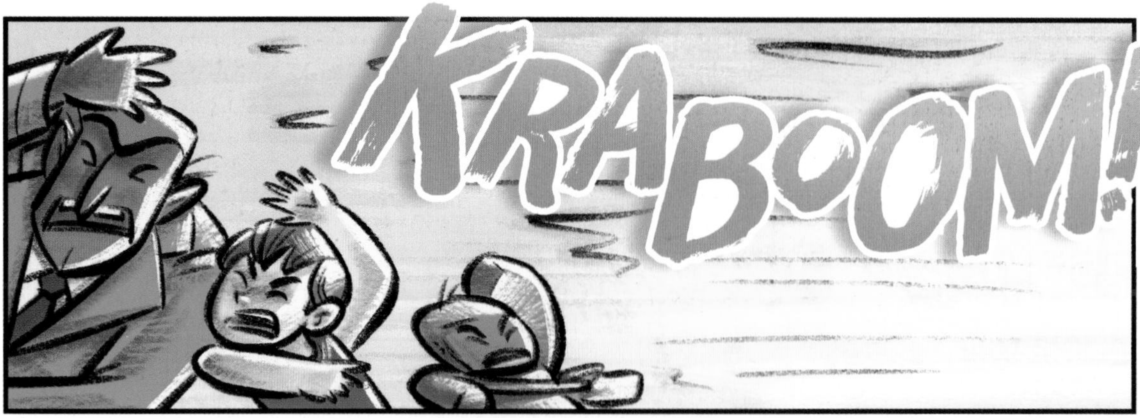
KRABOOM!

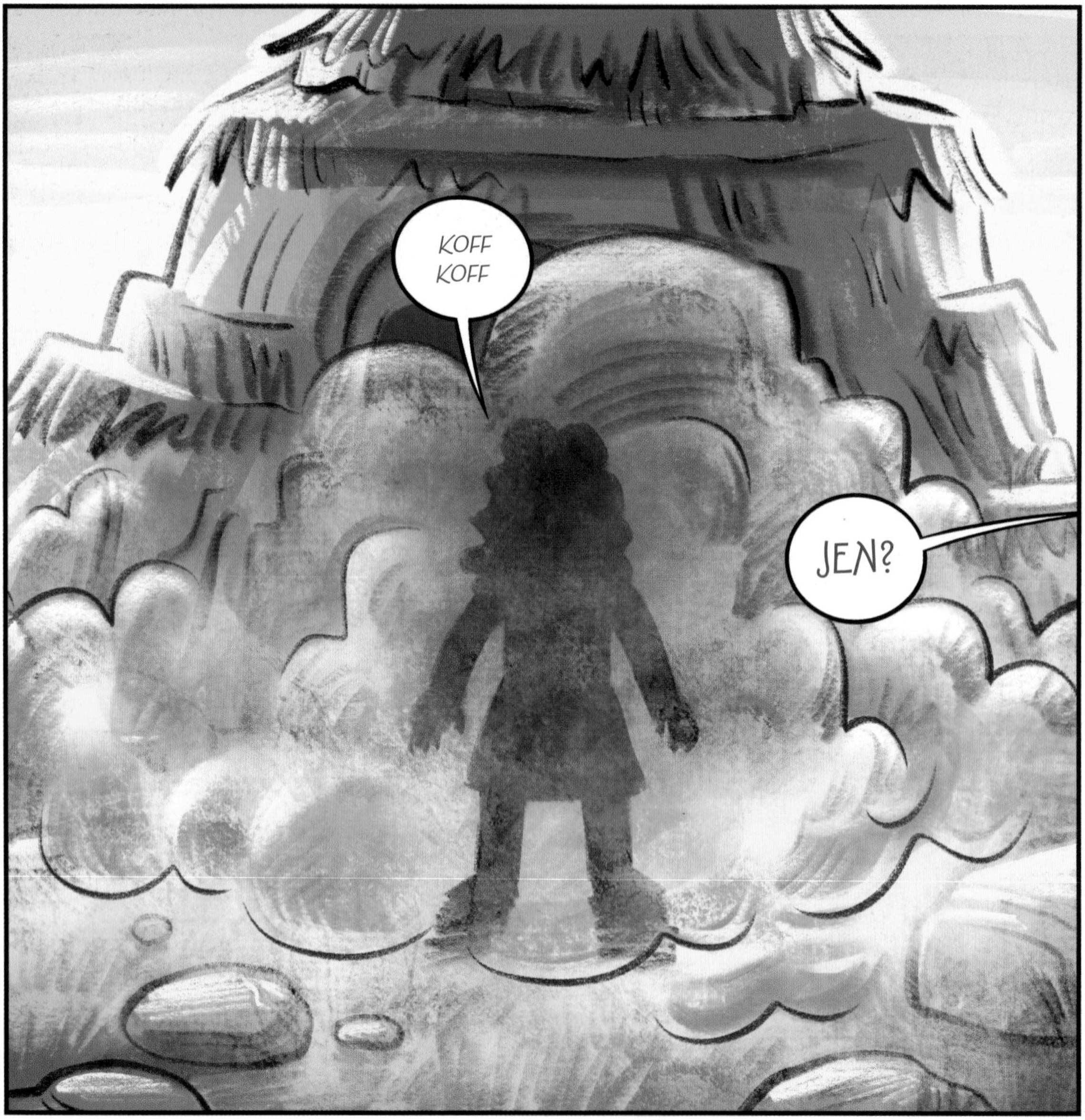
KOFF
KOFF
JEN?

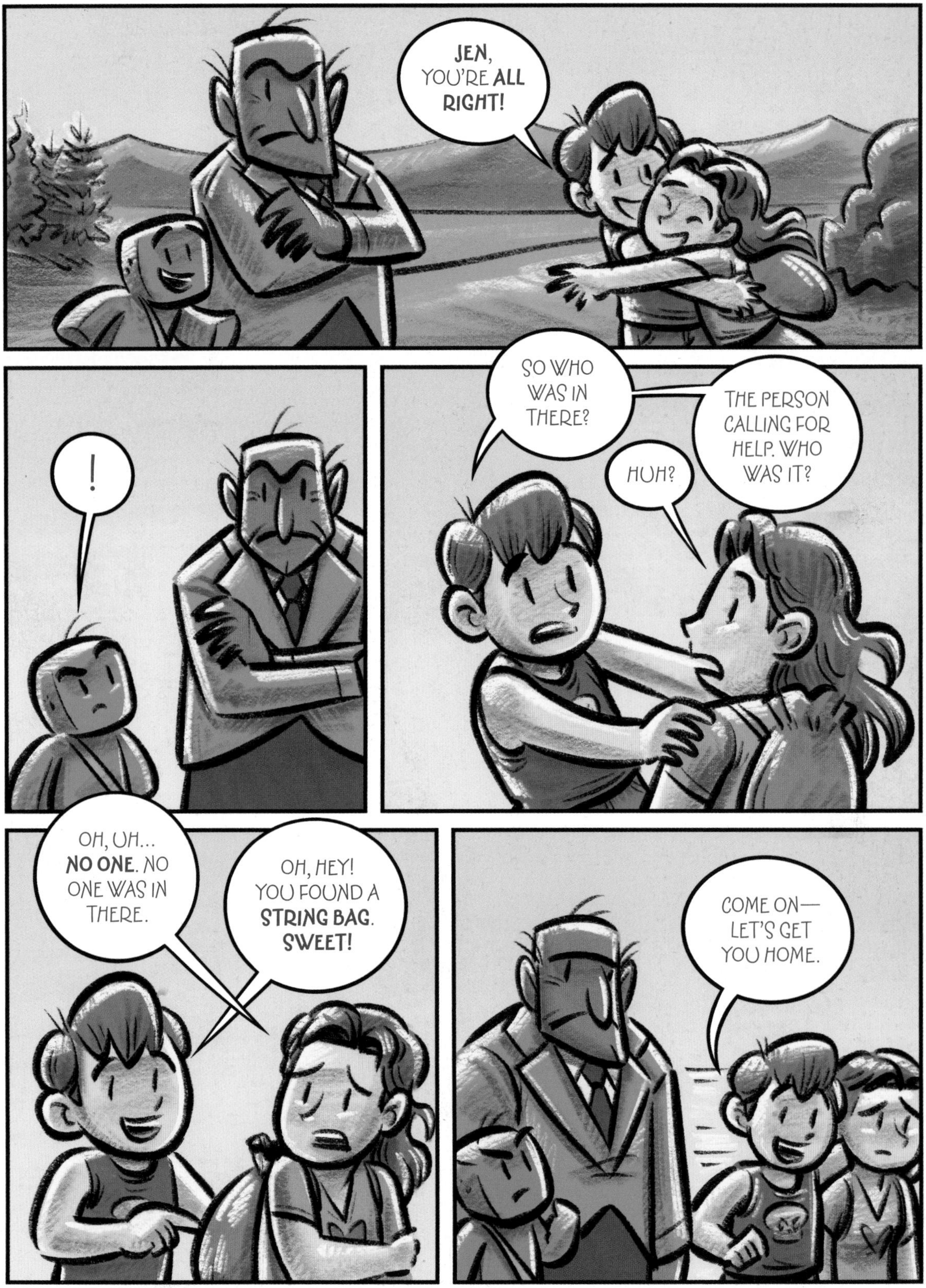
JEN, YOU'RE ALL RIGHT!
!
SO WHO WAS IN THERE?
HUH?
THE PERSON CALLING FOR HELP. WHO WAS IT?
OH, UH... NO ONE. NO ONE WAS IN THERE.
OH, HEY! YOU FOUND A STRING BAG. SWEET!
COME ON— LET'S GET YOU HOME.

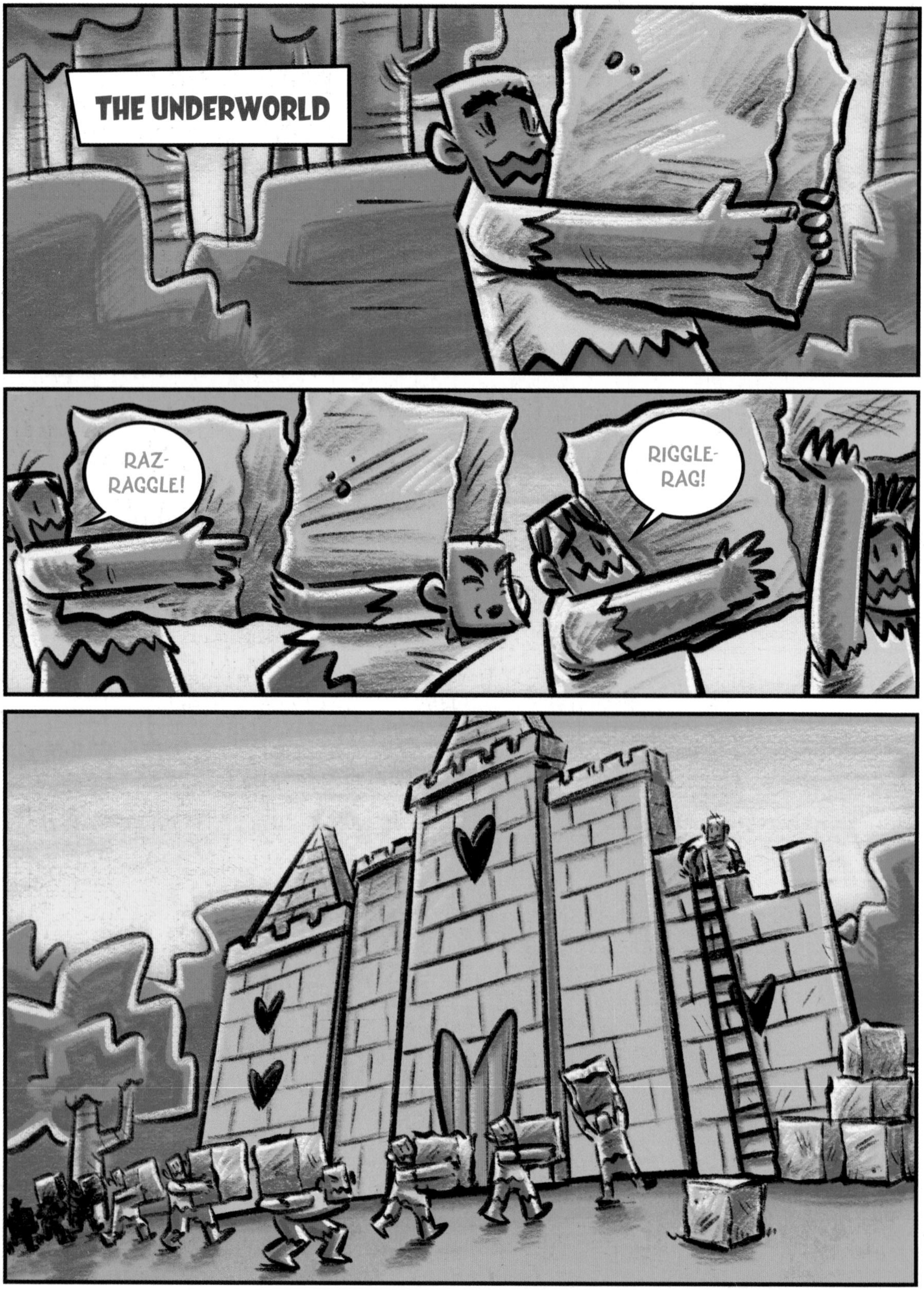
THE UNDERWORLD
RAZ-RAGGLE!
RIGGLE-RAG!

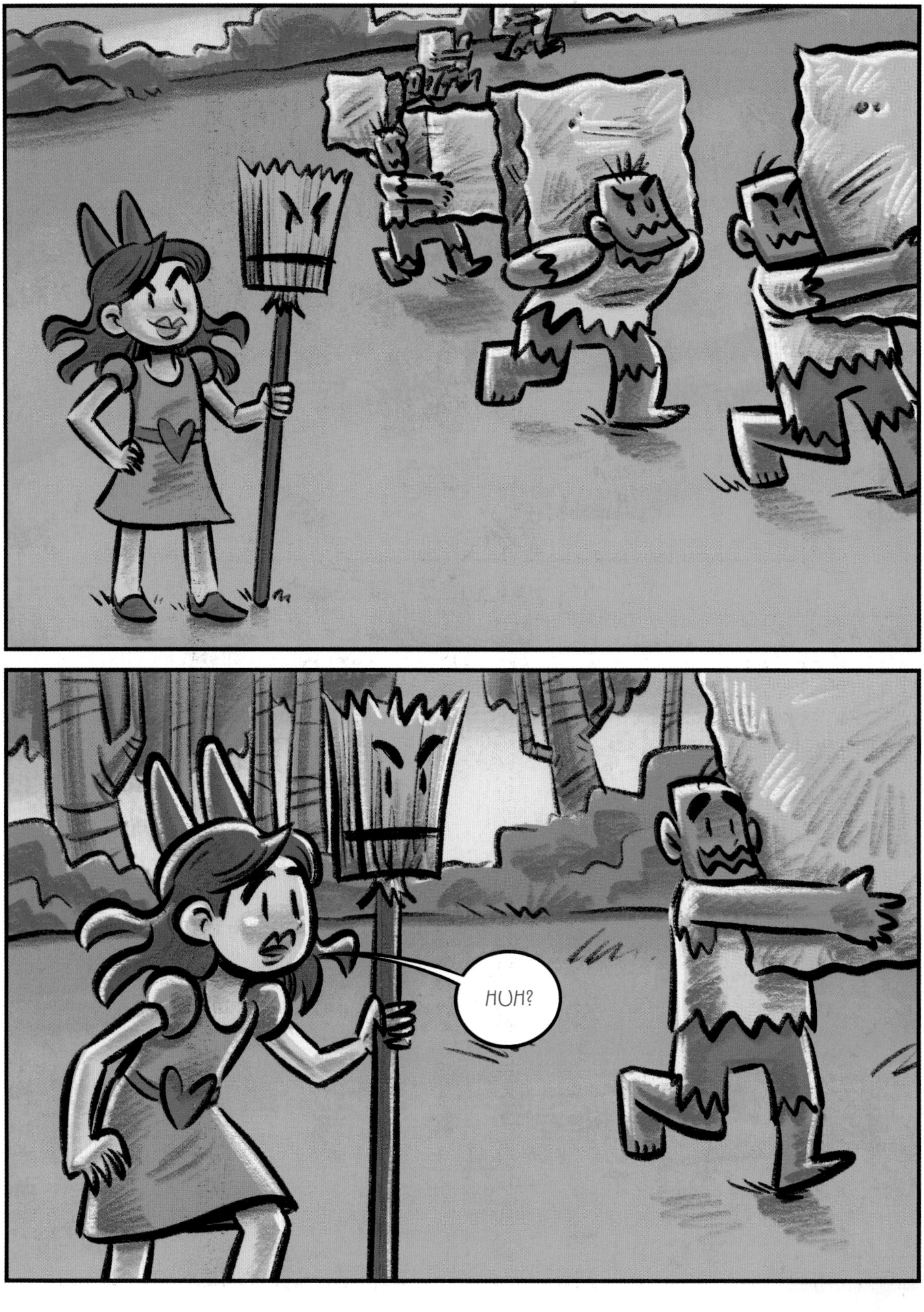
HUH?

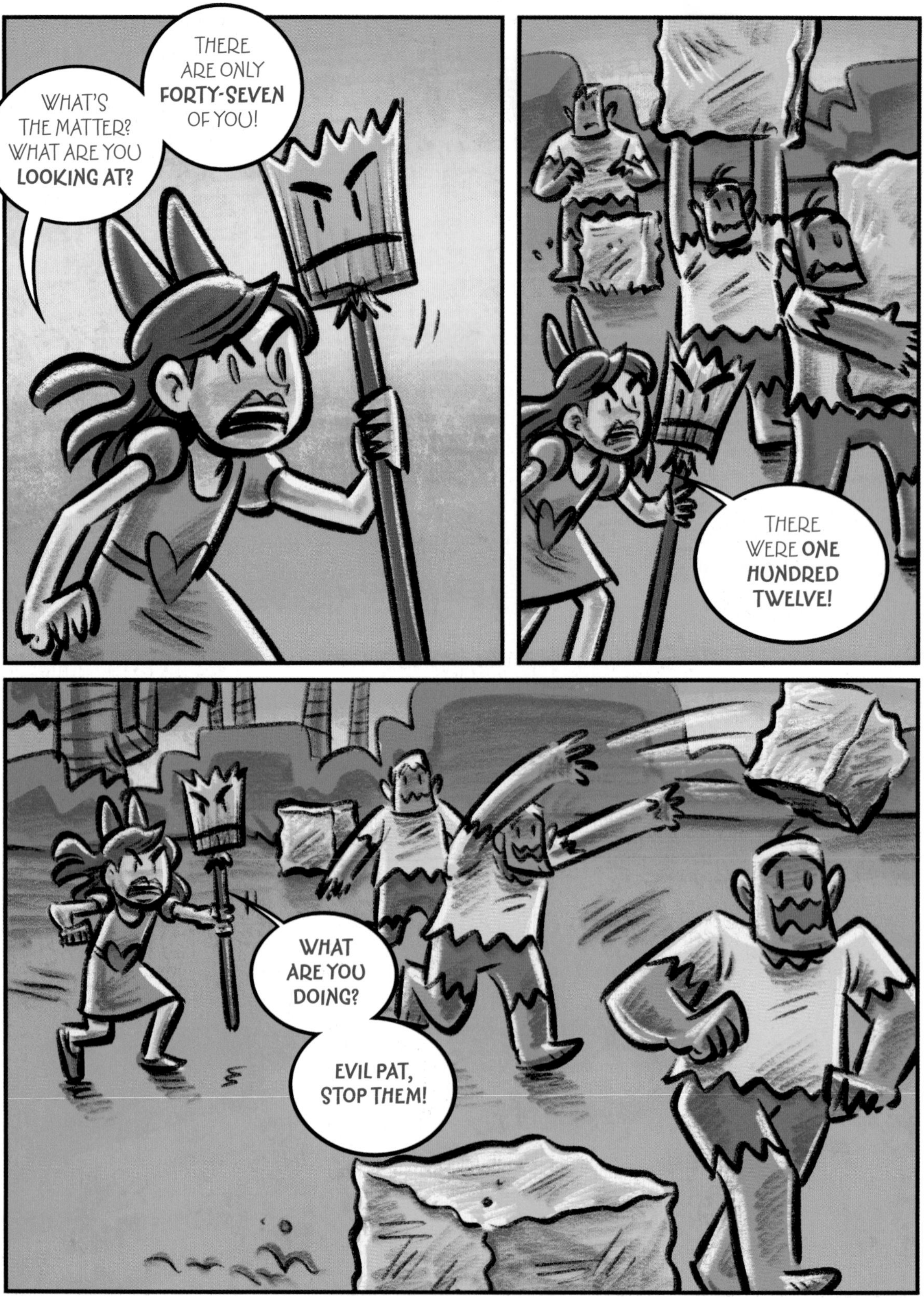
WHAT'S THE MATTER? WHAT ARE YOU LOOKING AT?
THERE ARE ONLY FORTY-SEVEN OF YOU!
THERE WERE ONE HUNDRED TWELVE!
WHAT ARE YOU DOING?
EVIL PAT, STOP THEM!

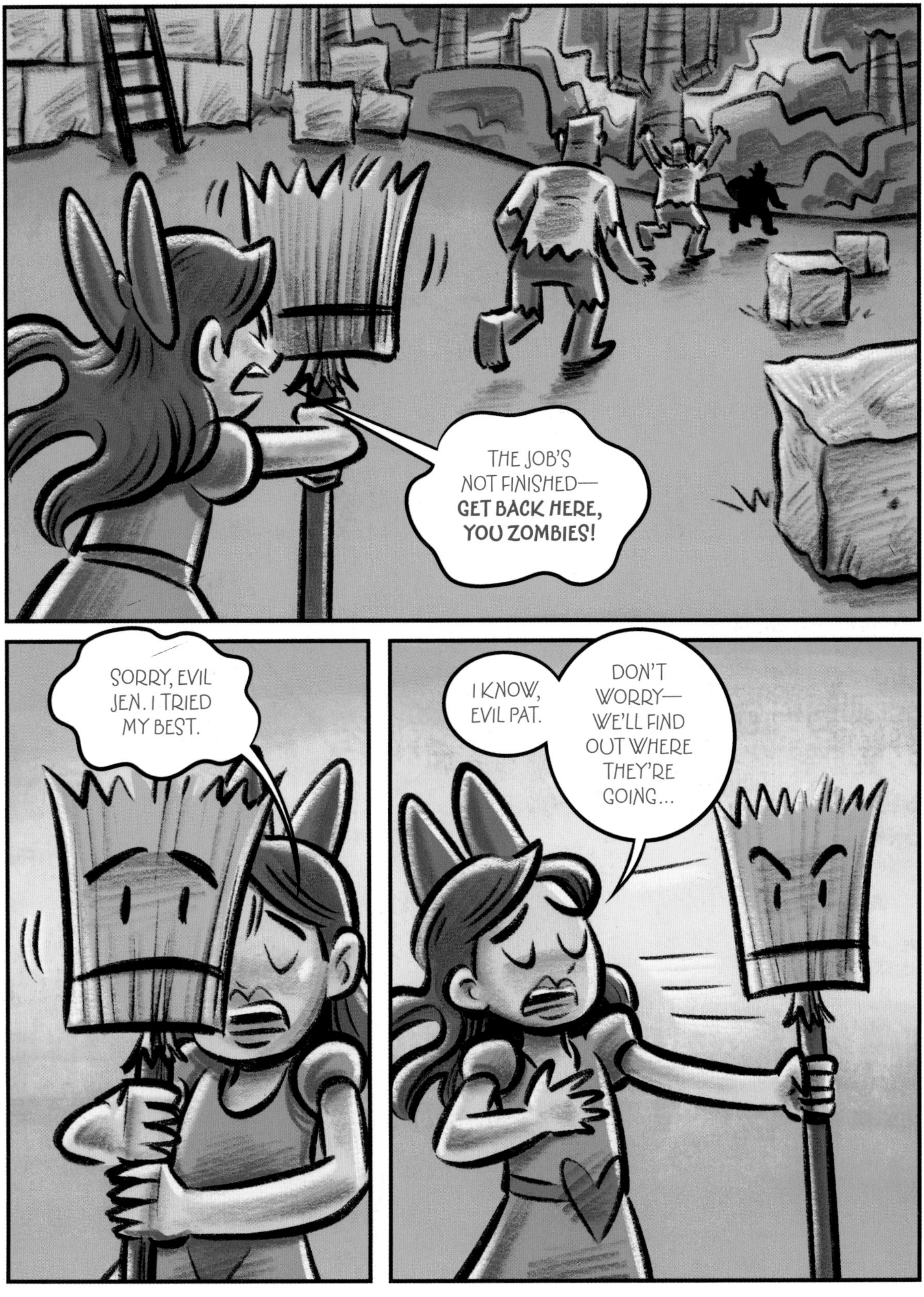
THE JOB'S NOT FINISHED— **GET BACK HERE, YOU ZOMBIES!**
SORRY, EVIL JEN. I TRIED MY BEST.
I KNOW, EVIL PAT.
DON'T WORRY— WE'LL FIND OUT WHERE THEY'RE GOING...

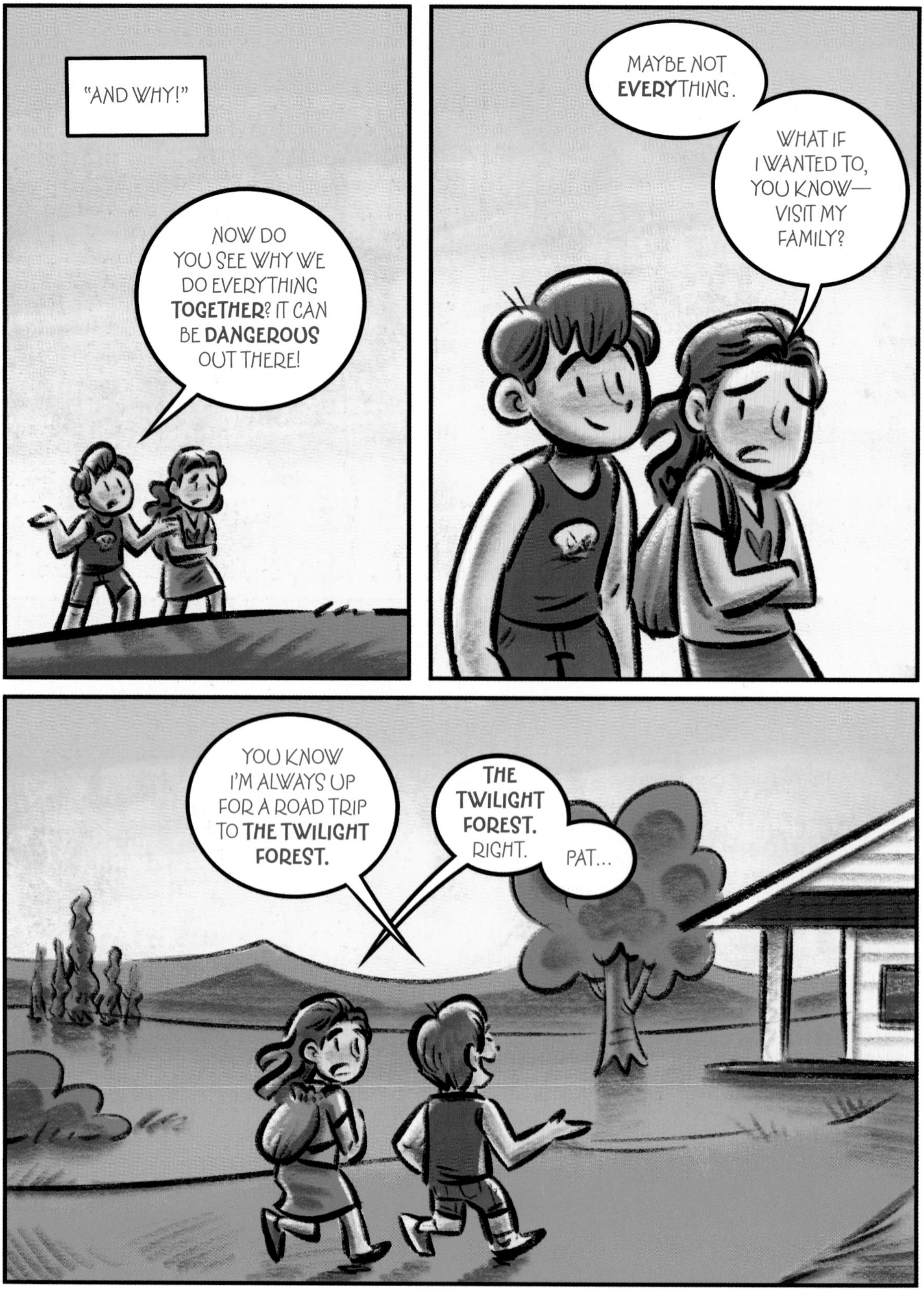
"AND WHY!"
NOW DO YOU SEE WHY WE DO EVERYTHING **TOGETHER**? IT CAN BE **DANGEROUS** OUT THERE!
MAYBE NOT **EVERY**THING.
WHAT IF I WANTED TO, YOU KNOW— VISIT MY FAMILY?
YOU KNOW I'M ALWAYS UP FOR A ROAD TRIP TO **THE TWILIGHT FOREST.**
THE TWILIGHT FOREST. RIGHT.
PAT...

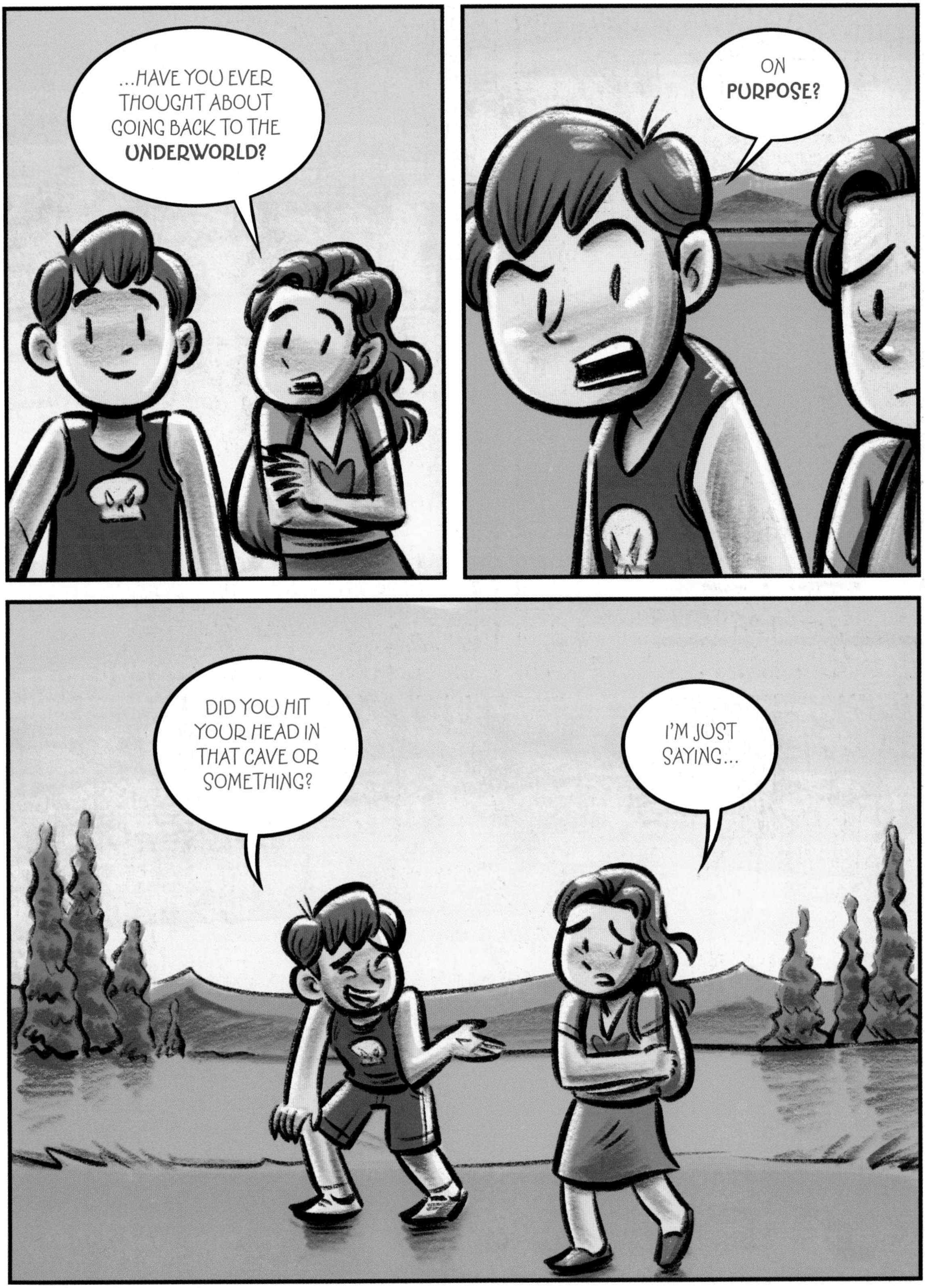
...HAVE YOU EVER THOUGHT ABOUT GOING BACK TO THE **UNDERWORLD?**
ON **PURPOSE?**
DID YOU HIT YOUR HEAD IN THAT CAVE OR SOMETHING?
I'M JUST SAYING...

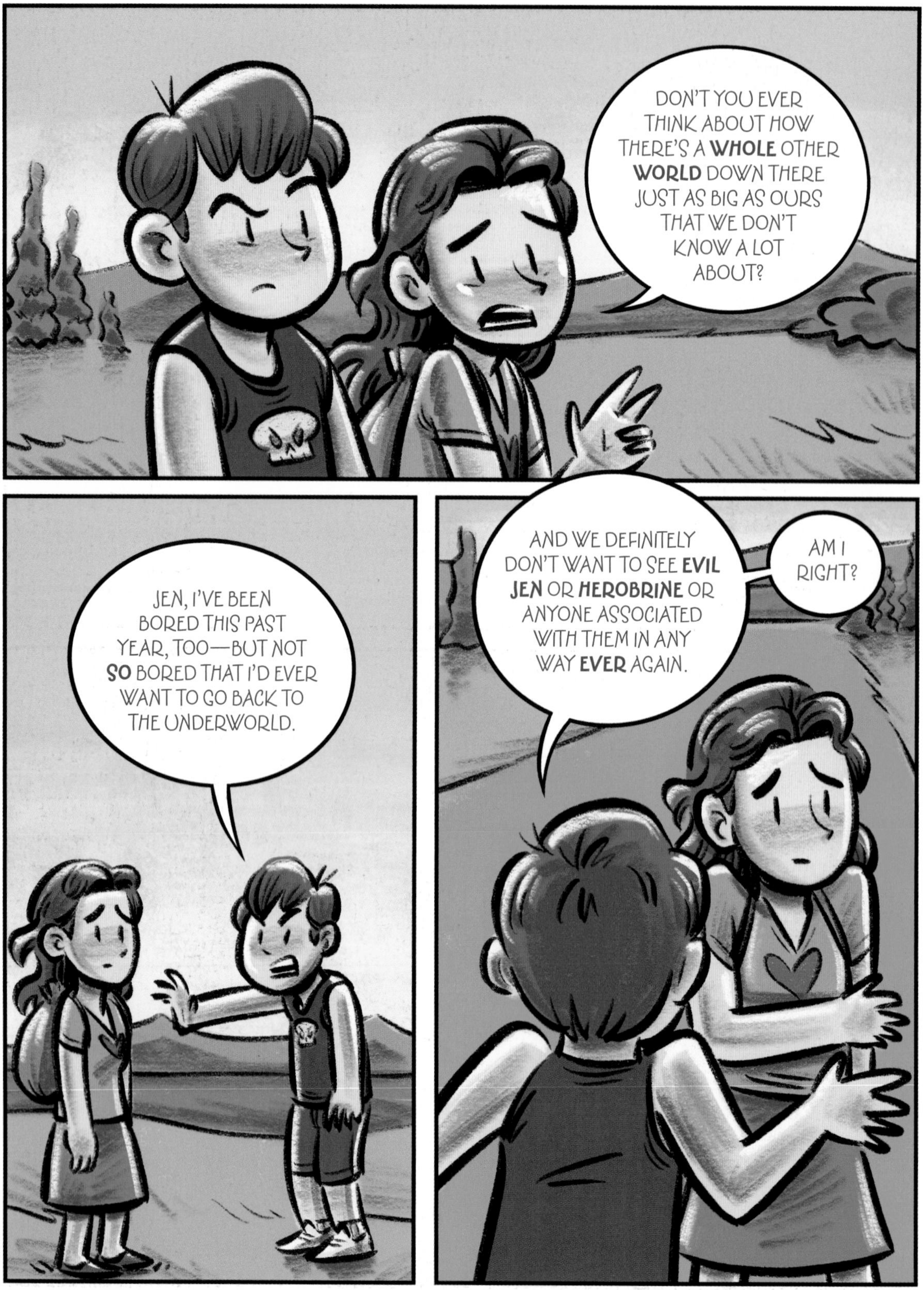
DON'T YOU EVER THINK ABOUT HOW THERE'S A WHOLE OTHER WORLD DOWN THERE JUST AS BIG AS OURS THAT WE DON'T KNOW A LOT ABOUT?
JEN, I'VE BEEN BORED THIS PAST YEAR, TOO—BUT NOT SO BORED THAT I'D EVER WANT TO GO BACK TO THE UNDERWORLD.
AND WE DEFINITELY DON'T WANT TO SEE EVIL JEN OR HEROBRINE OR ANYONE ASSOCIATED WITH THEM IN ANY WAY EVER AGAIN.
AM I RIGHT?

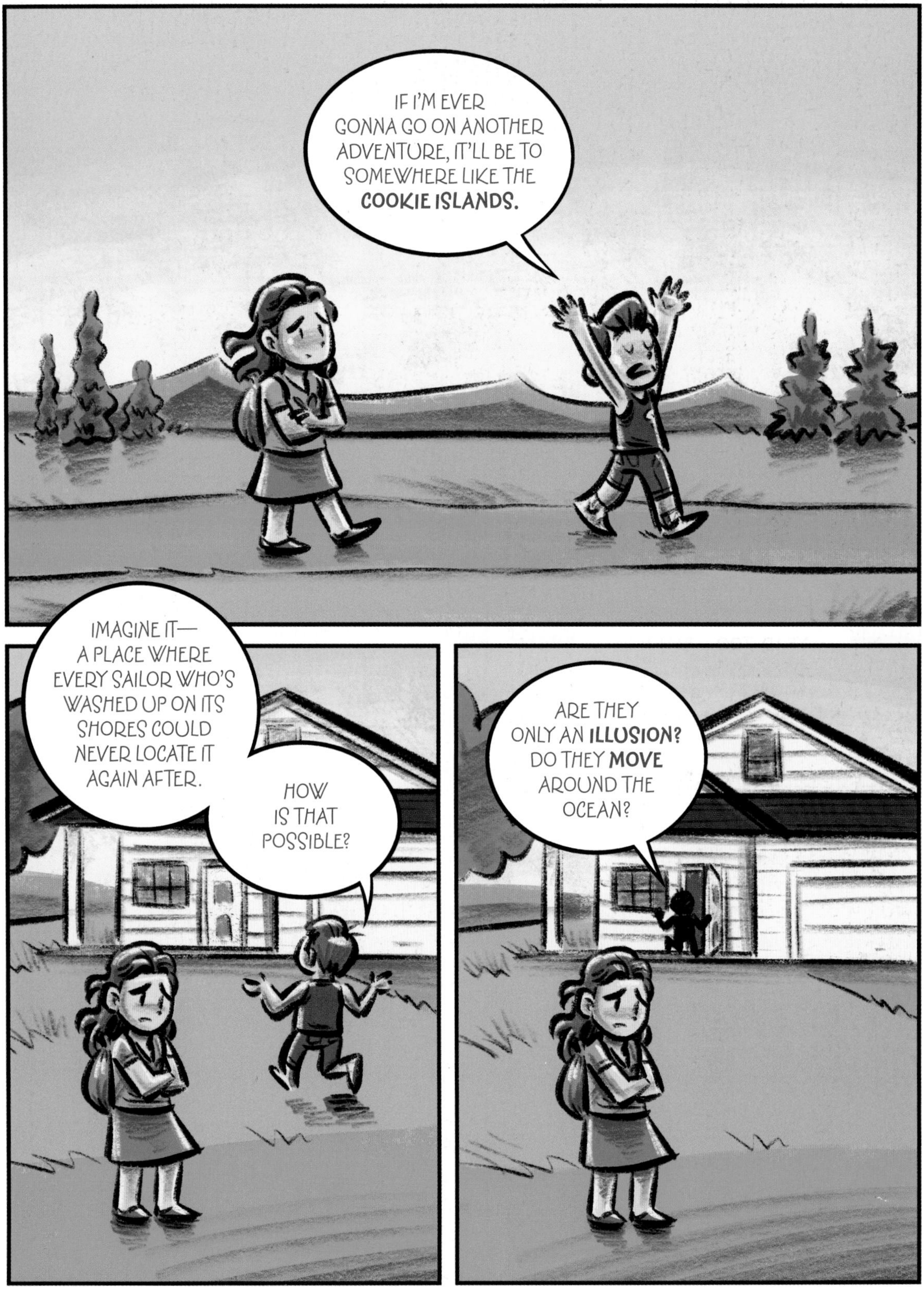
IF I'M EVER GONNA GO ON ANOTHER ADVENTURE, IT'LL BE TO SOMEWHERE LIKE THE **COOKIE ISLANDS.**
IMAGINE IT— A PLACE WHERE EVERY SAILOR WHO'S WASHED UP ON ITS SHORES COULD NEVER LOCATE IT AGAIN AFTER.
HOW IS THAT POSSIBLE?
ARE THEY ONLY AN **ILLUSION?** DO THEY **MOVE** AROUND THE OCEAN?

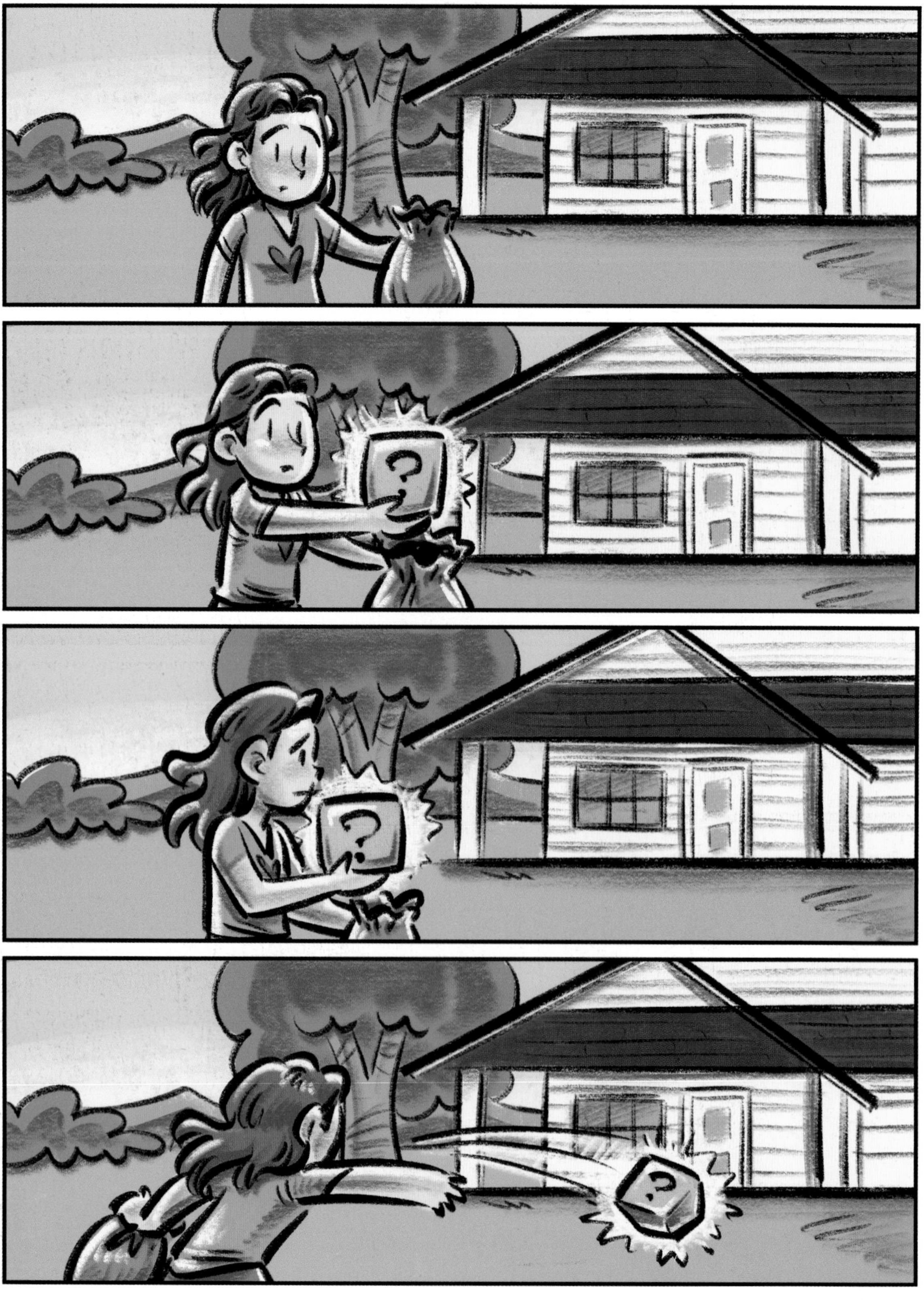

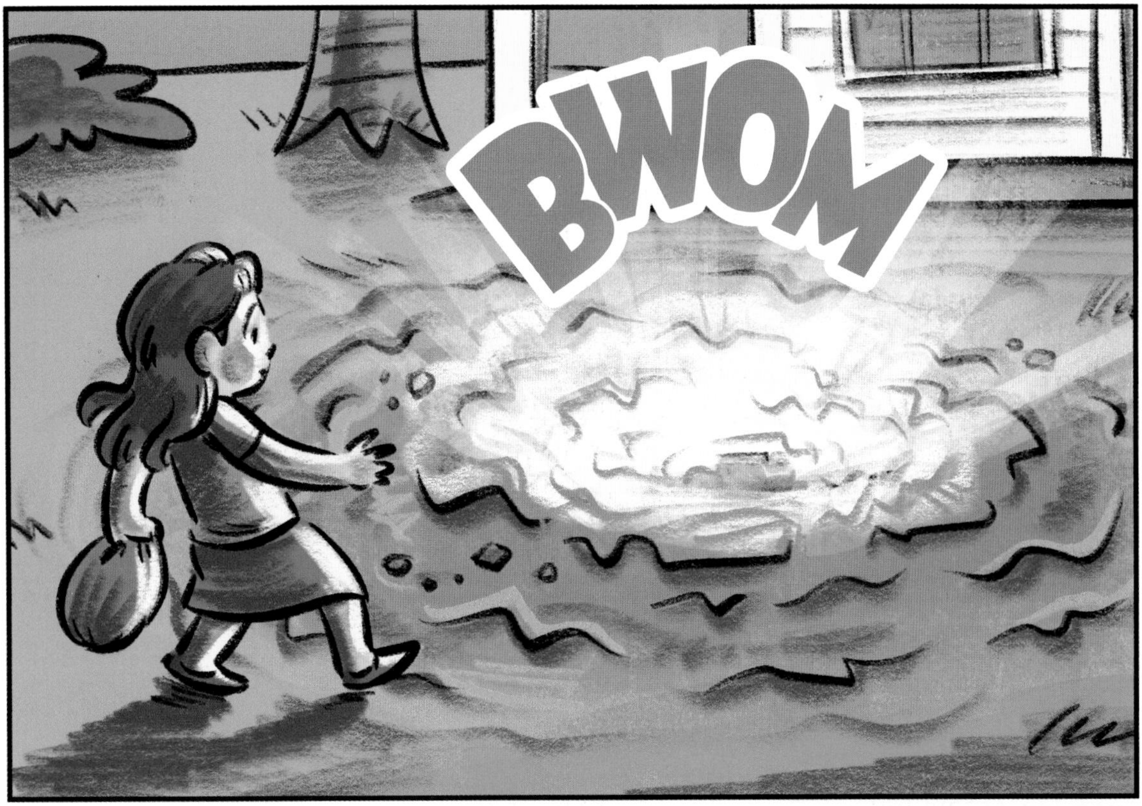
BWOM

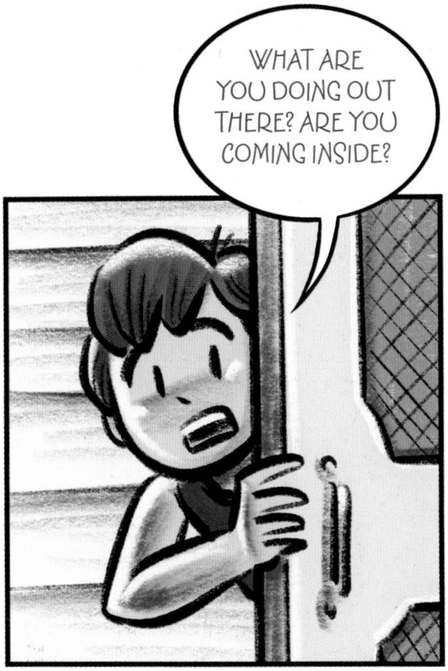
WHAT ARE YOU DOING OUT THERE? ARE YOU COMING INSIDE?

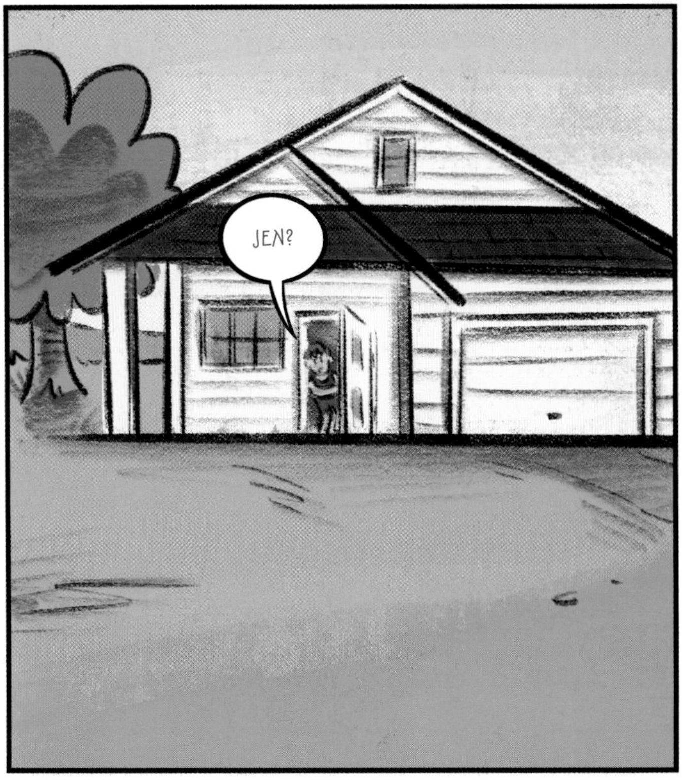
JEN?

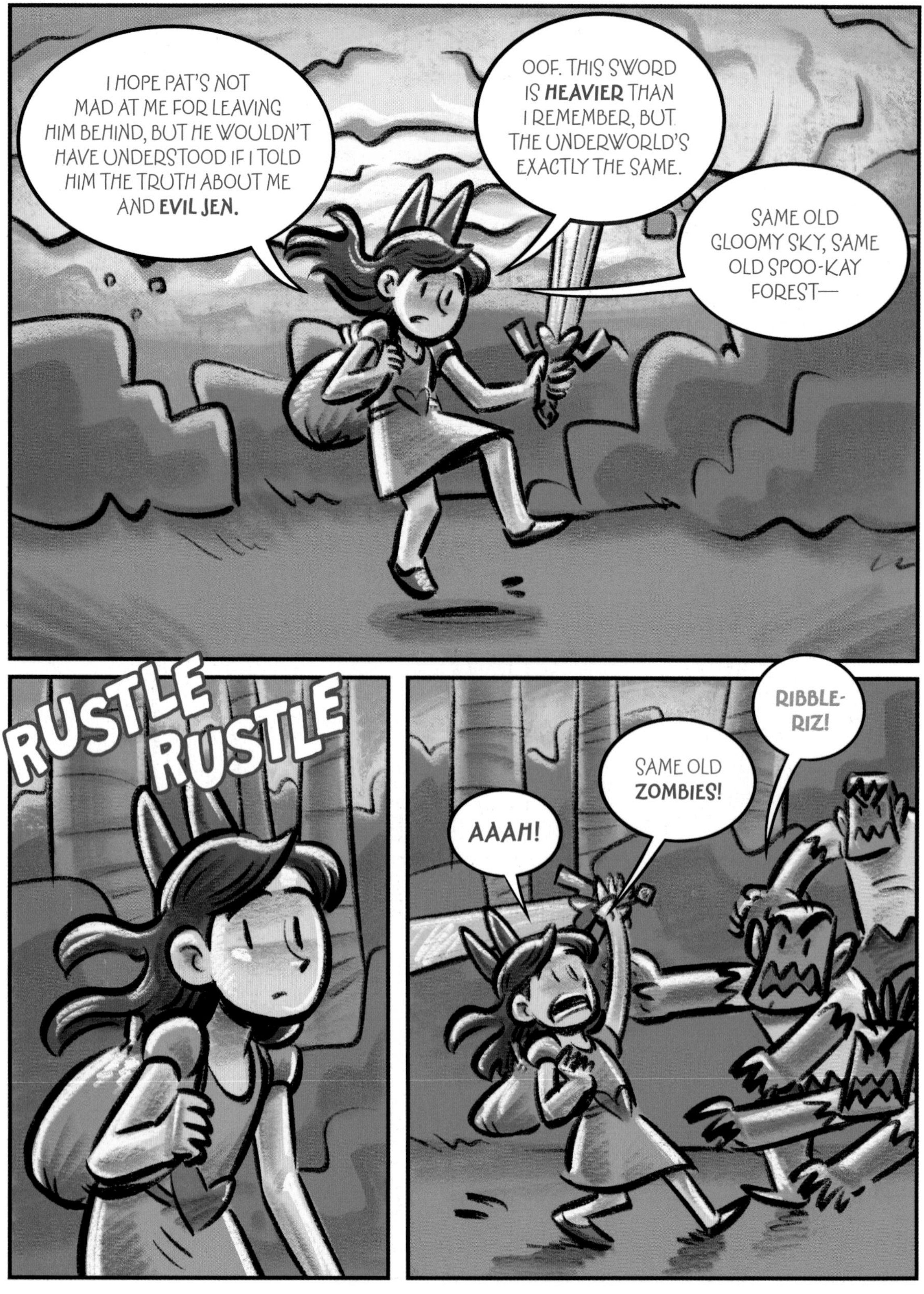
I HOPE PAT'S NOT MAD AT ME FOR LEAVING HIM BEHIND, BUT HE WOULDN'T HAVE UNDERSTOOD IF I TOLD HIM THE TRUTH ABOUT ME AND **EVIL JEN.**
OOF. THIS SWORD IS **HEAVIER** THAN I REMEMBER, BUT THE UNDERWORLD'S EXACTLY THE SAME.
SAME OLD GLOOMY SKY, SAME OLD SPOO-KAY FOREST—
RUSTLE RUSTLE
AAAH!
SAME OLD **ZOMBIES!**
RIBBLE-RIZ!

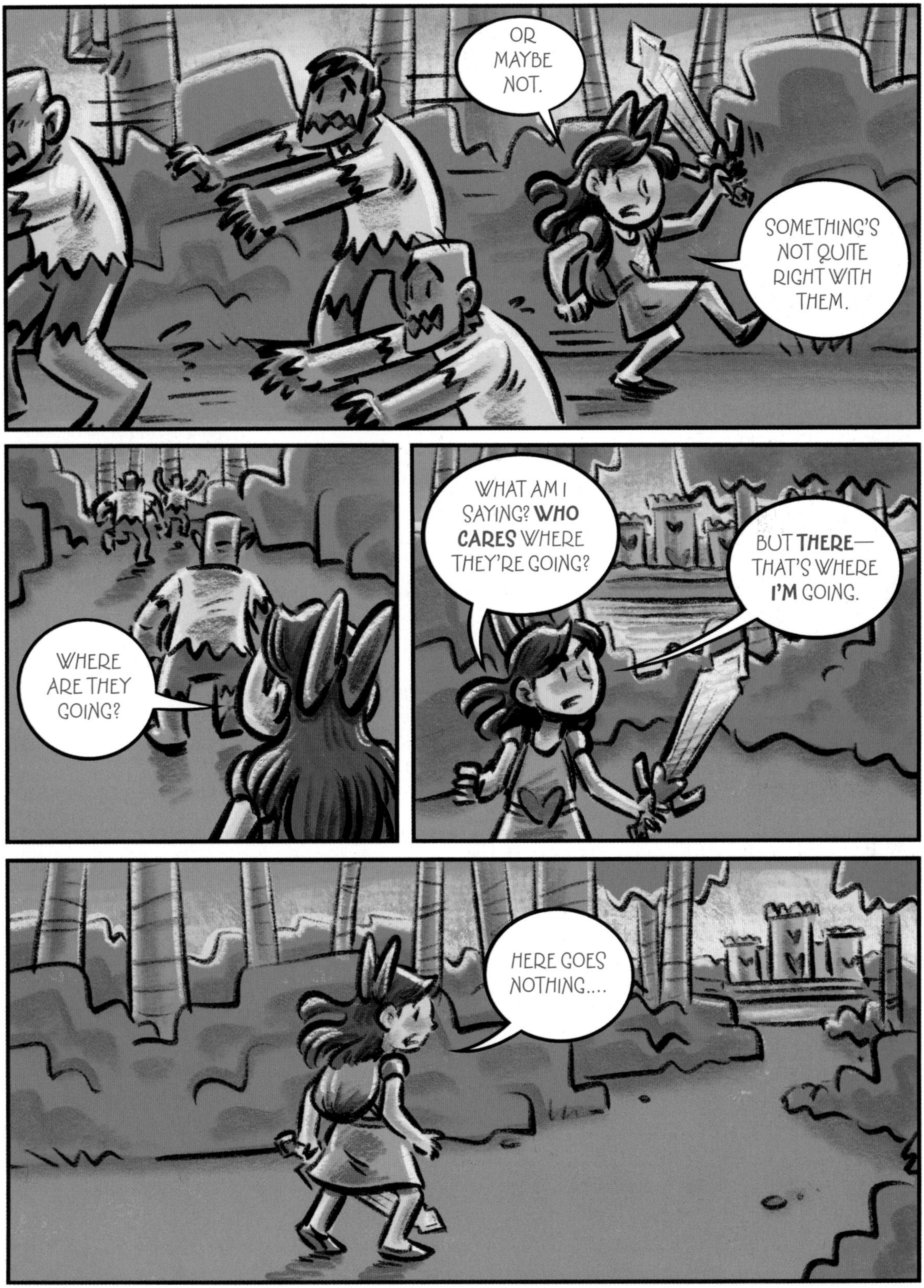
OR MAYBE NOT.
SOMETHING'S NOT QUITE RIGHT WITH THEM.
WHERE ARE THEY GOING?
WHAT AM I SAYING? **WHO CARES** WHERE THEY'RE GOING?
BUT **THERE**—THAT'S WHERE **I'M** GOING.
HERE GOES NOTHING....

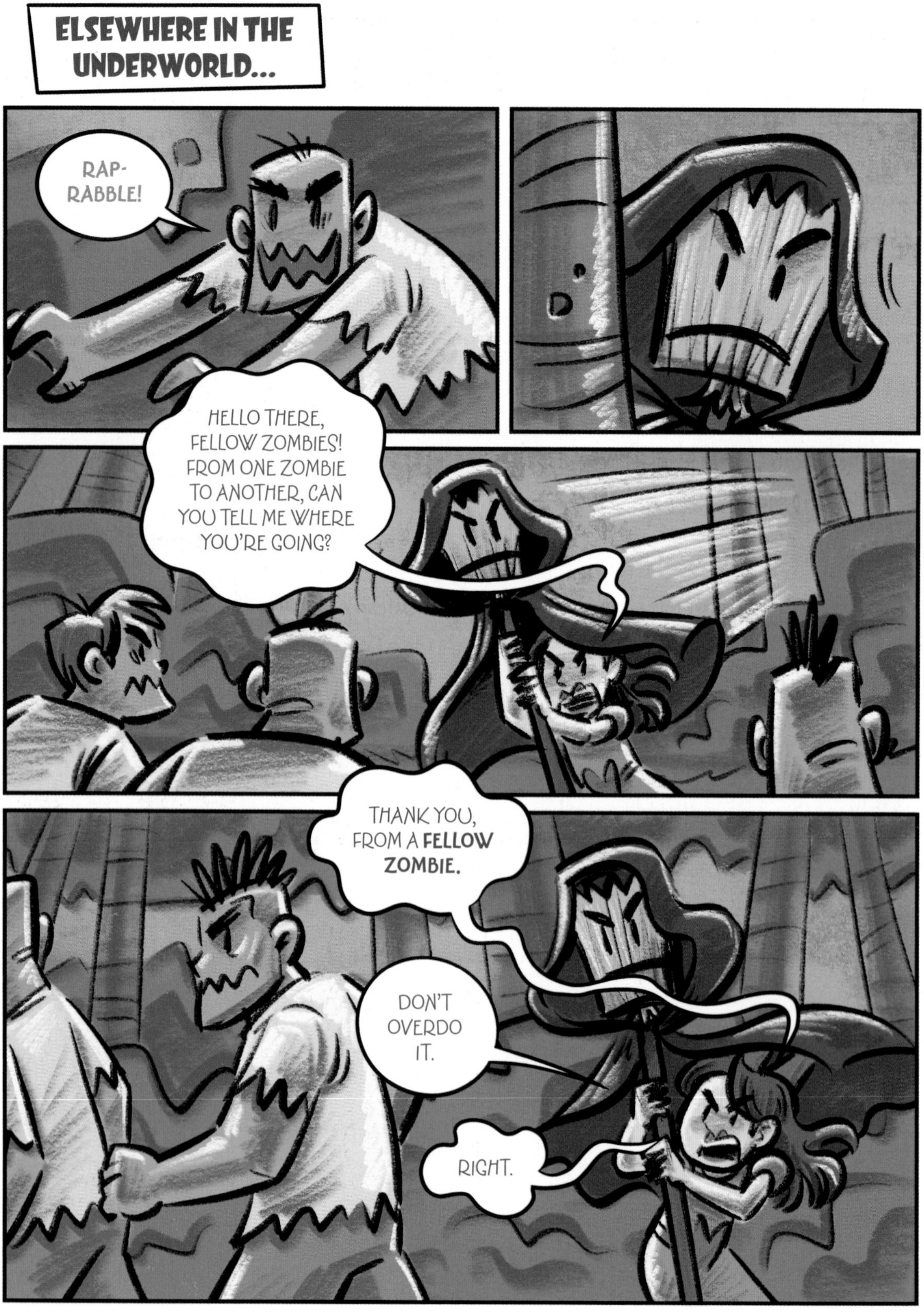
ELSEWHERE IN THE UNDERWORLD...
RAP-RABBLE!
HELLO THERE, FELLOW ZOMBIES! FROM ONE ZOMBIE TO ANOTHER, CAN YOU TELL ME WHERE YOU'RE GOING?
THANK YOU, FROM A **FELLOW ZOMBIE.**
DON'T OVERDO IT.
RIGHT.

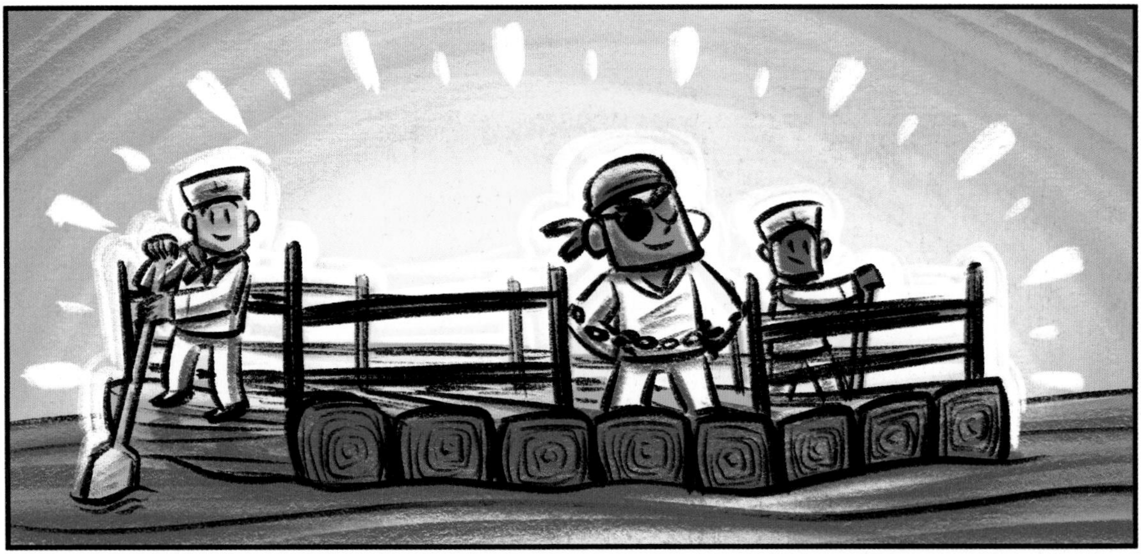

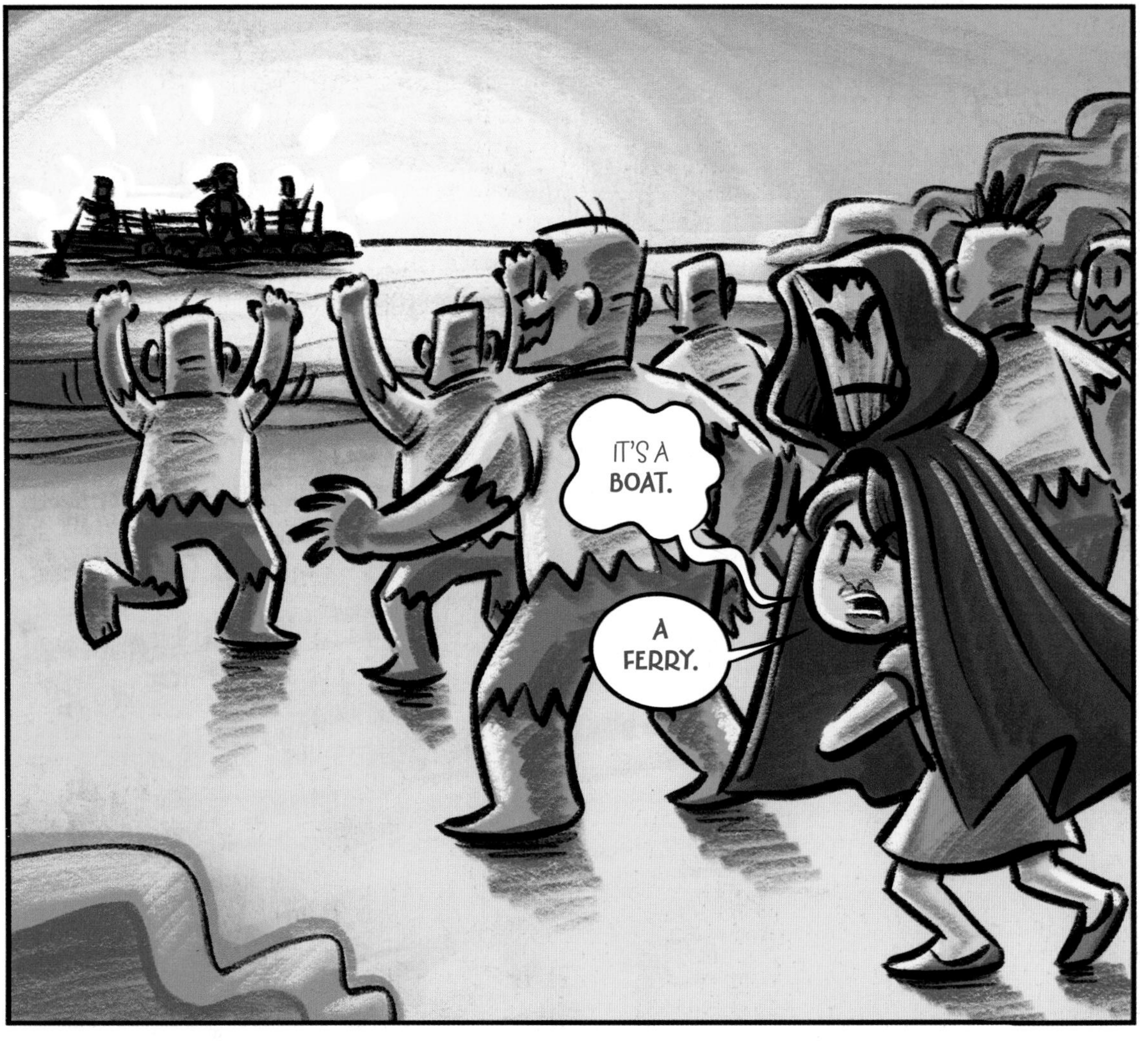

IT'S A BOAT.
A FERRY.

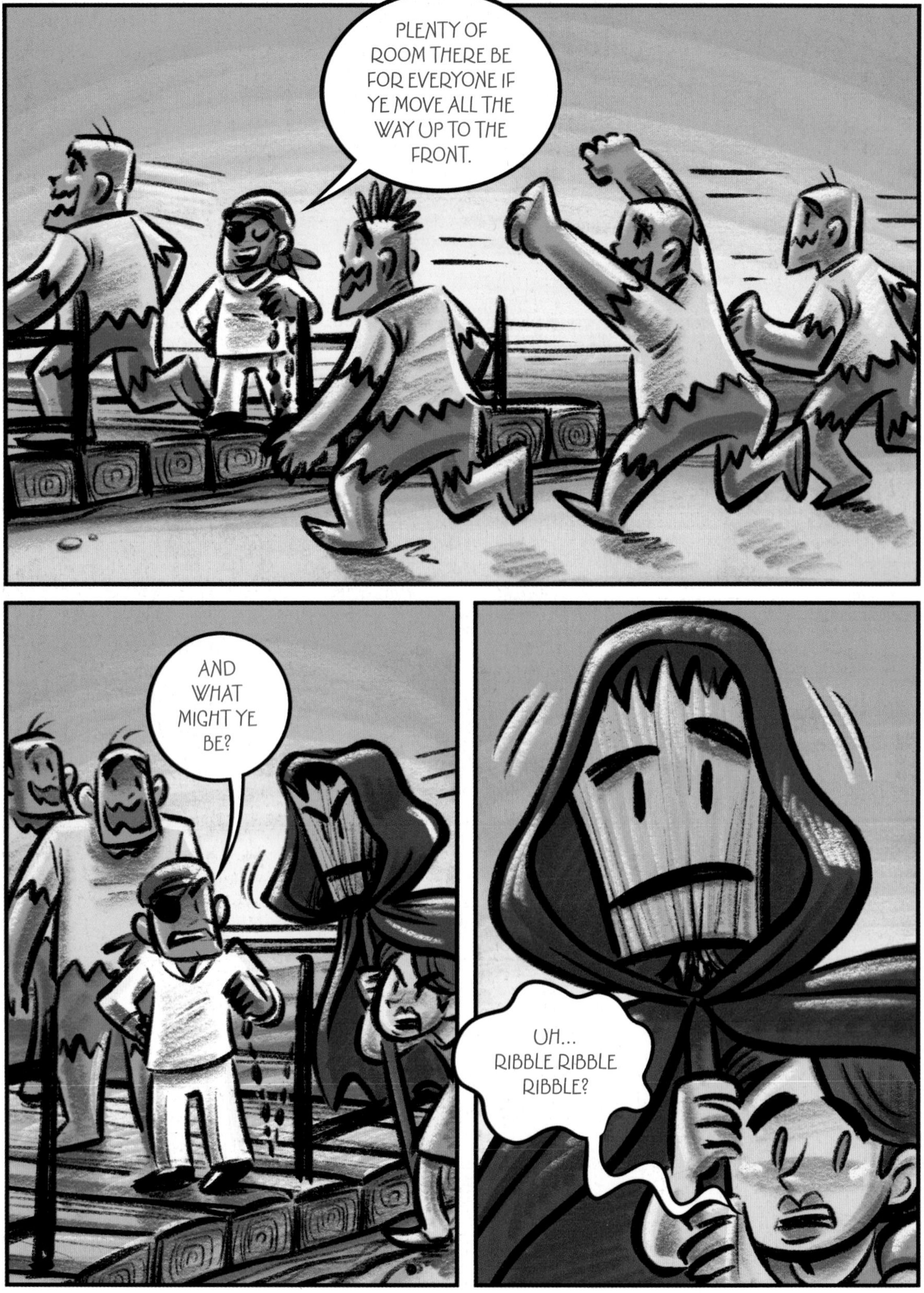
PLENTY OF ROOM THERE BE FOR EVERYONE IF YE MOVE ALL THE WAY UP TO THE FRONT.
AND WHAT MIGHT YE BE?
UH... RIBBLE RIBBLE RIBBLE?

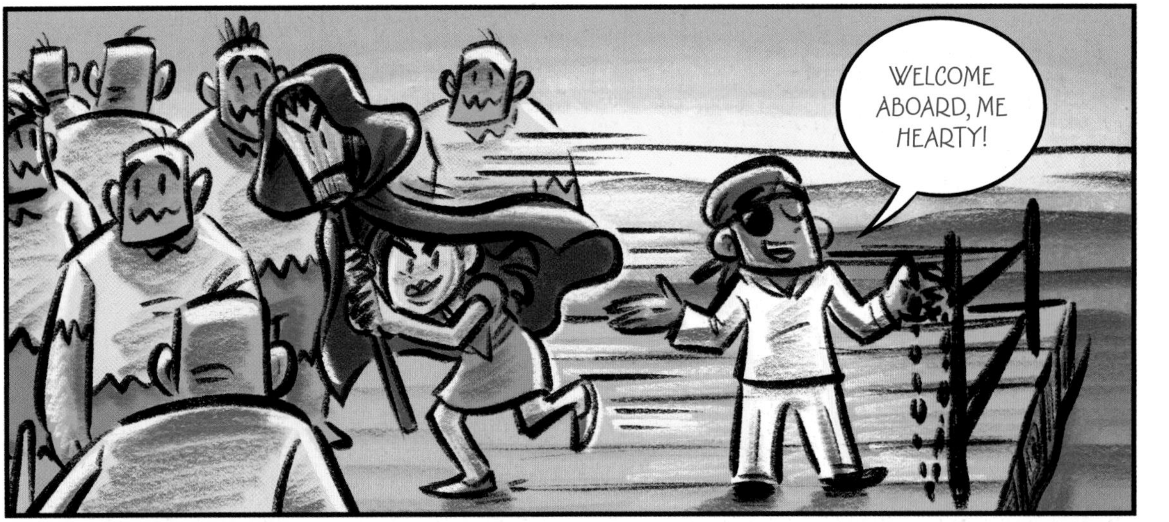
WELCOME ABOARD, ME HEARTY!

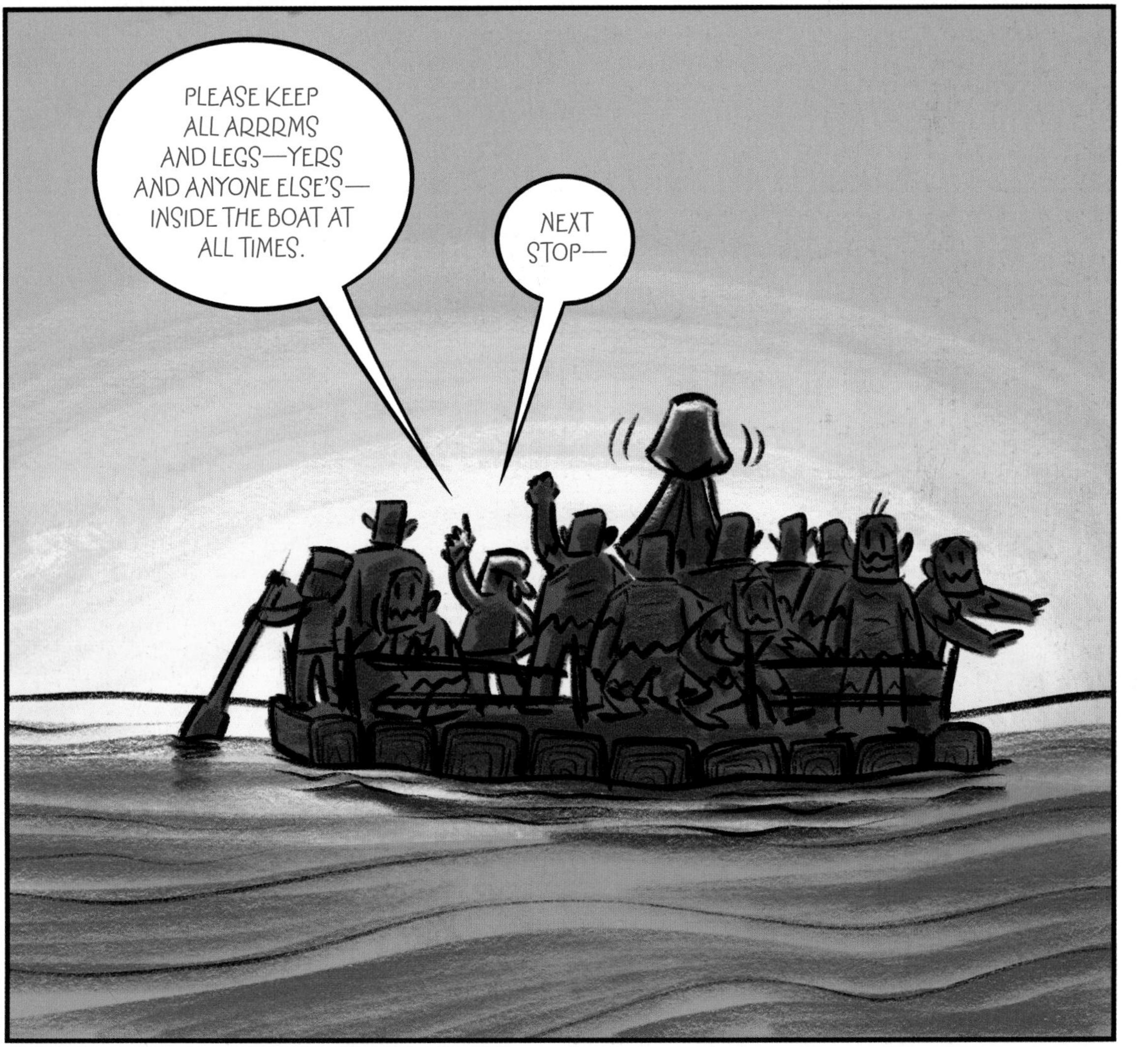
PLEASE KEEP ALL ARRRMS AND LEGS—YERS AND ANYONE ELSE'S—INSIDE THE BOAT AT ALL TIMES.
NEXT STOP—

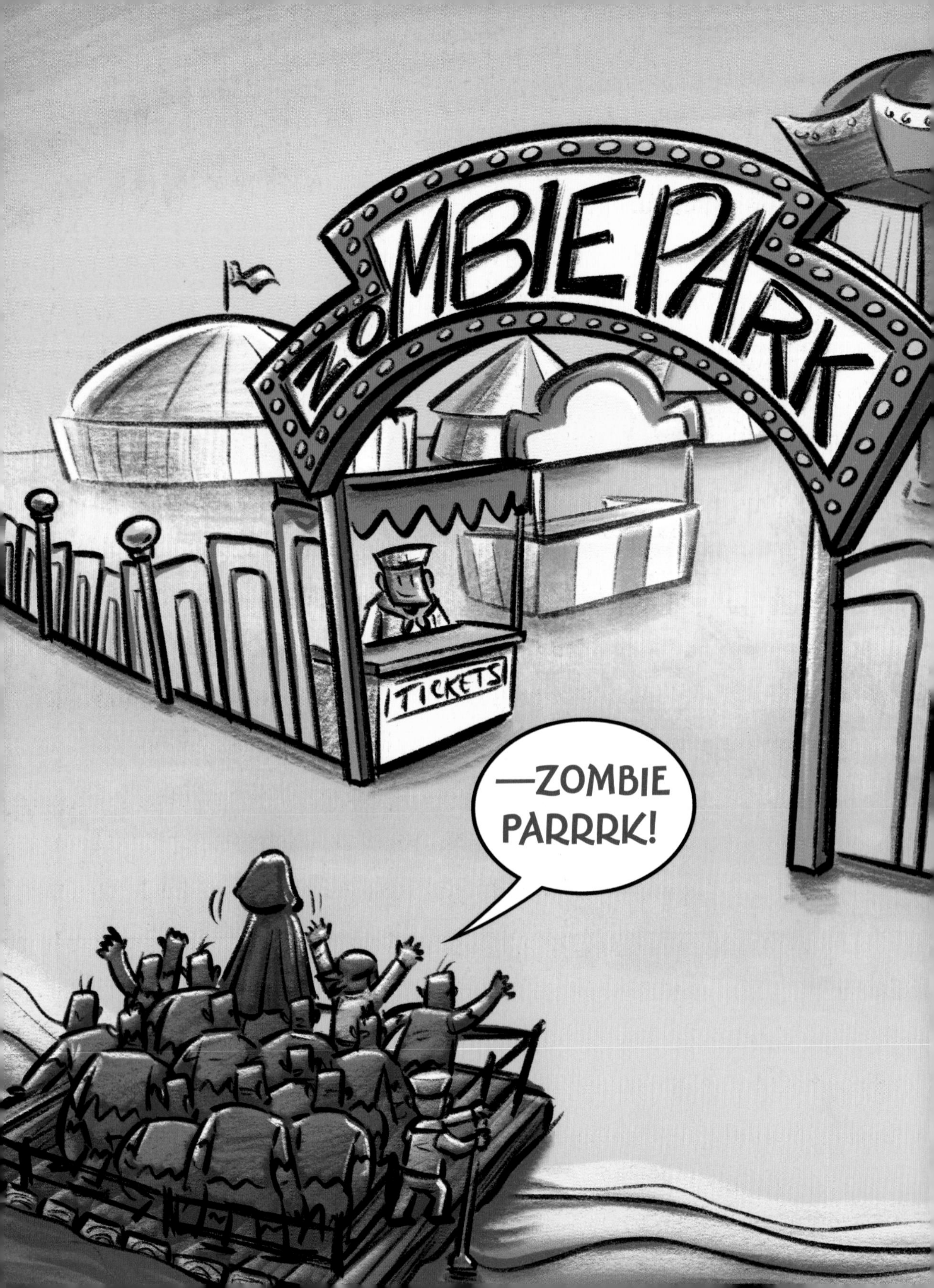
ZOMBIE PARK
TICKETS
—ZOMBIE PARRRK!

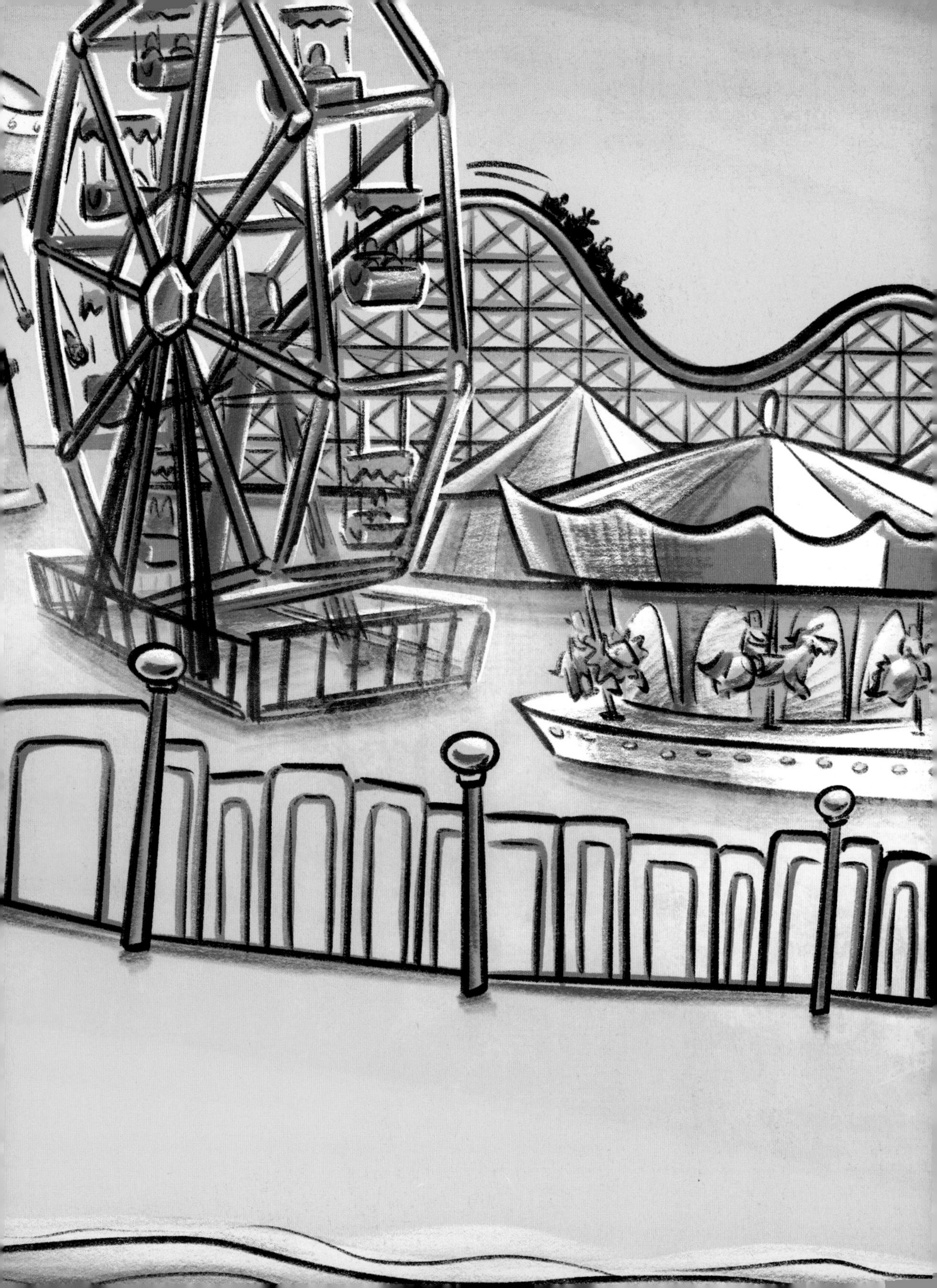

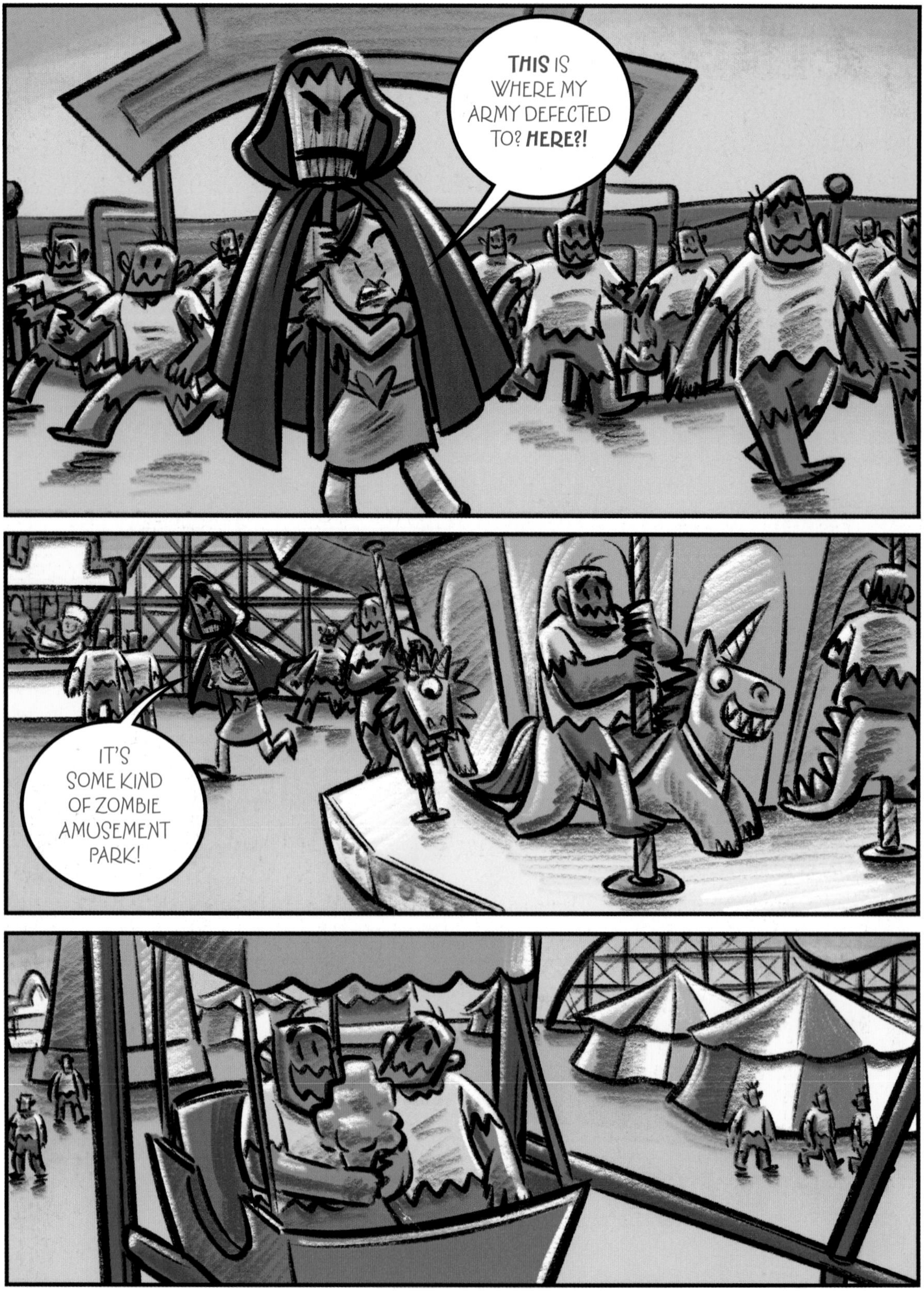
THIS IS WHERE MY ARMY DEFECTED TO? HERE?!
IT'S SOME KIND OF ZOMBIE AMUSEMENT PARK!

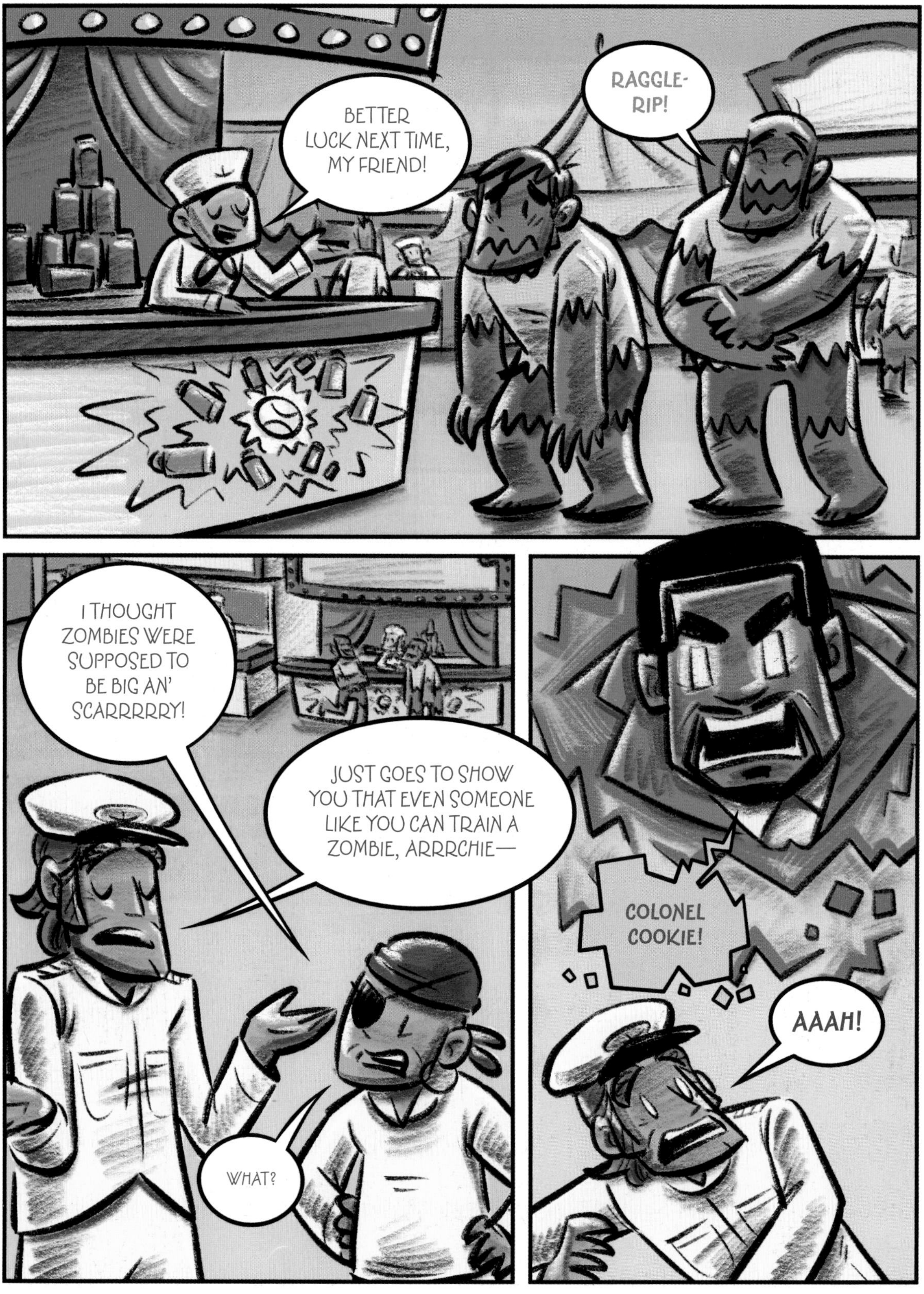
BETTER LUCK NEXT TIME, MY FRIEND!
RAGGLE-RIP!
I THOUGHT ZOMBIES WERE SUPPOSED TO BE BIG AN' SCARRRRRRY!
JUST GOES TO SHOW YOU THAT EVEN SOMEONE LIKE YOU CAN TRAIN A ZOMBIE, ARRRCHIE—
WHAT?
COLONEL COOKIE!
AAAH!

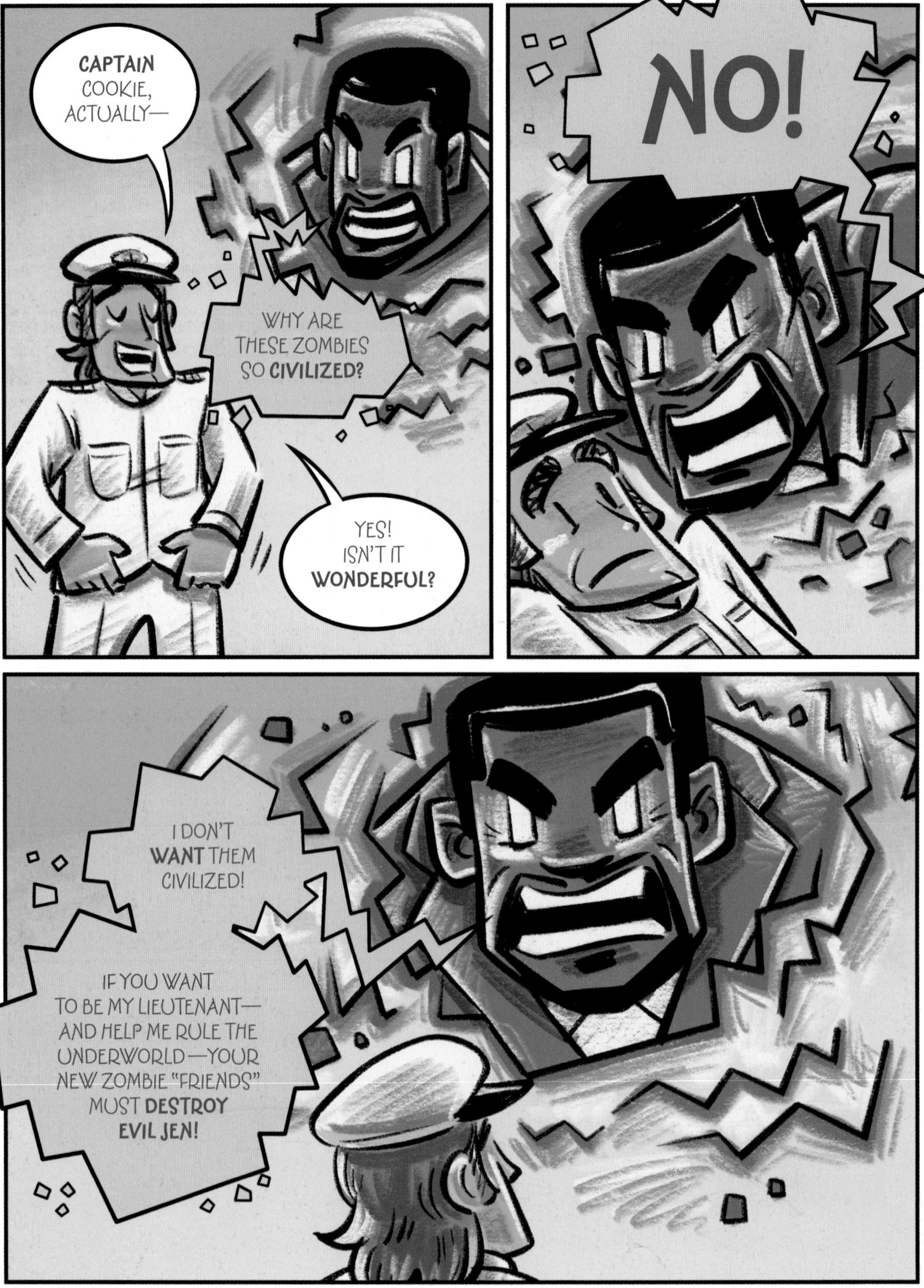

CAPTAIN COOKIE, ACTUALLY—
WHY ARE THESE ZOMBIES SO CIVILIZED?
YES! ISN'T IT WONDERFUL?
NO!
I DON'T WANT THEM CIVILIZED!
IF YOU WANT TO BE MY LIEUTENANT—AND HELP ME RULE THE UNDERWORLD—YOUR NEW ZOMBIE "FRIENDS" MUST DESTROY EVIL JEN!

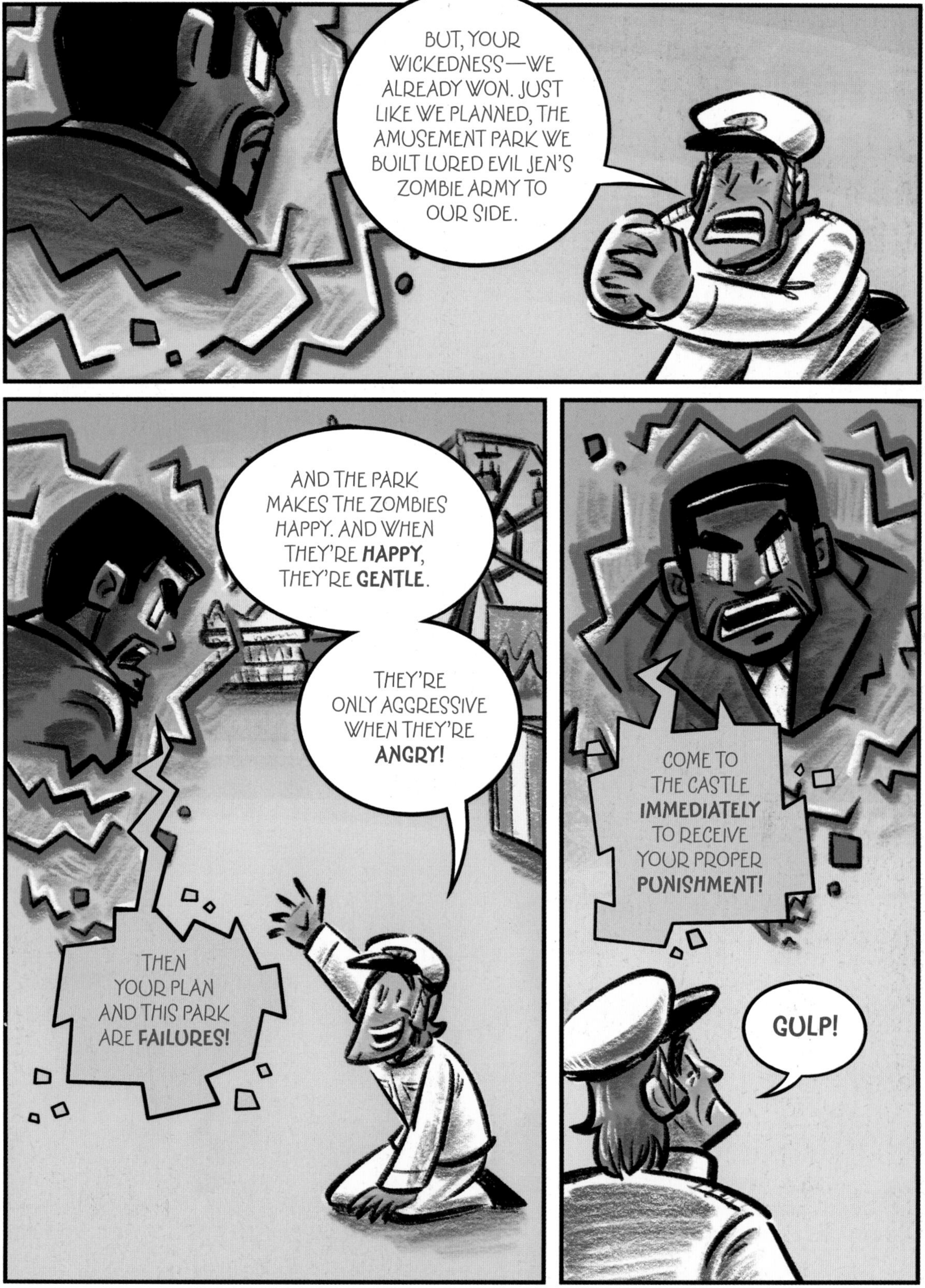
BUT, YOUR WICKEDNESS—WE ALREADY WON. JUST LIKE WE PLANNED, THE AMUSEMENT PARK WE BUILT LURED EVIL JEN'S ZOMBIE ARMY TO OUR SIDE.
AND THE PARK MAKES THE ZOMBIES HAPPY. AND WHEN THEY'RE **HAPPY**, THEY'RE **GENTLE**.
THEY'RE ONLY AGGRESSIVE WHEN THEY'RE **ANGRY!**
THEN YOUR PLAN AND THIS PARK ARE **FAILURES!**
COME TO THE CASTLE **IMMEDIATELY** TO RECEIVE YOUR PROPER **PUNISHMENT!**
GULP!

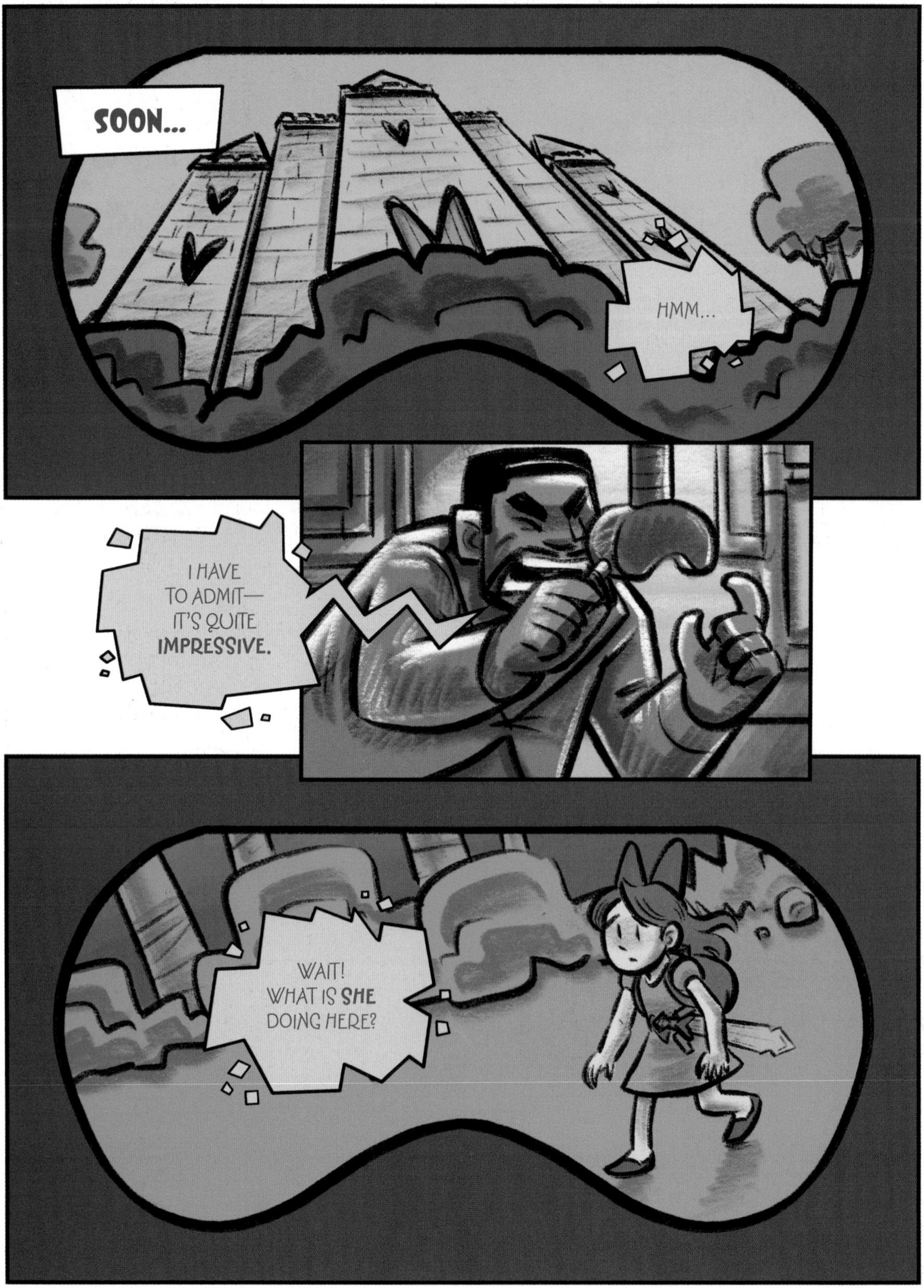
SOON...
HMM...
I HAVE TO ADMIT— IT'S QUITE **IMPRESSIVE.**
WAIT! WHAT IS **SHE** DOING HERE?

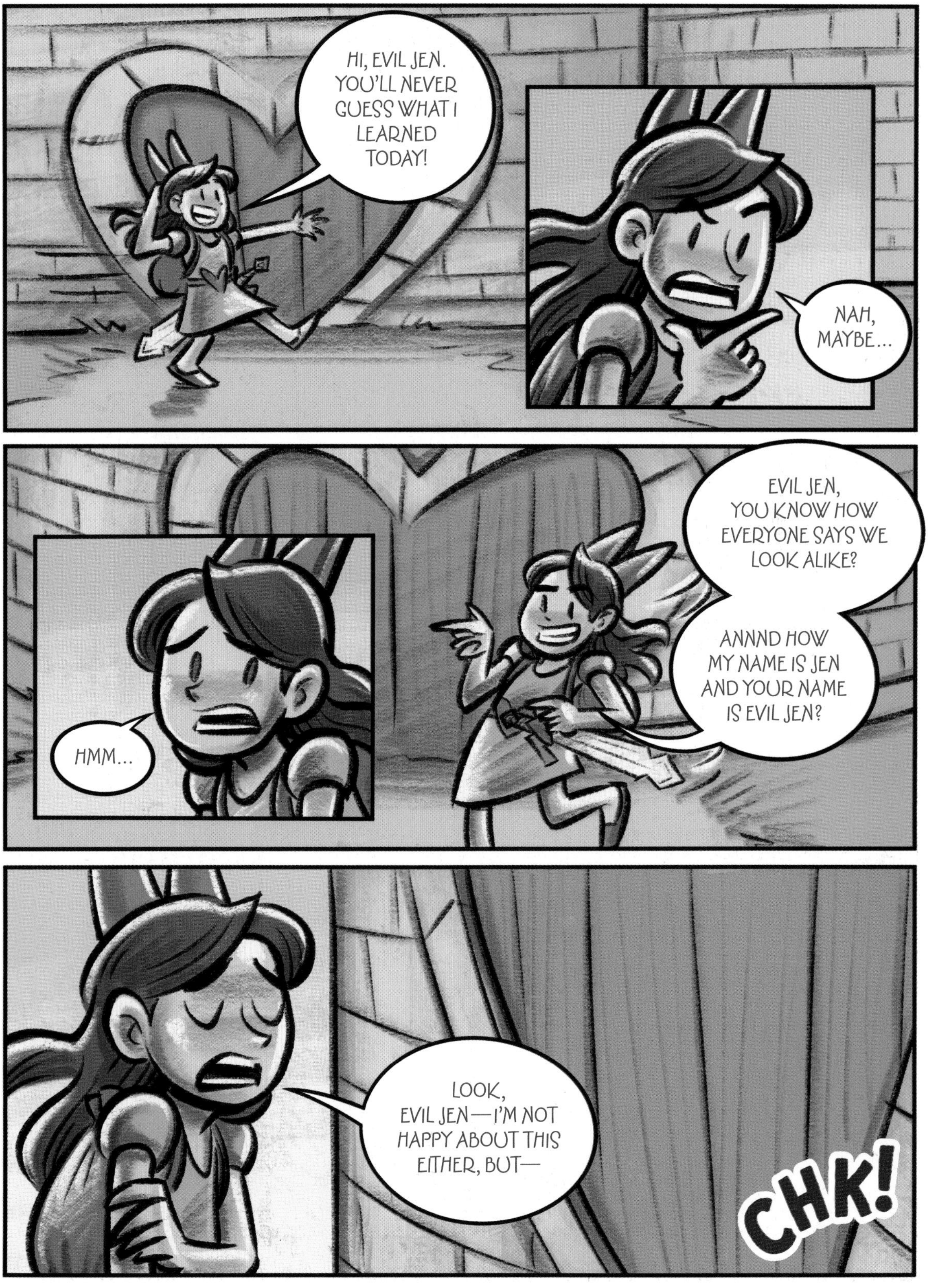
HI, EVIL JEN. YOU'LL NEVER GUESS WHAT I LEARNED TODAY!
NAH, MAYBE...
EVIL JEN, YOU KNOW HOW EVERYONE SAYS WE LOOK ALIKE?
ANNND HOW MY NAME IS JEN AND YOUR NAME IS EVIL JEN?
HMM...
LOOK, EVIL JEN—I'M NOT HAPPY ABOUT THIS EITHER, BUT—
CHK!

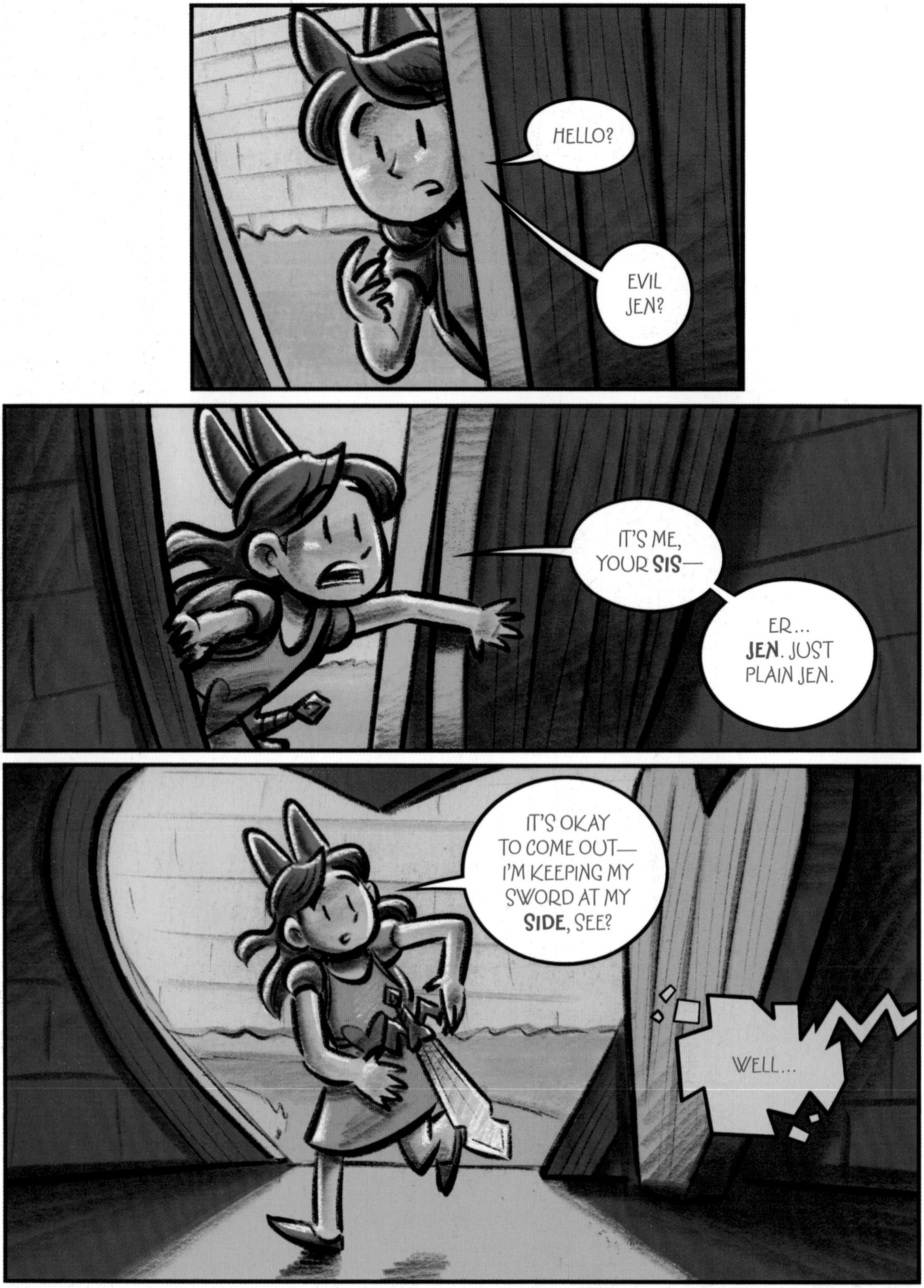

HELLO?
EVIL JEN?
IT'S ME, YOUR SIS—
ER... JEN. JUST PLAIN JEN.
IT'S OKAY TO COME OUT— I'M KEEPING MY SWORD AT MY SIDE, SEE?
WELL...

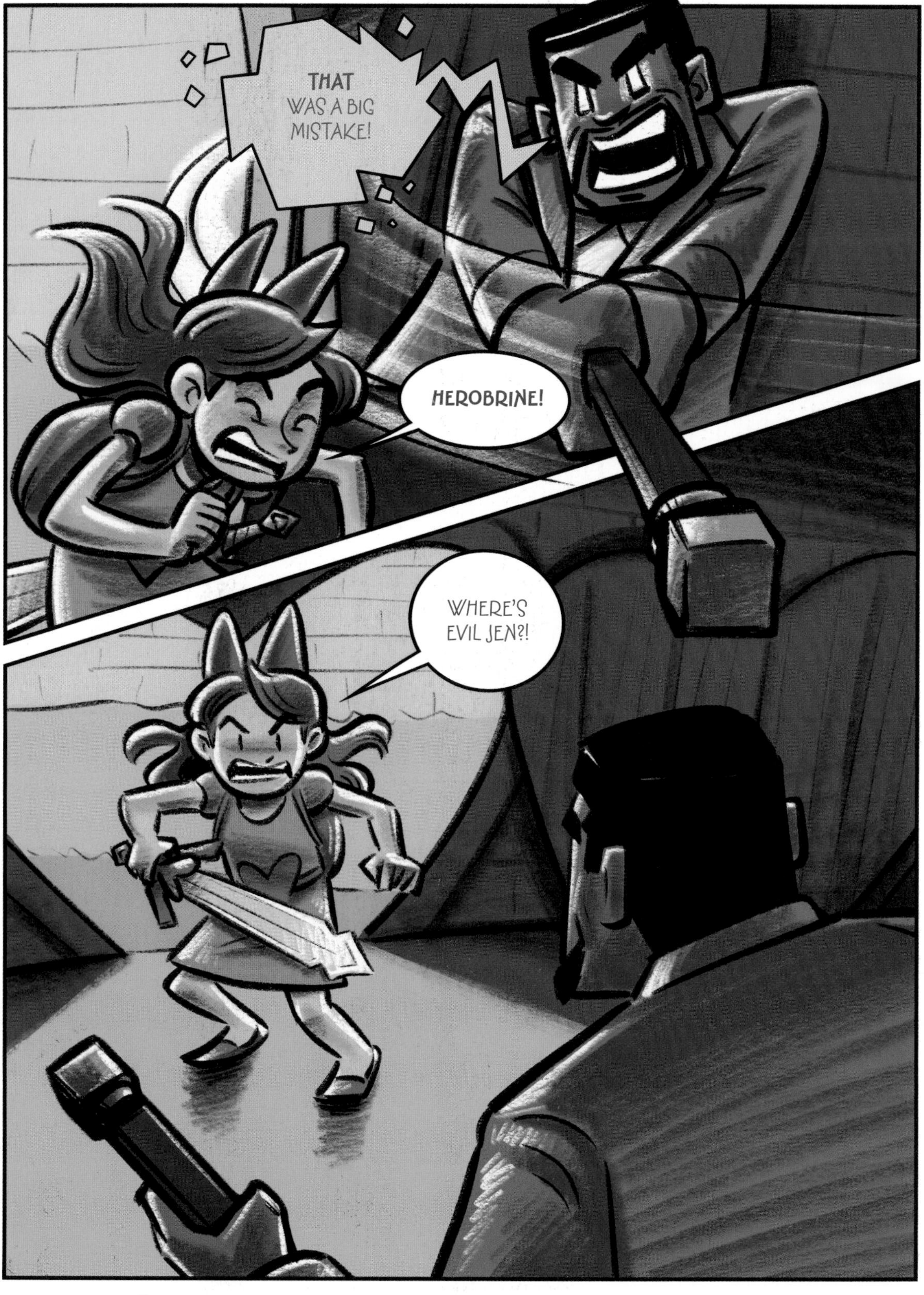
THAT WAS A BIG MISTAKE!
HEROBRINE!
WHERE'S EVIL JEN?!

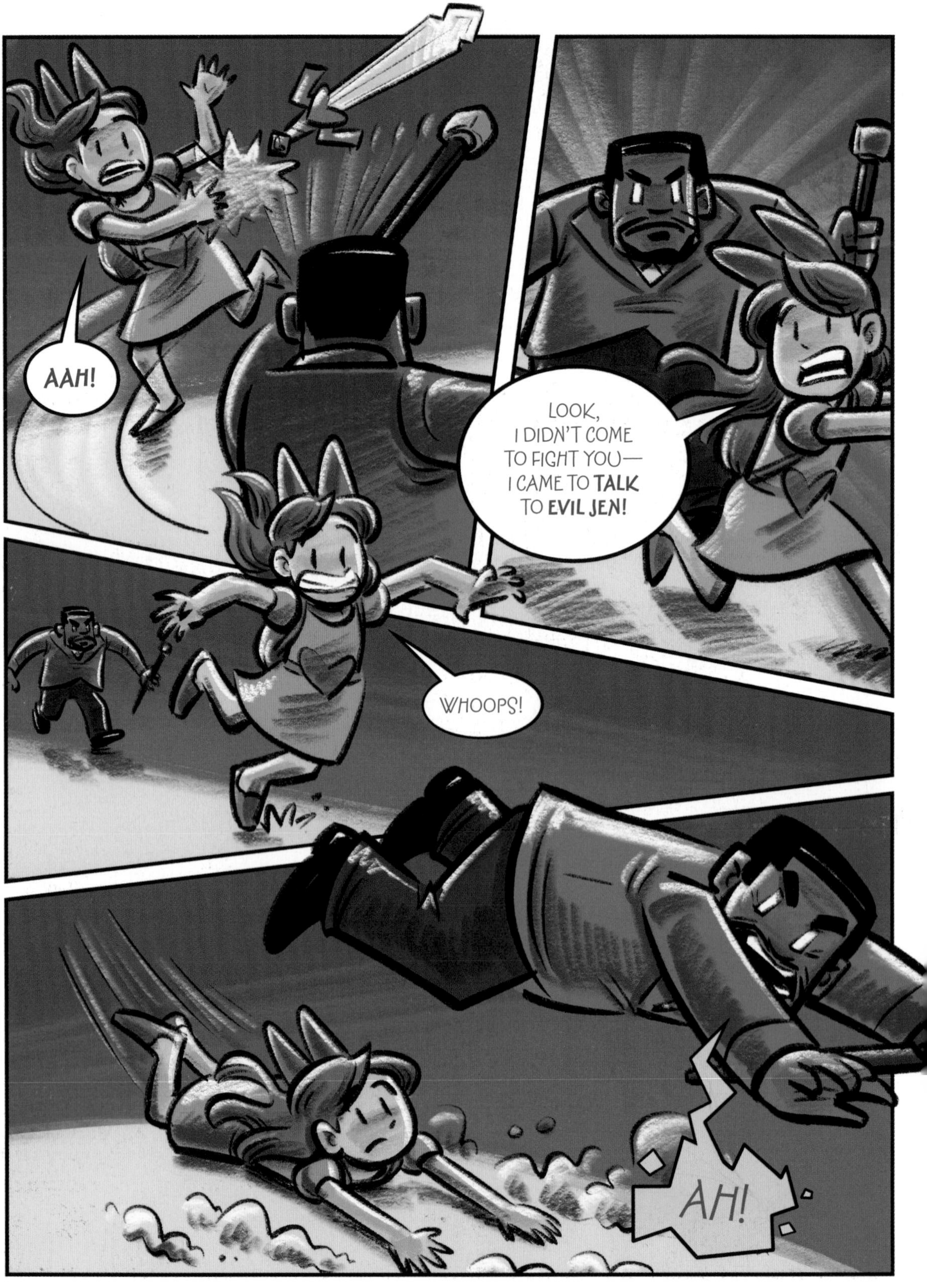
AAH!
LOOK, I DIDN'T COME TO FIGHT YOU— I CAME TO **TALK** TO **EVIL JEN!**
WHOOPS!
AH!

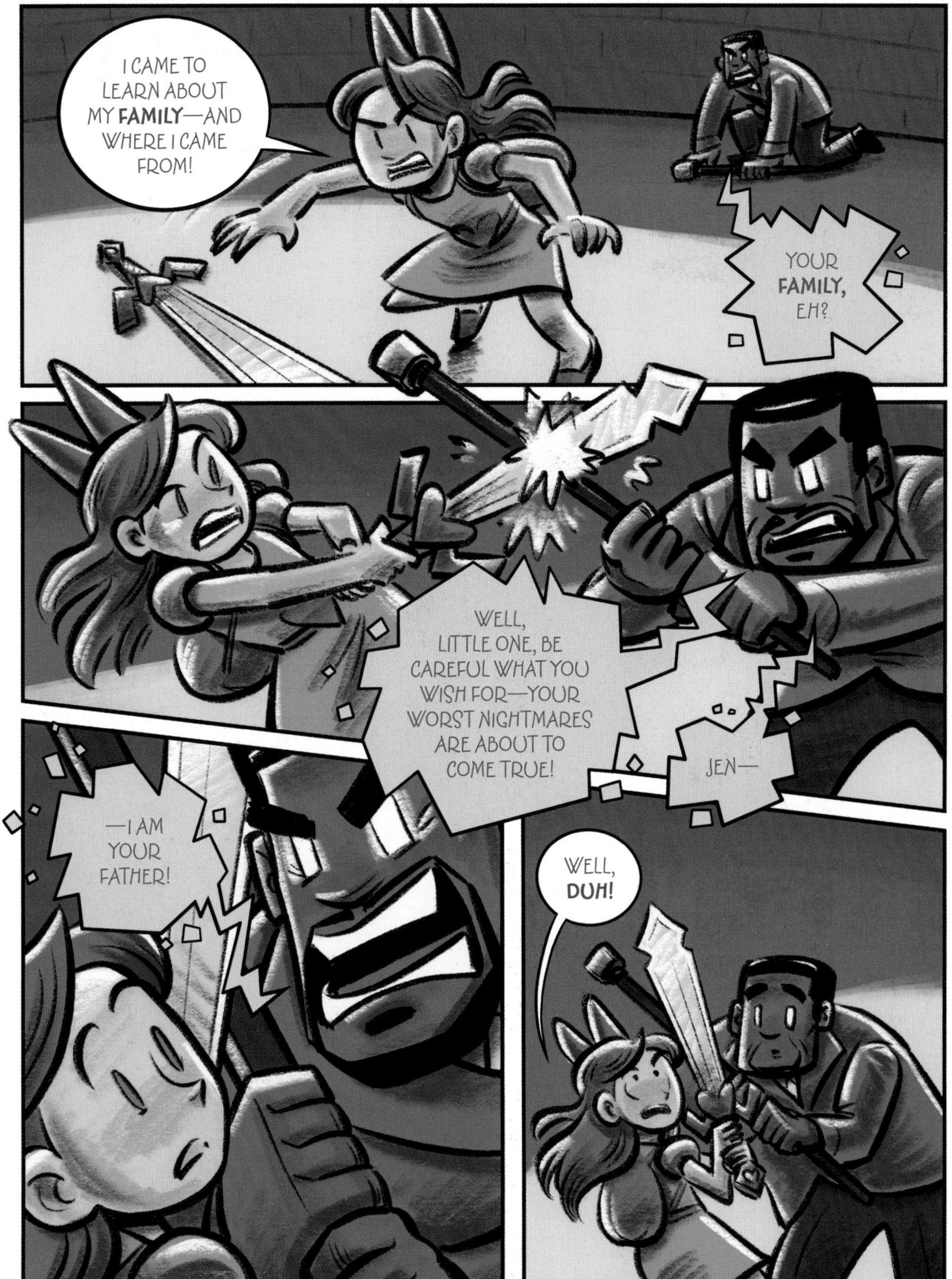
I CAME TO LEARN ABOUT MY FAMILY—AND WHERE I CAME FROM!
YOUR FAMILY, EH?
WELL, LITTLE ONE, BE CAREFUL WHAT YOU WISH FOR—YOUR WORST NIGHTMARES ARE ABOUT TO COME TRUE!
JEN—
—I AM YOUR FATHER!
WELL, DUH!

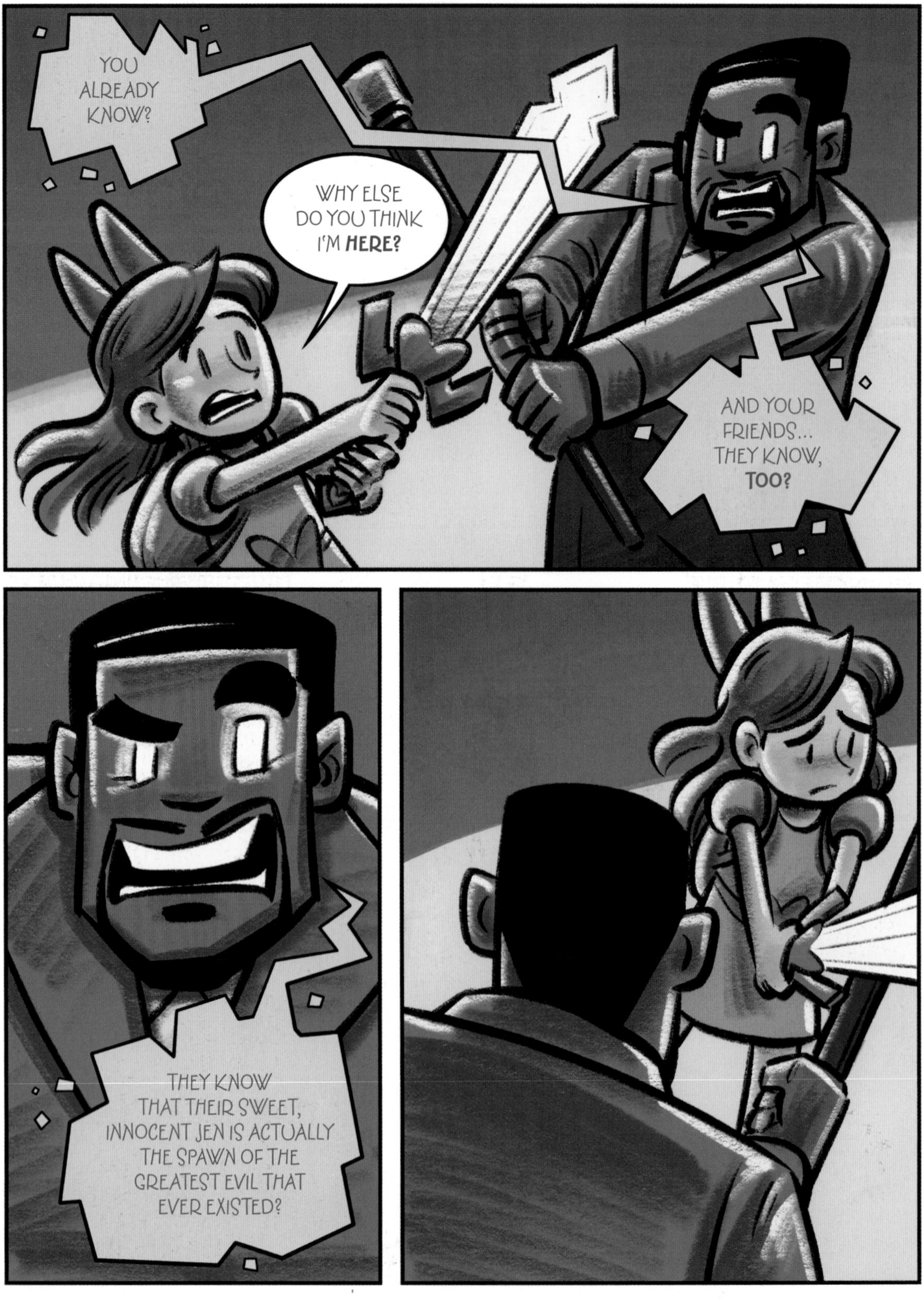
YOU ALREADY KNOW?
WHY ELSE DO YOU THINK I'M **HERE?**
AND YOUR FRIENDS... THEY KNOW, **TOO?**
THEY KNOW THAT THEIR SWEET, INNOCENT JEN IS ACTUALLY THE SPAWN OF THE GREATEST EVIL THAT EVER EXISTED?

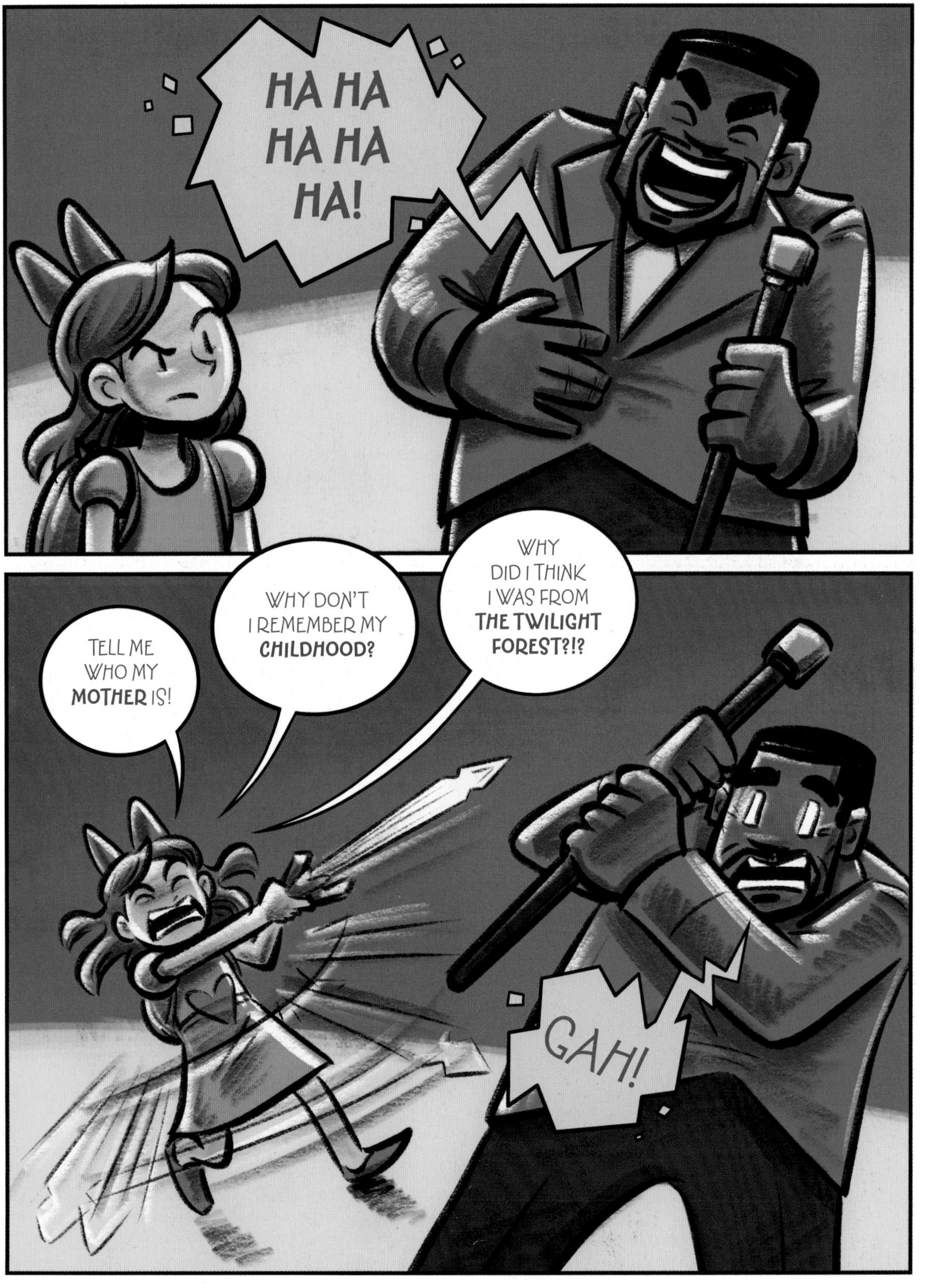

HA HA HA HA HA!
TELL ME WHO MY MOTHER IS!
WHY DON'T I REMEMBER MY CHILDHOOD?
WHY DID I THINK I WAS FROM THE TWILIGHT FOREST?!?
GAH!

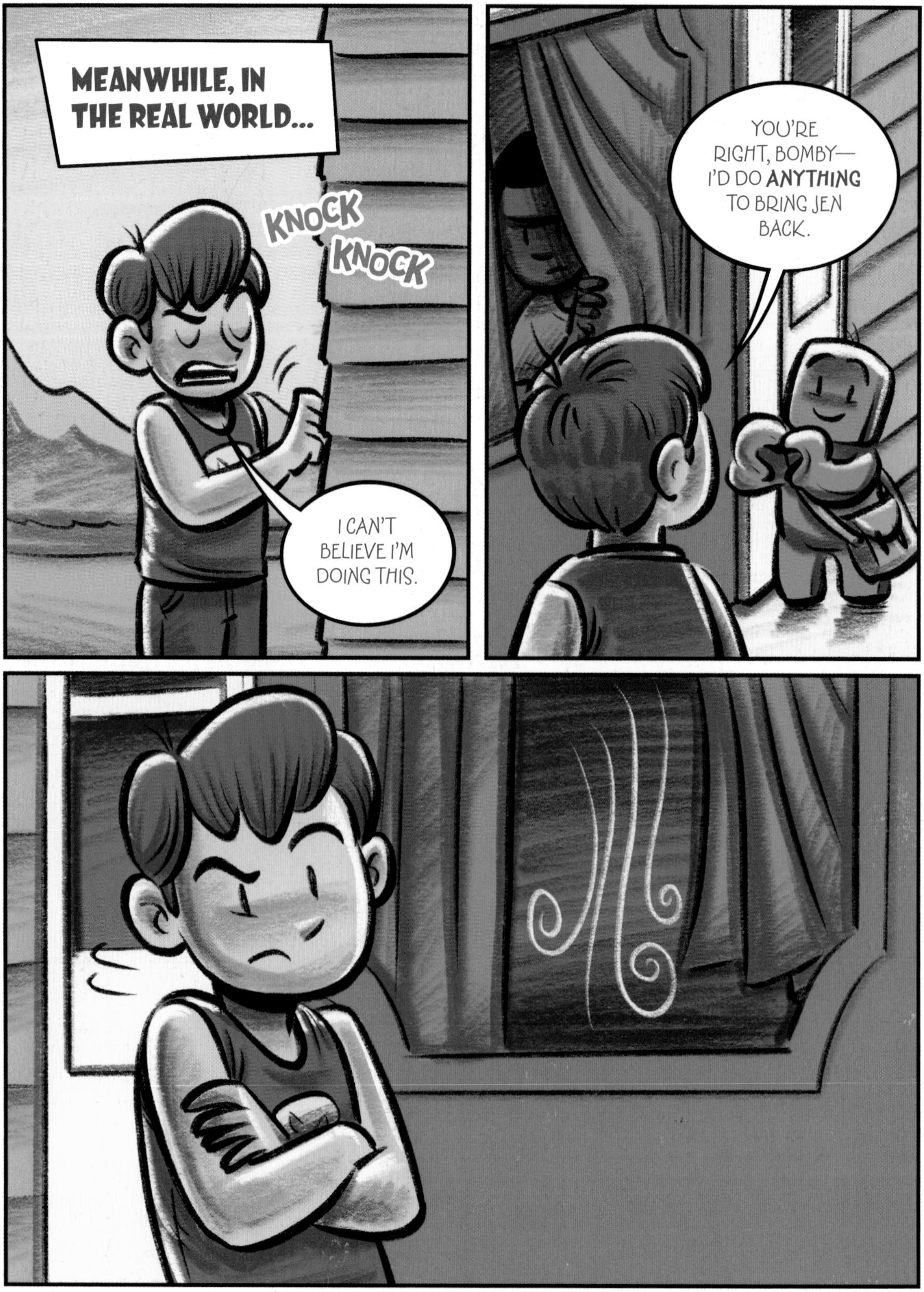
MEANWHILE, IN THE REAL WORLD...
KNOCK
KNOCK
I CAN'T BELIEVE I'M DOING THIS.
YOU'RE RIGHT, BOMBY— I'D DO ANYTHING TO BRING JEN BACK.

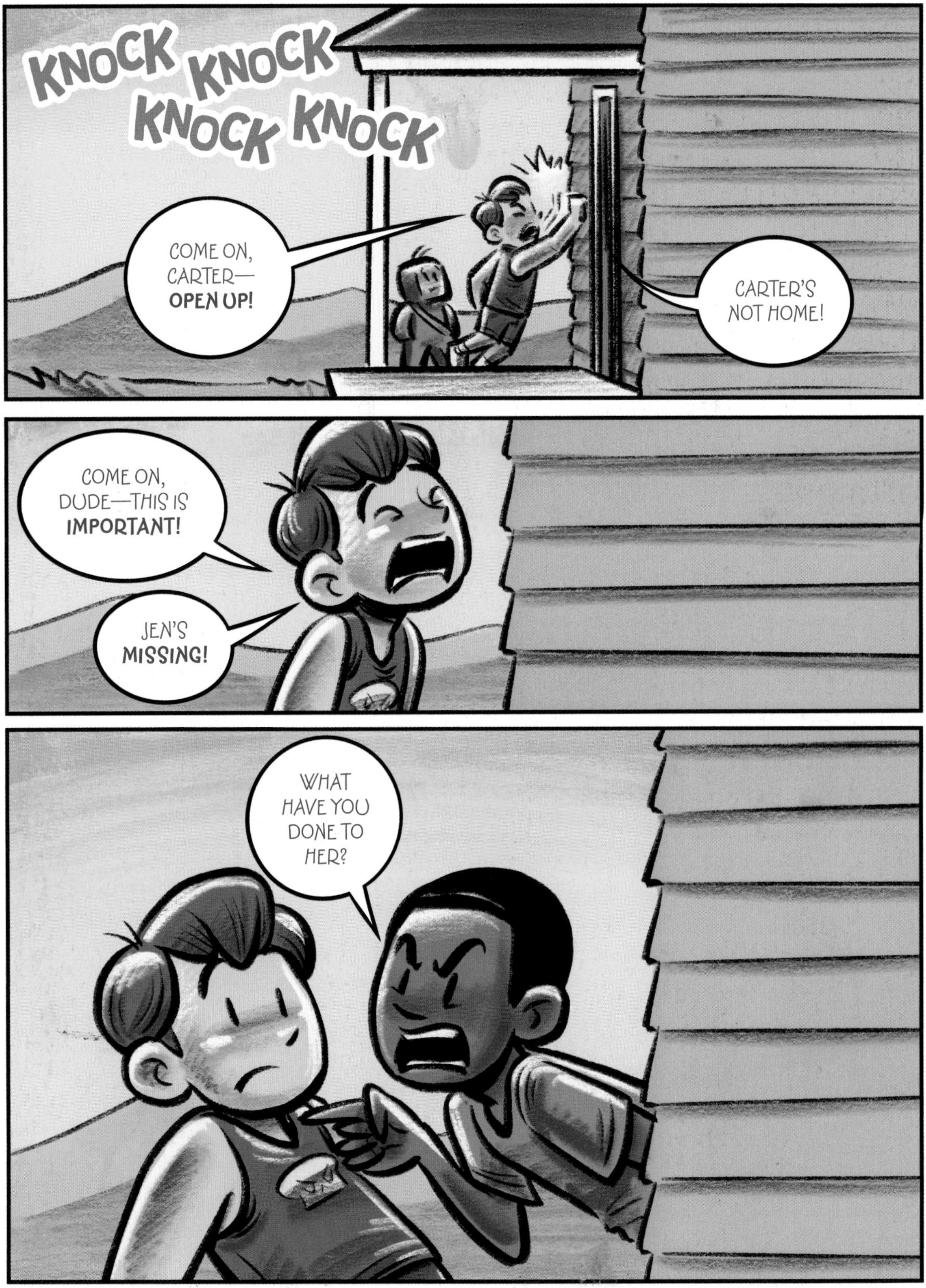
KNOCK KNOCK KNOCK KNOCK
COME ON, CARTER— **OPEN UP!**
CARTER'S NOT HOME!
COME ON, DUDE—THIS IS **IMPORTANT!**
JEN'S **MISSING!**
WHAT HAVE YOU DONE TO HER?

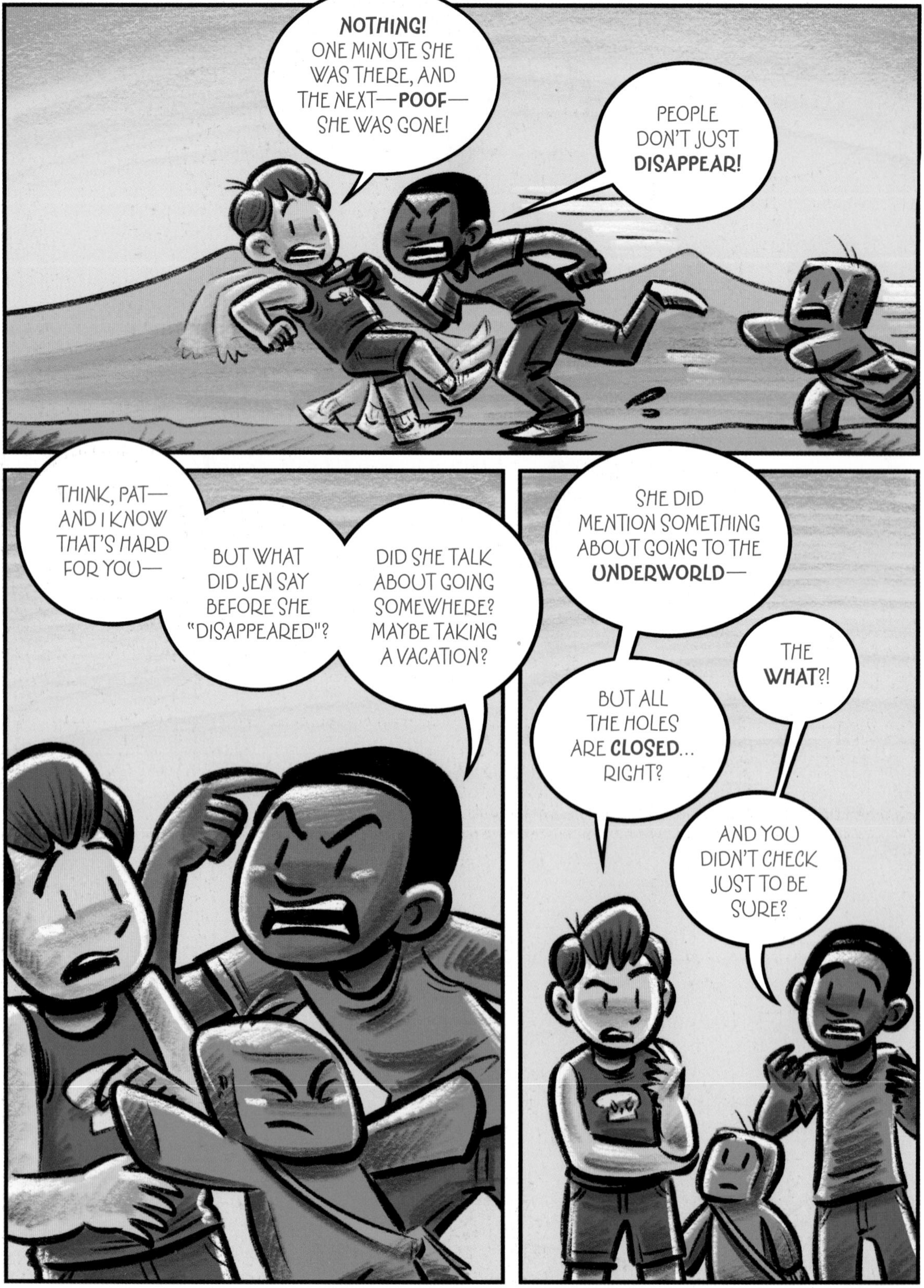
NOTHING! ONE MINUTE SHE WAS THERE, AND THE NEXT—POOF—SHE WAS GONE!
PEOPLE DON'T JUST DISAPPEAR!
THINK, PAT—AND I KNOW THAT'S HARD FOR YOU—
BUT WHAT DID JEN SAY BEFORE SHE "DISAPPEARED"?
DID SHE TALK ABOUT GOING SOMEWHERE? MAYBE TAKING A VACATION?
SHE DID MENTION SOMETHING ABOUT GOING TO THE UNDERWORLD—
THE WHAT?!
BUT ALL THE HOLES ARE CLOSED... RIGHT?
AND YOU DIDN'T CHECK JUST TO BE SURE?

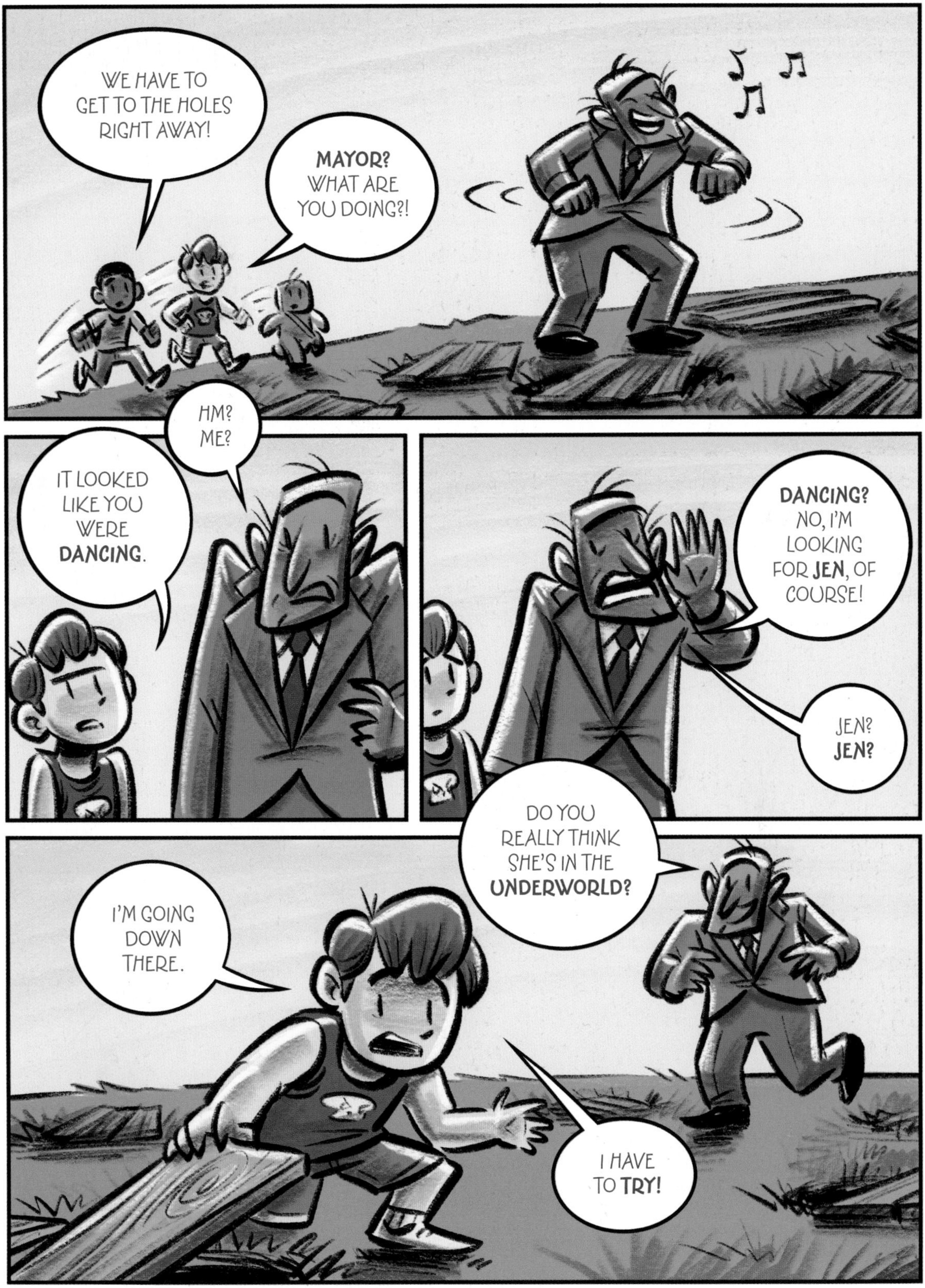
WE HAVE TO GET TO THE HOLES RIGHT AWAY!
MAYOR? WHAT ARE YOU DOING?!
IT LOOKED LIKE YOU WERE DANCING.
HM? ME?
DANCING? NO, I'M LOOKING FOR JEN, OF COURSE!
JEN? JEN?
DO YOU REALLY THINK SHE'S IN THE UNDERWORLD?
I'M GOING DOWN THERE.
I HAVE TO TRY!

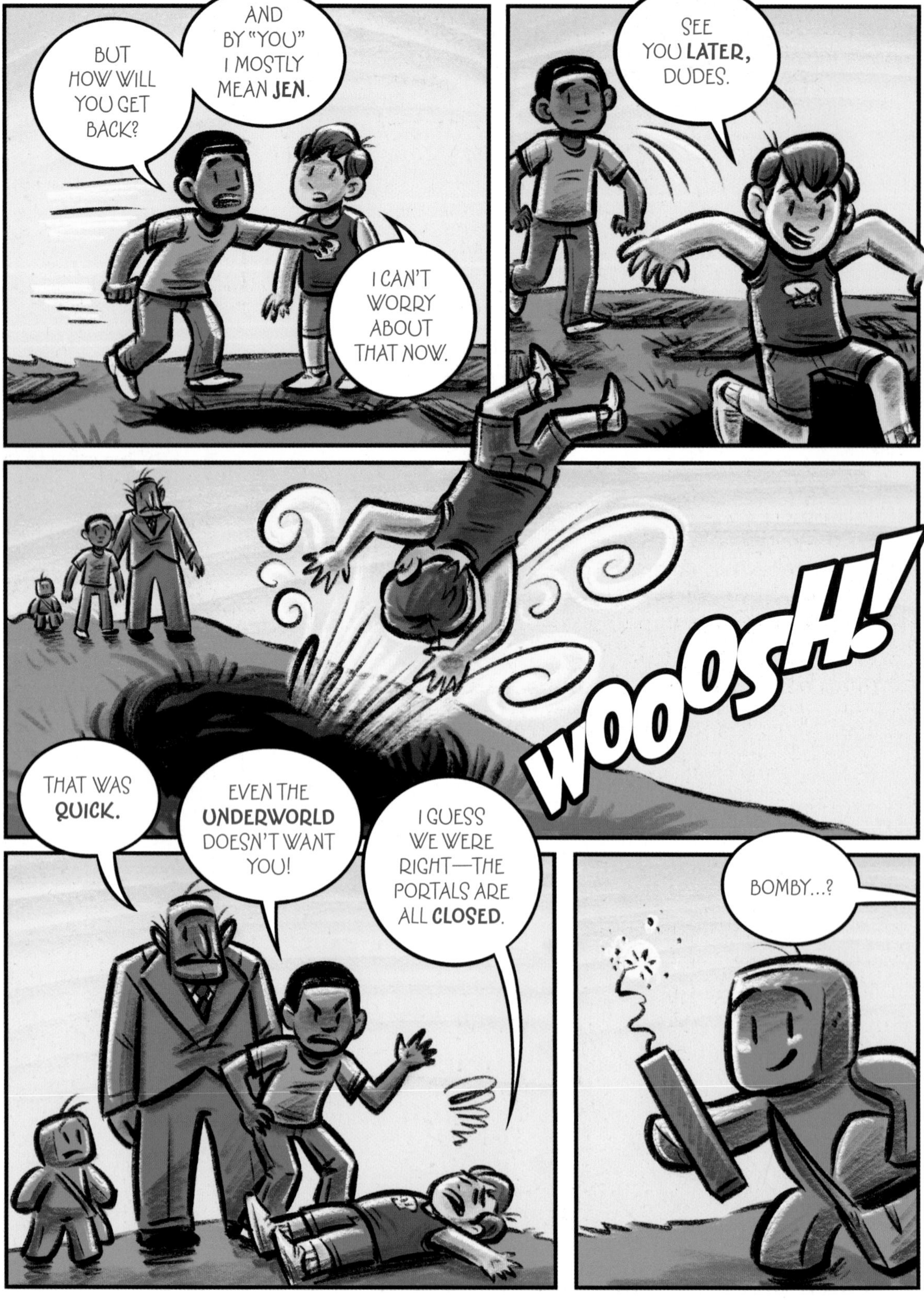
BUT HOW WILL YOU GET BACK?
AND BY "YOU" I MOSTLY MEAN **JEN**.
I CAN'T WORRY ABOUT THAT NOW.
SEE YOU **LATER,** DUDES.
WOOOSH!
THAT WAS **QUICK.**
EVEN THE **UNDERWORLD** DOESN'T WANT YOU!
I GUESS WE WERE RIGHT—THE PORTALS ARE ALL **CLOSED**.
BOMBY...?

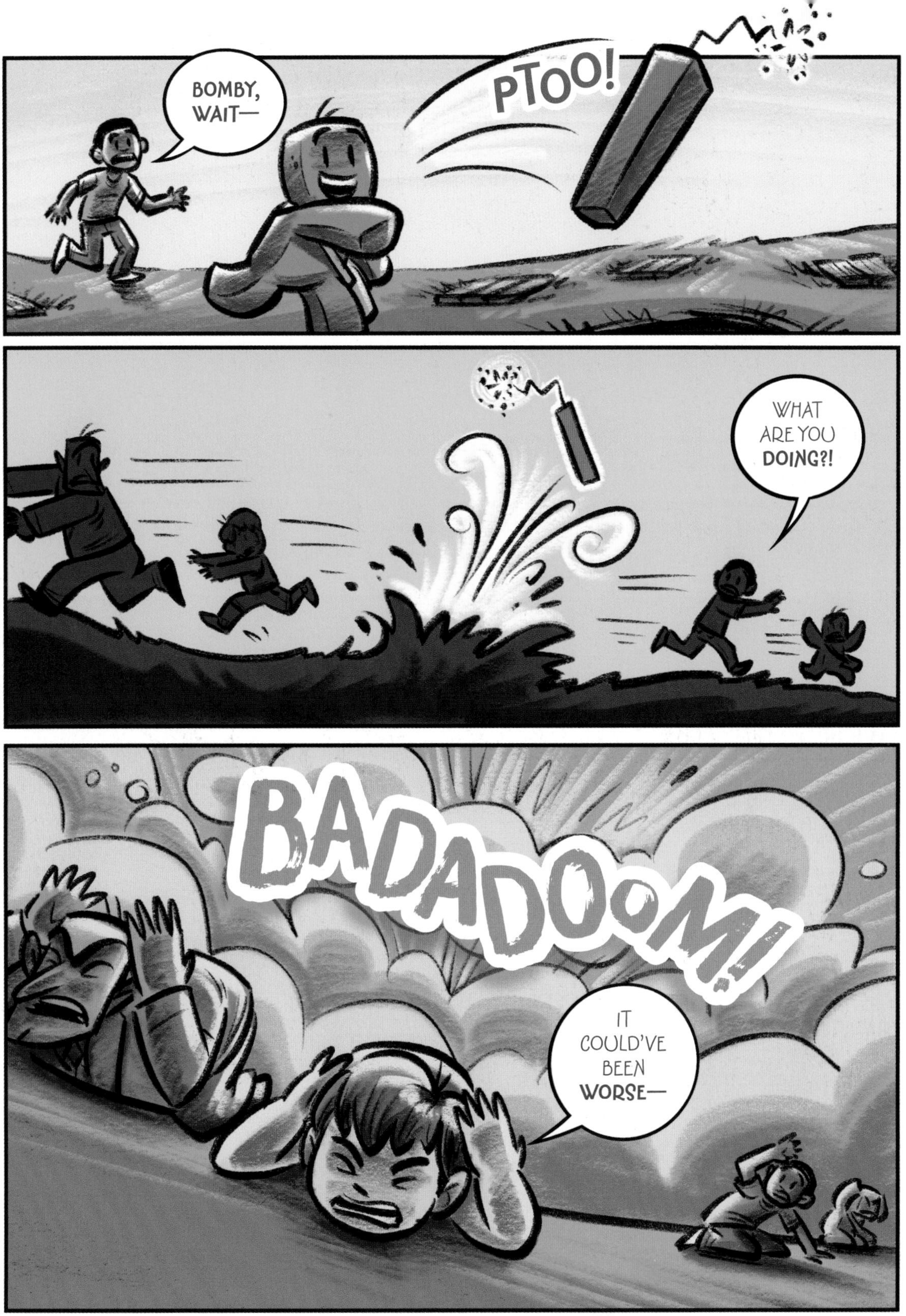
BOMBY, WAIT—
PTOO!
WHAT ARE YOU DOING?!
BADADOOM!
IT COULD'VE BEEN WORSE—

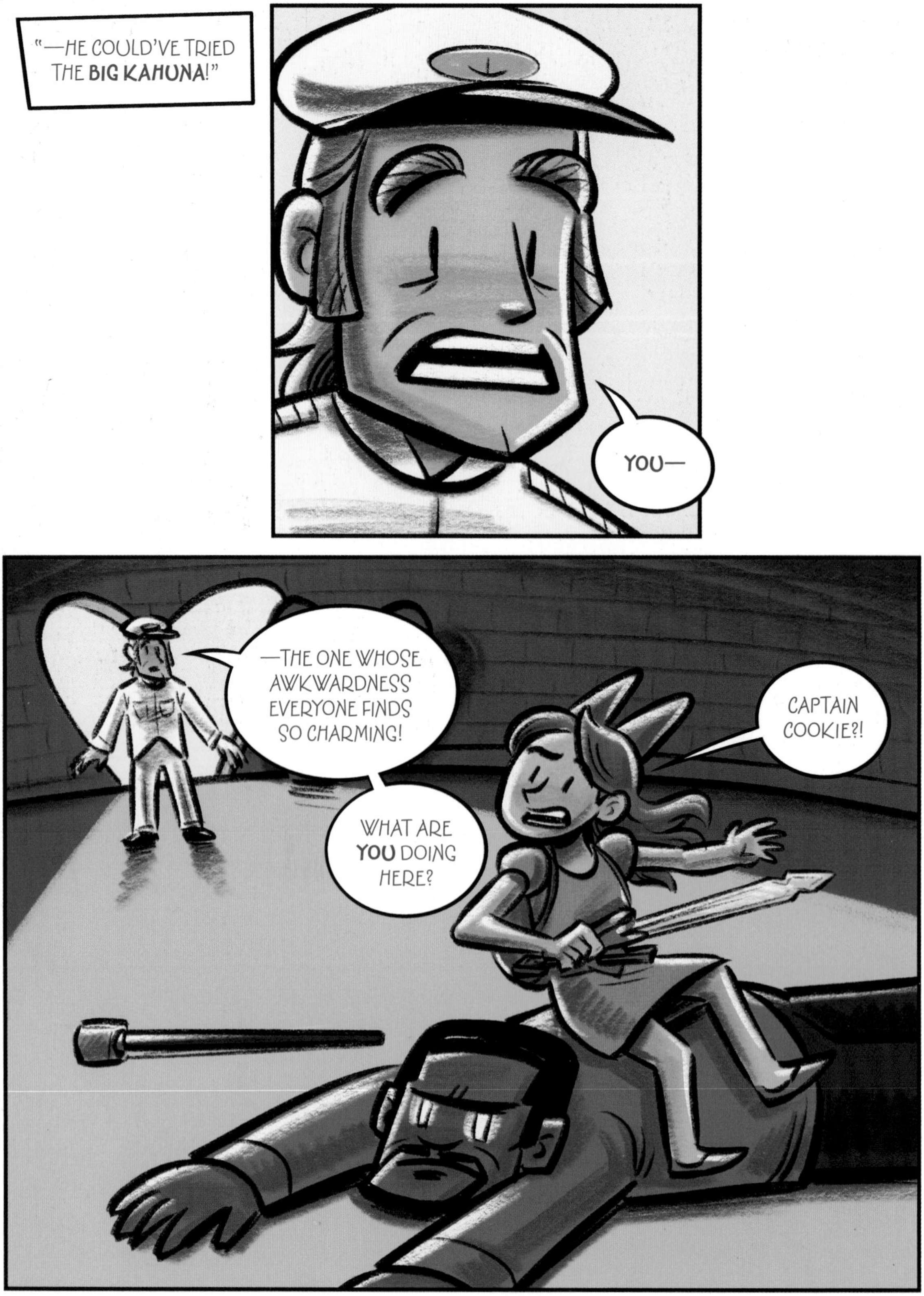
"—HE COULD'VE TRIED THE BIG KAHUNA!"
YOU—
—THE ONE WHOSE AWKWARDNESS EVERYONE FINDS SO CHARMING!
CAPTAIN COOKIE?!
WHAT ARE YOU DOING HERE?

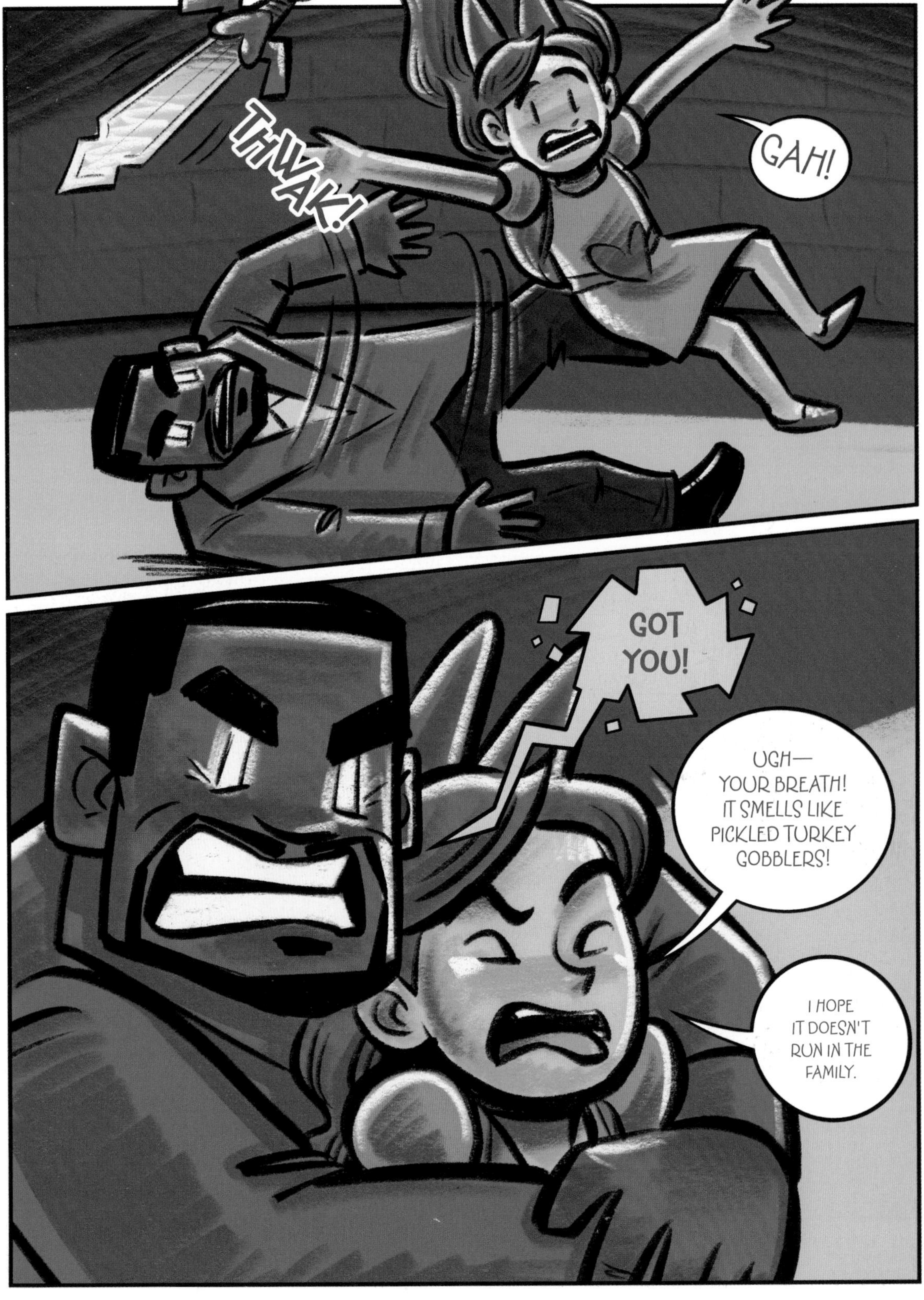
THWAK!
GAH!
GOT YOU!
UGH— YOUR BREATH! IT SMELLS LIKE PICKLED TURKEY GOBBLERS!
I HOPE IT DOESN'T RUN IN THE FAMILY.

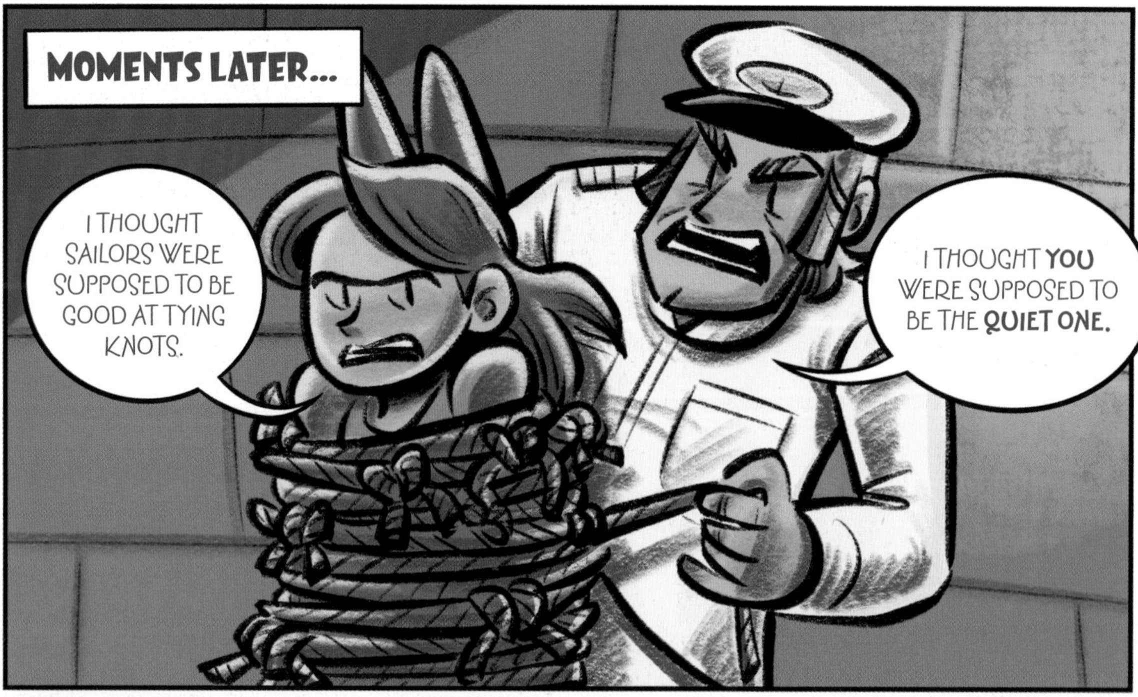
MOMENTS LATER...
I THOUGHT SAILORS WERE SUPPOSED TO BE GOOD AT TYING KNOTS.
I THOUGHT **YOU** WERE SUPPOSED TO BE THE **QUIET ONE.**

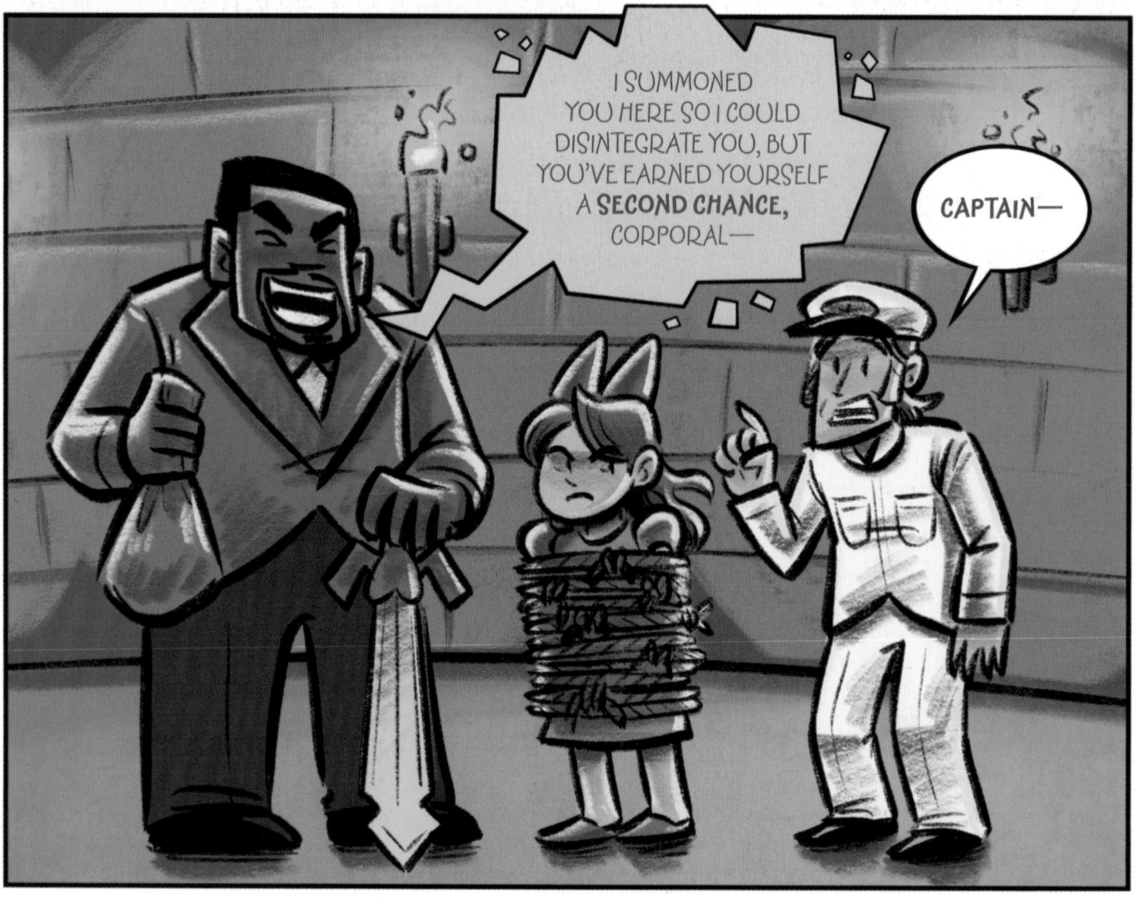
I SUMMONED YOU HERE SO I COULD DISINTEGRATE YOU, BUT YOU'VE EARNED YOURSELF A **SECOND CHANCE,** CORPORAL—
CAPTAIN—

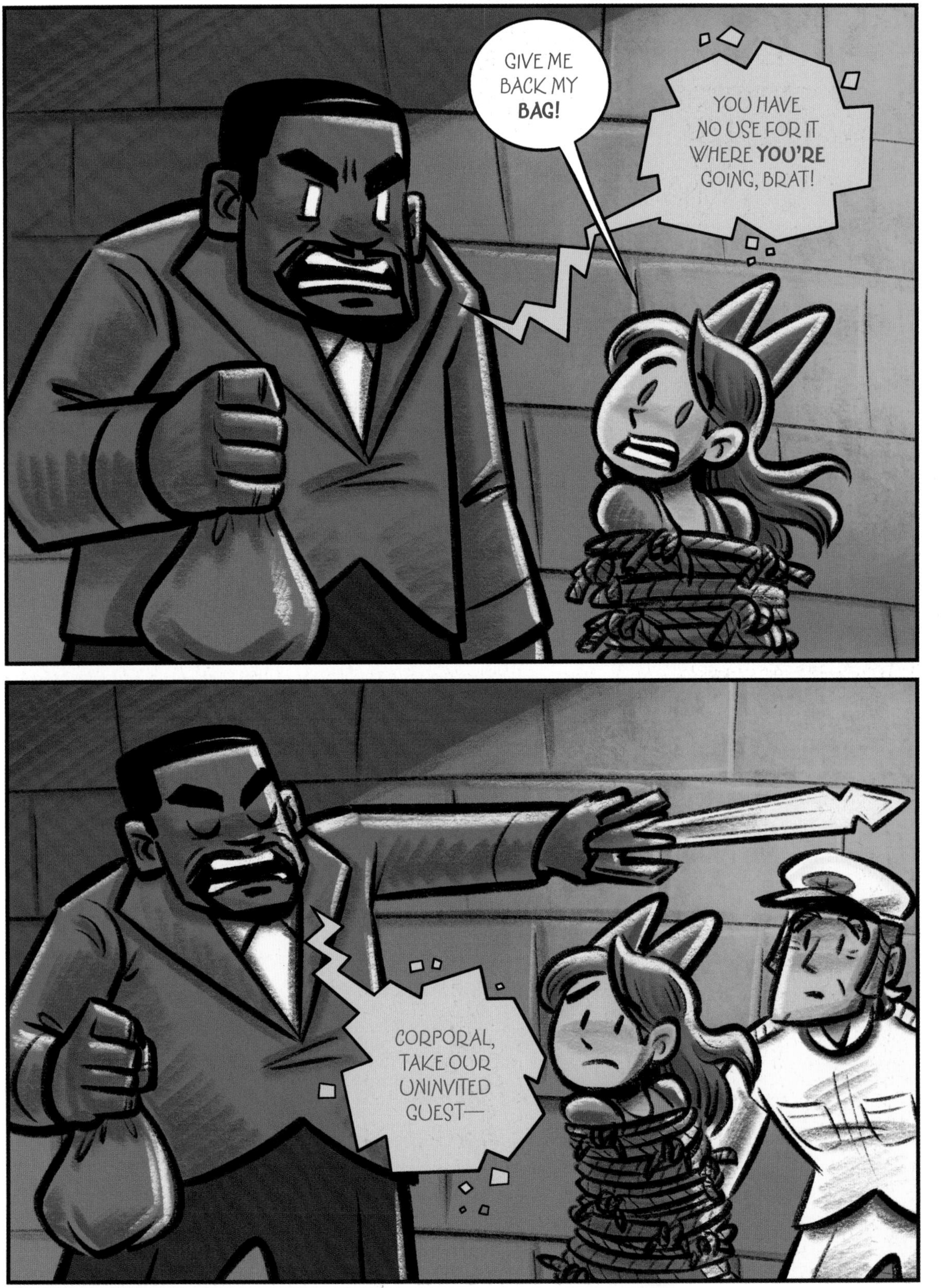
GIVE ME BACK MY **BAG!**
YOU HAVE NO USE FOR IT WHERE **YOU'RE** GOING, BRAT!
CORPORAL, TAKE OUR UNINVITED GUEST—

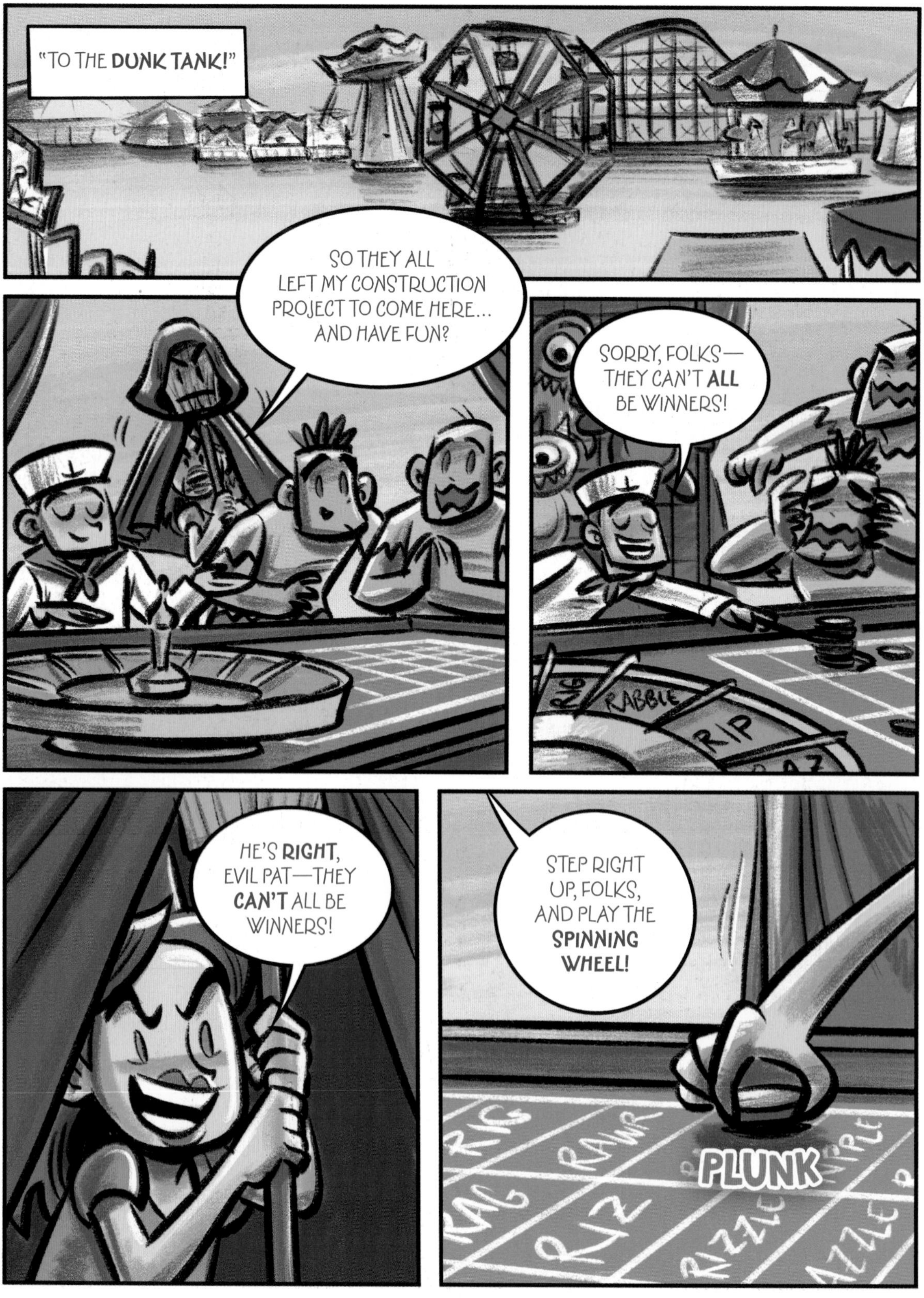
"TO THE **DUNK TANK!**"
SO THEY ALL LEFT MY CONSTRUCTION PROJECT TO COME HERE... AND HAVE FUN?
SORRY, FOLKS— THEY CAN'T **ALL** BE WINNERS!
RIG
RABBLE
RIP
HE'S **RIGHT**, EVIL PAT—THEY **CAN'T** ALL BE WINNERS!
STEP RIGHT UP, FOLKS, AND PLAY THE **SPINNING WHEEL!**
RIG
RAWR
RAG
RIZ
RIZZLE
PLUNK

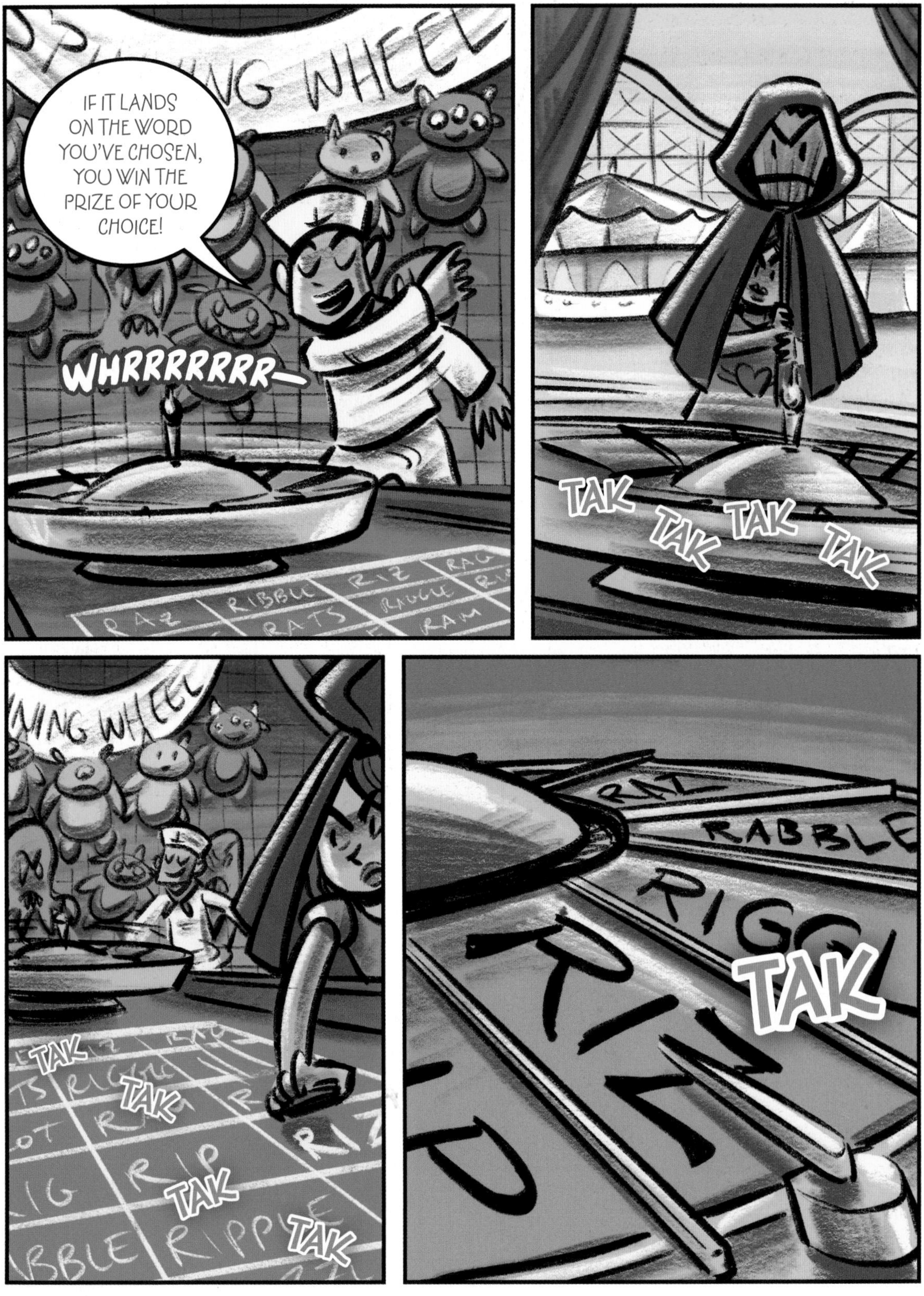
IF IT LANDS ON THE WORD YOU'VE CHOSEN, YOU WIN THE PRIZE OF YOUR CHOICE!
WHRRRRRRR—
TAK
TAK
TAK
TAK
TAK
TAK
TAK
TAK
TAK

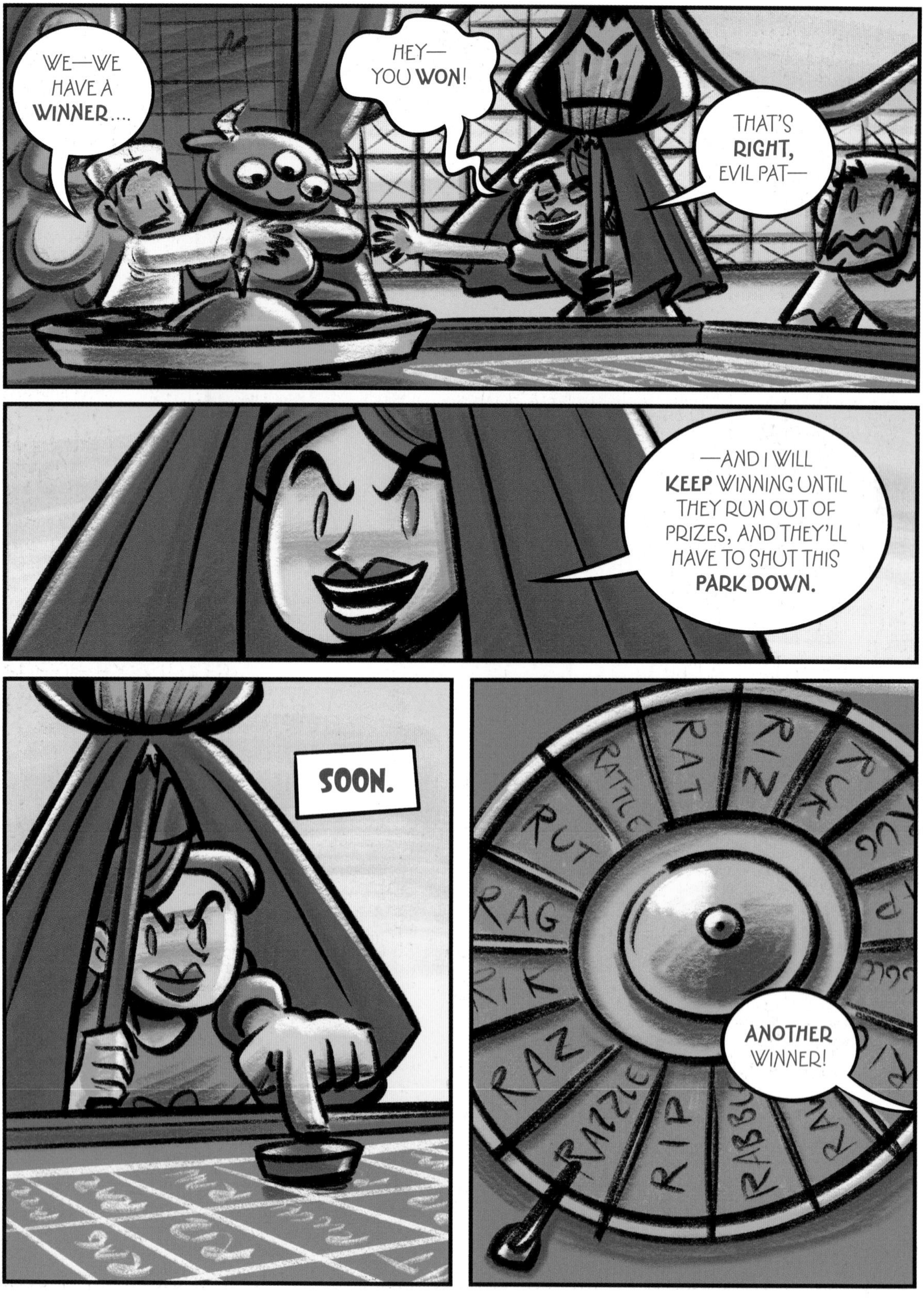
WE—WE HAVE A WINNER....
HEY— YOU WON!
THAT'S RIGHT, EVIL PAT—
—AND I WILL KEEP WINNING UNTIL THEY RUN OUT OF PRIZES, AND THEY'LL HAVE TO SHUT THIS PARK DOWN.
SOON.
RATTLE
RAT
RIZ
RUK
RUT
RAG
RIK
RAZ
RAZZLE
RIP
ANOTHER WINNER!

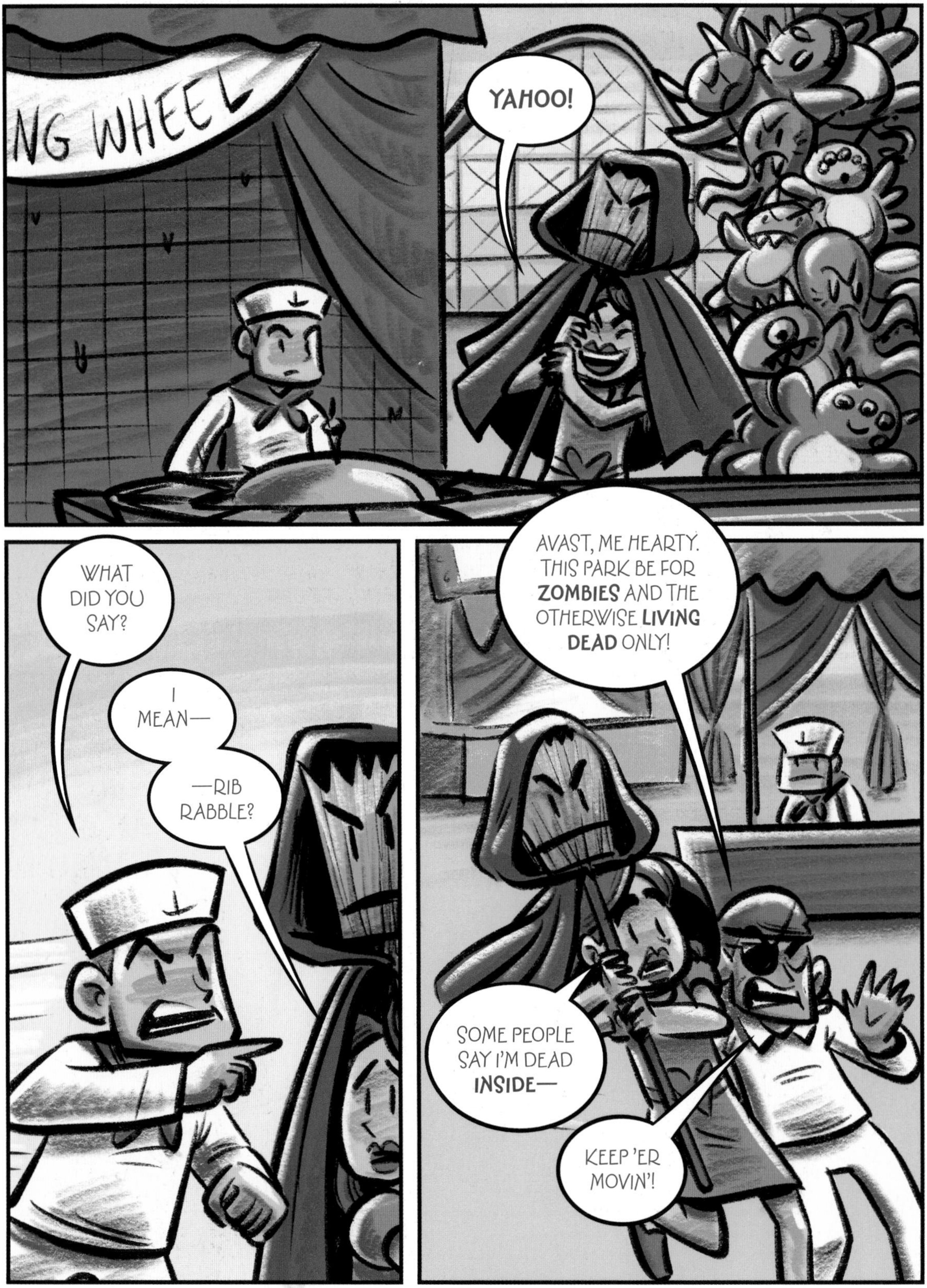
NG WHEEL
YAHOO!
WHAT DID YOU SAY?
I MEAN—
—RIB RABBLE?
AVAST, ME HEARTY. THIS PARK BE FOR **ZOMBIES** AND THE OTHERWISE **LIVING DEAD** ONLY!
SOME PEOPLE SAY I'M DEAD **INSIDE**—
KEEP 'ER MOVIN'!

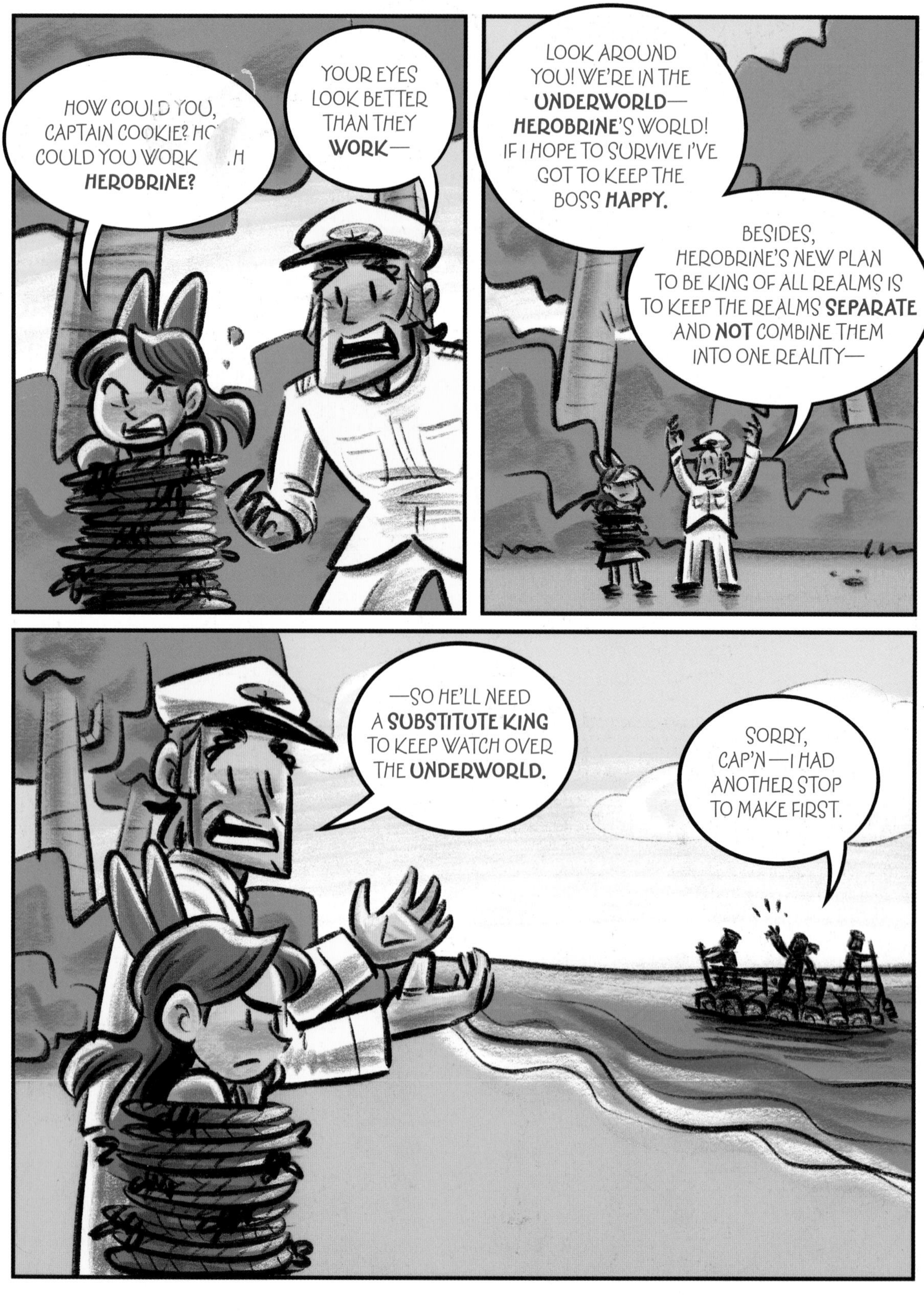
HOW COULD YOU, CAPTAIN COOKIE? HO COULD YOU WORK H **HEROBRINE?**
YOUR EYES LOOK BETTER THAN THEY **WORK**—
LOOK AROUND YOU! WE'RE IN THE **UNDERWORLD**— **HEROBRINE**'S WORLD! IF I HOPE TO SURVIVE I'VE GOT TO KEEP THE BOSS **HAPPY.**
BESIDES, HEROBRINE'S NEW PLAN TO BE KING OF ALL REALMS IS TO KEEP THE REALMS **SEPARATE** AND **NOT** COMBINE THEM INTO ONE REALITY—
—SO HE'LL NEED A **SUBSTITUTE KING** TO KEEP WATCH OVER THE **UNDERWORLD.**
SORRY, CAP'N—I HAD ANOTHER STOP TO MAKE FIRST.

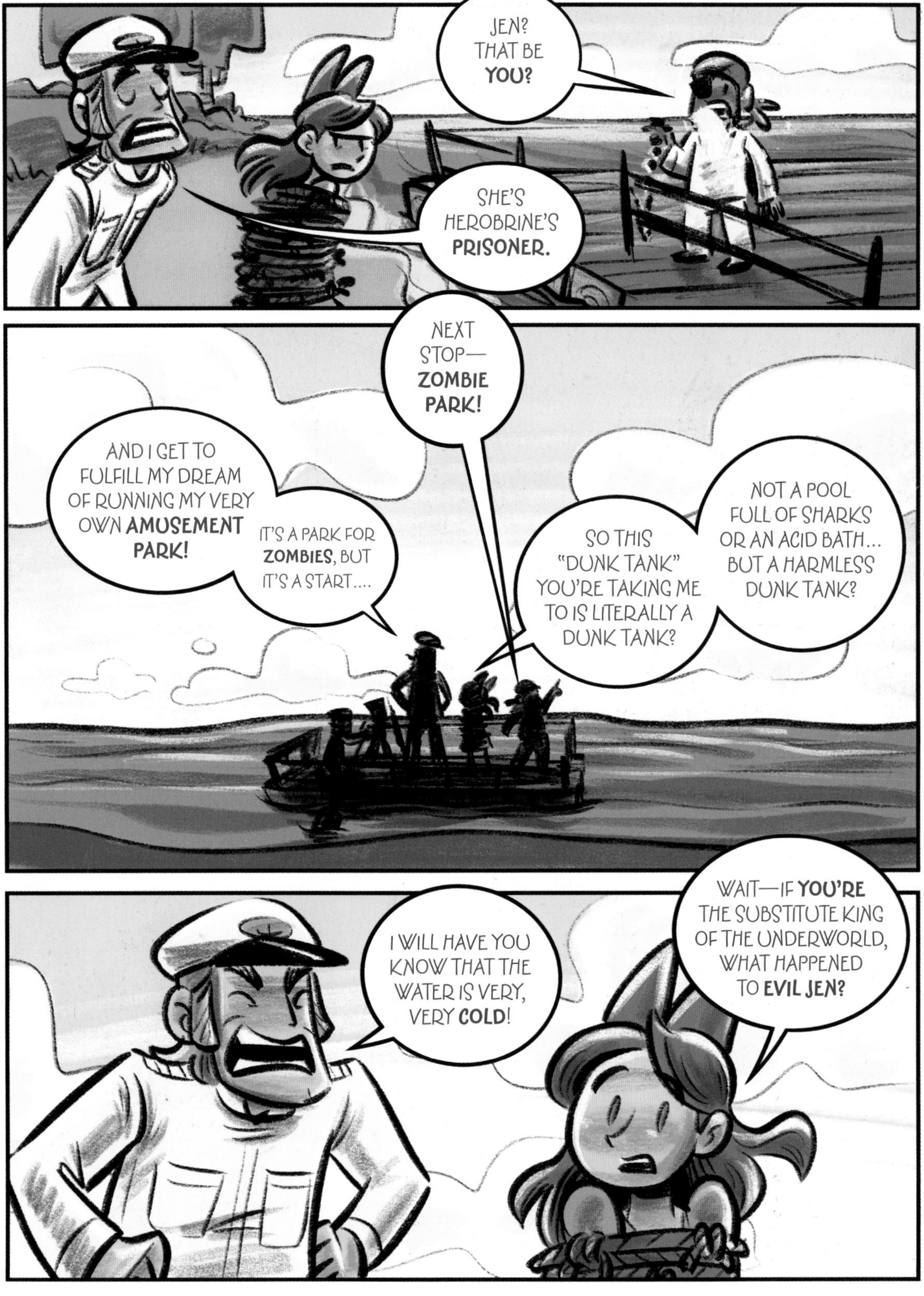
JEN? THAT BE YOU?
SHE'S HEROBRINE'S PRISONER.
NEXT STOP— ZOMBIE PARK!
AND I GET TO FULFILL MY DREAM OF RUNNING MY VERY OWN AMUSEMENT PARK!
IT'S A PARK FOR ZOMBIES, BUT IT'S A START....
SO THIS "DUNK TANK" YOU'RE TAKING ME TO IS LITERALLY A DUNK TANK?
NOT A POOL FULL OF SHARKS OR AN ACID BATH... BUT A HARMLESS DUNK TANK?
I WILL HAVE YOU KNOW THAT THE WATER IS VERY, VERY COLD!
WAIT—IF YOU'RE THE SUBSTITUTE KING OF THE UNDERWORLD, WHAT HAPPENED TO EVIL JEN?

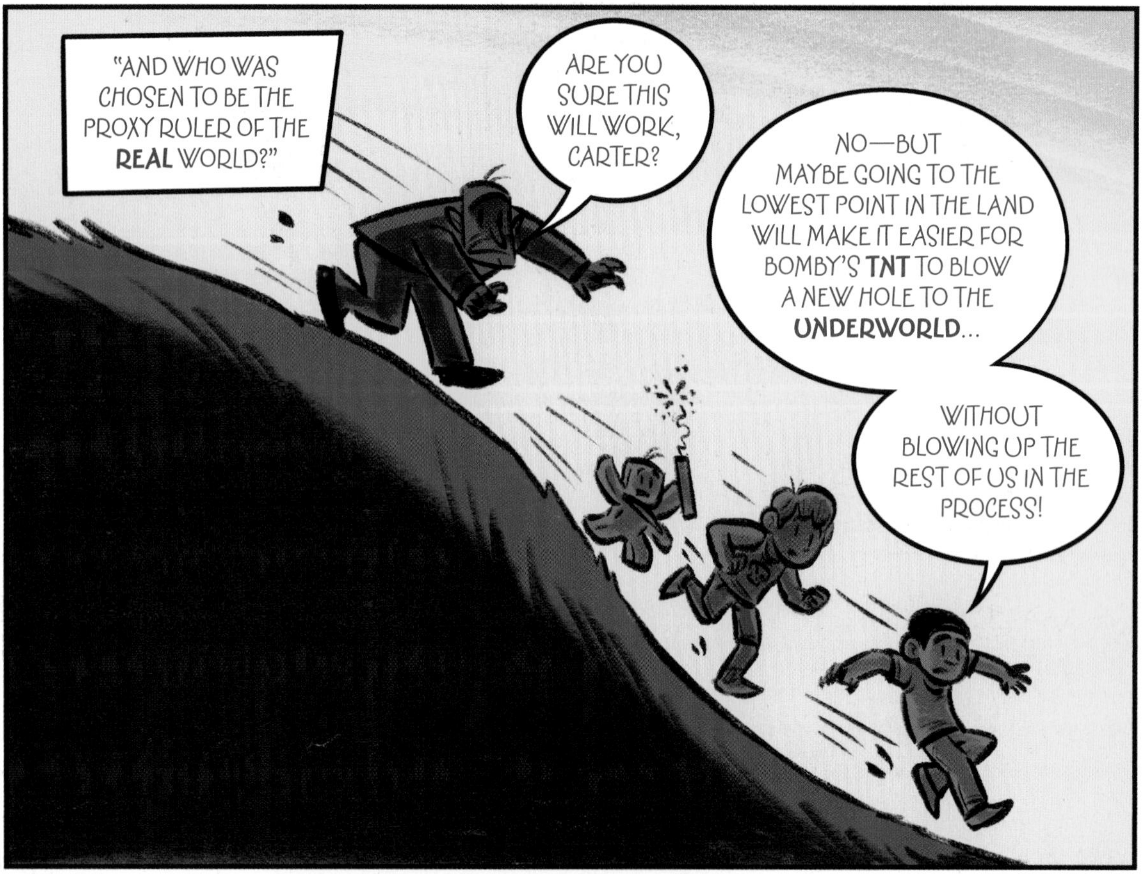
"AND WHO WAS CHOSEN TO BE THE PROXY RULER OF THE **REAL** WORLD?"
ARE YOU SURE THIS WILL WORK, CARTER?
NO—BUT MAYBE GOING TO THE LOWEST POINT IN THE LAND WILL MAKE IT EASIER FOR BOMBY'S **TNT** TO BLOW A NEW HOLE TO THE **UNDERWORLD**...
WITHOUT BLOWING UP THE REST OF US IN THE PROCESS!

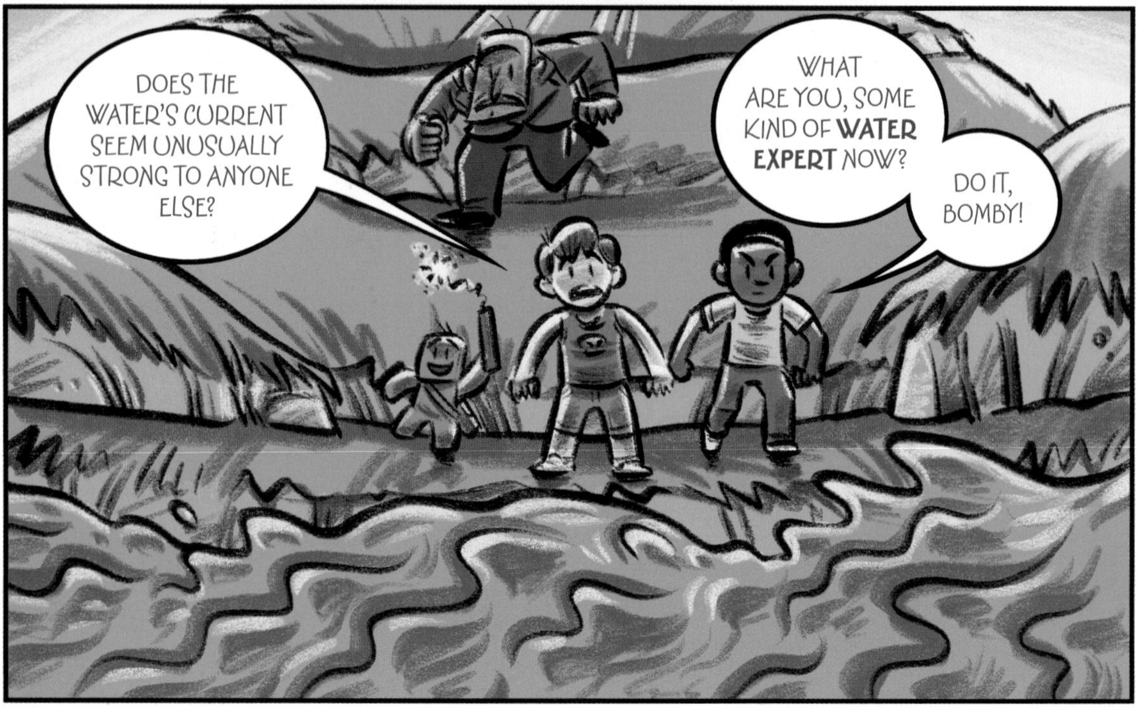
DOES THE WATER'S CURRENT SEEM UNUSUALLY STRONG TO ANYONE ELSE?
WHAT ARE YOU, SOME KIND OF **WATER EXPERT** NOW?
DO IT, BOMBY!

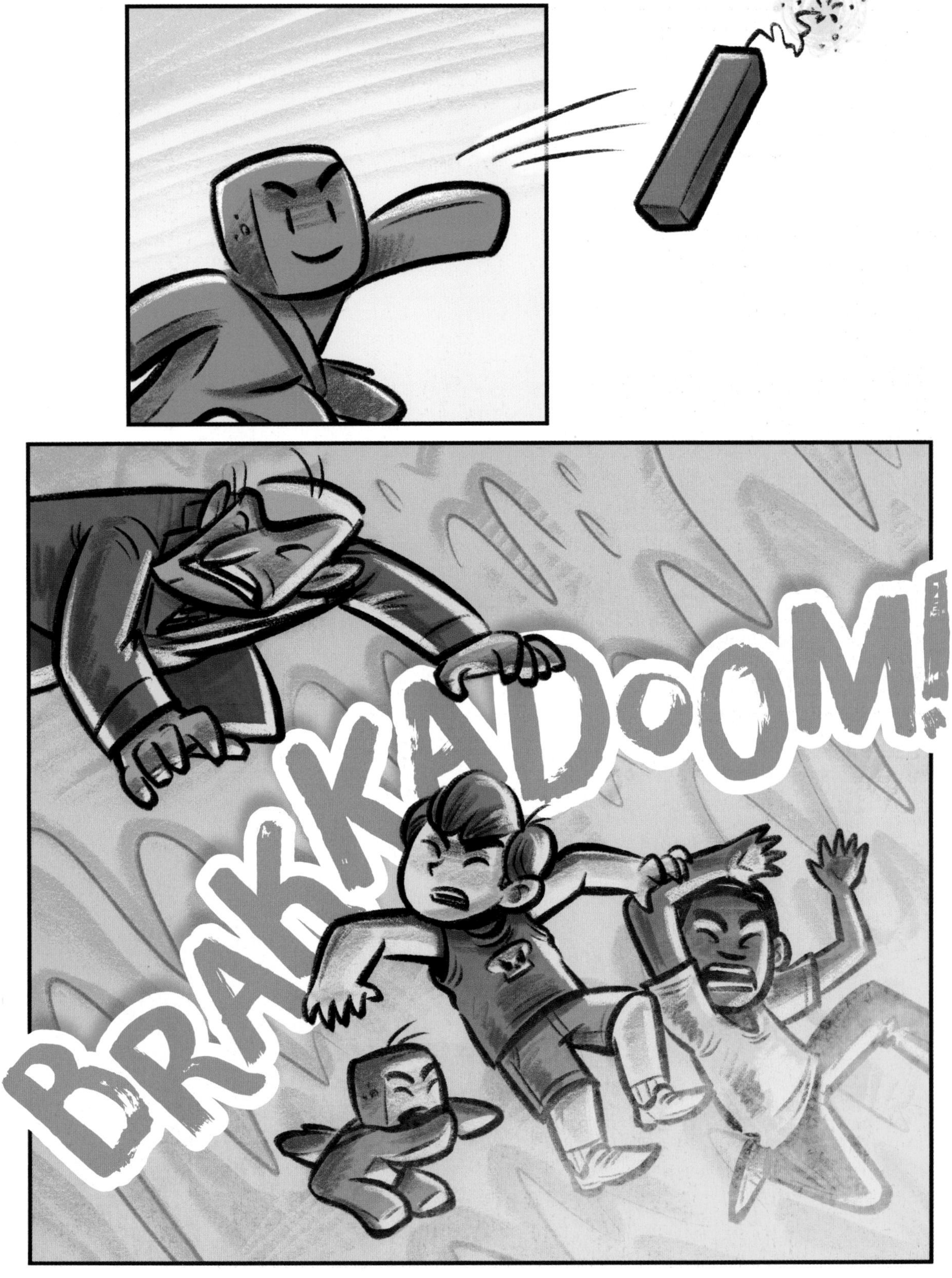
BRAKKADOOM!

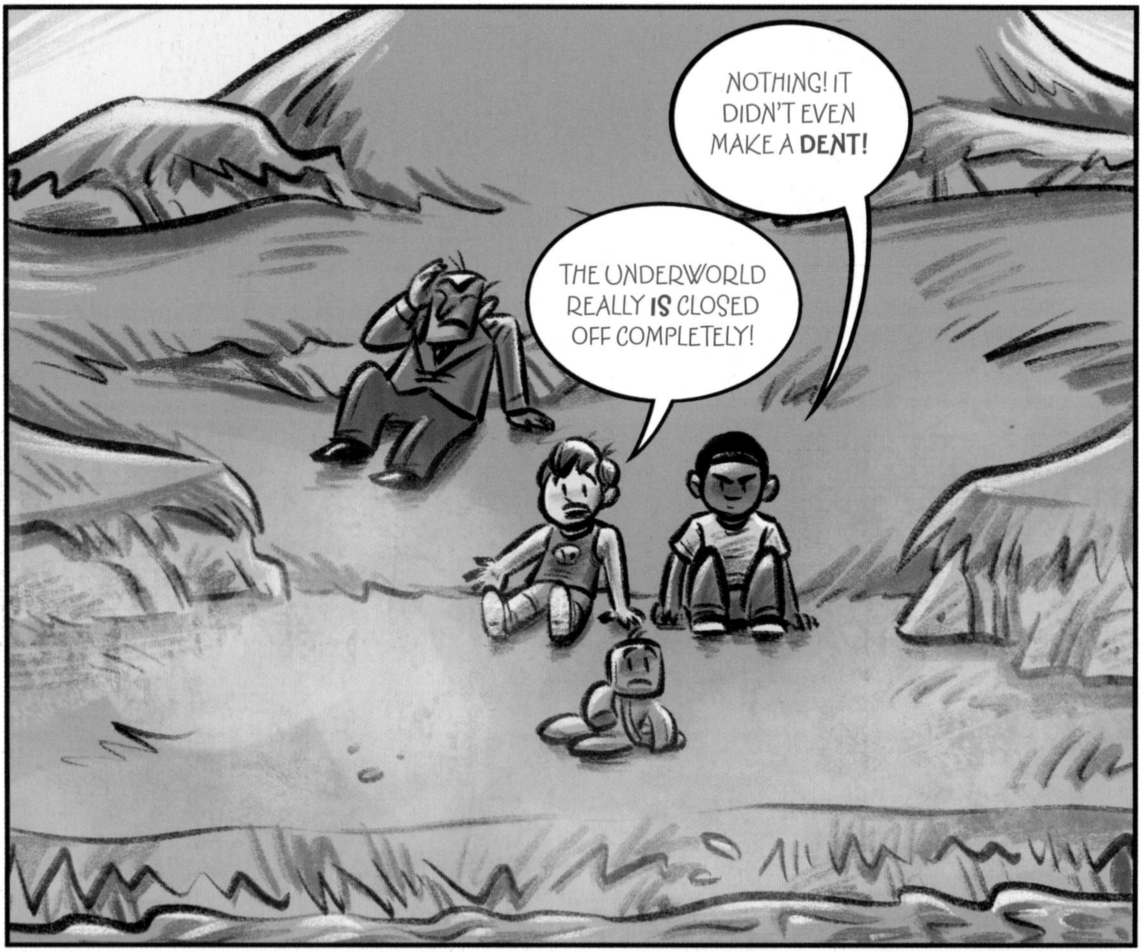
NOTHING! IT DIDN'T EVEN MAKE A **DENT!**
THE UNDERWORLD REALLY **IS** CLOSED OFF COMPLETELY!

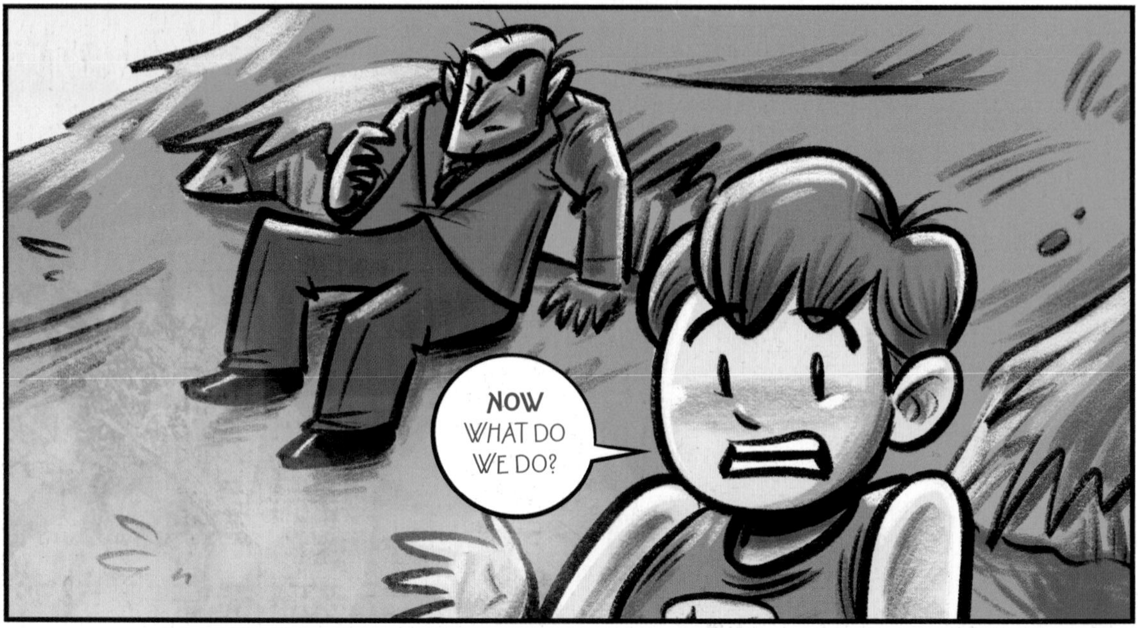
NOW WHAT DO WE DO?

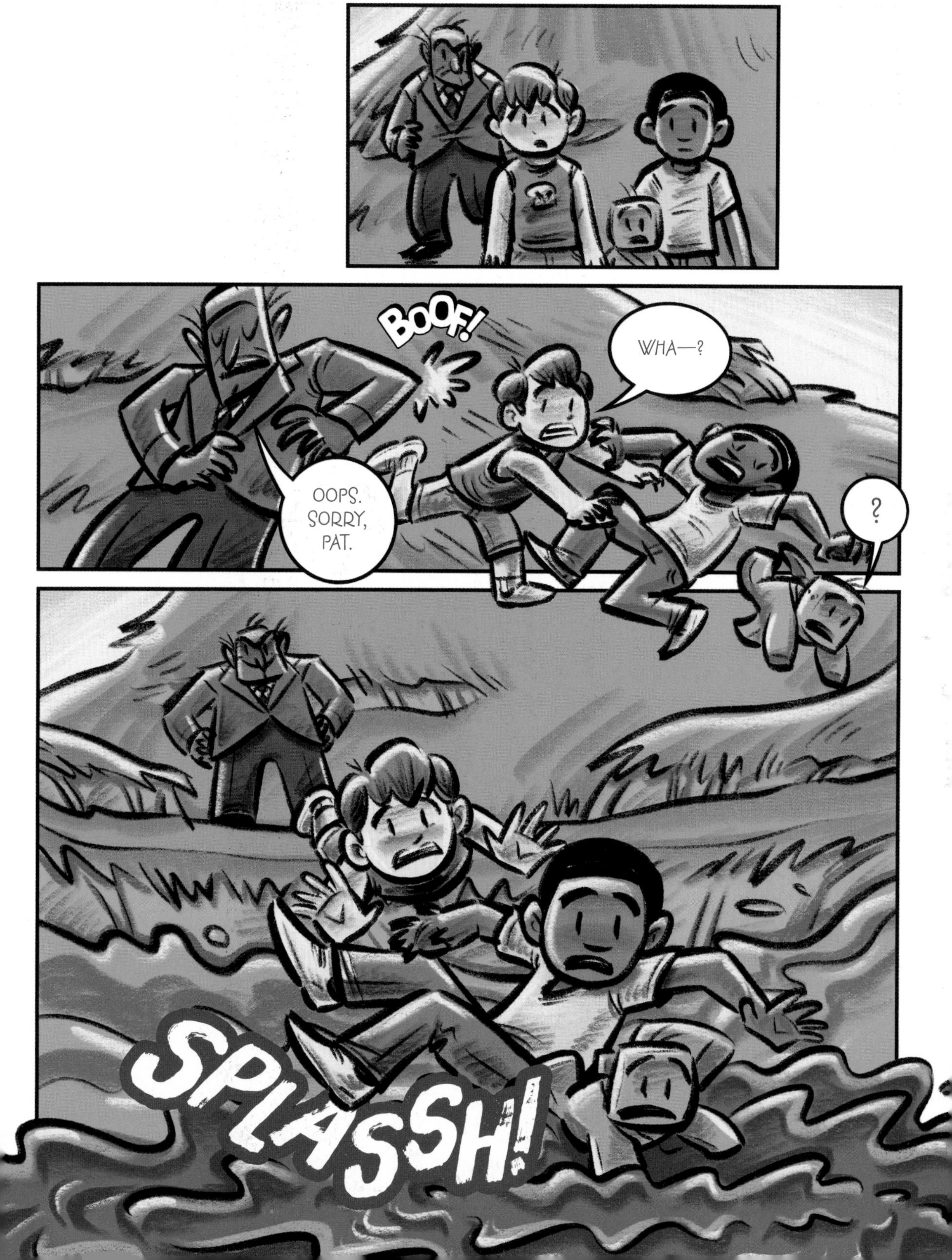
BOOF!
WHA—?
OOPS. SORRY, PAT.
?
SPLASSH!

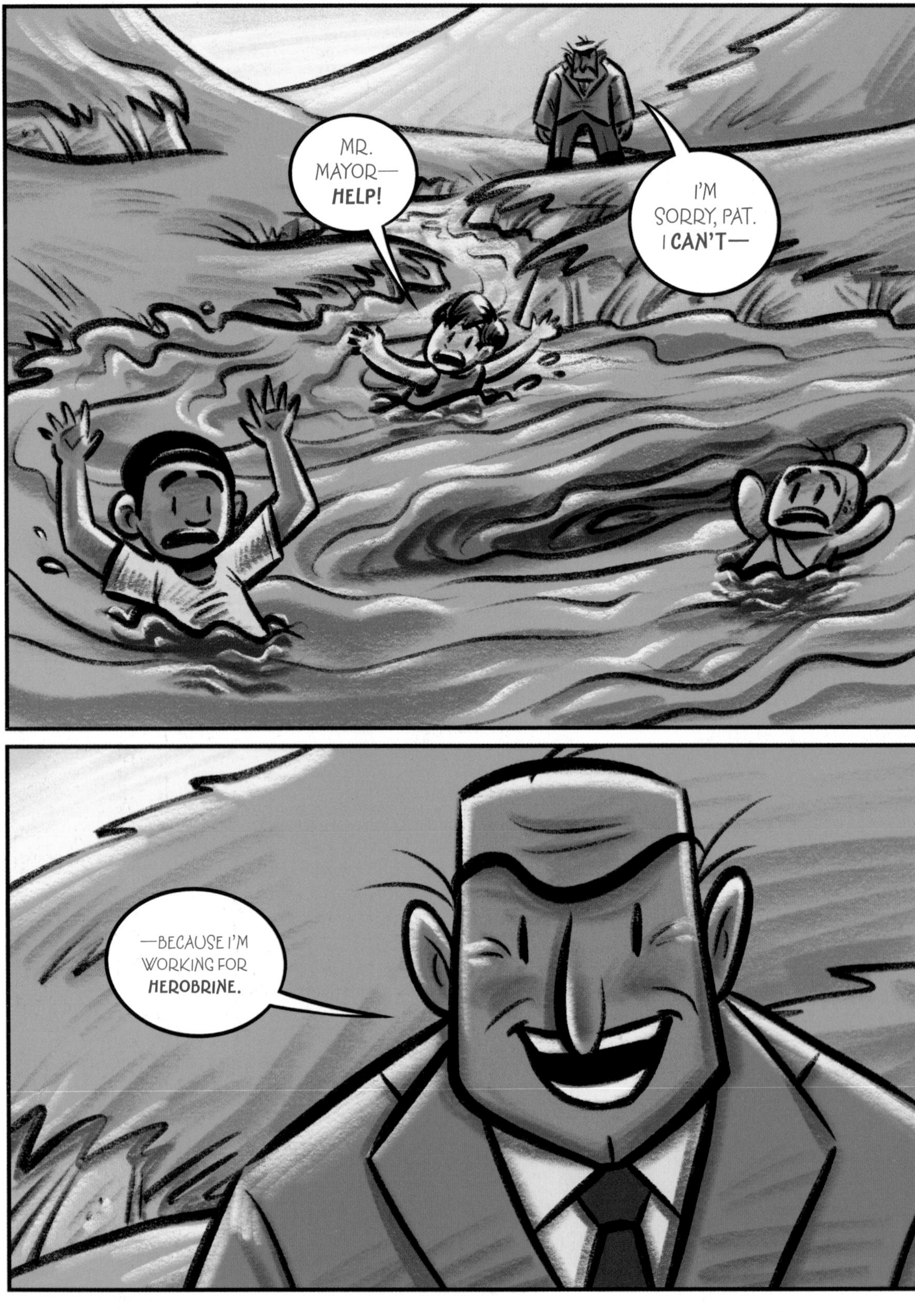
MR. MAYOR— HELP!
I'M SORRY, PAT. I CAN'T—
—BECAUSE I'M WORKING FOR HEROBRINE.

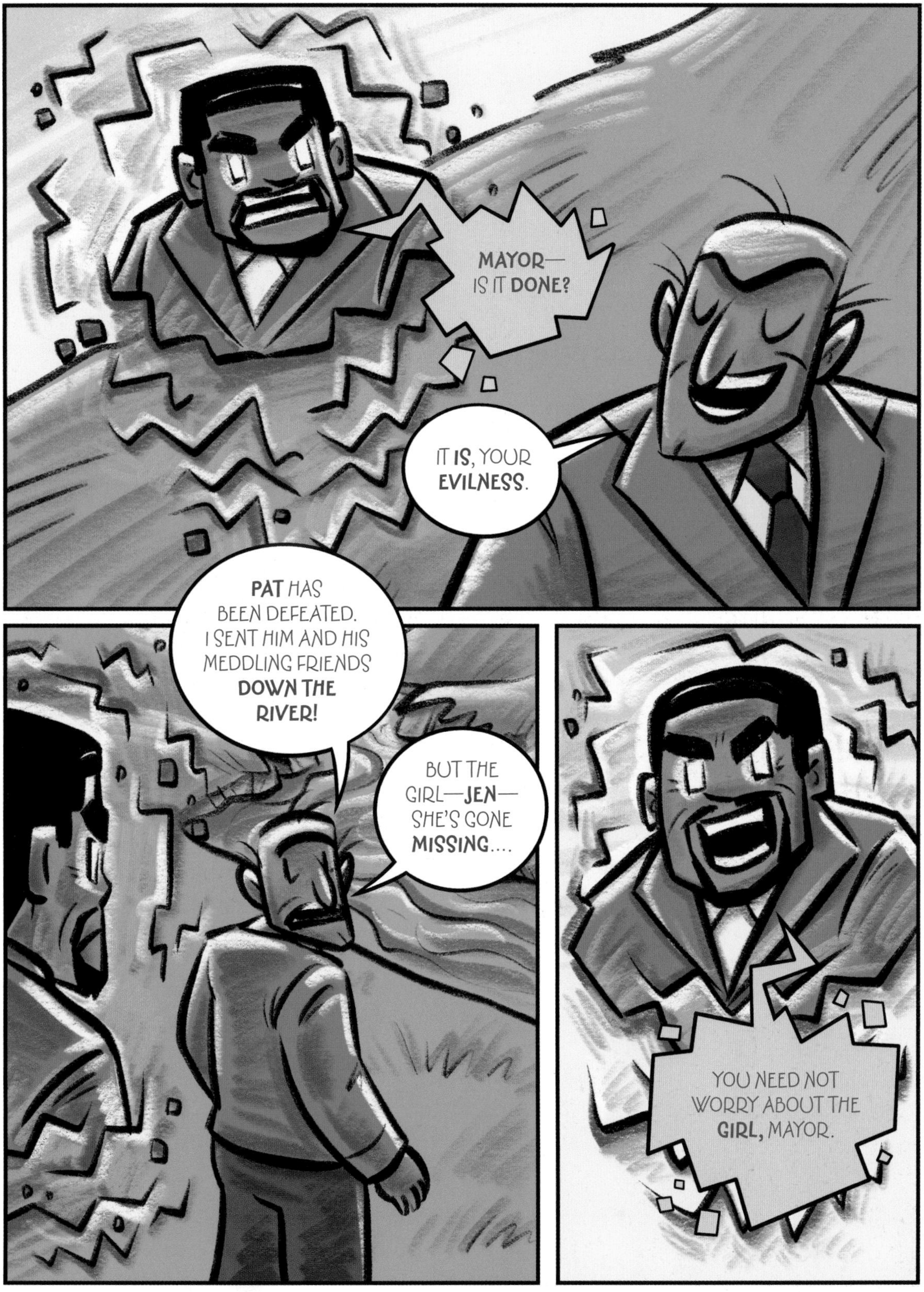
MAYOR—
IS IT DONE?
IT IS, YOUR EVILNESS.
PAT HAS BEEN DEFEATED. I SENT HIM AND HIS MEDDLING FRIENDS DOWN THE RIVER!
BUT THE GIRL—JEN—SHE'S GONE MISSING....
YOU NEED NOT WORRY ABOUT THE GIRL, MAYOR.

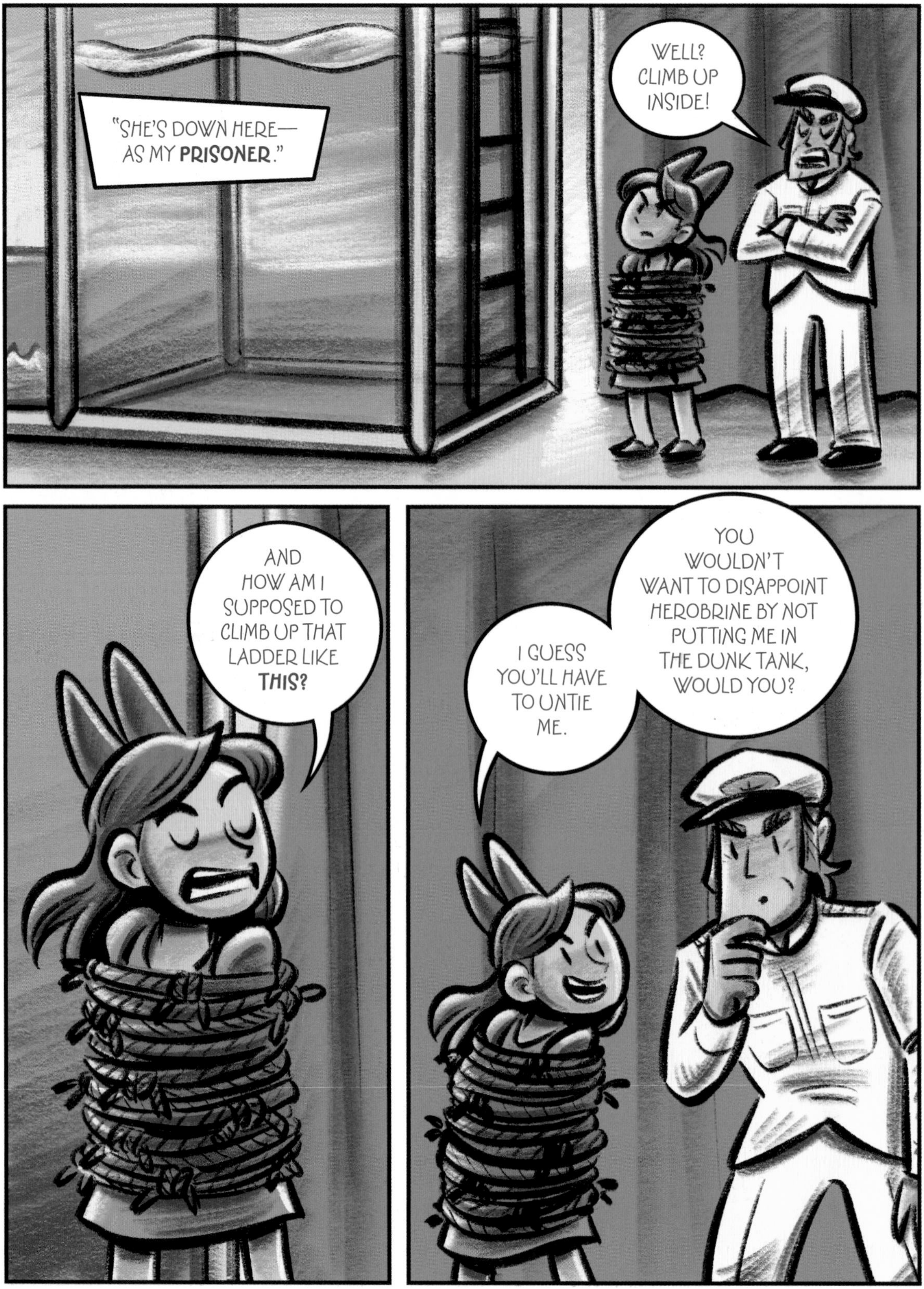
"SHE'S DOWN HERE— AS MY **PRISONER**."
WELL? CLIMB UP INSIDE!
AND HOW AM I SUPPOSED TO CLIMB UP THAT LADDER LIKE **THIS?**
I GUESS YOU'LL HAVE TO UNTIE ME.
YOU WOULDN'T WANT TO DISAPPOINT HEROBRINE BY NOT PUTTING ME IN THE DUNK TANK, WOULD YOU?

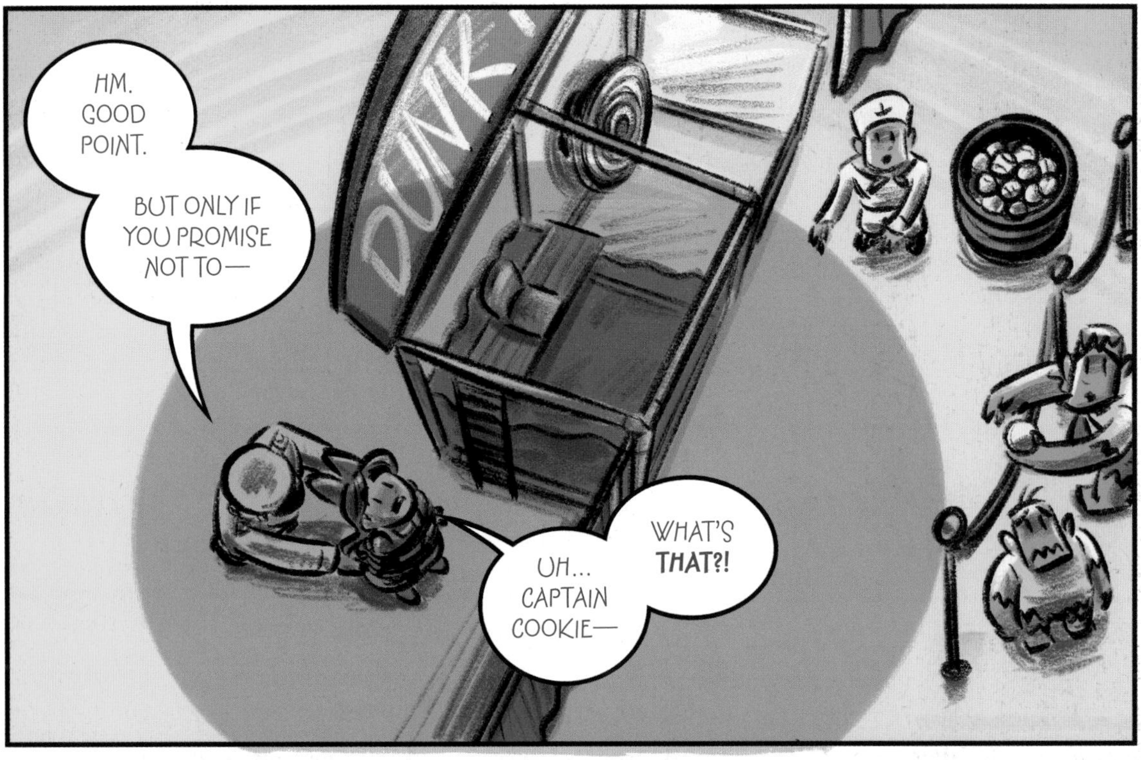
DUNK
HM. GOOD POINT.
BUT ONLY IF YOU PROMISE NOT TO—
UH... CAPTAIN COOKIE—
WHAT'S THAT?!

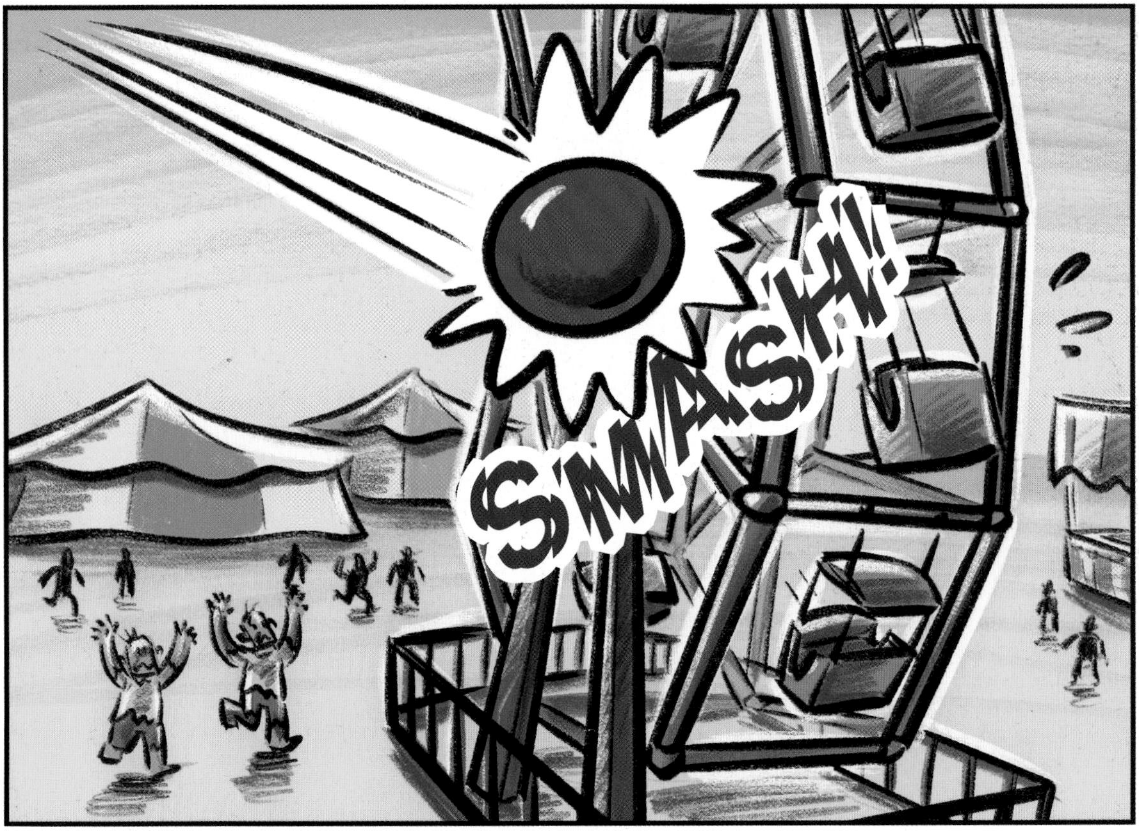
SMASH!

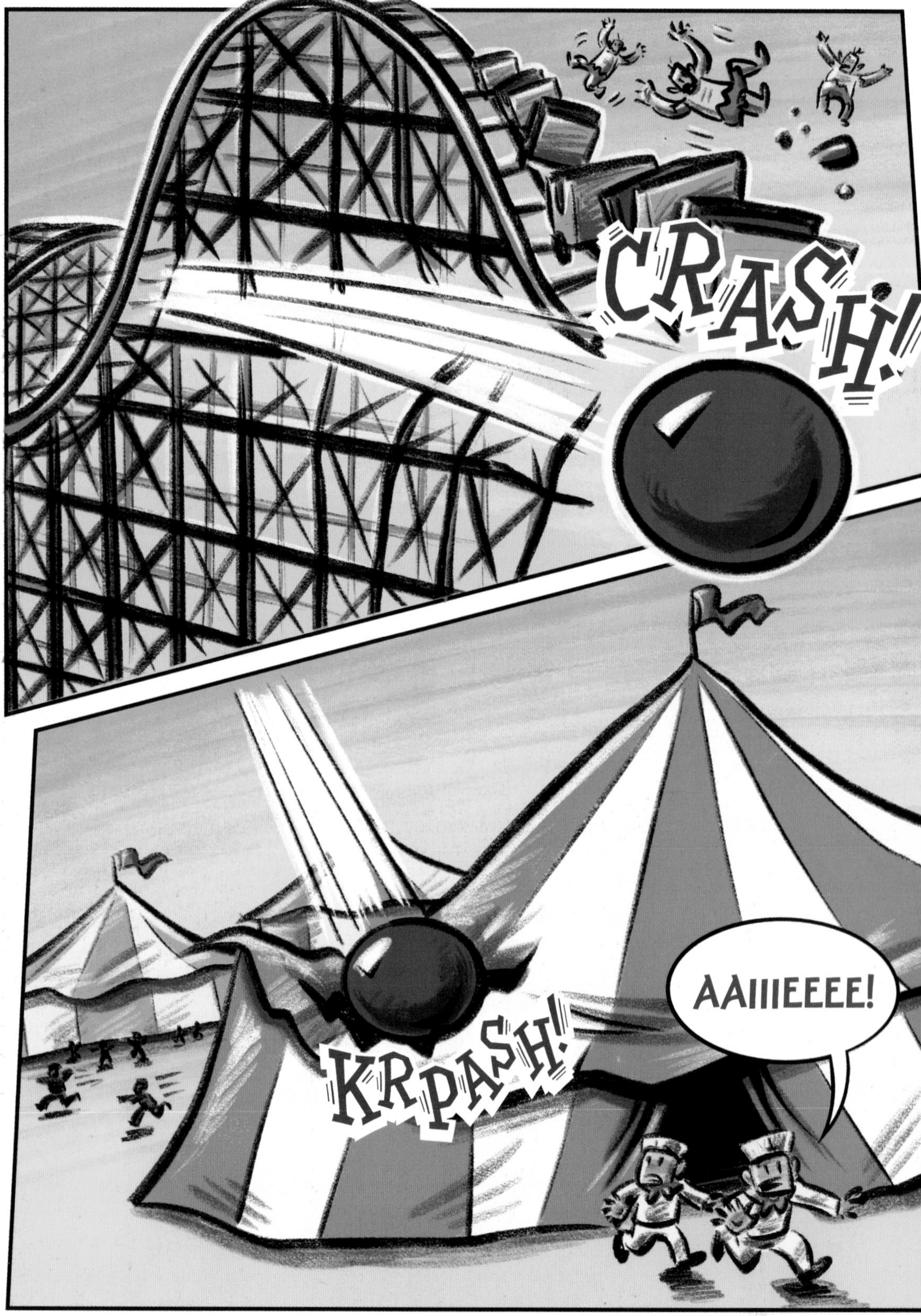

CRASH!
KRPASH!
AAIIIEEEE!

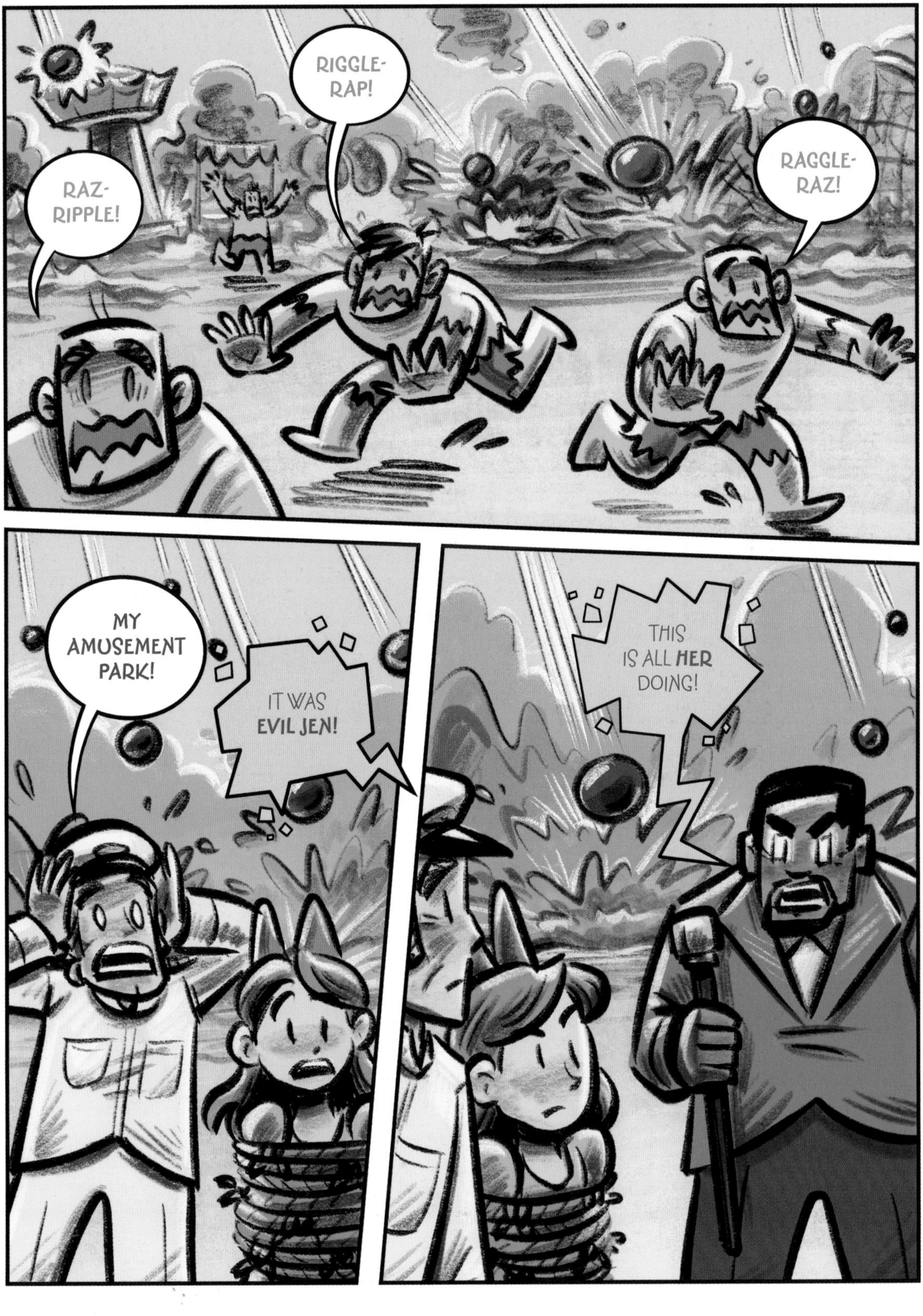
RAZ-
RIPPLE!
RIGGLE-
RAP!
RAGGLE-
RAZ!
MY
AMUSEMENT
PARK!
IT WAS
EVIL JEN!
THIS
IS ALL HER
DOING!

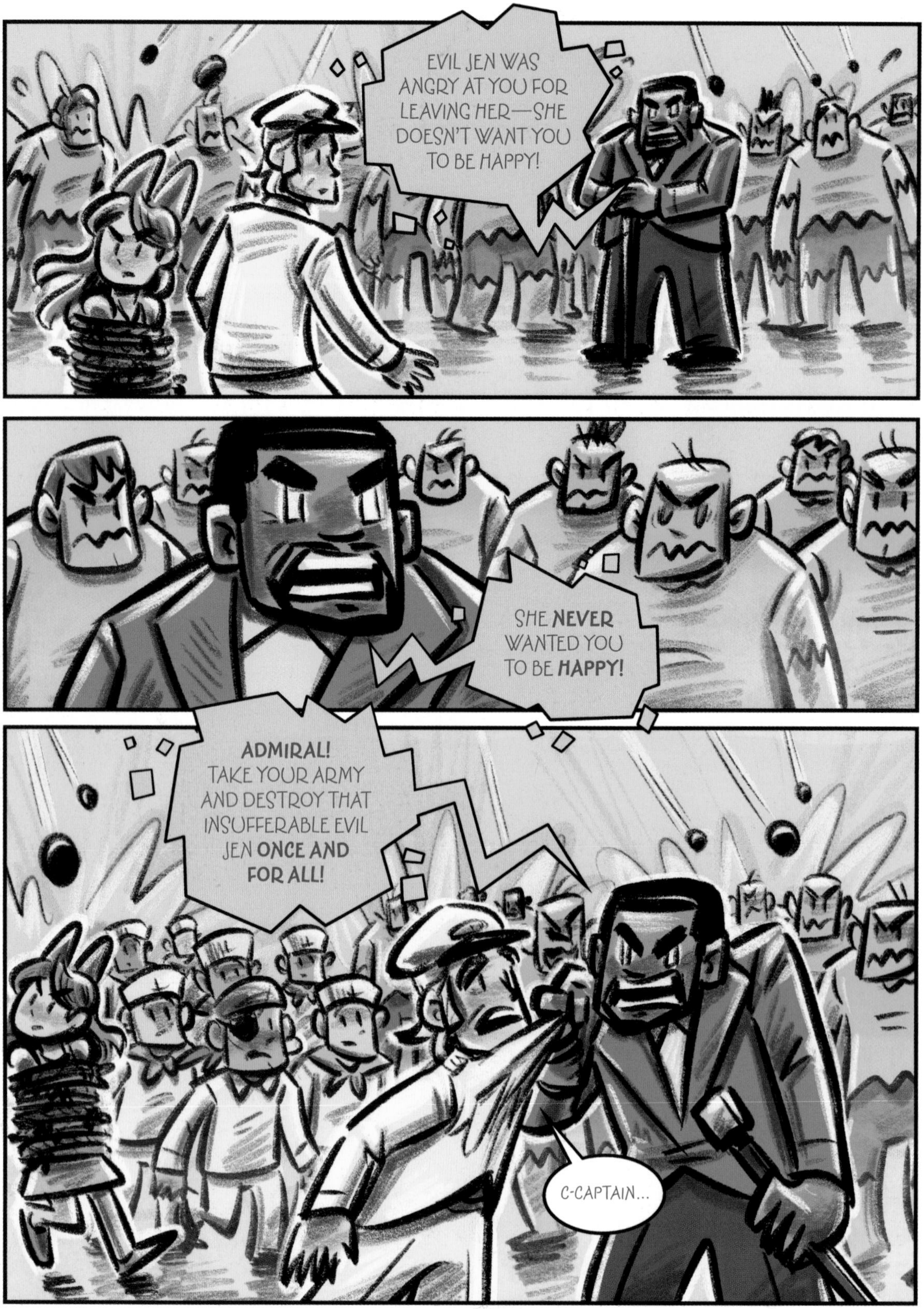
EVIL JEN WAS ANGRY AT YOU FOR LEAVING HER—SHE DOESN'T WANT YOU TO BE HAPPY!
SHE NEVER WANTED YOU TO BE HAPPY!
ADMIRAL! TAKE YOUR ARMY AND DESTROY THAT INSUFFERABLE EVIL JEN ONCE AND FOR ALL!
C-CAPTAIN...

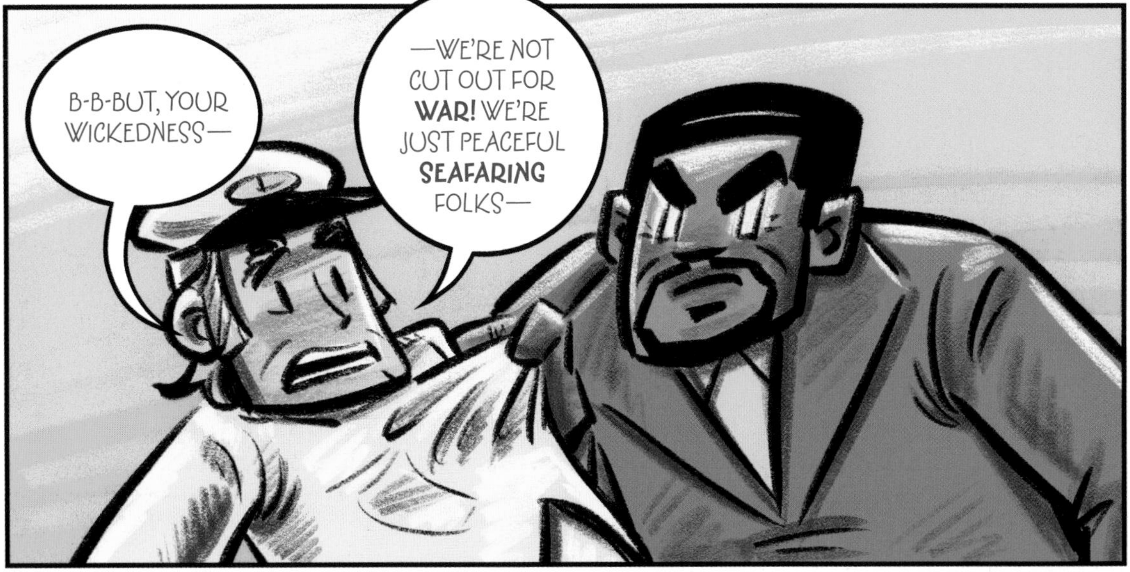
B-B-BUT, YOUR WICKEDNESS—
—WE'RE NOT CUT OUT FOR WAR! WE'RE JUST PEACEFUL SEAFARING FOLKS—

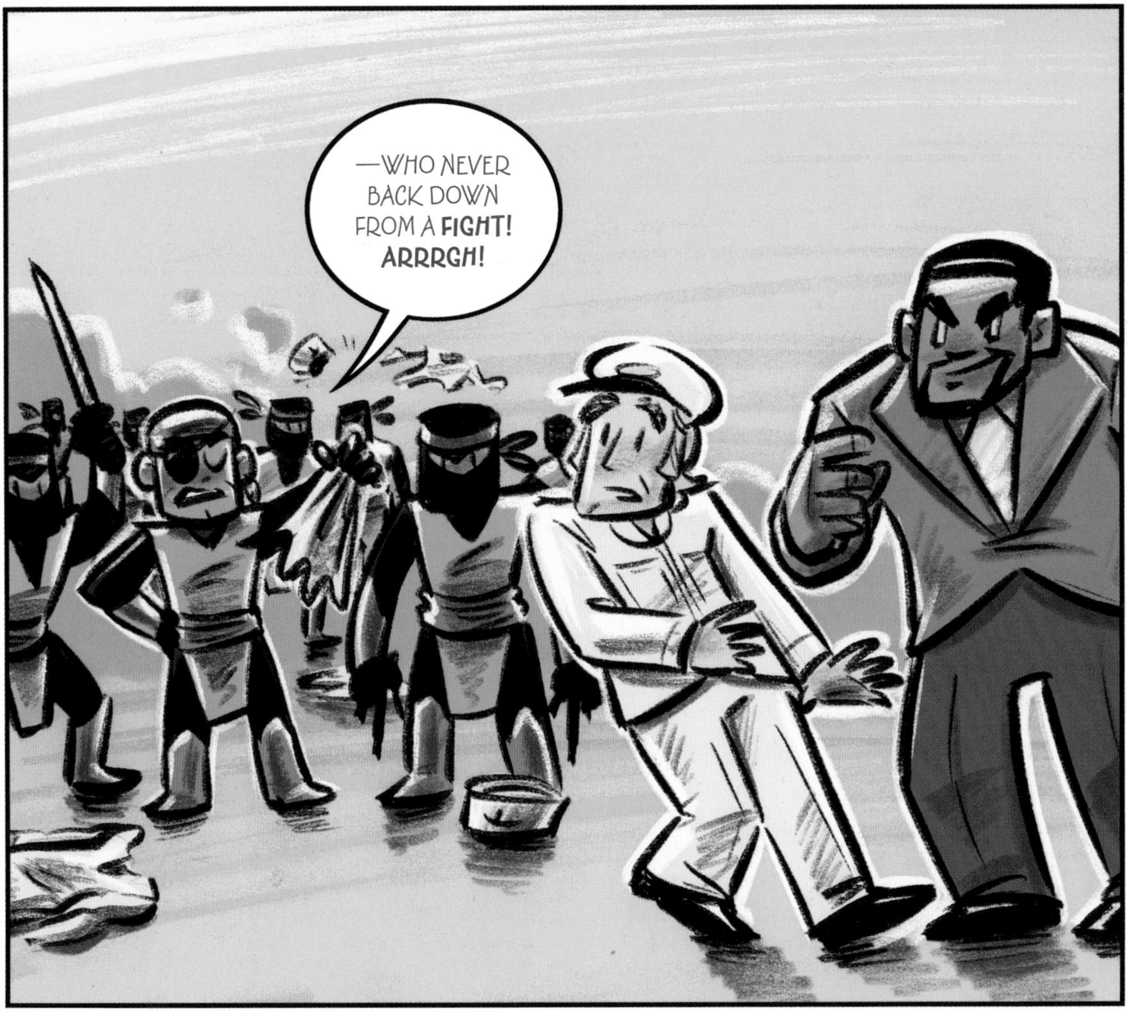
—WHO NEVER BACK DOWN FROM A FIGHT! ARRRGH!

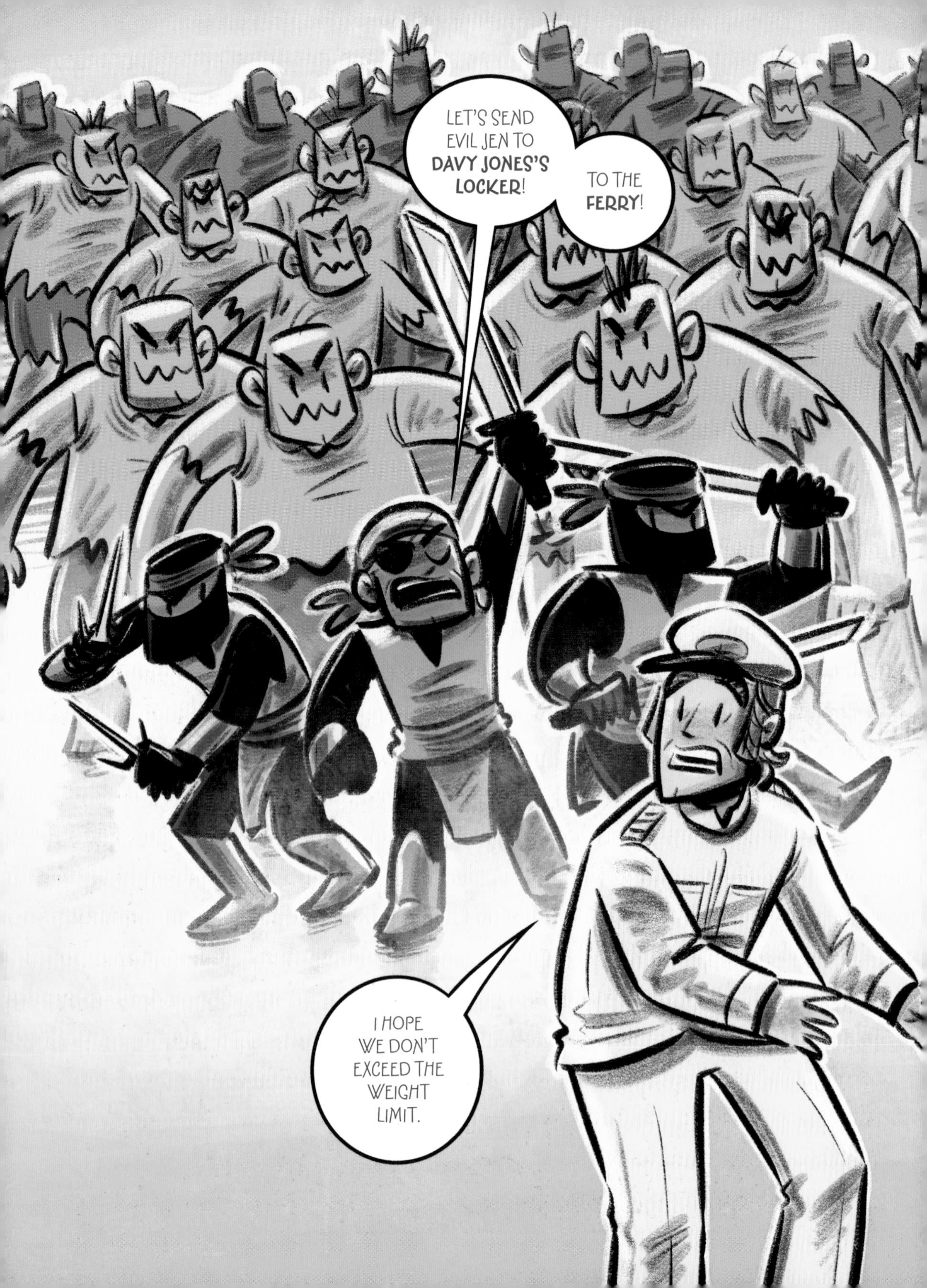
LET'S SEND EVIL JEN TO **DAVY JONES'S LOCKER**!
TO THE **FERRY**!
I HOPE WE DON'T EXCEED THE WEIGHT LIMIT.

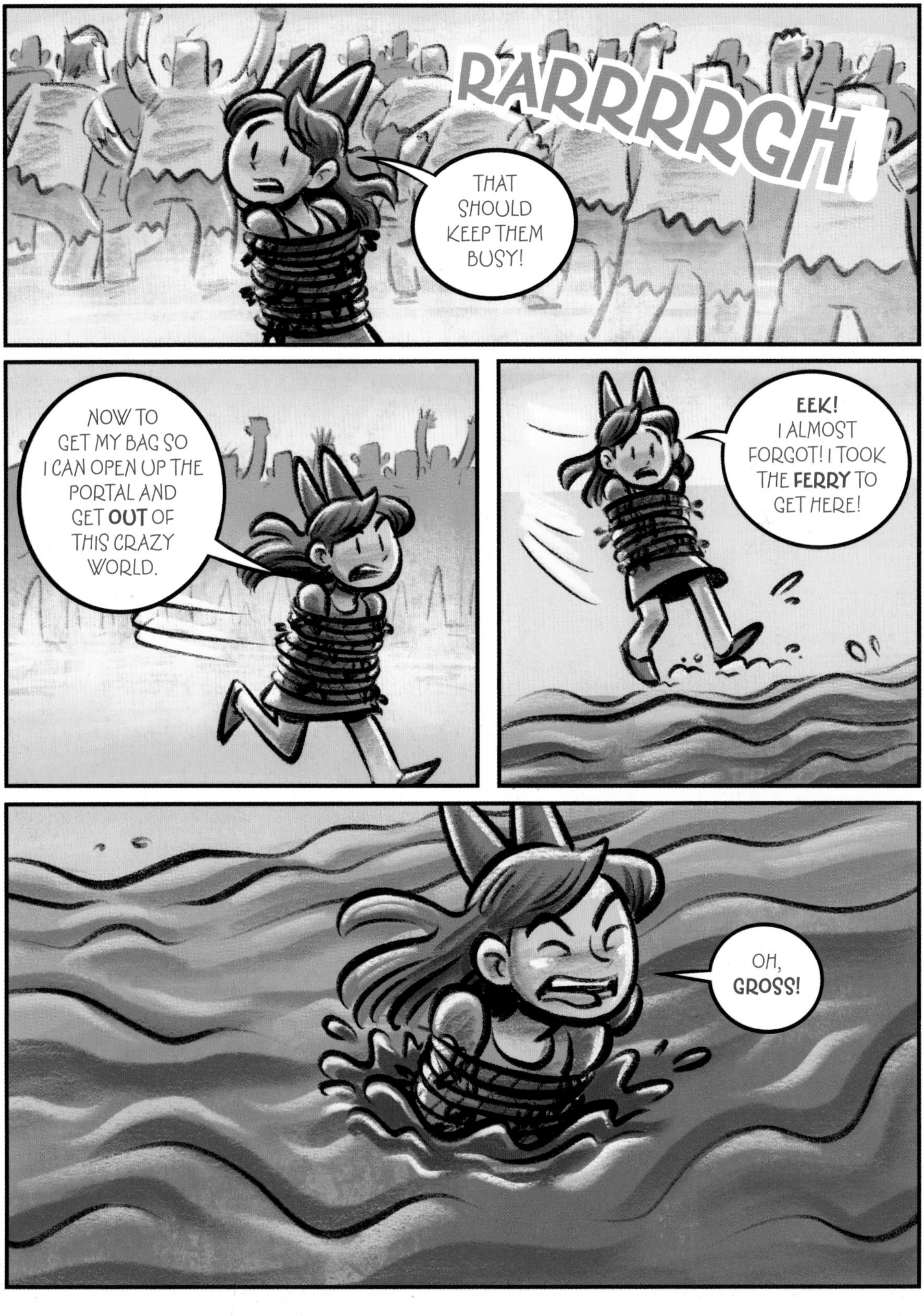
RARRRRGH!
THAT SHOULD KEEP THEM BUSY!
NOW TO GET MY BAG SO I CAN OPEN UP THE PORTAL AND GET **OUT** OF THIS CRAZY WORLD.
EEK! I ALMOST FORGOT! I TOOK THE **FERRY** TO GET HERE!
OH, **GROSS!**

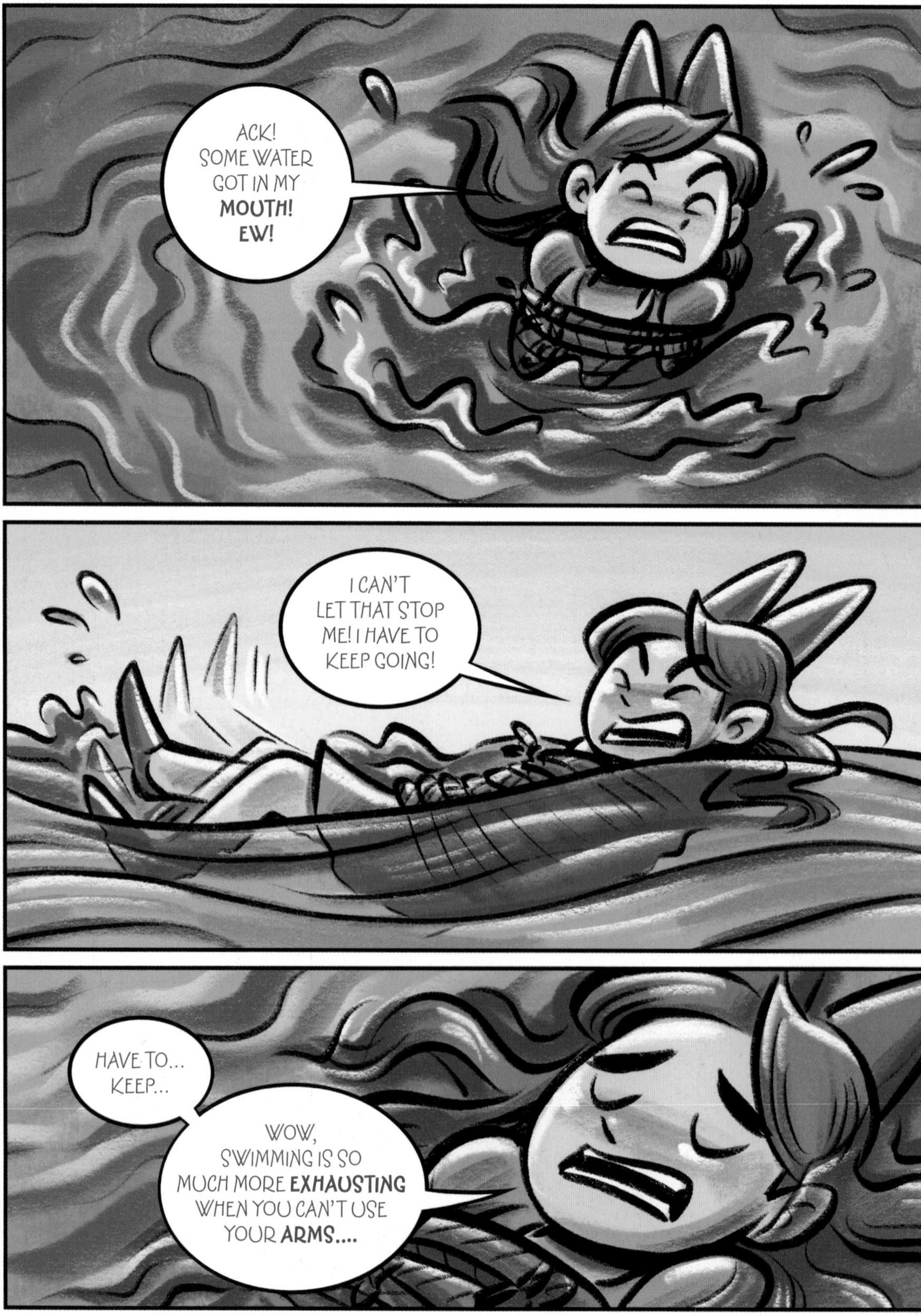
ACK! SOME WATER GOT IN MY **MOUTH! EW!**
I CAN'T LET THAT STOP ME! I HAVE TO KEEP GOING!
HAVE TO... KEEP...
WOW, SWIMMING IS SO MUCH MORE **EXHAUSTING** WHEN YOU CAN'T USE YOUR **ARMS....**

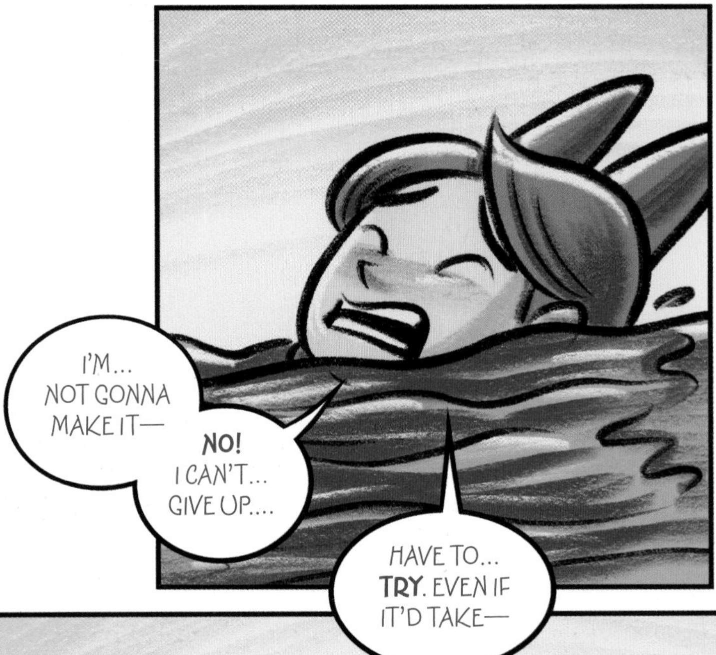
I'M... NOT GONNA MAKE IT—
NO! I CAN'T... GIVE UP....
HAVE TO... TRY. EVEN IF IT'D TAKE—

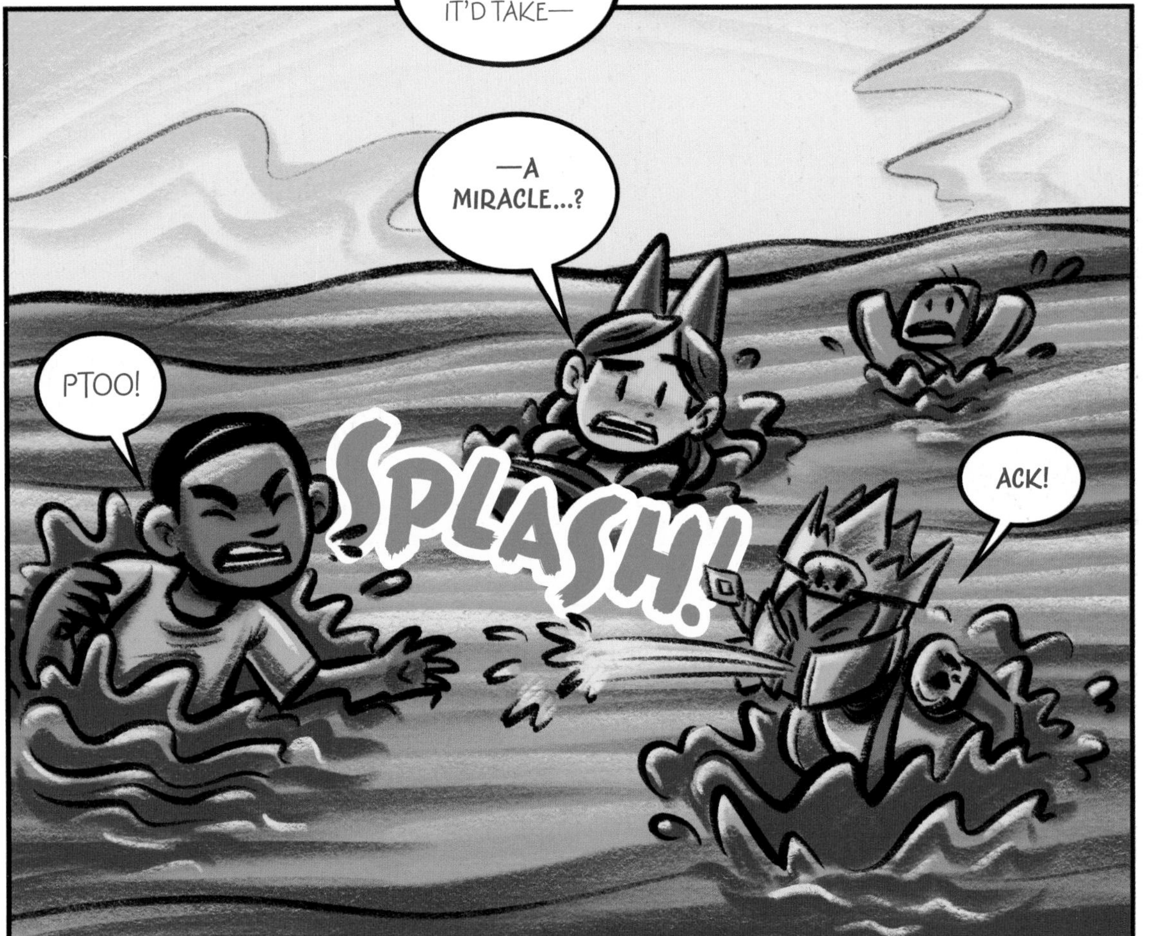
—A MIRACLE...?
PTOO!
SPLASH!
ACK!

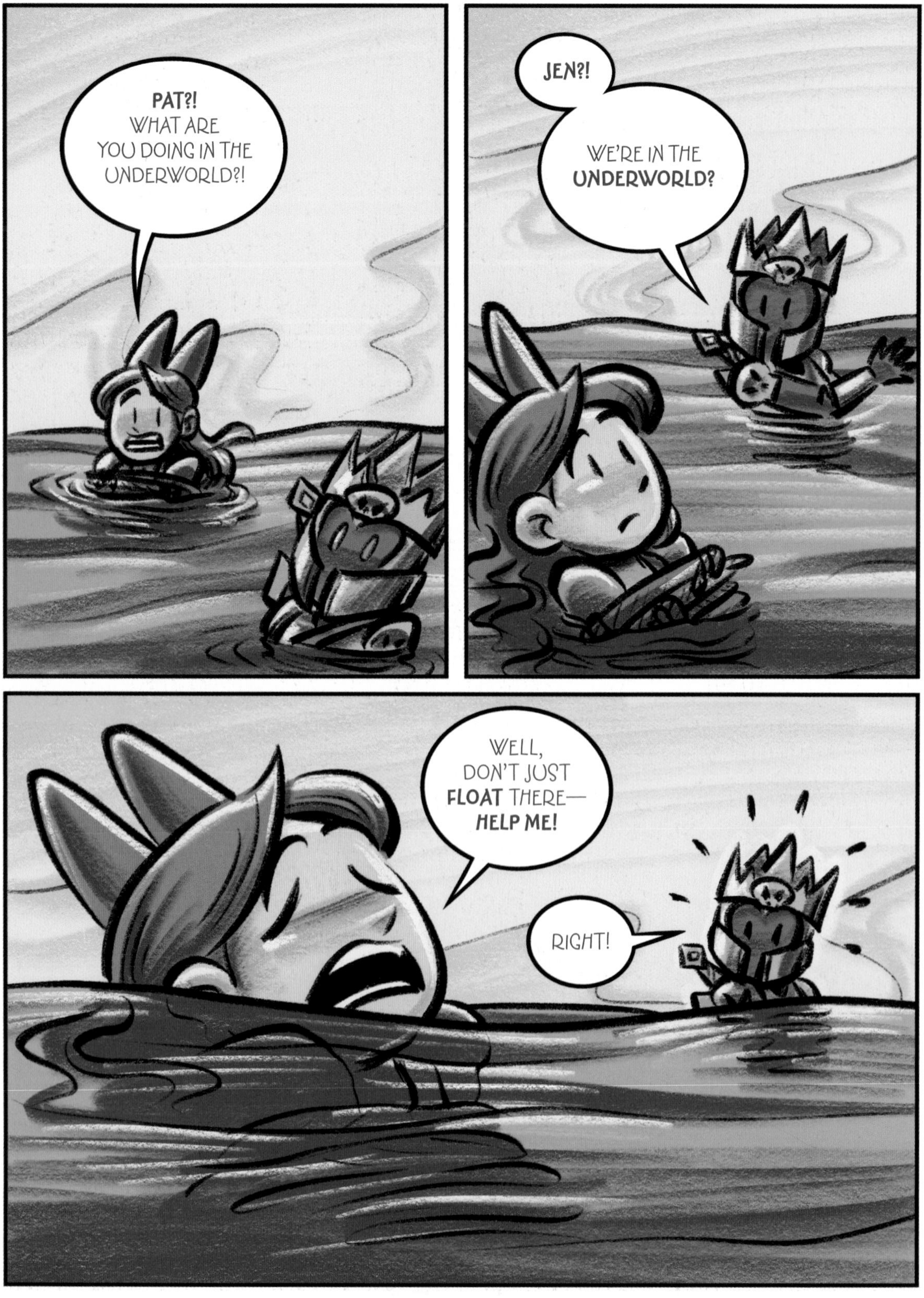

PAT?! WHAT ARE YOU DOING IN THE UNDERWORLD?!
JEN?!
WE'RE IN THE UNDERWORLD?
WELL, DON'T JUST FLOAT THERE— HELP ME!
RIGHT!

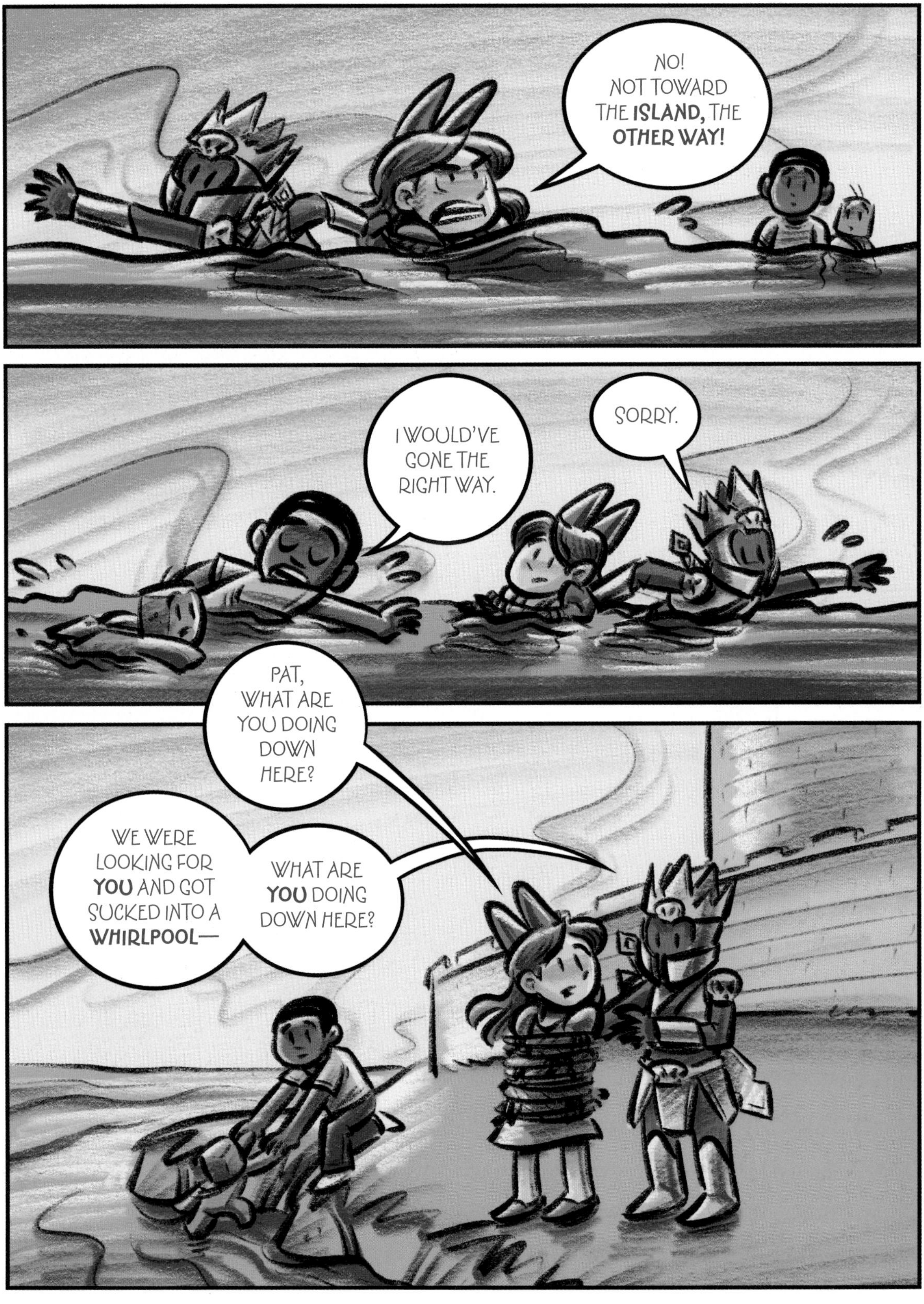
NO! NOT TOWARD THE **ISLAND,** THE **OTHER WAY!**
I WOULD'VE GONE THE RIGHT WAY.
SORRY.
PAT, WHAT ARE YOU DOING DOWN HERE?
WE WERE LOOKING FOR **YOU** AND GOT SUCKED INTO A **WHIRLPOOL**—
WHAT ARE **YOU** DOING DOWN HERE?

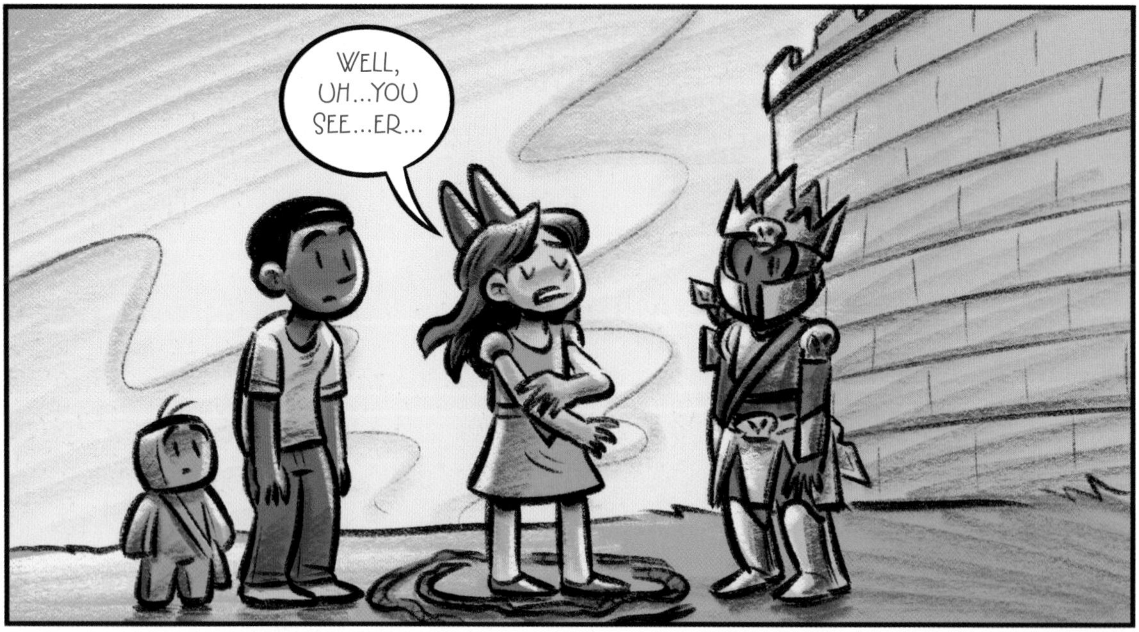
WELL, UH...YOU SEE...ER...

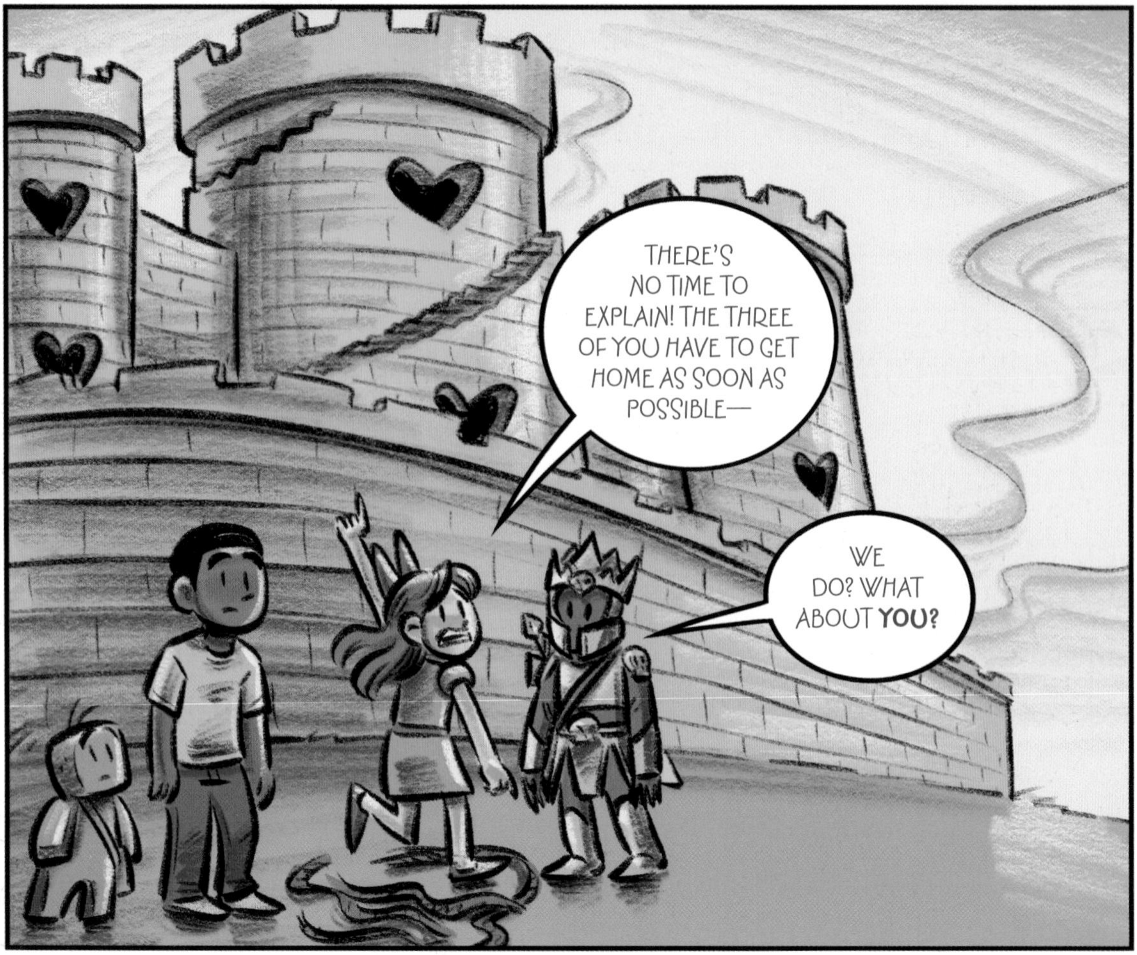
THERE'S NO TIME TO EXPLAIN! THE THREE OF YOU HAVE TO GET HOME AS SOON AS POSSIBLE—
WE DO? WHAT ABOUT **YOU?**

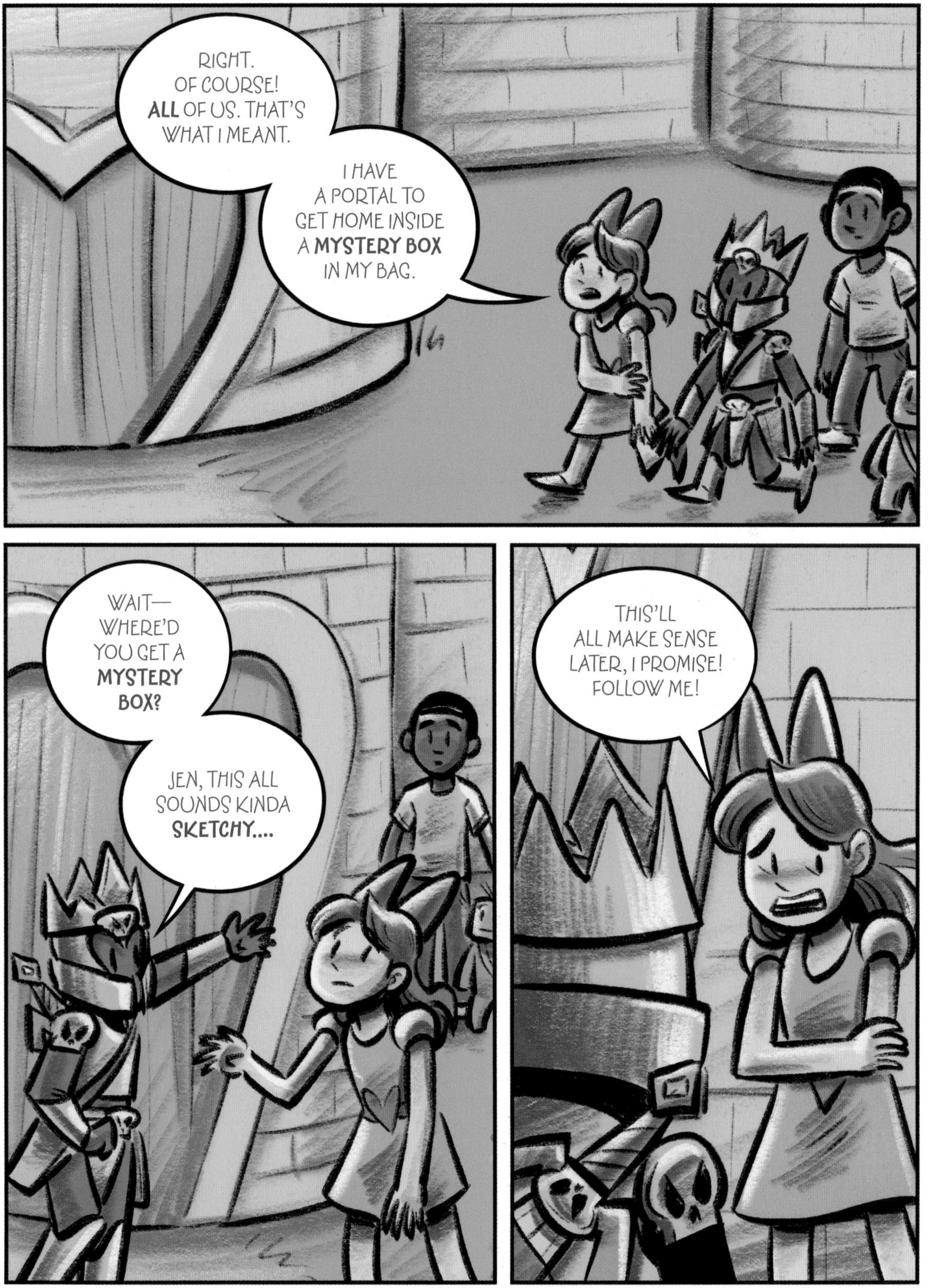
RIGHT. OF COURSE! ALL OF US. THAT'S WHAT I MEANT.
I HAVE A PORTAL TO GET HOME INSIDE A MYSTERY BOX IN MY BAG.
WAIT— WHERE'D YOU GET A MYSTERY BOX?
JEN, THIS ALL SOUNDS KINDA SKETCHY....
THIS'LL ALL MAKE SENSE LATER, I PROMISE! FOLLOW ME!

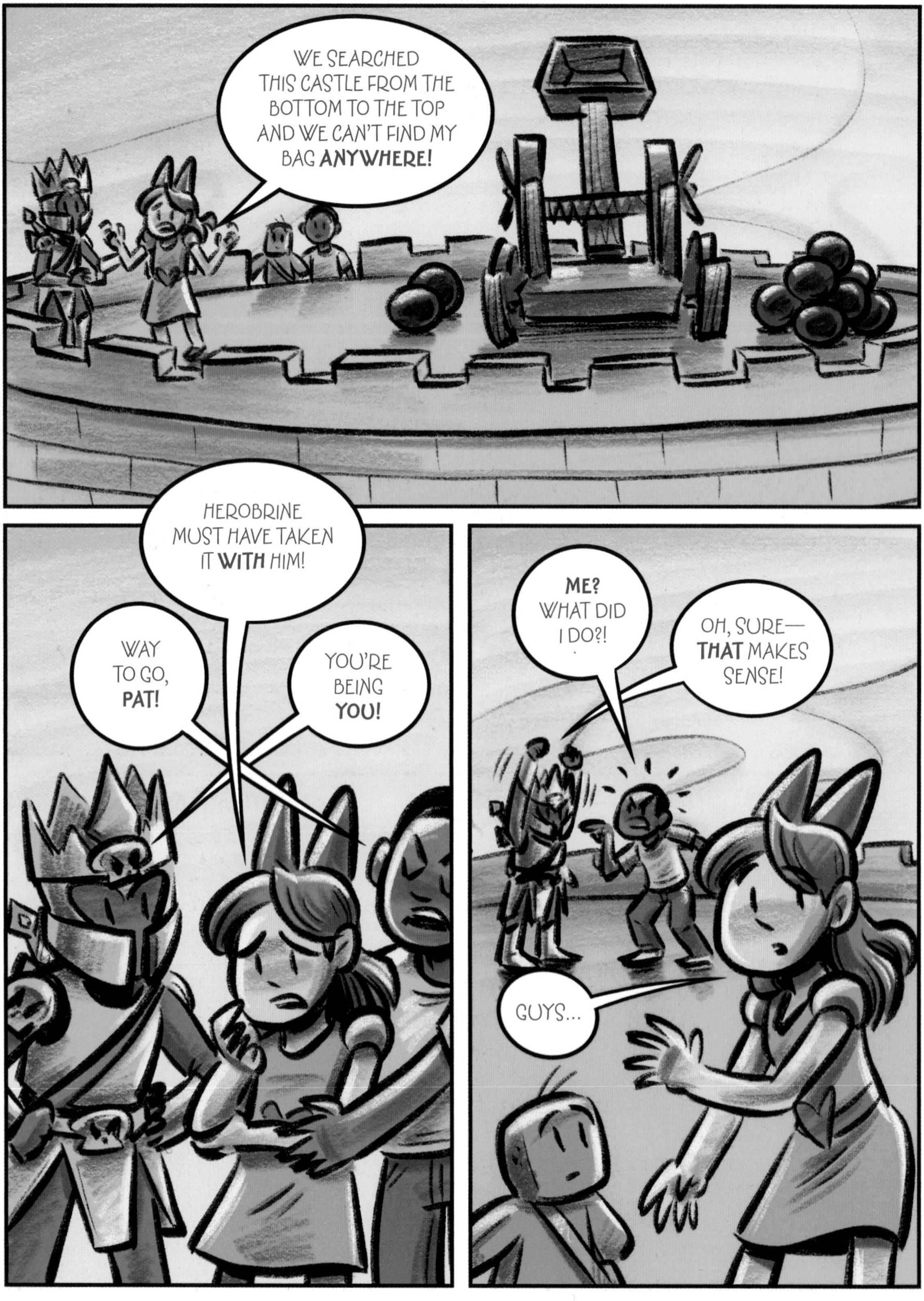
WE SEARCHED THIS CASTLE FROM THE BOTTOM TO THE TOP AND WE CAN'T FIND MY BAG **ANYWHERE!**
HEROBRINE MUST HAVE TAKEN IT **WITH** HIM!
WAY TO GO, **PAT!**
YOU'RE BEING **YOU!**
ME? WHAT DID I DO?!
OH, SURE— **THAT** MAKES SENSE!
GUYS...

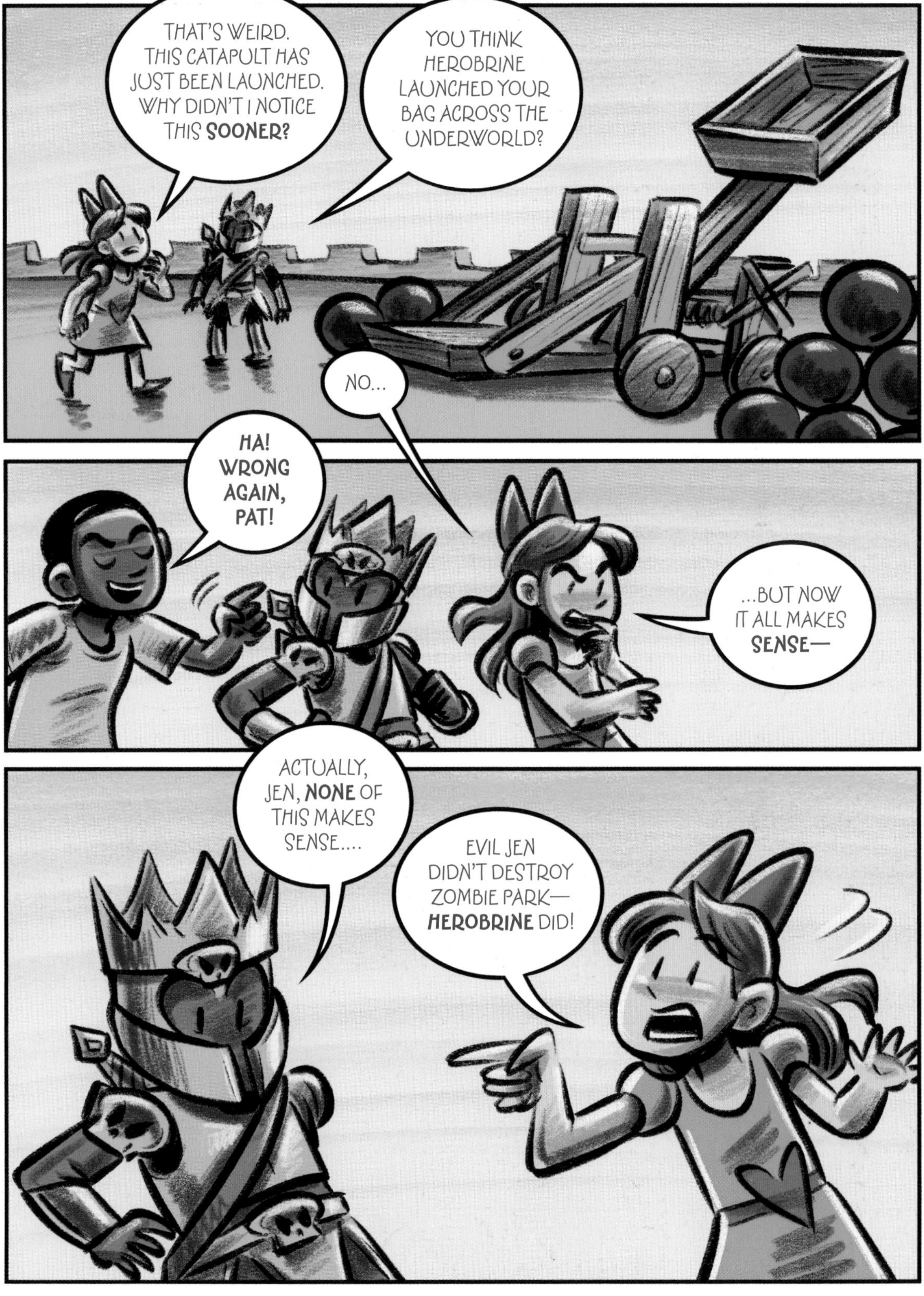
THAT'S WEIRD. THIS CATAPULT HAS JUST BEEN LAUNCHED. WHY DIDN'T I NOTICE THIS **SOONER?**
YOU THINK HEROBRINE LAUNCHED YOUR BAG ACROSS THE UNDERWORLD?
NO...
HA! WRONG AGAIN, PAT!
...BUT NOW IT ALL MAKES **SENSE**—
ACTUALLY, JEN, **NONE** OF THIS MAKES SENSE....
EVIL JEN DIDN'T DESTROY ZOMBIE PARK— **HEROBRINE** DID!

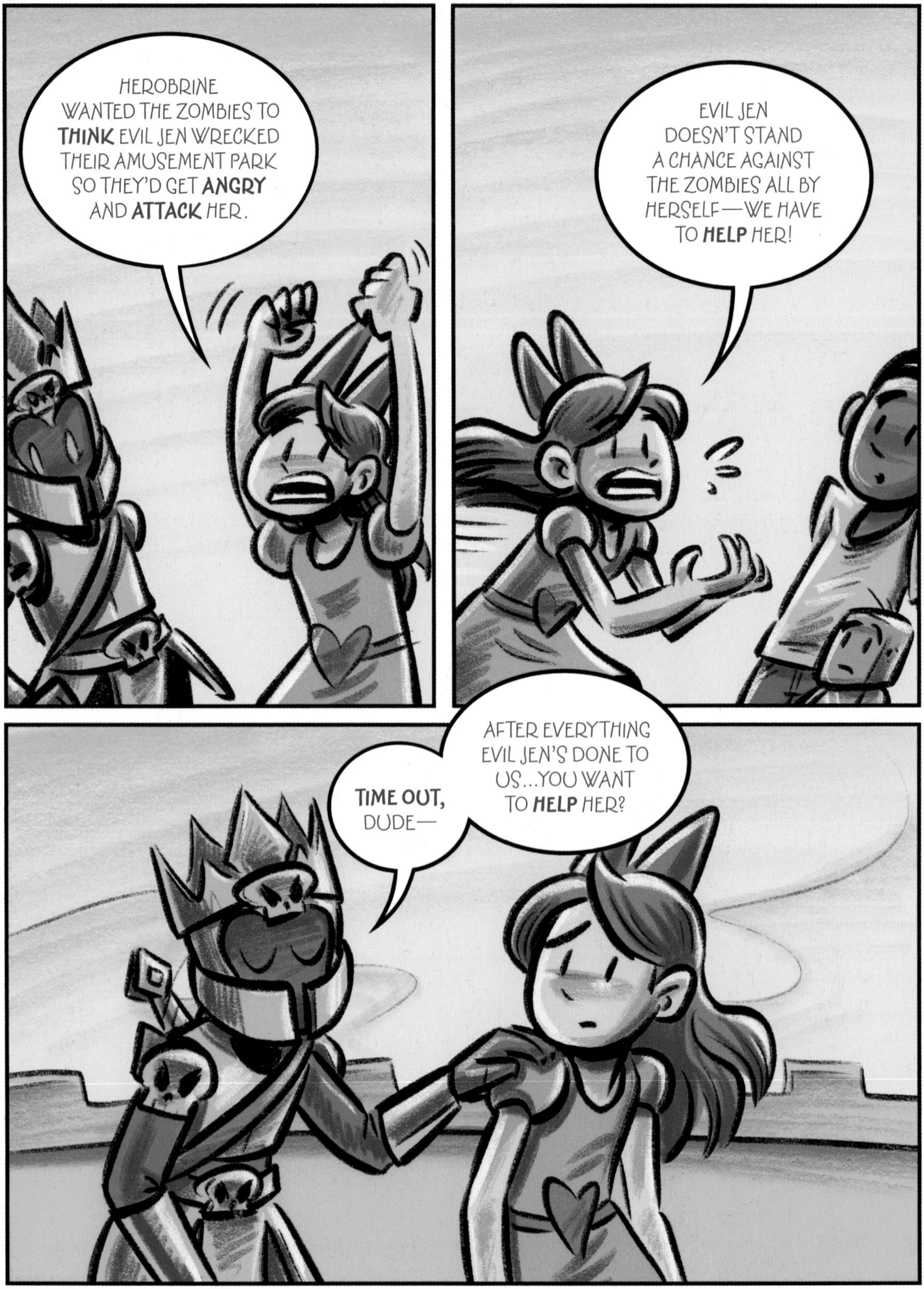
HEROBRINE WANTED THE ZOMBIES TO **THINK** EVIL JEN WRECKED THEIR AMUSEMENT PARK SO THEY'D GET **ANGRY** AND **ATTACK** HER.
EVIL JEN DOESN'T STAND A CHANCE AGAINST THE ZOMBIES ALL BY HERSELF—WE HAVE TO **HELP** HER!
TIME OUT, DUDE—
AFTER EVERYTHING EVIL JEN'S DONE TO US...YOU WANT TO **HELP** HER?

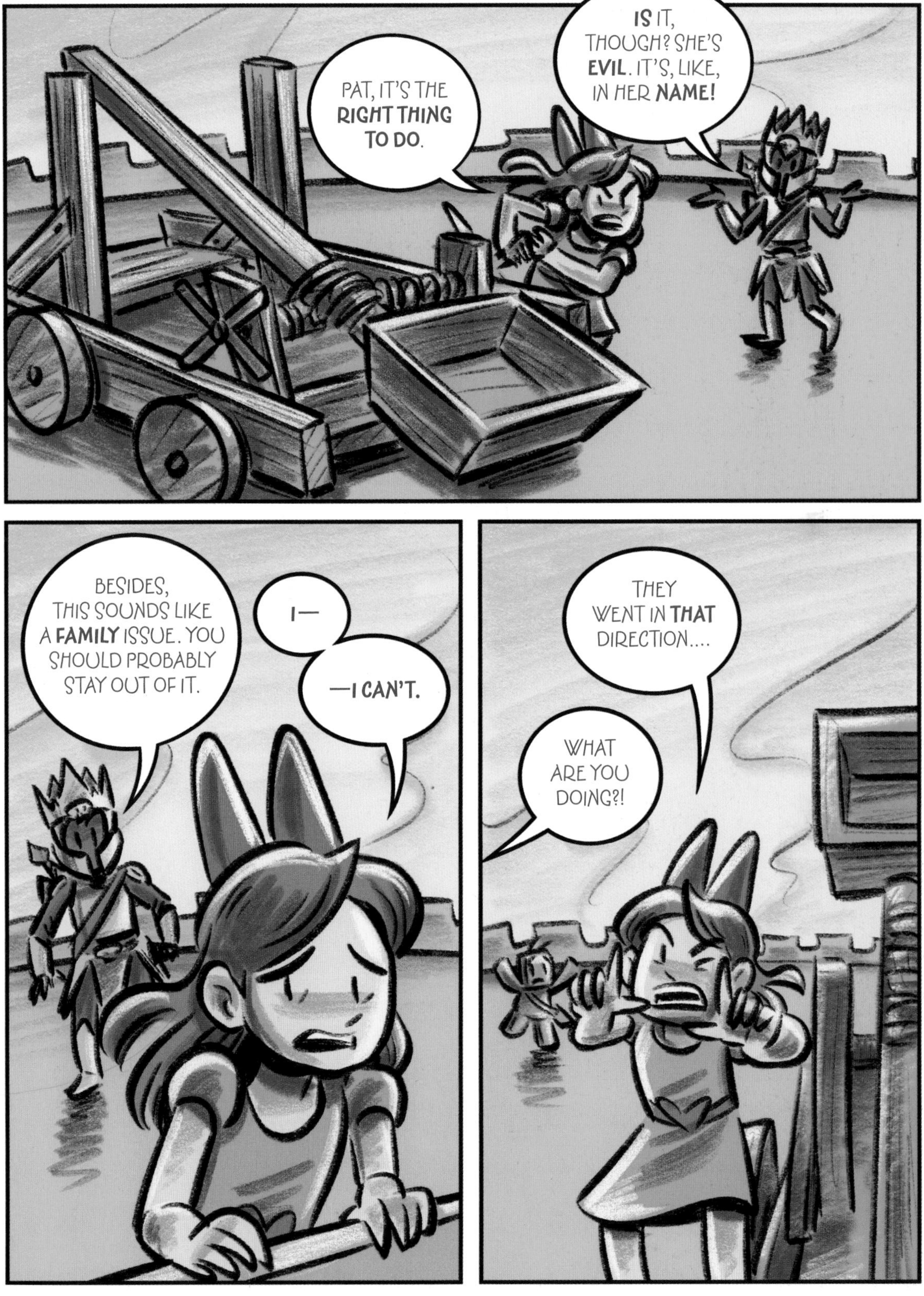
PAT, IT'S THE **RIGHT THING** TO DO.
IS IT, THOUGH? SHE'S **EVIL**. IT'S, LIKE, IN HER **NAME!**
BESIDES, THIS SOUNDS LIKE A **FAMILY** ISSUE. YOU SHOULD PROBABLY STAY OUT OF IT.
I—
—**I CAN'T.**
THEY WENT IN **THAT** DIRECTION....
WHAT ARE YOU DOING?!

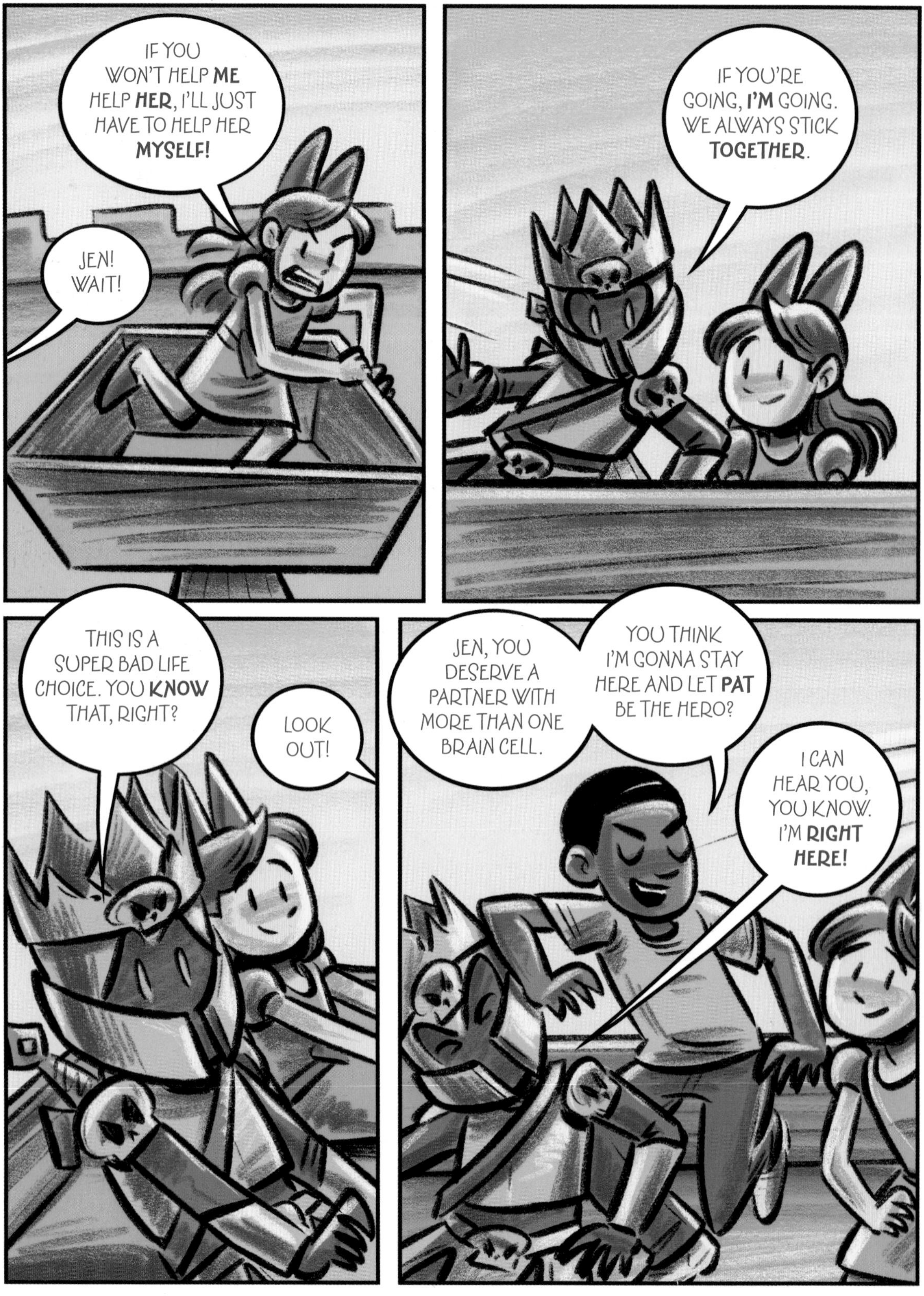
IF YOU WON'T HELP ME HELP HER, I'LL JUST HAVE TO HELP HER MYSELF!
JEN! WAIT!
IF YOU'RE GOING, I'M GOING. WE ALWAYS STICK TOGETHER.
THIS IS A SUPER BAD LIFE CHOICE. YOU KNOW THAT, RIGHT?
LOOK OUT!
JEN, YOU DESERVE A PARTNER WITH MORE THAN ONE BRAIN CELL.
YOU THINK I'M GONNA STAY HERE AND LET PAT BE THE HERO?
I CAN HEAR YOU, YOU KNOW. I'M RIGHT HERE!

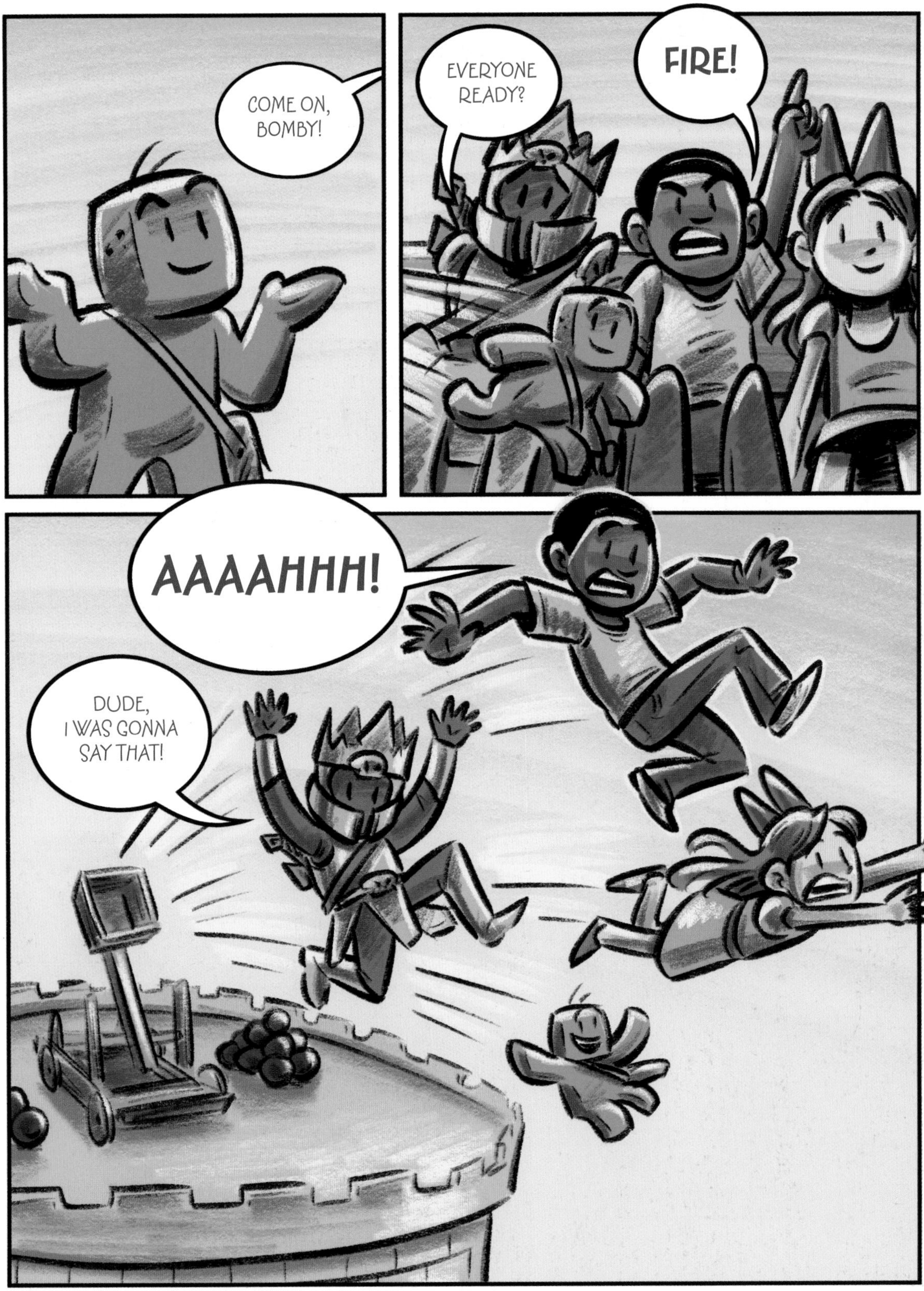
COME ON, BOMBY!
EVERYONE READY?
FIRE!
AAAAHHH!
DUDE, I WAS GONNA SAY THAT!

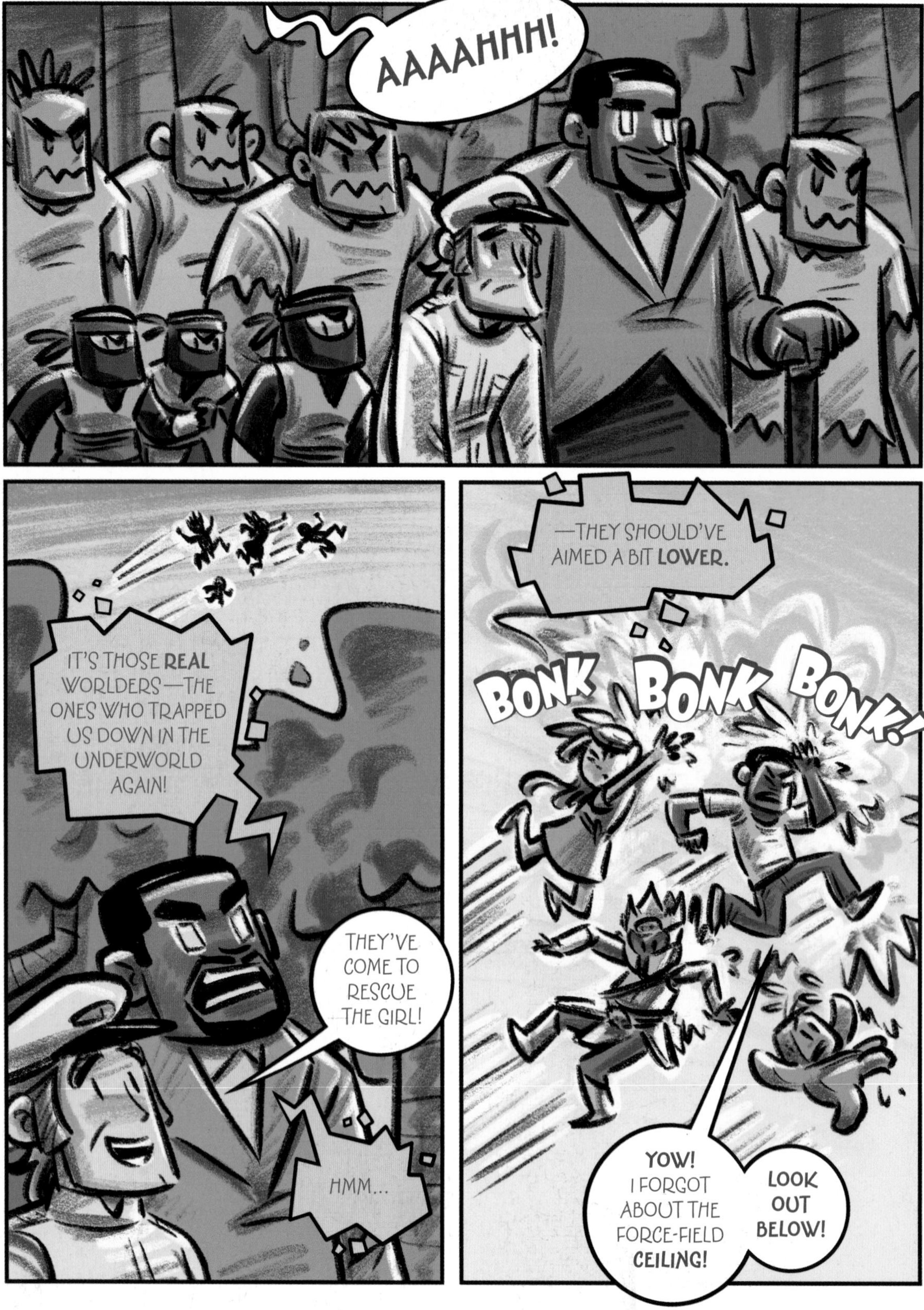
AAAAHHH!
IT'S THOSE **REAL** WORLDERS—THE ONES WHO TRAPPED US DOWN IN THE UNDERWORLD AGAIN!
THEY'VE COME TO RESCUE THE GIRL!
HMM...
—THEY SHOULD'VE AIMED A BIT **LOWER.**
BONK BONK BONK!
YOW! I FORGOT ABOUT THE FORCE-FIELD **CEILING!**
LOOK OUT BELOW!

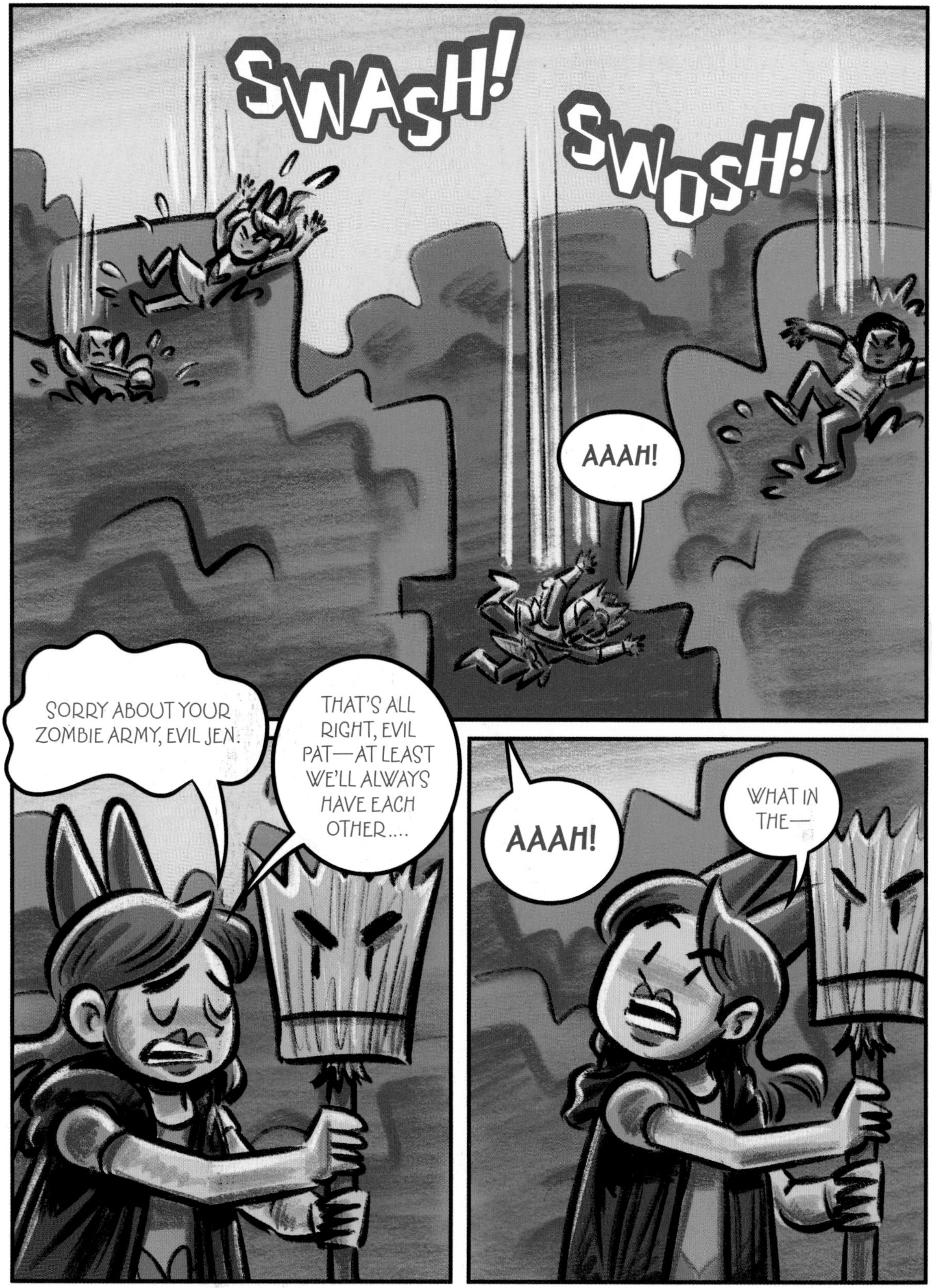
SWASH!
SWOSH!
AAAH!
SORRY ABOUT YOUR ZOMBIE ARMY, EVIL JEN.
THAT'S ALL RIGHT, EVIL PAT—AT LEAST WE'LL ALWAYS HAVE EACH OTHER....
AAAH!
WHAT IN THE—

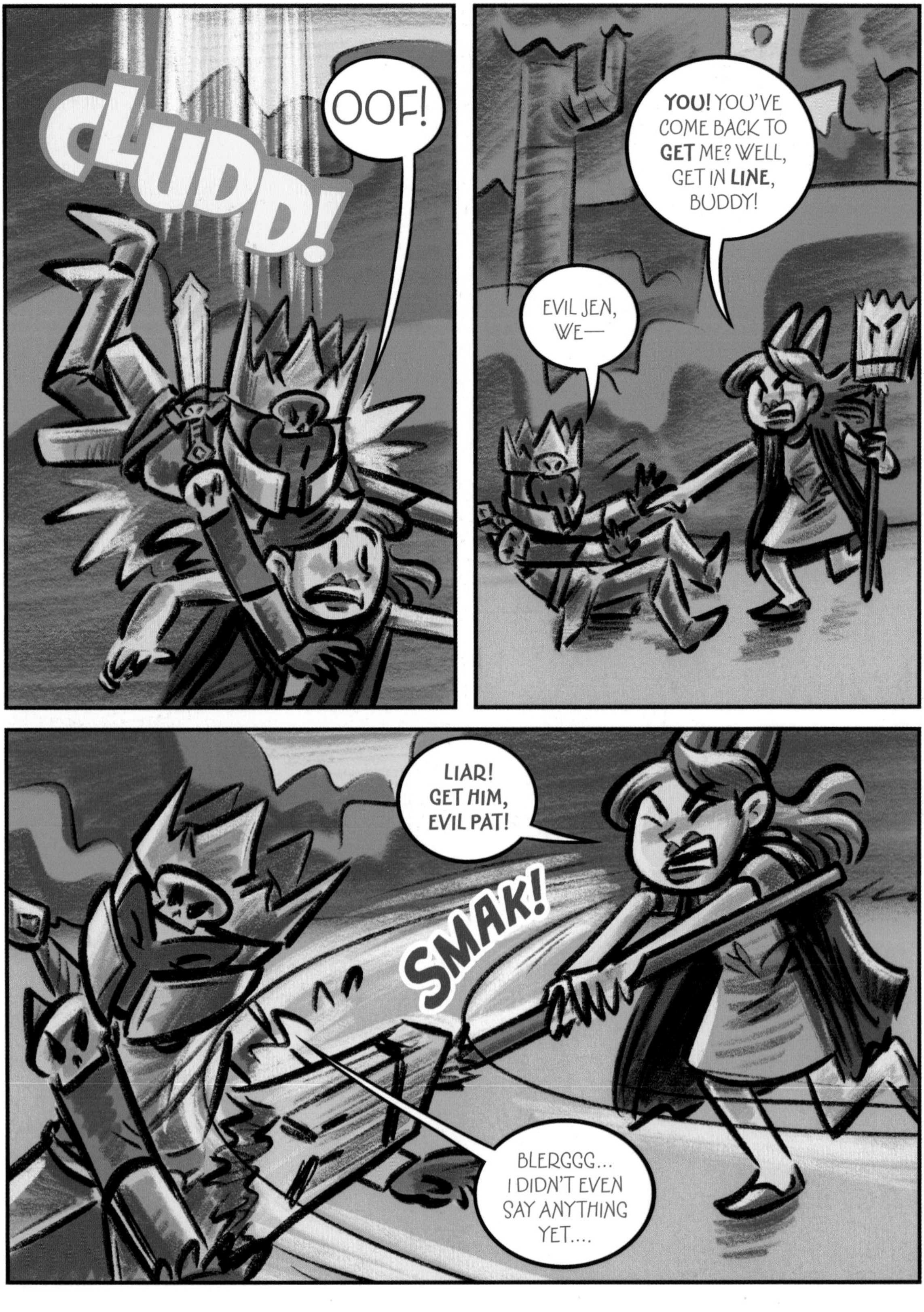
CLUDD!
OOF!
YOU! YOU'VE COME BACK TO GET ME? WELL, GET IN LINE, BUDDY!
EVIL JEN, WE—
LIAR! GET HIM, EVIL PAT!
SMAK!
BLERGGG... I DIDN'T EVEN SAY ANYTHING YET....

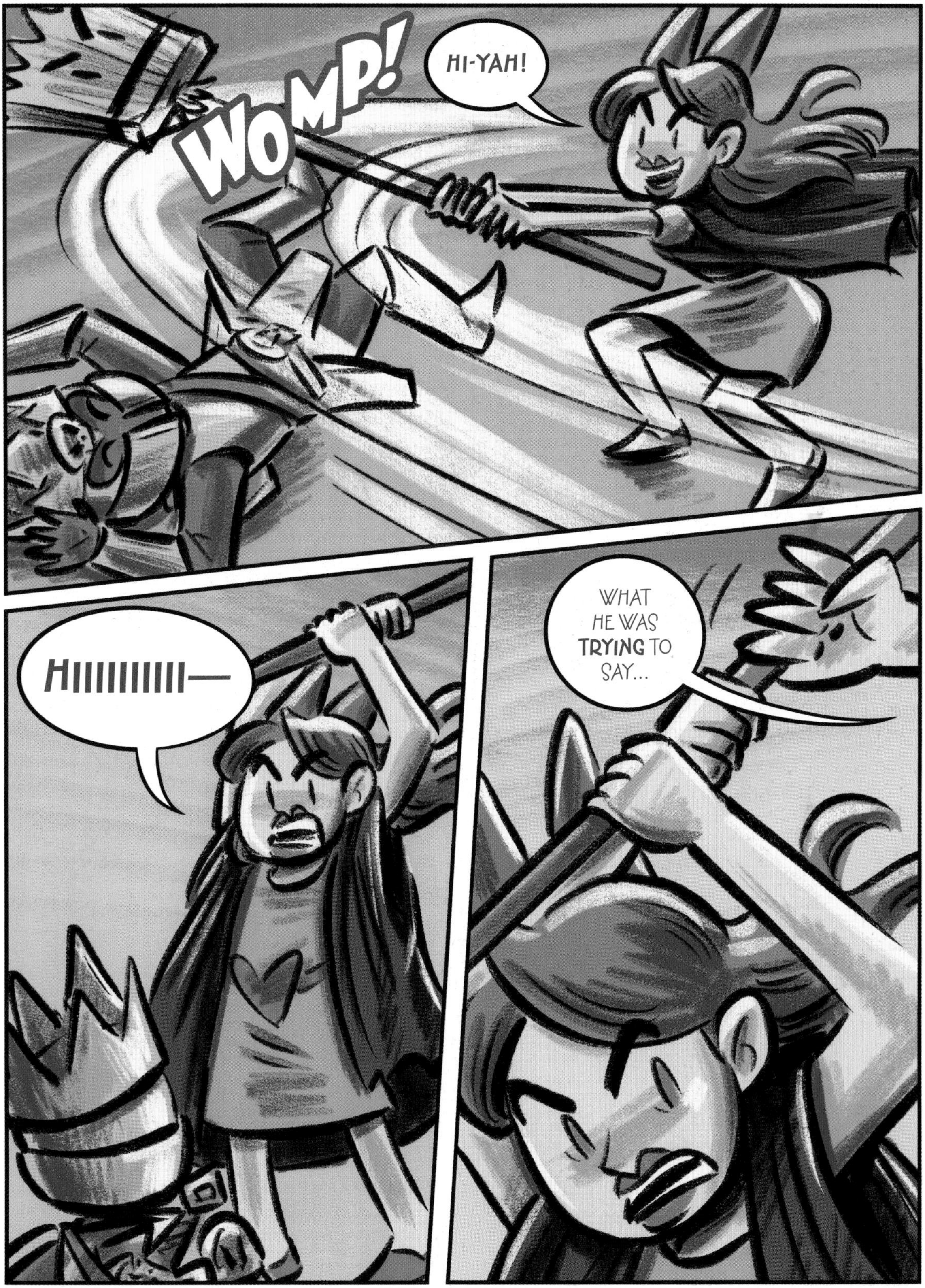
WOMP!
HI-YAH!
HIIIIIIIIII—
WHAT HE WAS TRYING TO SAY...

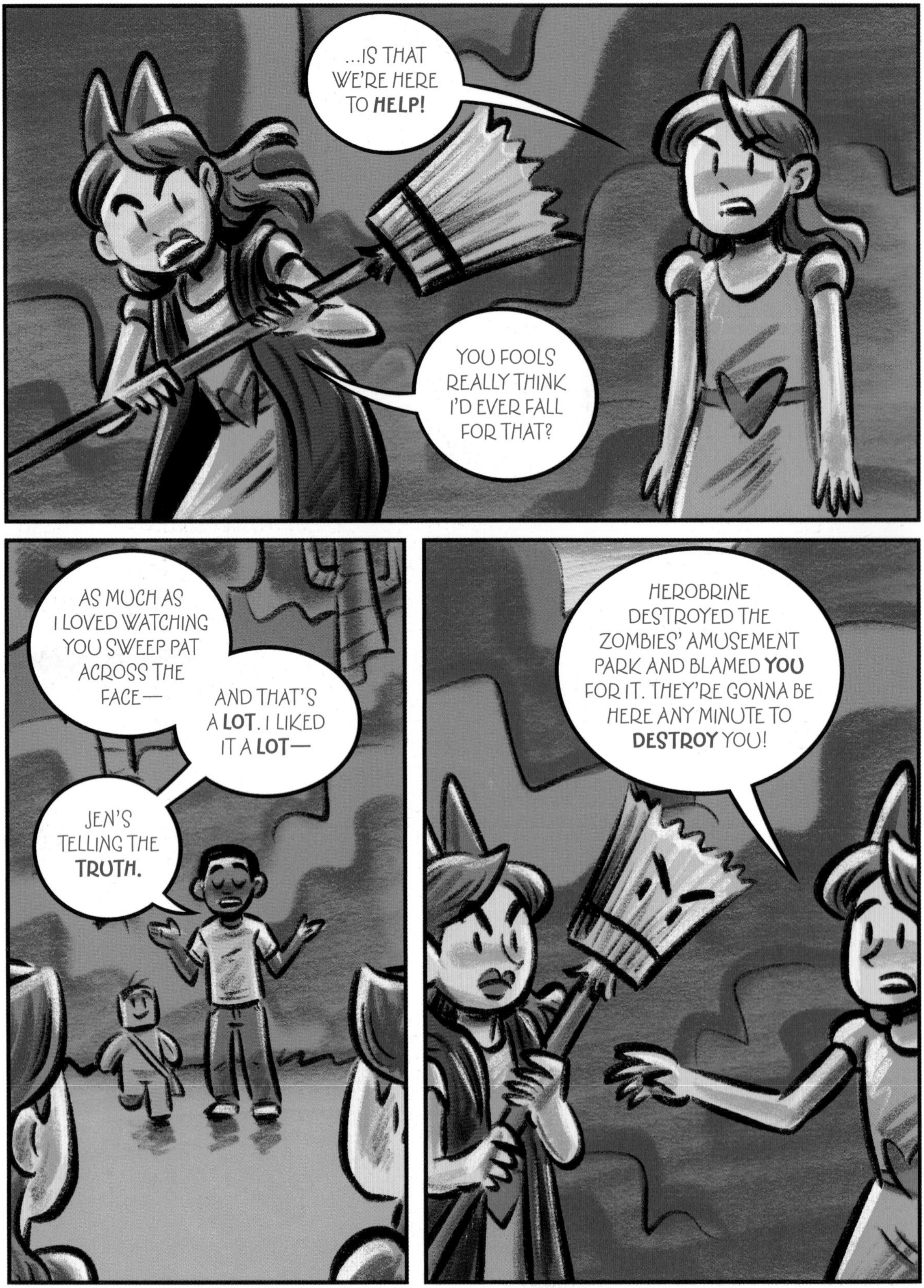
...IS THAT WE'RE HERE TO HELP!
YOU FOOLS REALLY THINK I'D EVER FALL FOR THAT?
AS MUCH AS I LOVED WATCHING YOU SWEEP PAT ACROSS THE FACE—
AND THAT'S A LOT. I LIKED IT A LOT—
JEN'S TELLING THE TRUTH.
HEROBRINE DESTROYED THE ZOMBIES' AMUSEMENT PARK AND BLAMED YOU FOR IT. THEY'RE GONNA BE HERE ANY MINUTE TO DESTROY YOU!

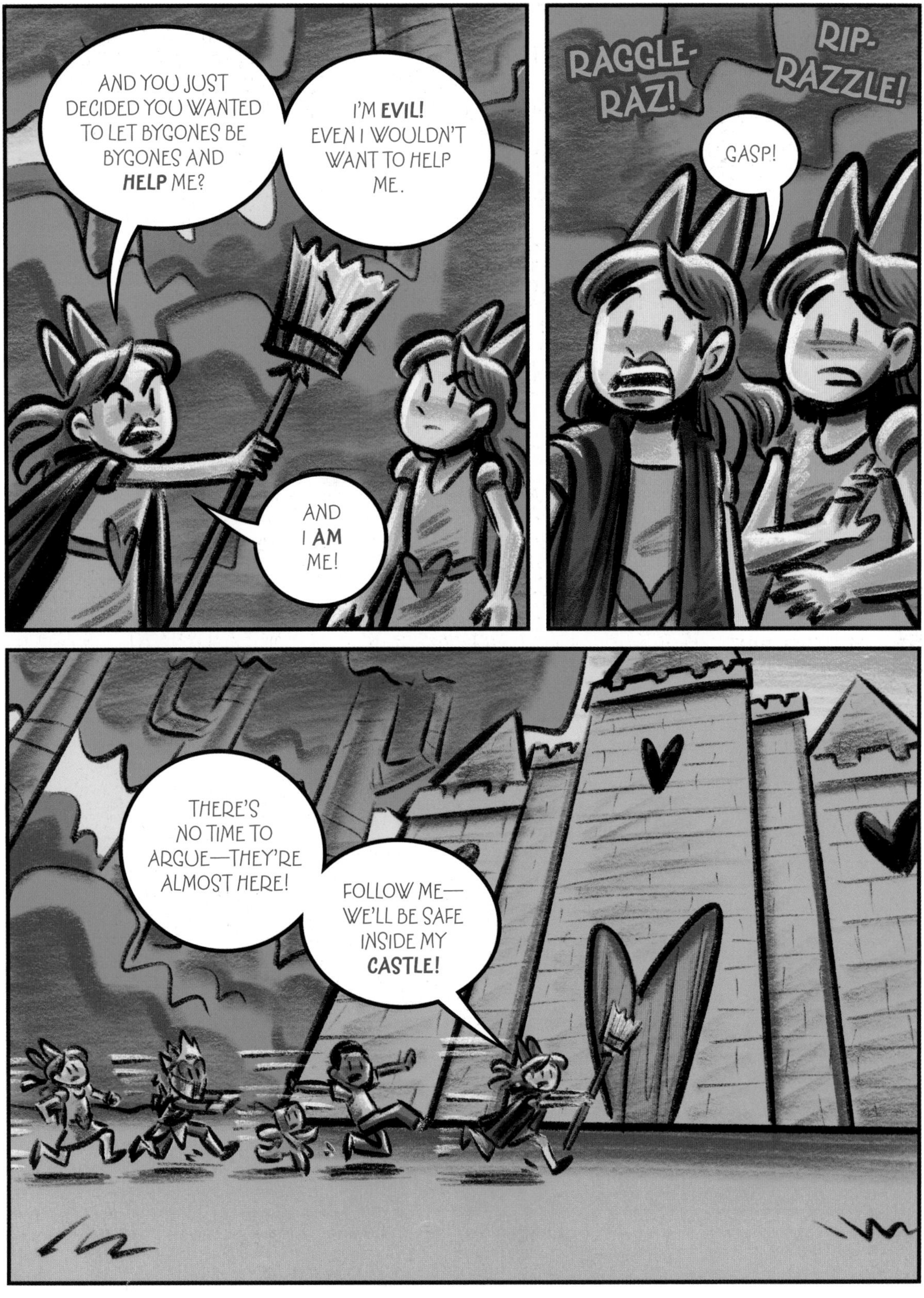
AND YOU JUST DECIDED YOU WANTED TO LET BYGONES BE BYGONES AND **HELP** ME?
I'M **EVIL!** EVEN I WOULDN'T WANT TO HELP ME.
AND I **AM** ME!
RAGGLE-RAZ!
RIP-RAZZLE!
GASP!
THERE'S NO TIME TO ARGUE—THEY'RE ALMOST HERE!
FOLLOW ME—WE'LL BE SAFE INSIDE MY **CASTLE!**

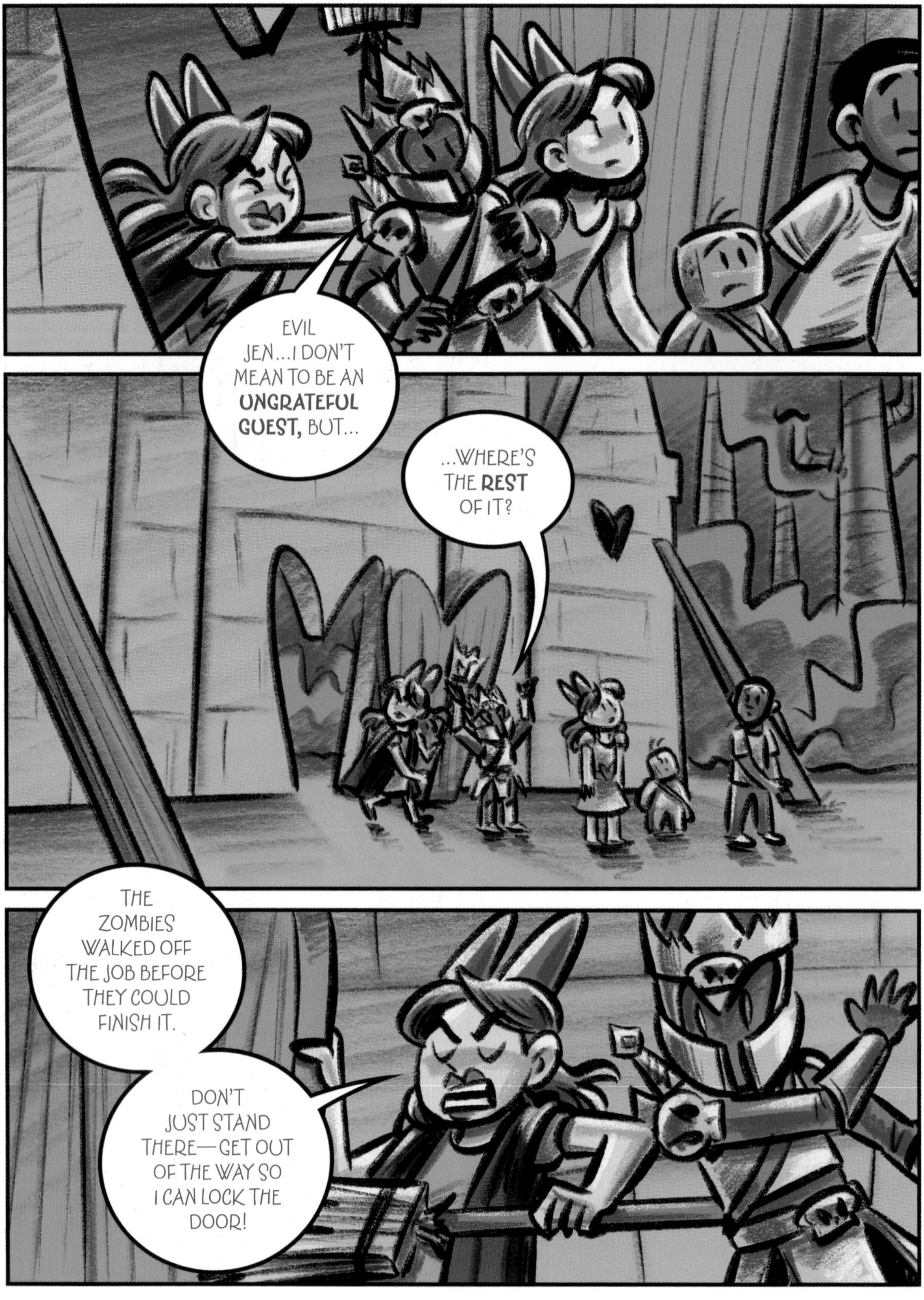
EVIL JEN...I DON'T MEAN TO BE AN **UNGRATEFUL GUEST,** BUT...
...WHERE'S THE **REST** OF IT?
THE ZOMBIES WALKED OFF THE JOB BEFORE THEY COULD FINISH IT.
DON'T JUST STAND THERE—GET OUT OF THE WAY SO I CAN LOCK THE DOOR!

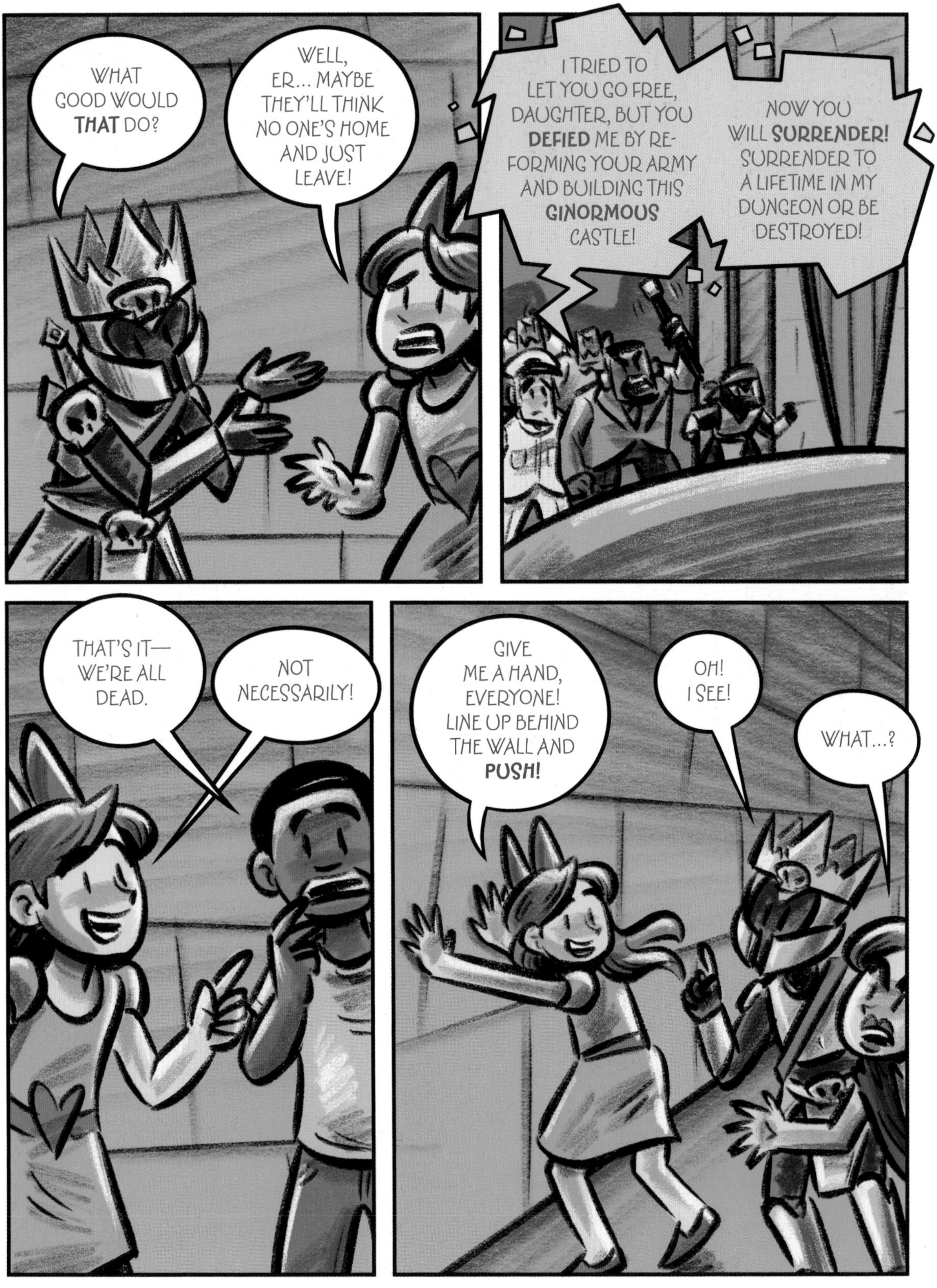
WHAT GOOD WOULD **THAT** DO?
WELL, ER... MAYBE THEY'LL THINK NO ONE'S HOME AND JUST LEAVE!
I TRIED TO LET YOU GO FREE, DAUGHTER, BUT YOU **DEFIED** ME BY RE-FORMING YOUR ARMY AND BUILDING THIS **GINORMOUS** CASTLE!
NOW YOU WILL **SURRENDER!** SURRENDER TO A LIFETIME IN MY DUNGEON OR BE DESTROYED!
THAT'S IT— WE'RE ALL DEAD.
NOT NECESSARILY!
GIVE ME A HAND, EVERYONE! LINE UP BEHIND THE WALL AND **PUSH!**
OH! I SEE!
WHAT...?

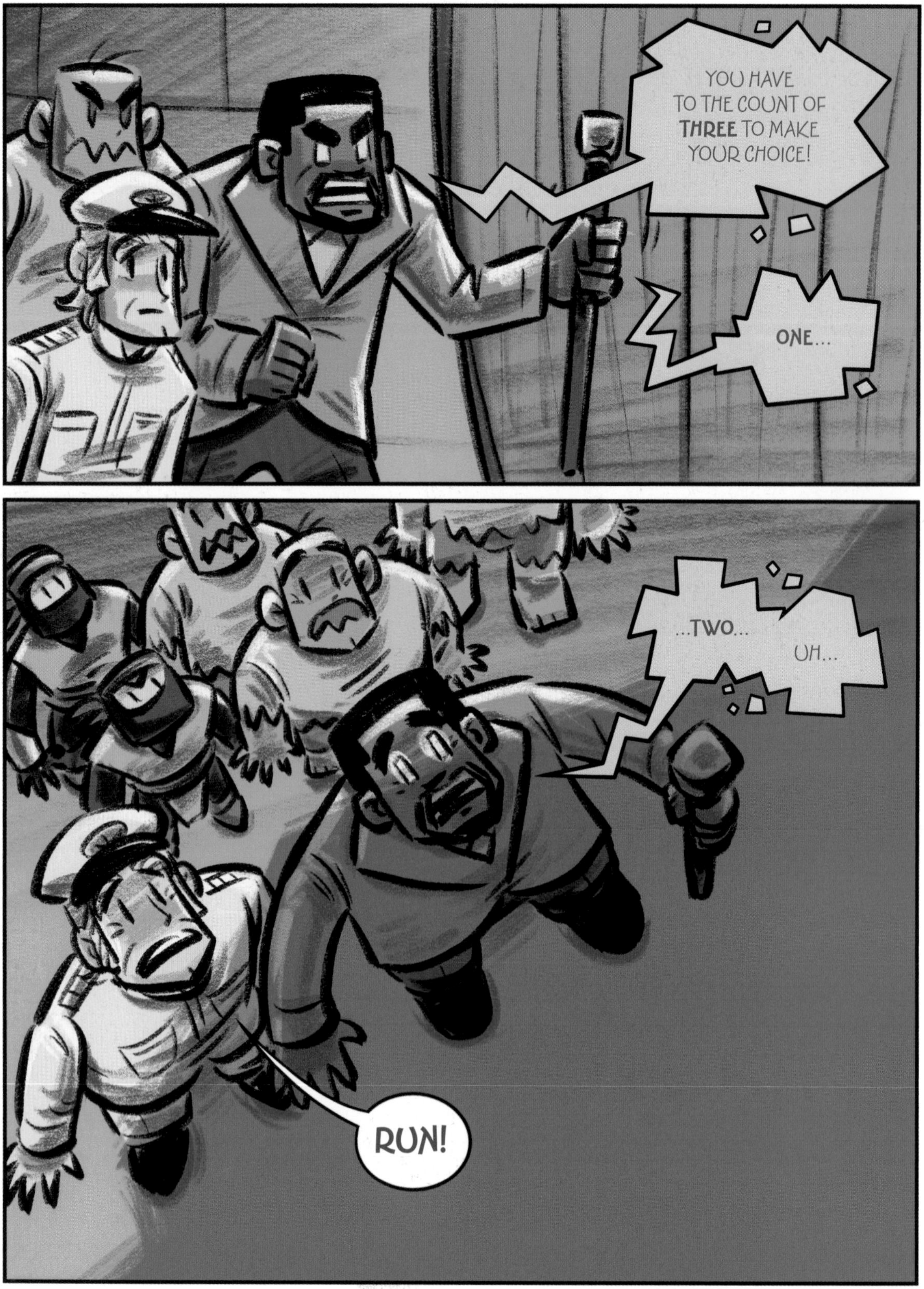
YOU HAVE TO THE COUNT OF THREE TO MAKE YOUR CHOICE!
ONE...
...TWO... UH...
RUN!

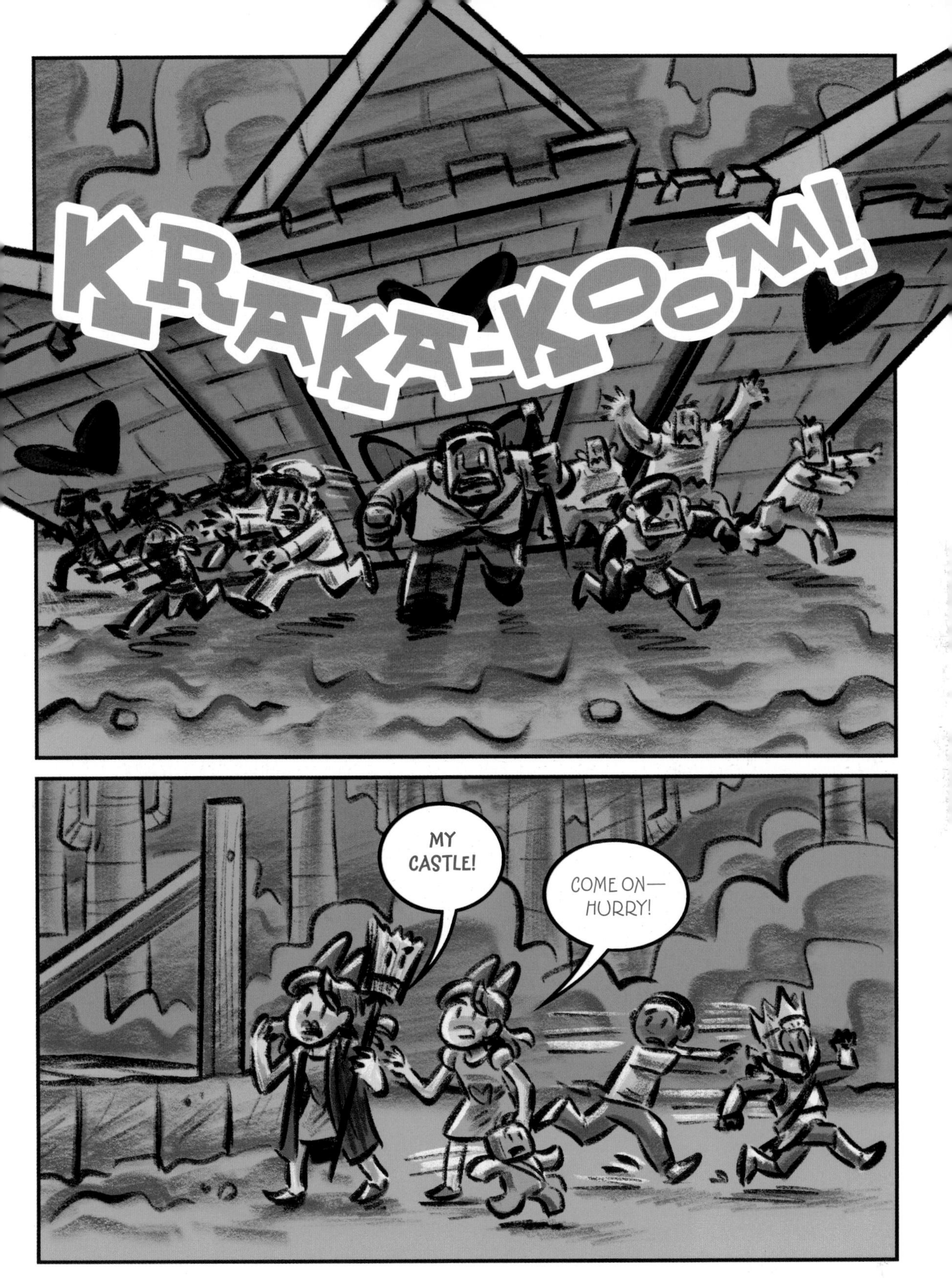
KRAKA-KOOM!
MY CASTLE!
COME ON—
HURRY!

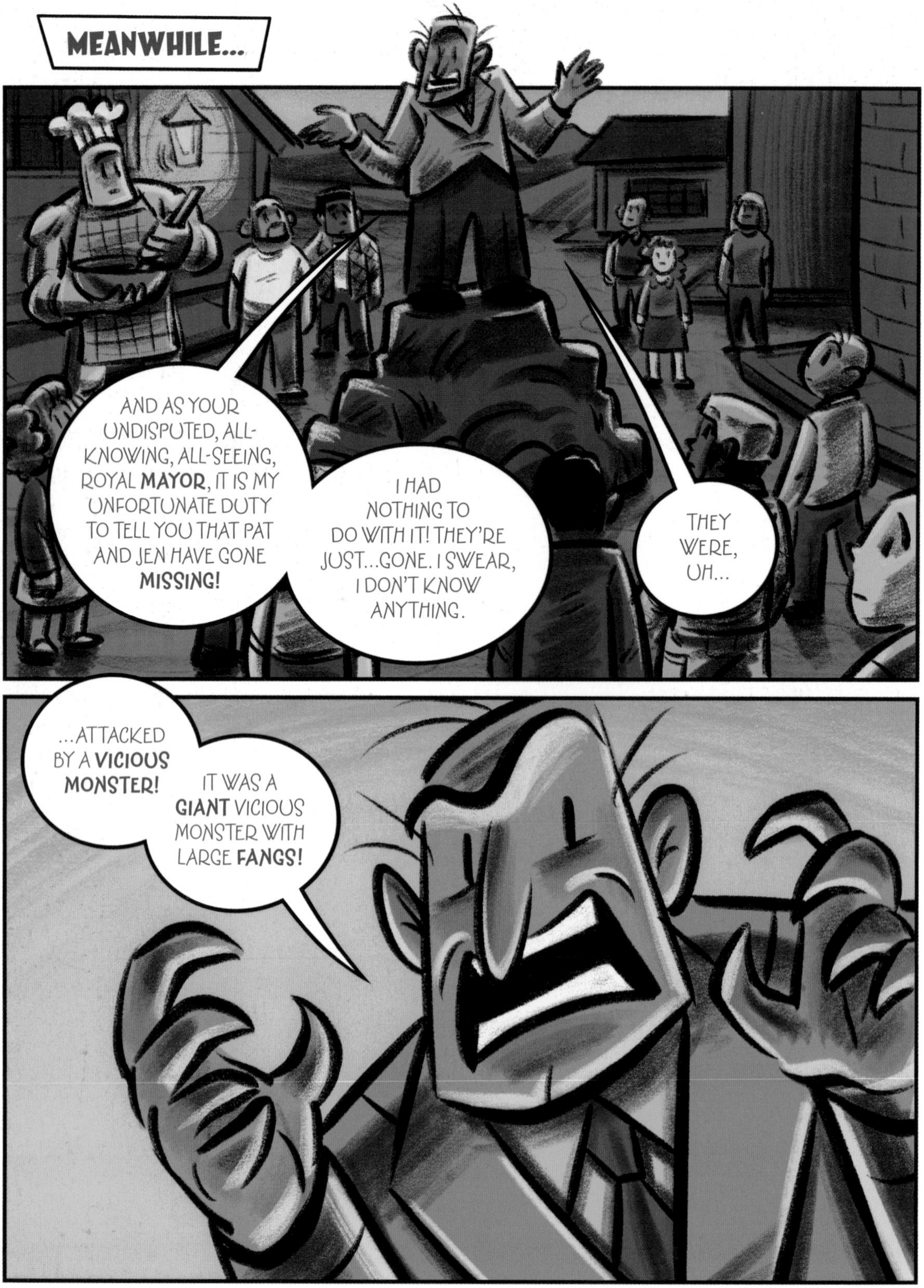
MEANWHILE...
AND AS YOUR UNDISPUTED, ALL-KNOWING, ALL-SEEING, ROYAL MAYOR, IT IS MY UNFORTUNATE DUTY TO TELL YOU THAT PAT AND JEN HAVE GONE MISSING!
I HAD NOTHING TO DO WITH IT! THEY'RE JUST...GONE. I SWEAR, I DON'T KNOW ANYTHING.
THEY WERE, UH...
...ATTACKED BY A VICIOUS MONSTER!
IT WAS A GIANT VICIOUS MONSTER WITH LARGE FANGS!

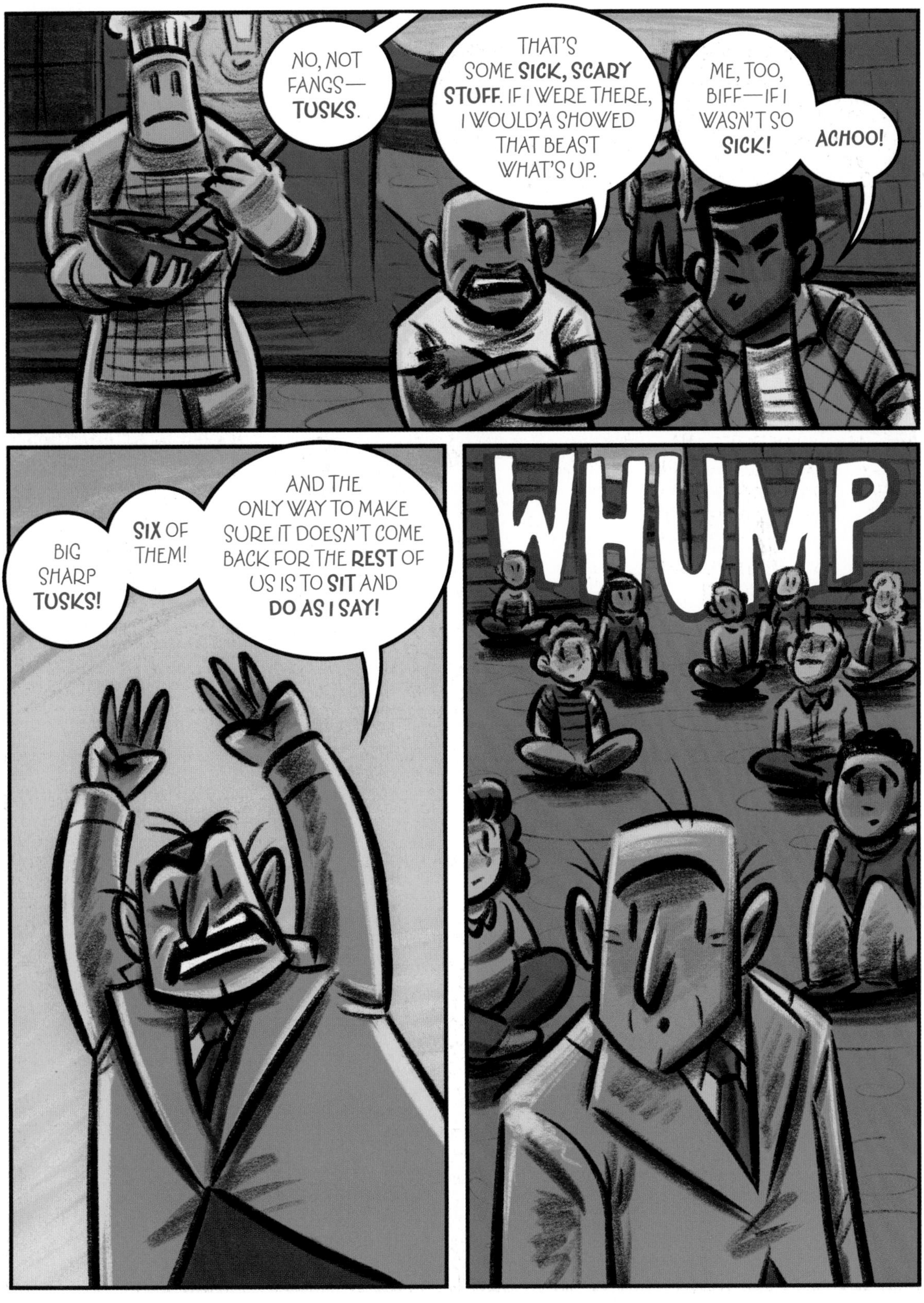
NO, NOT FANGS— TUSKS.
THAT'S SOME SICK, SCARY STUFF. IF I WERE THERE, I WOULD'A SHOWED THAT BEAST WHAT'S UP.
ME, TOO, BIFF—IF I WASN'T SO SICK!
ACHOO!
BIG SHARP TUSKS!
SIX OF THEM!
AND THE ONLY WAY TO MAKE SURE IT DOESN'T COME BACK FOR THE REST OF US IS TO SIT AND DO AS I SAY!
WHUMP

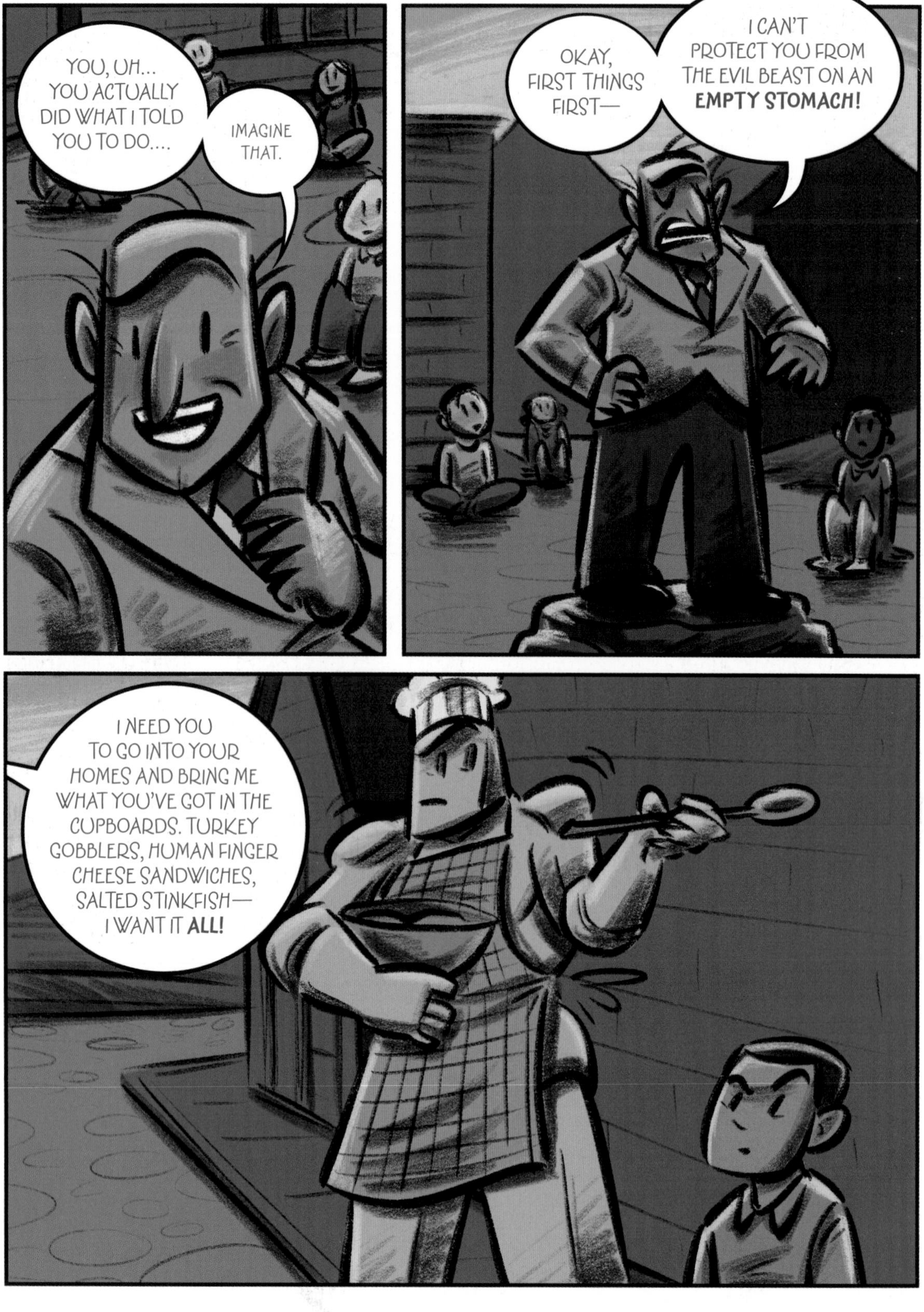
YOU, UH...
YOU ACTUALLY DID WHAT I TOLD YOU TO DO....
IMAGINE THAT.
OKAY, FIRST THINGS FIRST—
I CAN'T PROTECT YOU FROM THE EVIL BEAST ON AN **EMPTY STOMACH!**
I NEED YOU TO GO INTO YOUR HOMES AND BRING ME WHAT YOU'VE GOT IN THE CUPBOARDS. TURKEY GOBBLERS, HUMAN FINGER CHEESE SANDWICHES, SALTED STINKFISH— I WANT IT **ALL!**

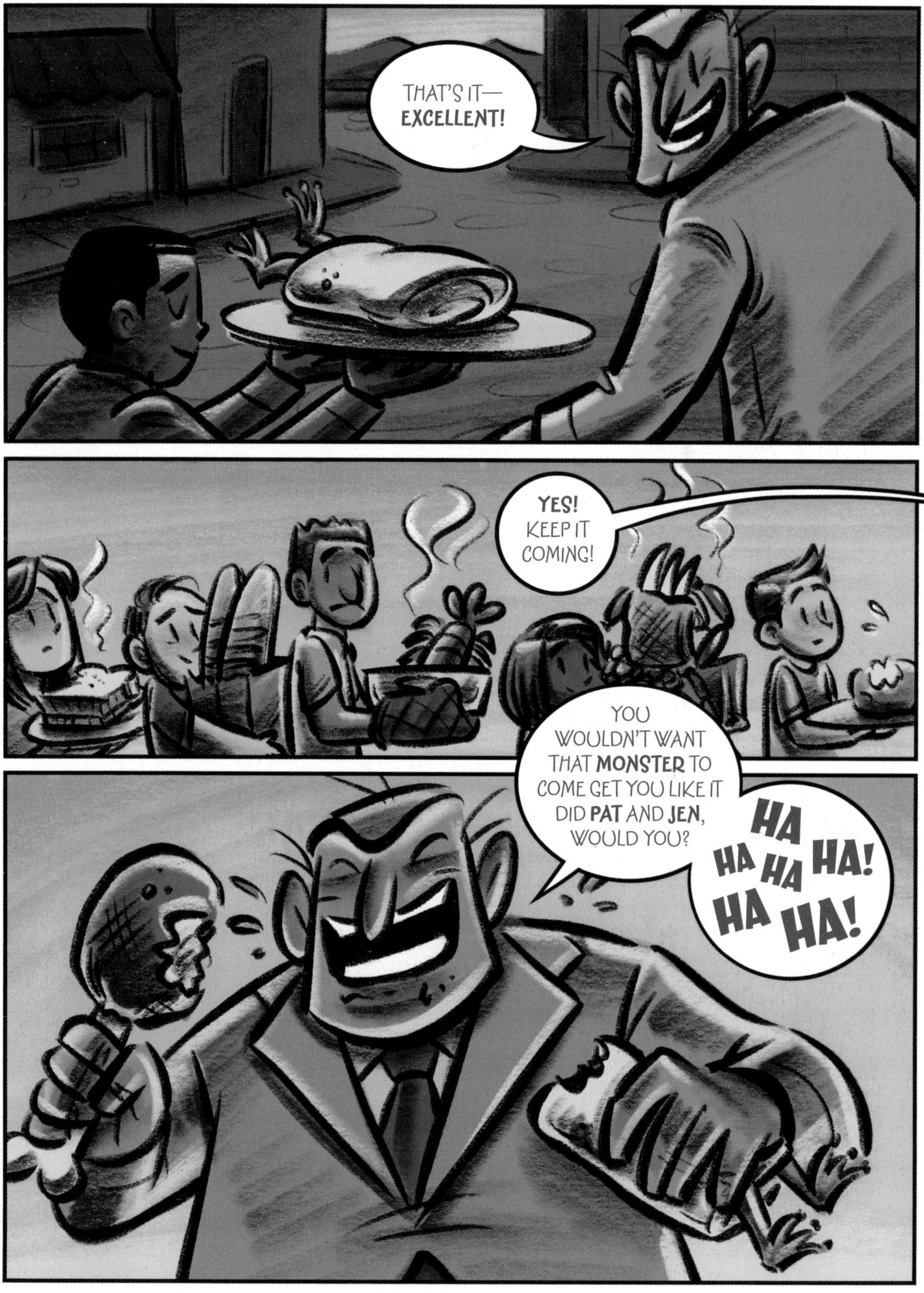
THAT'S IT—
EXCELLENT!
YES! KEEP IT COMING!
YOU WOULDN'T WANT THAT MONSTER TO COME GET YOU LIKE IT DID PAT AND JEN, WOULD YOU?
HA HA HA HA! HA HA!

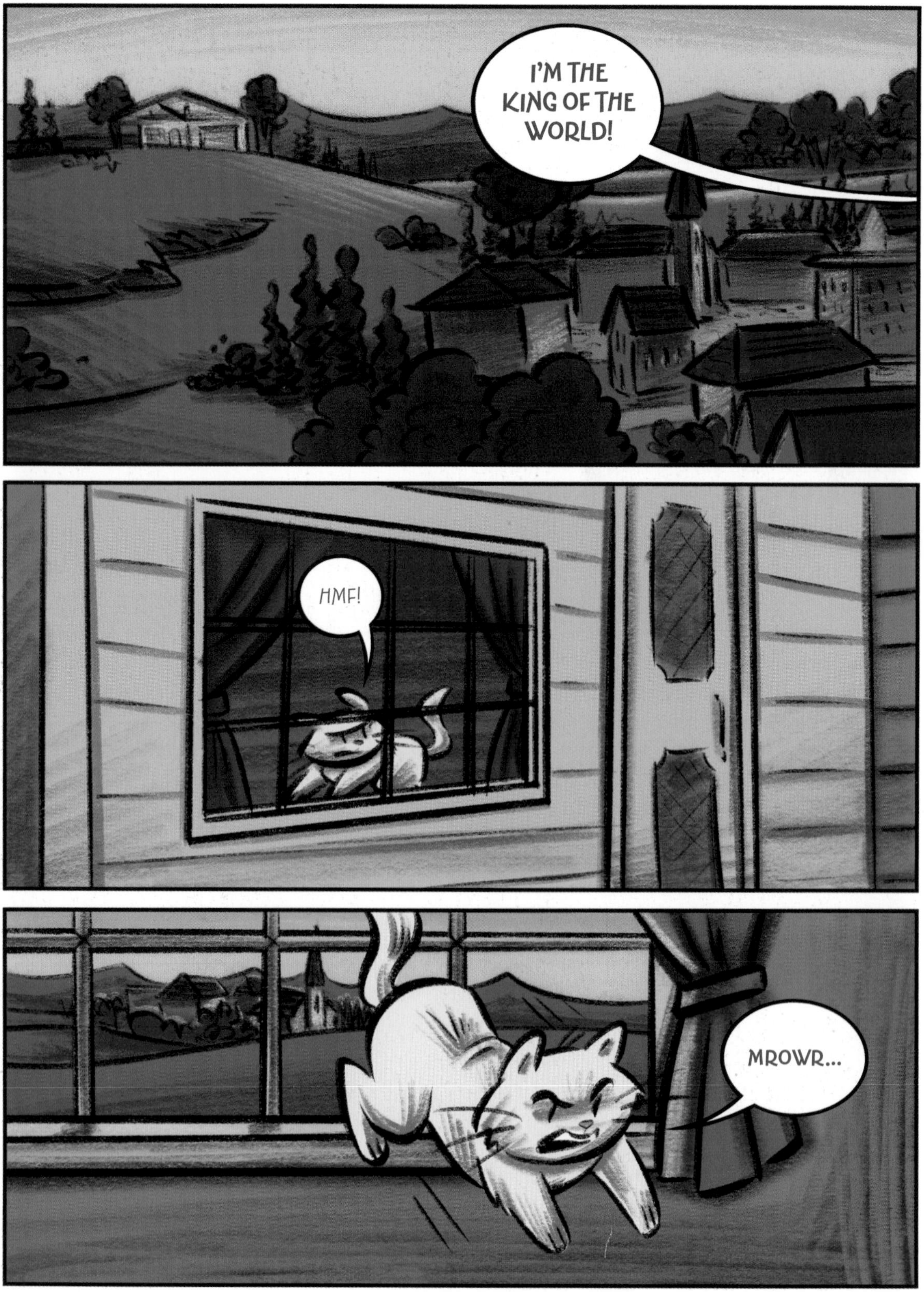
I'M THE KING OF THE WORLD!
HMF!
MROWR...

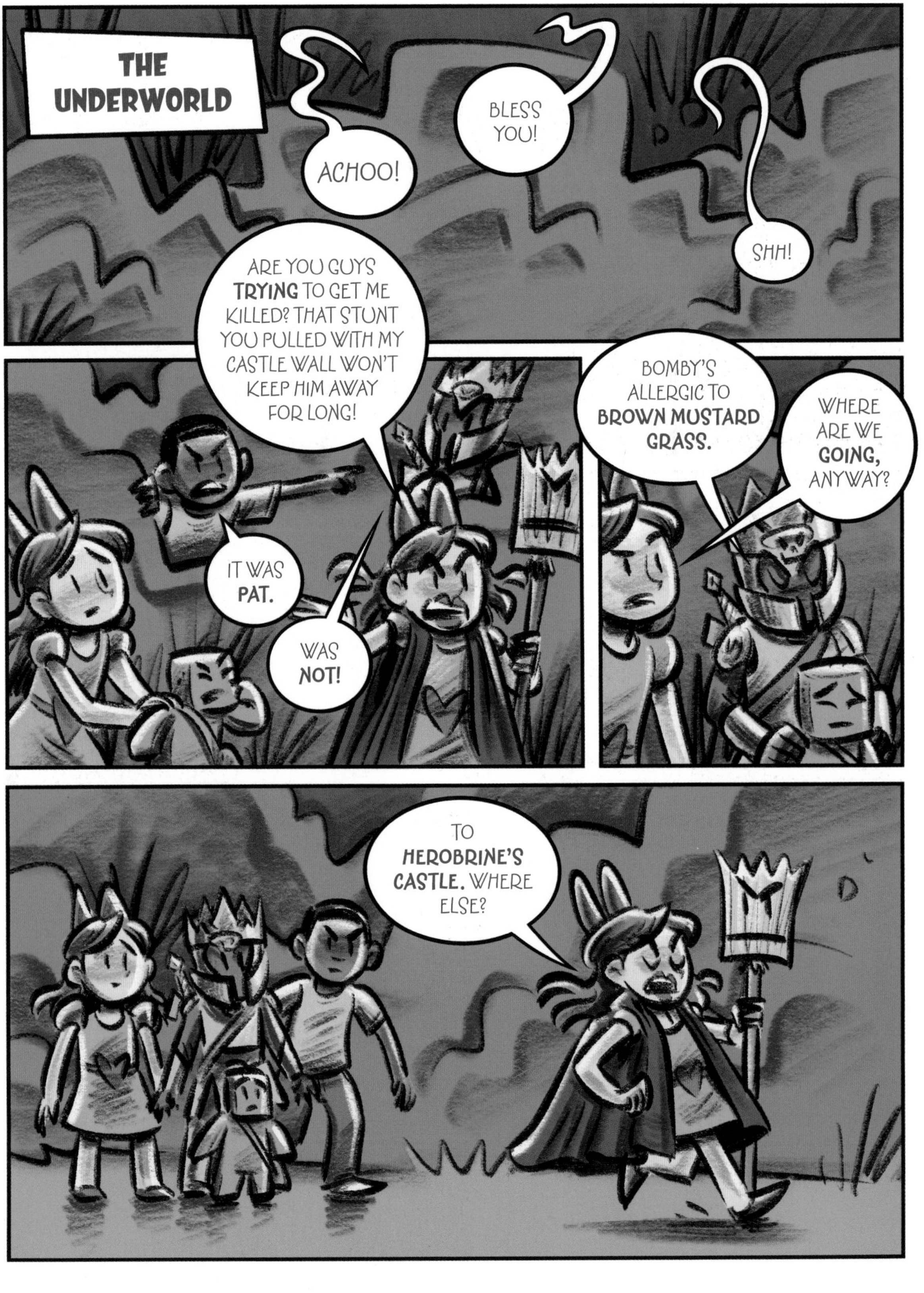
THE UNDERWORLD
ACHOO!
BLESS YOU!
SHH!
ARE YOU GUYS **TRYING** TO GET ME KILLED? THAT STUNT YOU PULLED WITH MY CASTLE WALL WON'T KEEP HIM AWAY FOR LONG!
IT WAS **PAT.**
WAS **NOT!**
BOMBY'S ALLERGIC TO **BROWN MUSTARD GRASS.**
WHERE ARE WE **GOING,** ANYWAY?
TO **HEROBRINE'S CASTLE.** WHERE ELSE?

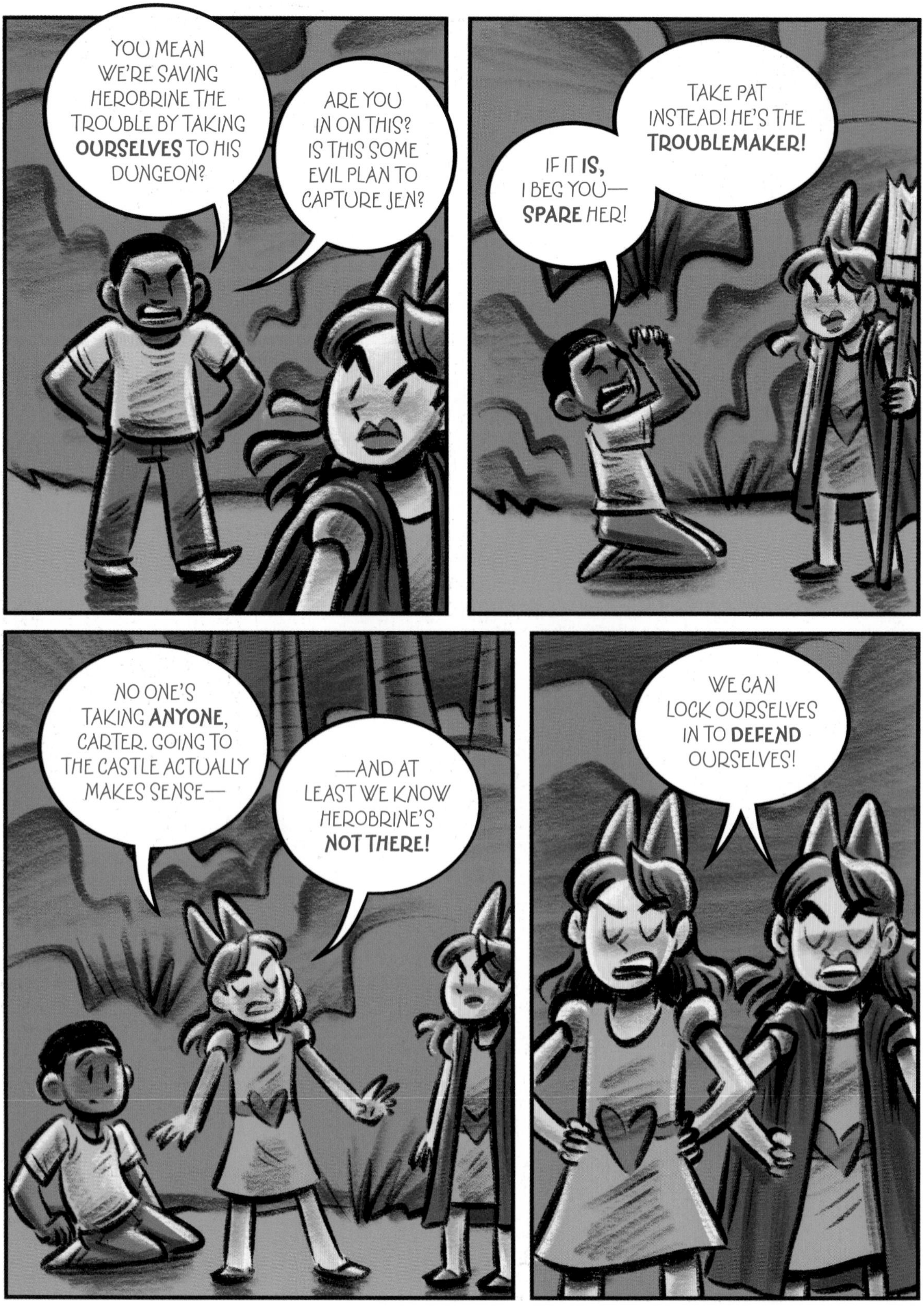
YOU MEAN WE'RE SAVING HEROBRINE THE TROUBLE BY TAKING **OURSELVES** TO HIS DUNGEON?
ARE YOU IN ON THIS? IS THIS SOME EVIL PLAN TO CAPTURE JEN?
TAKE PAT INSTEAD! HE'S THE **TROUBLEMAKER!**
IF IT **IS,** I BEG YOU— **SPARE** HER!
NO ONE'S TAKING **ANYONE,** CARTER. GOING TO THE CASTLE ACTUALLY MAKES SENSE—
—AND AT LEAST WE KNOW HEROBRINE'S **NOT THERE!**
WE CAN LOCK OURSELVES IN TO **DEFEND** OURSELVES!

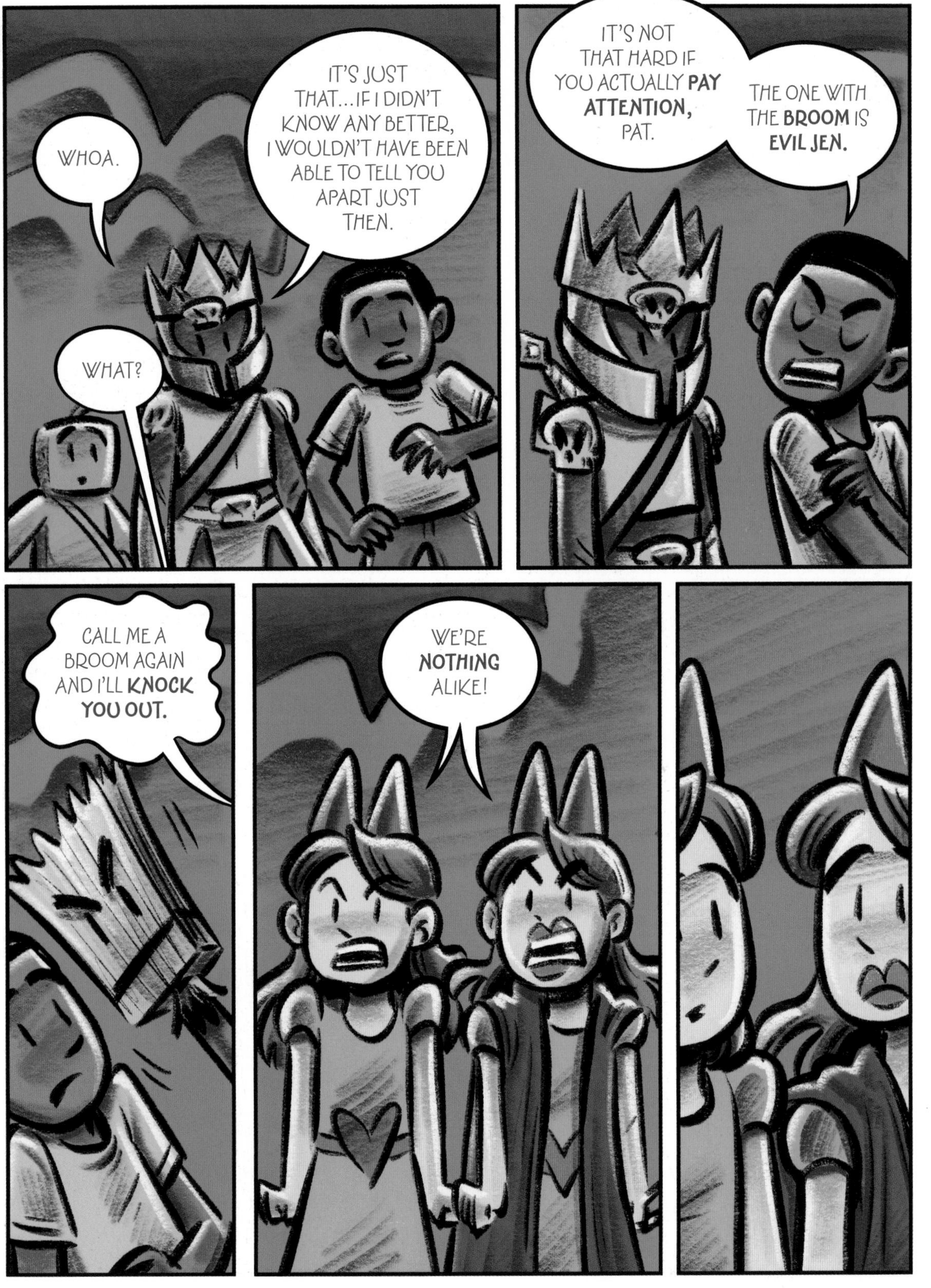
WHOA.
IT'S JUST THAT... IF I DIDN'T KNOW ANY BETTER, I WOULDN'T HAVE BEEN ABLE TO TELL YOU APART JUST THEN.
WHAT?
IT'S NOT THAT HARD IF YOU ACTUALLY PAY ATTENTION, PAT.
THE ONE WITH THE BROOM IS EVIL JEN.
CALL ME A BROOM AGAIN AND I'LL KNOCK YOU OUT.
WE'RE NOTHING ALIKE!

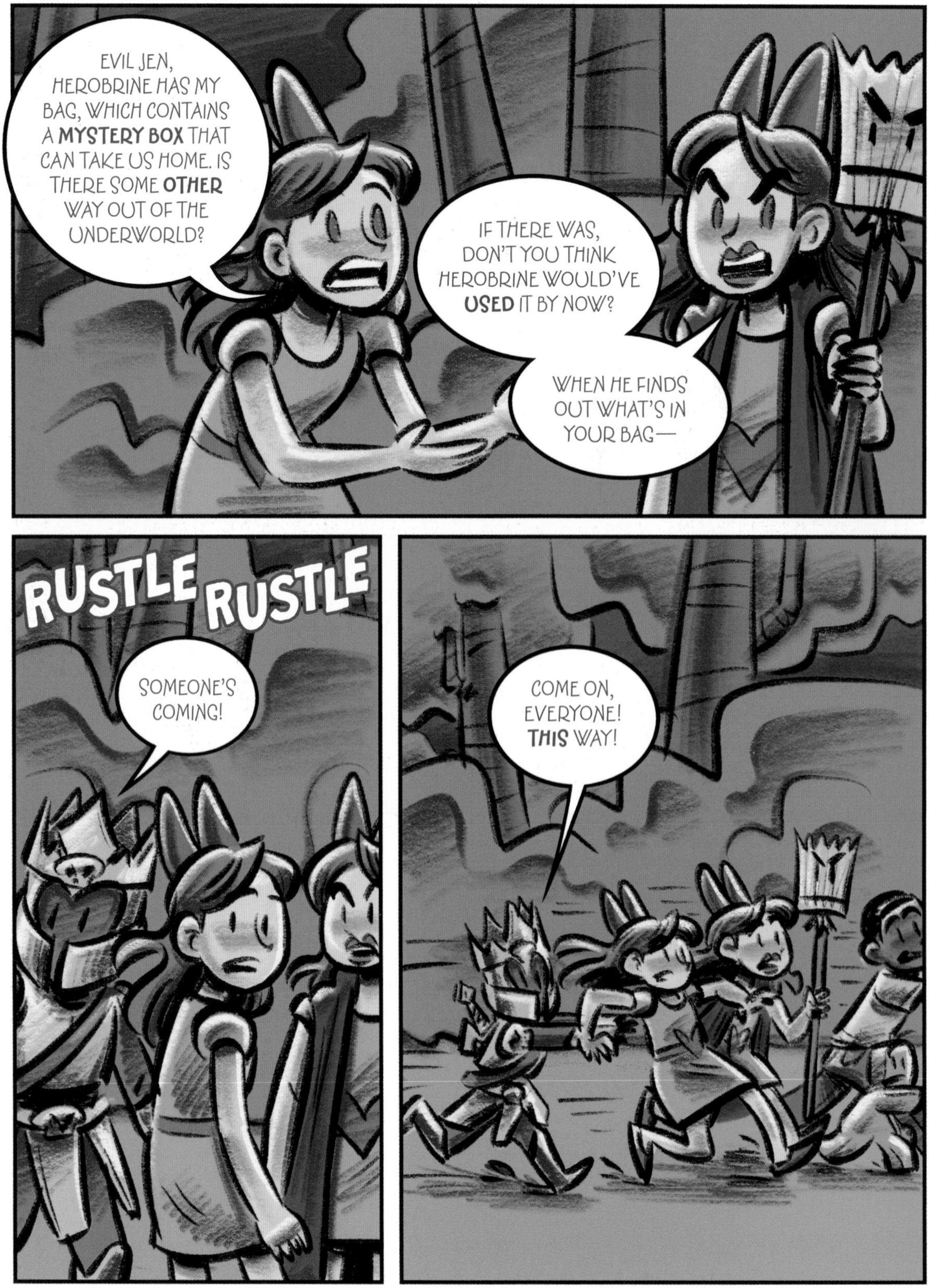
EVIL JEN, HEROBRINE HAS MY BAG, WHICH CONTAINS A **MYSTERY BOX** THAT CAN TAKE US HOME. IS THERE SOME **OTHER** WAY OUT OF THE UNDERWORLD?
IF THERE WAS, DON'T YOU THINK HEROBRINE WOULD'VE **USED** IT BY NOW?
WHEN HE FINDS OUT WHAT'S IN YOUR BAG—
RUSTLE RUSTLE
SOMEONE'S COMING!
COME ON, EVERYONE! **THIS** WAY!

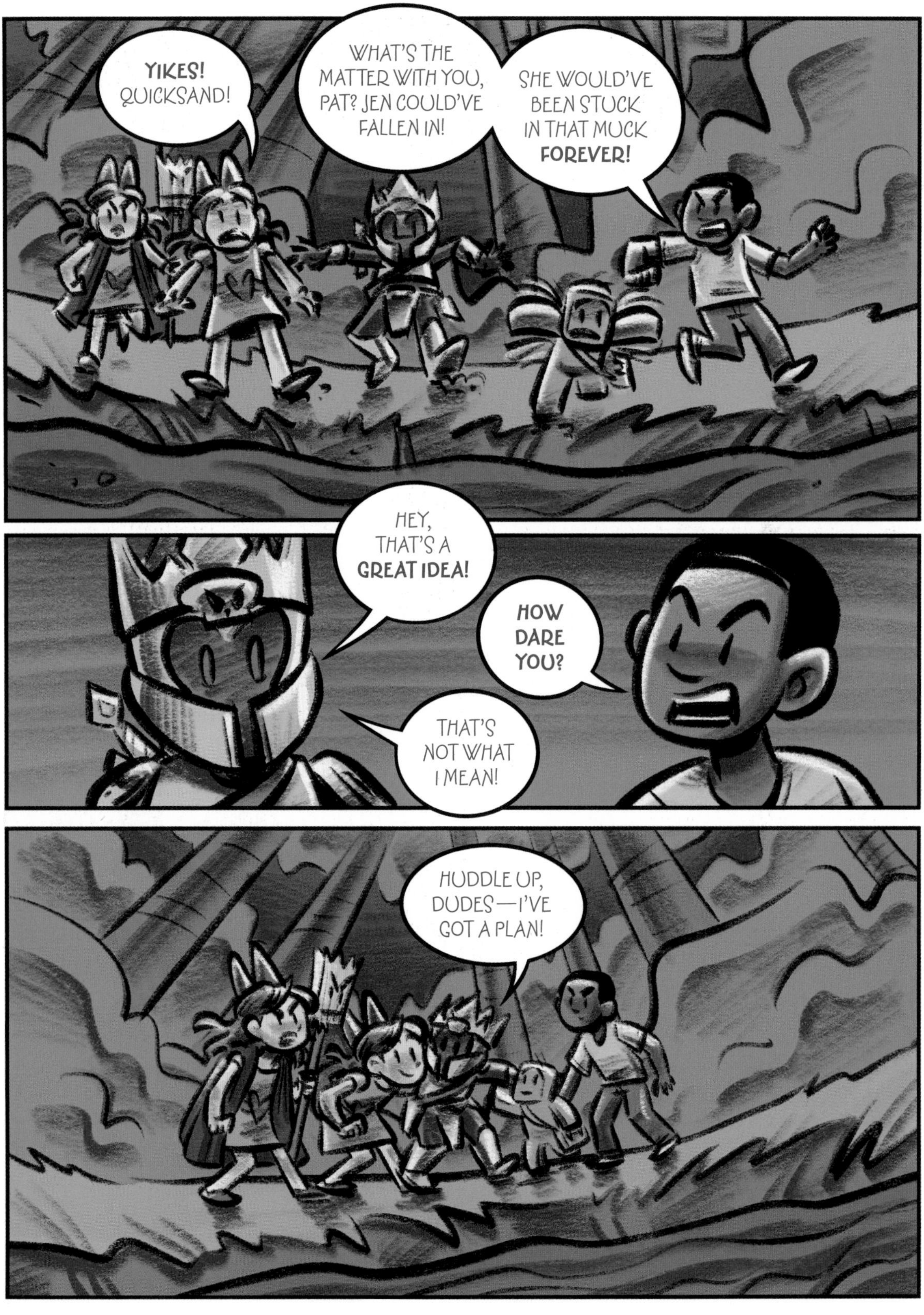
YIKES! QUICKSAND!
WHAT'S THE MATTER WITH YOU, PAT? JEN COULD'VE FALLEN IN!
SHE WOULD'VE BEEN STUCK IN THAT MUCK **FOREVER!**
HEY, THAT'S A **GREAT IDEA!**
HOW DARE YOU?
THAT'S NOT WHAT I MEAN!
HUDDLE UP, DUDES—I'VE GOT A PLAN!

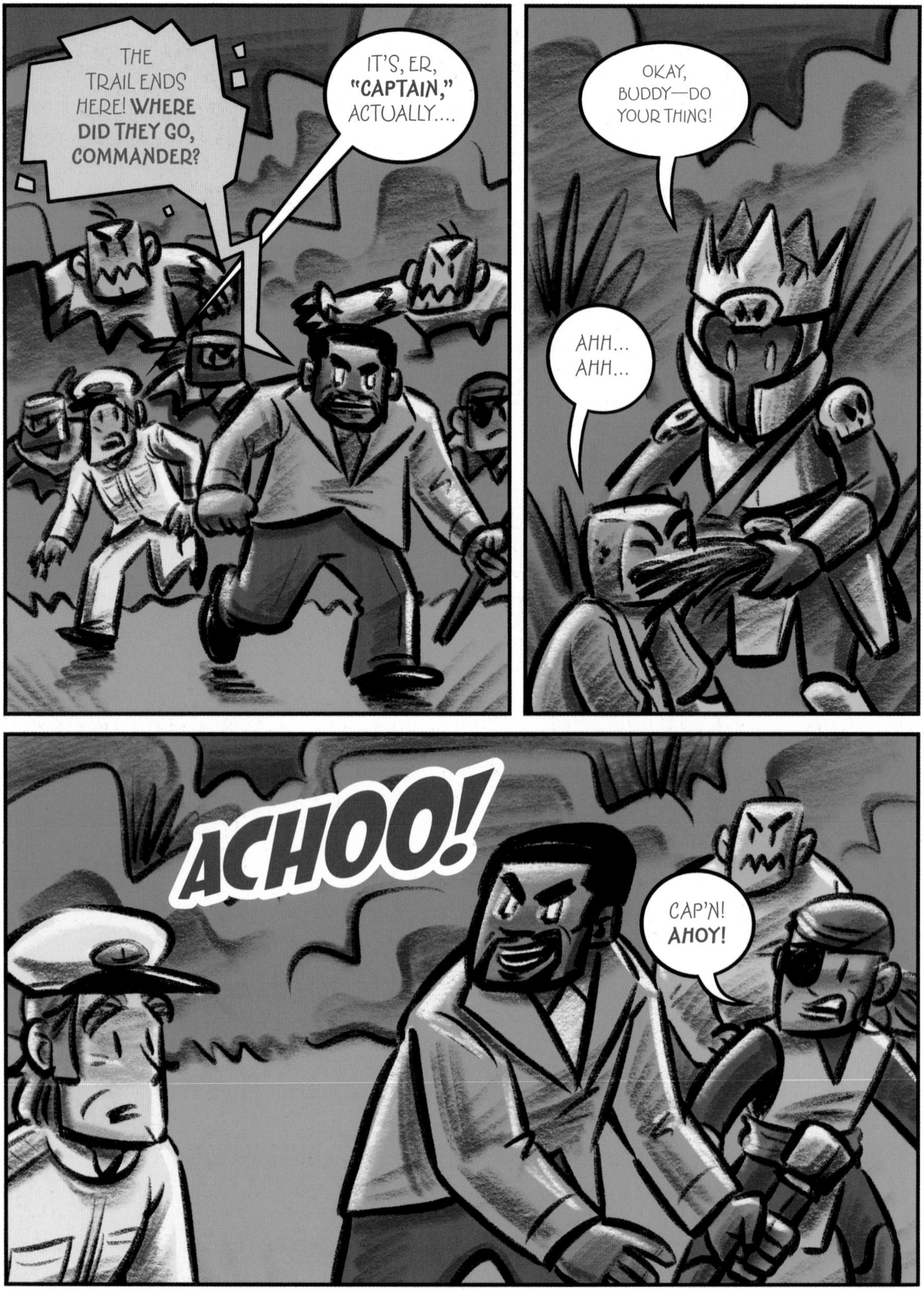
THE TRAIL ENDS HERE! WHERE DID THEY GO, COMMANDER?
IT'S, ER, "CAPTAIN," ACTUALLY....
OKAY, BUDDY—DO YOUR THING!
AHH... AHH...
ACHOO!
CAP'N! AHOY!

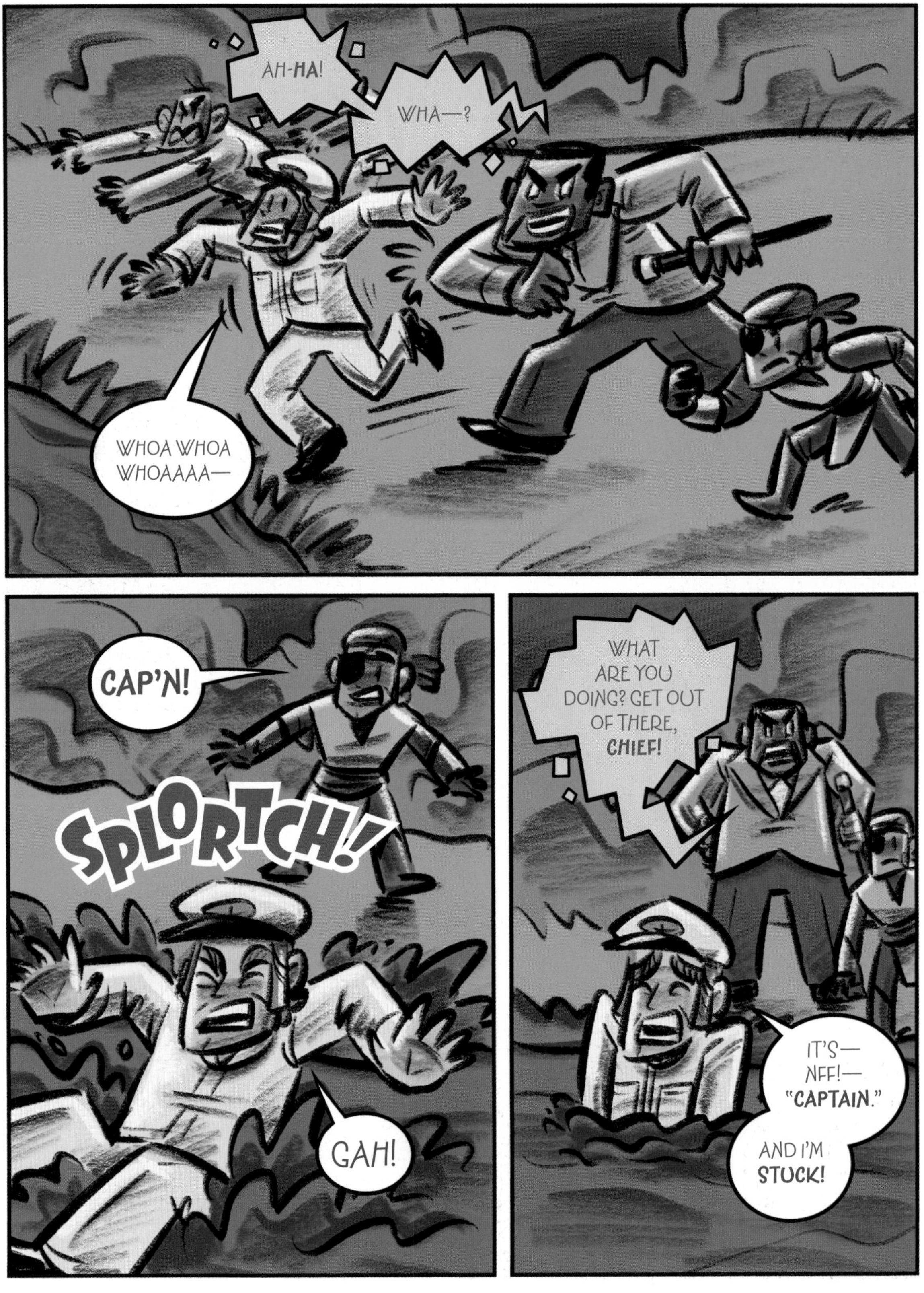
AH-HA!
WHA—?
WHOA WHOA WHOAAAA—
CAP'N!
SPLORTCH!
GAH!
WHAT ARE YOU DOING? GET OUT OF THERE, CHIEF!
IT'S—NFF!—"CAPTAIN."
AND I'M STUCK!

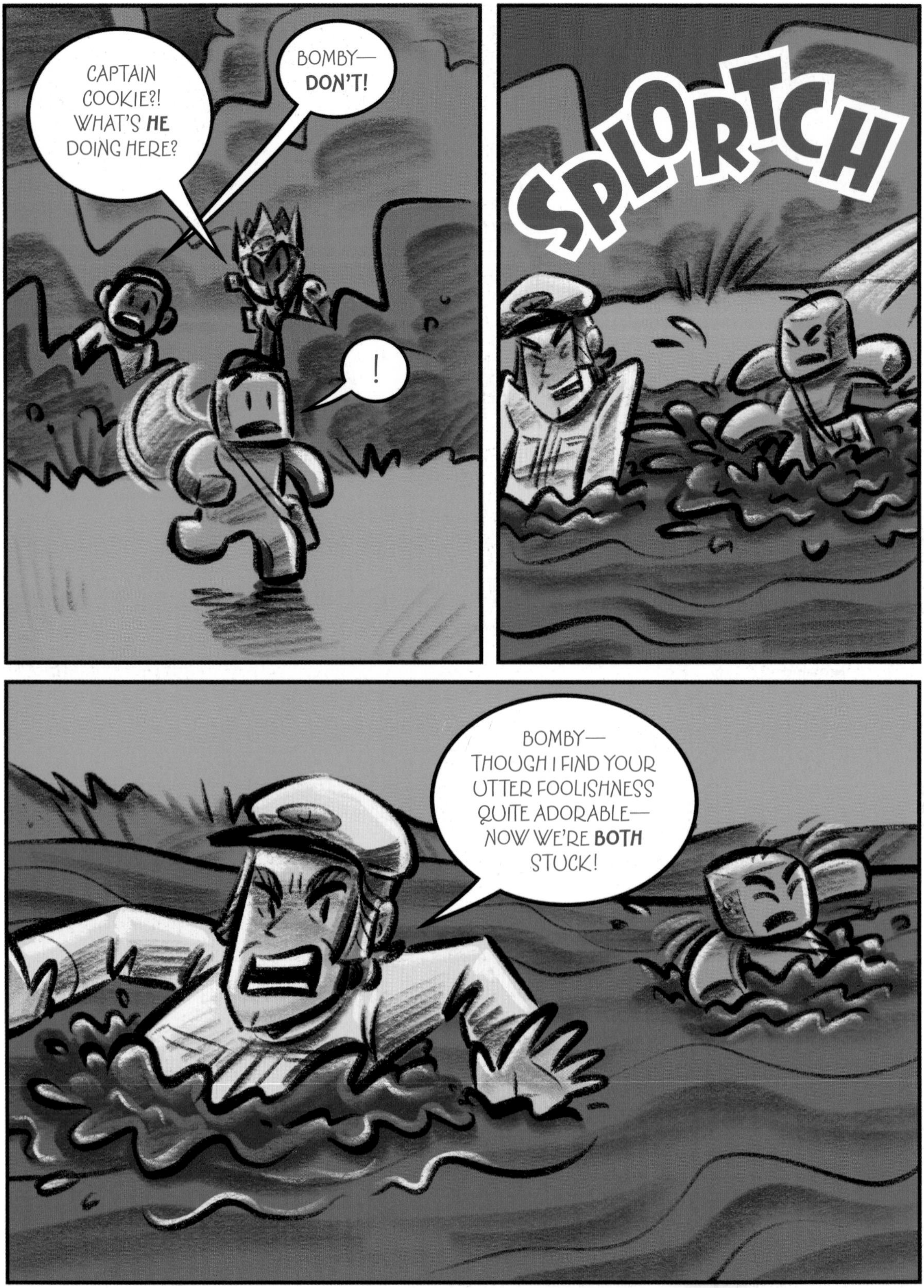
CAPTAIN COOKIE?! WHAT'S **HE** DOING HERE?
BOMBY— **DON'T!**
!
SPLORTCH
BOMBY— THOUGH I FIND YOUR UTTER FOOLISHNESS QUITE ADORABLE— NOW WE'RE **BOTH** STUCK!

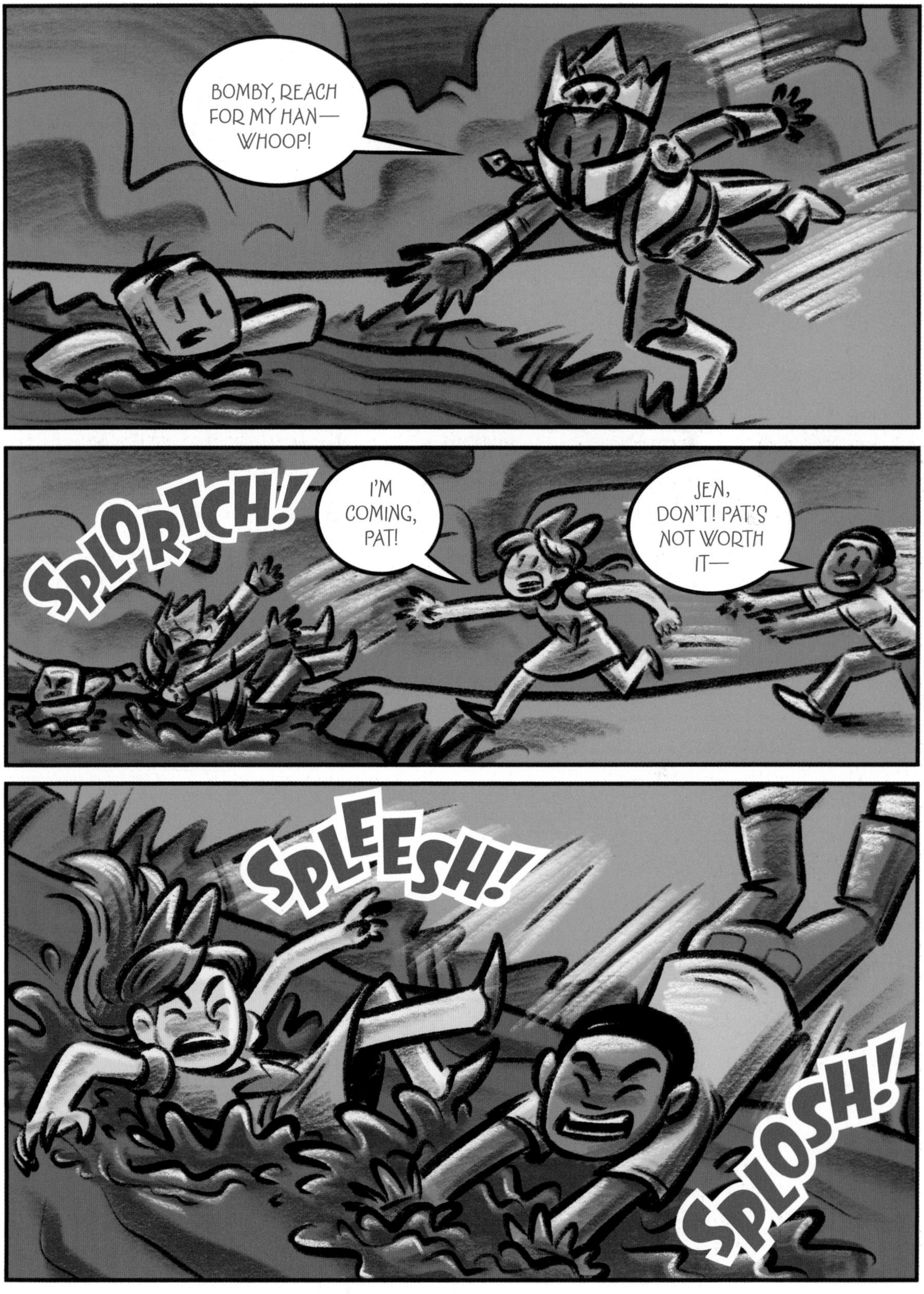
BOMBY, REACH FOR MY HAN— WHOOP!
SPLORTCH!
I'M COMING, PAT!
JEN, DON'T! PAT'S NOT WORTH IT—
SPLEESH!
SPLOSH!

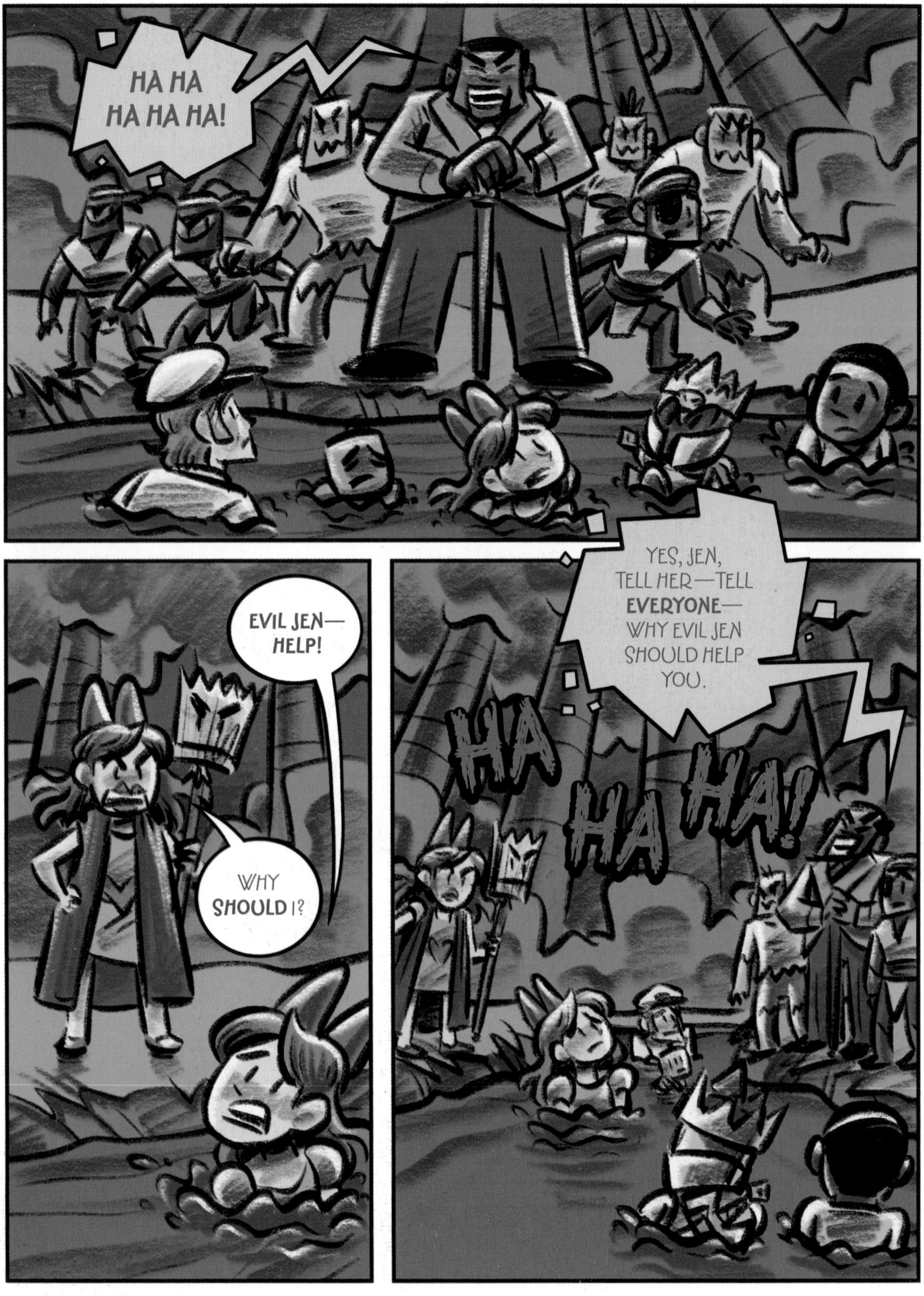
HA HA
HA HA HA!
EVIL JEN—
HELP!
WHY
SHOULD I?
YES, JEN,
TELL HER—TELL
EVERYONE—
WHY EVIL JEN
SHOULD HELP
YOU.
HA
HA HA HA!

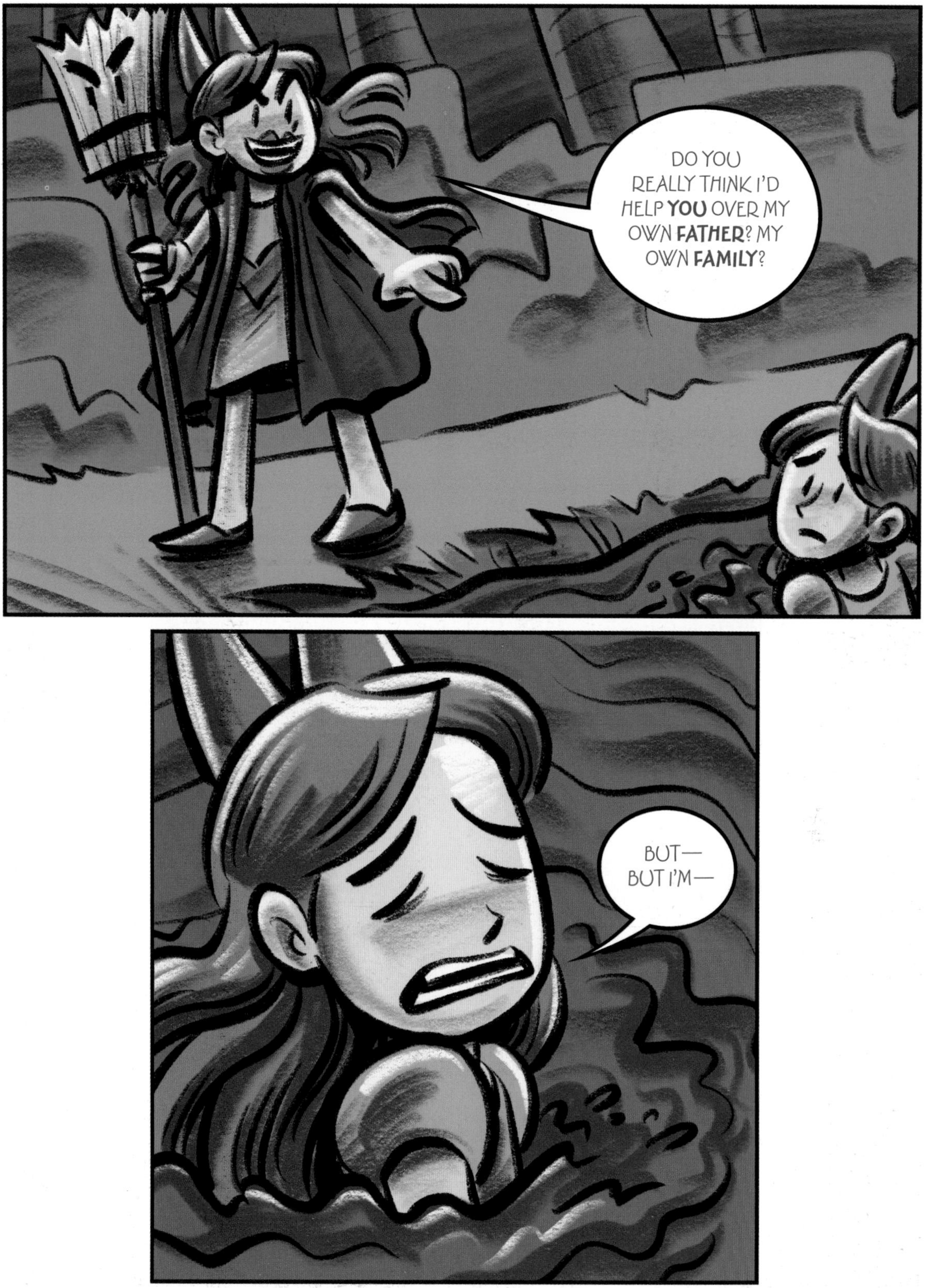
DO YOU REALLY THINK I'D HELP **YOU** OVER MY OWN **FATHER**? MY OWN **FAMILY**?
BUT— BUT I'M—

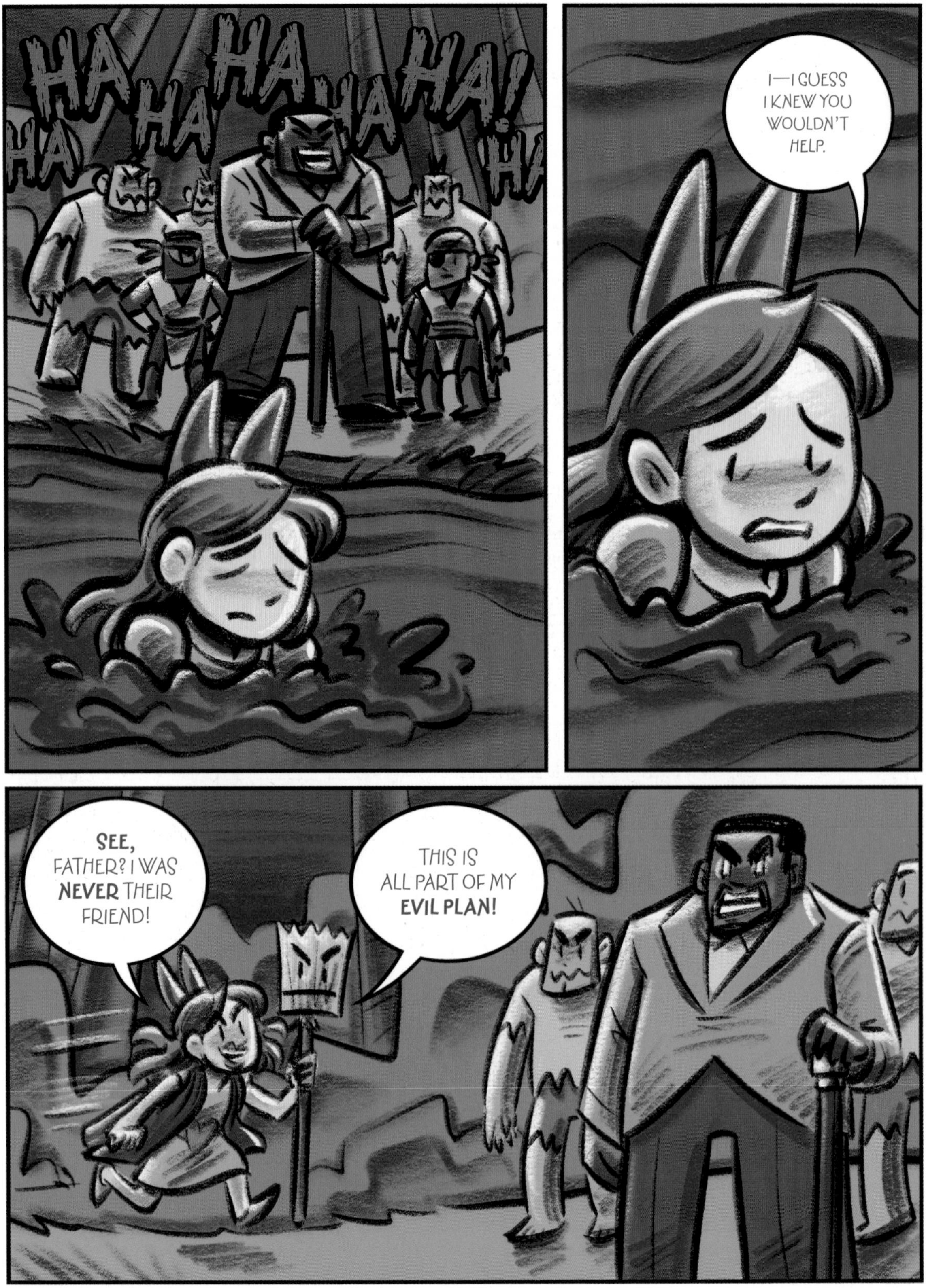
HA HA HA HA HA HA! HA HA
I—I GUESS I KNEW YOU WOULDN'T HELP.
SEE, FATHER? I WAS **NEVER** THEIR FRIEND!
THIS IS ALL PART OF MY **EVIL PLAN!**

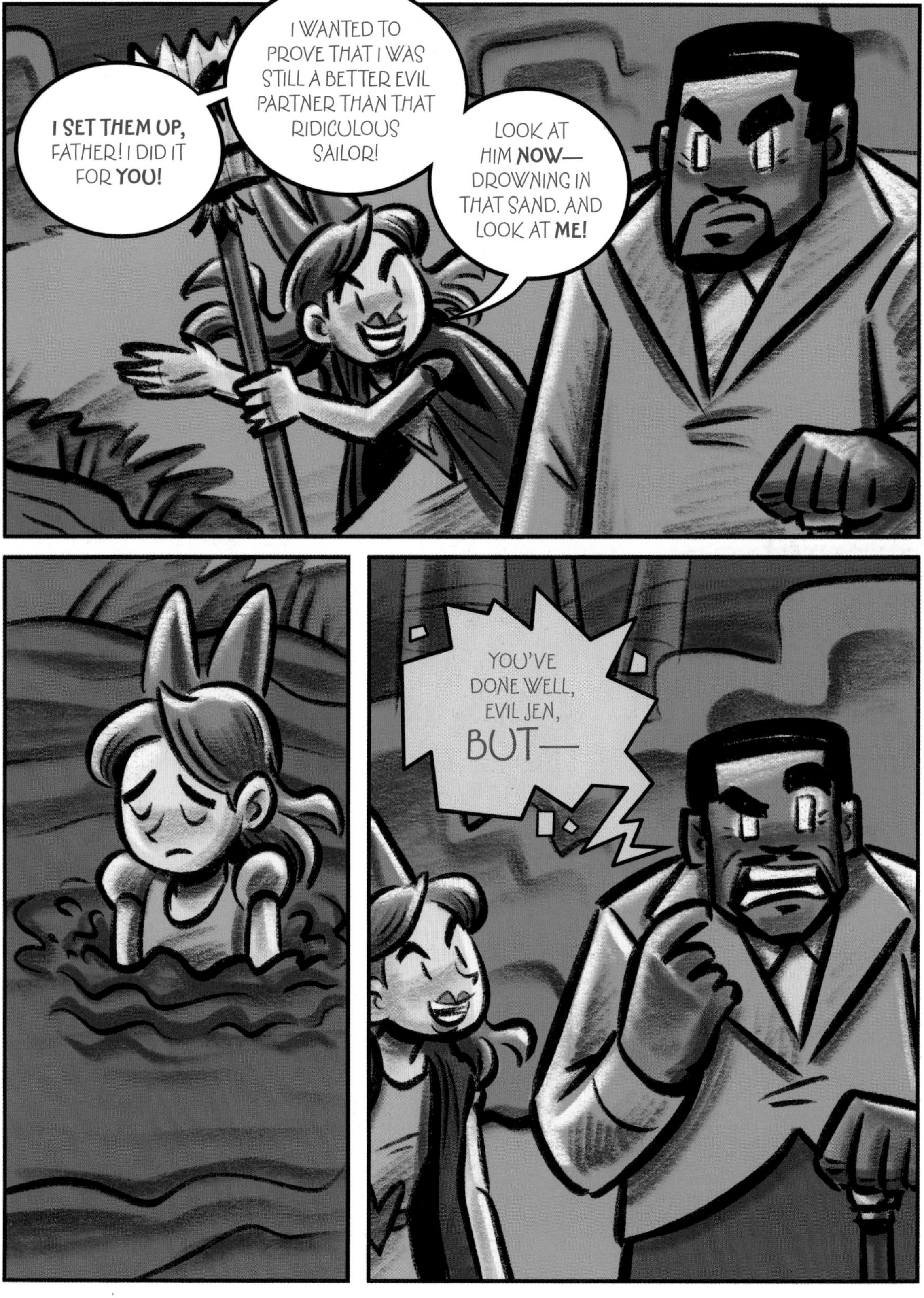
I SET THEM UP, FATHER! I DID IT FOR YOU!
I WANTED TO PROVE THAT I WAS STILL A BETTER EVIL PARTNER THAN THAT RIDICULOUS SAILOR!
LOOK AT HIM NOW— DROWNING IN THAT SAND. AND LOOK AT ME!
YOU'VE DONE WELL, EVIL JEN, BUT—

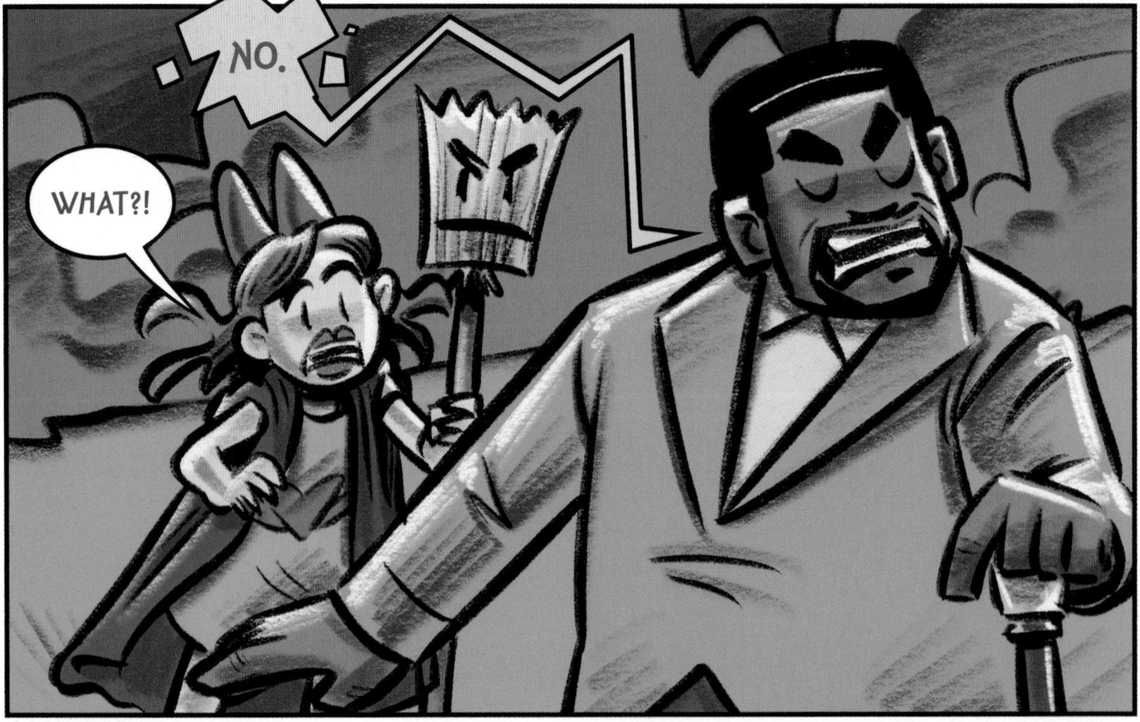
NO.
WHAT?!

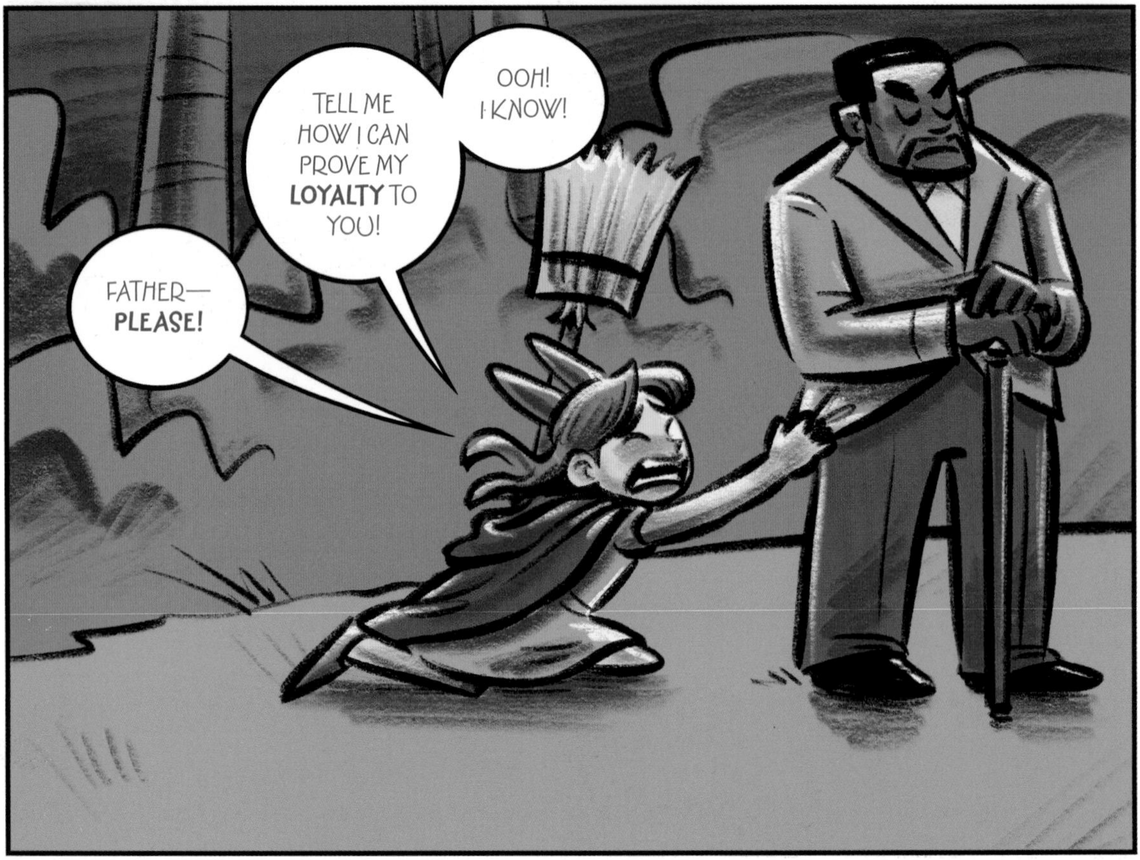
OOH! I KNOW!
TELL ME HOW I CAN PROVE MY **LOYALTY** TO YOU!
FATHER— **PLEASE!**

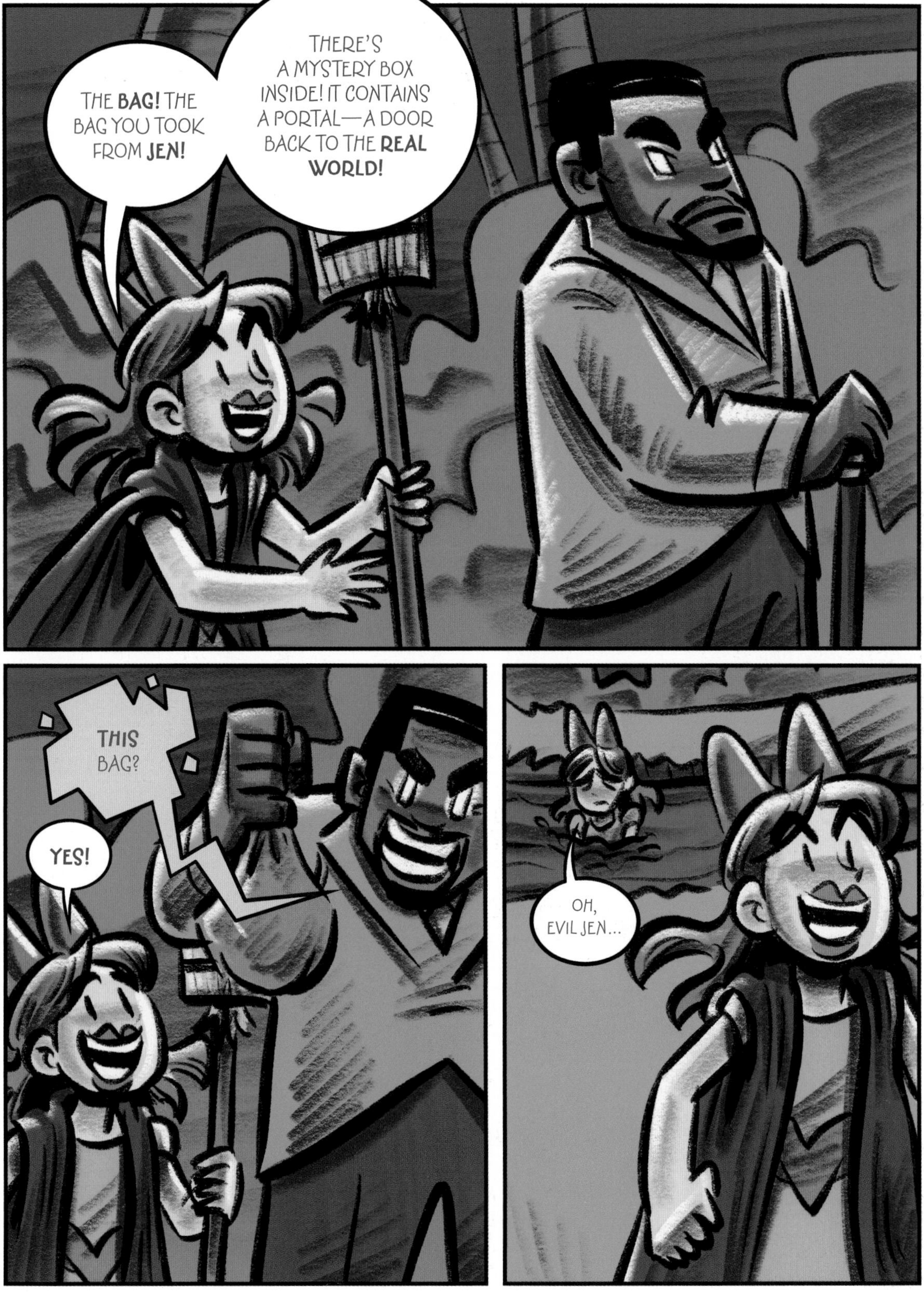
THE BAG! THE BAG YOU TOOK FROM JEN!
THERE'S A MYSTERY BOX INSIDE! IT CONTAINS A PORTAL—A DOOR BACK TO THE REAL WORLD!
THIS BAG?
YES!
OH, EVIL JEN...

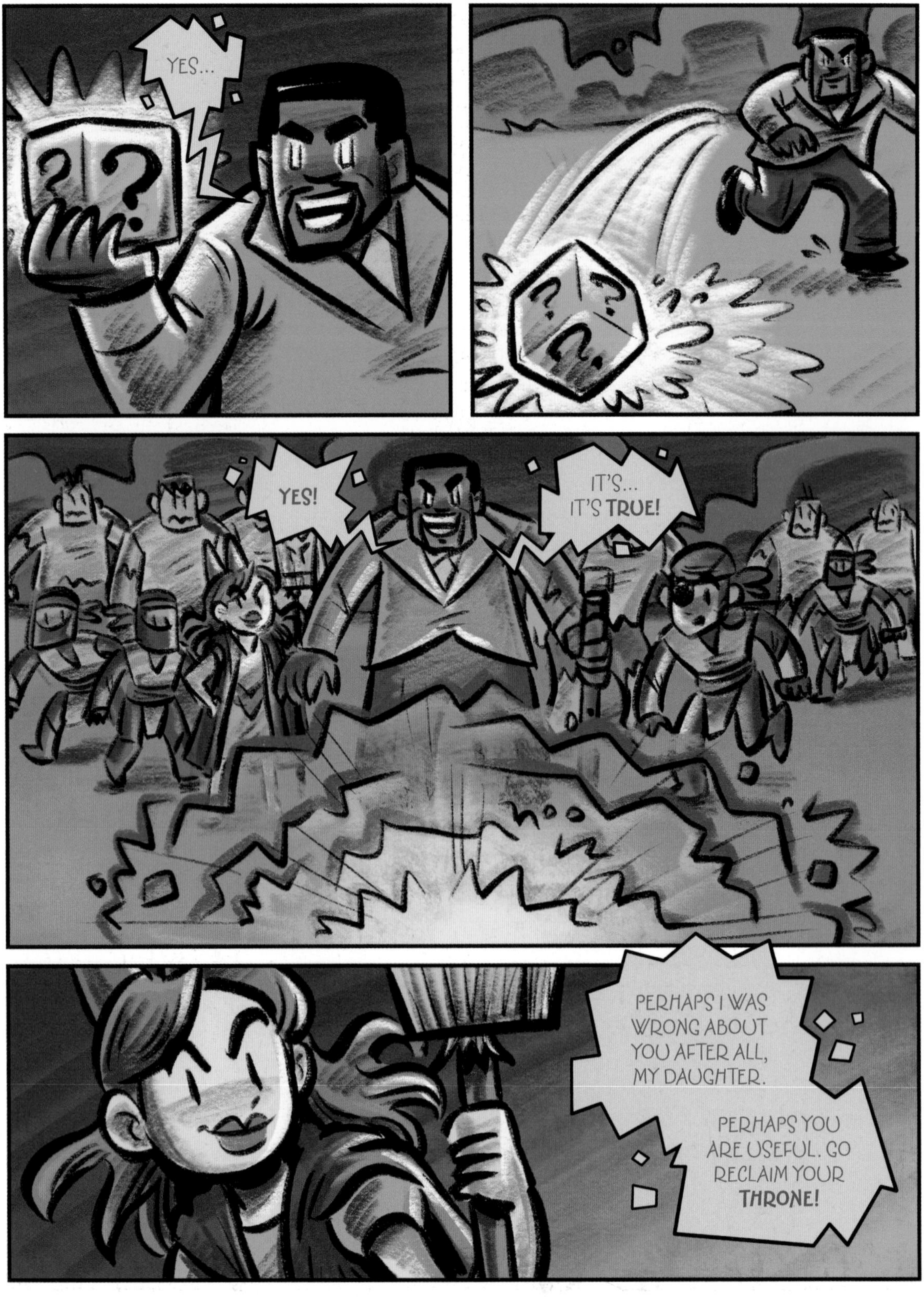
YES...
YES!
IT'S... IT'S **TRUE!**
PERHAPS I WAS WRONG ABOUT YOU AFTER ALL, MY DAUGHTER.
PERHAPS YOU ARE USEFUL. GO RECLAIM YOUR **THRONE!**

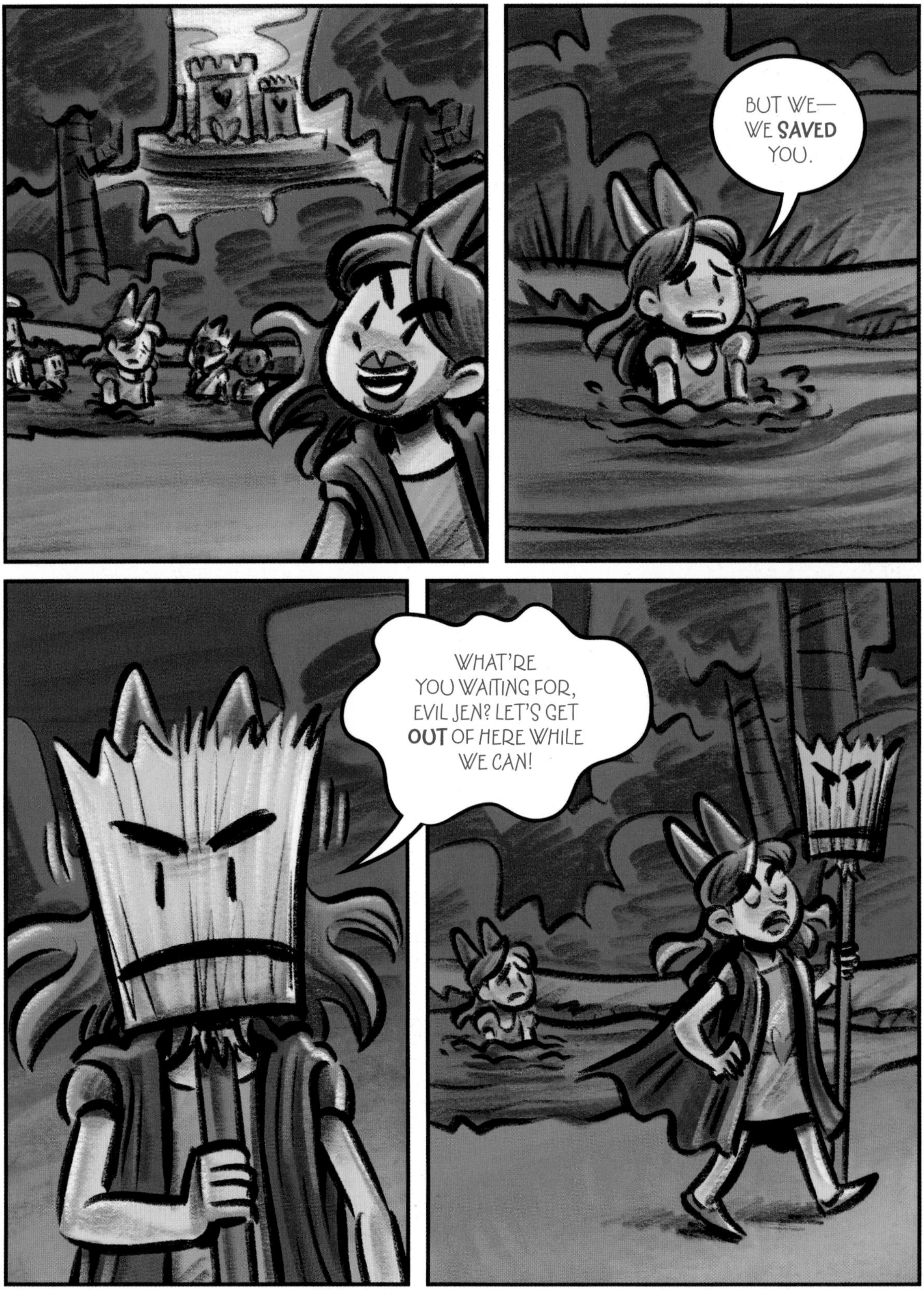
BUT WE—
WE **SAVED**
YOU.
WHAT'RE
YOU WAITING FOR,
EVIL JEN? LET'S GET
OUT OF HERE WHILE
WE CAN!

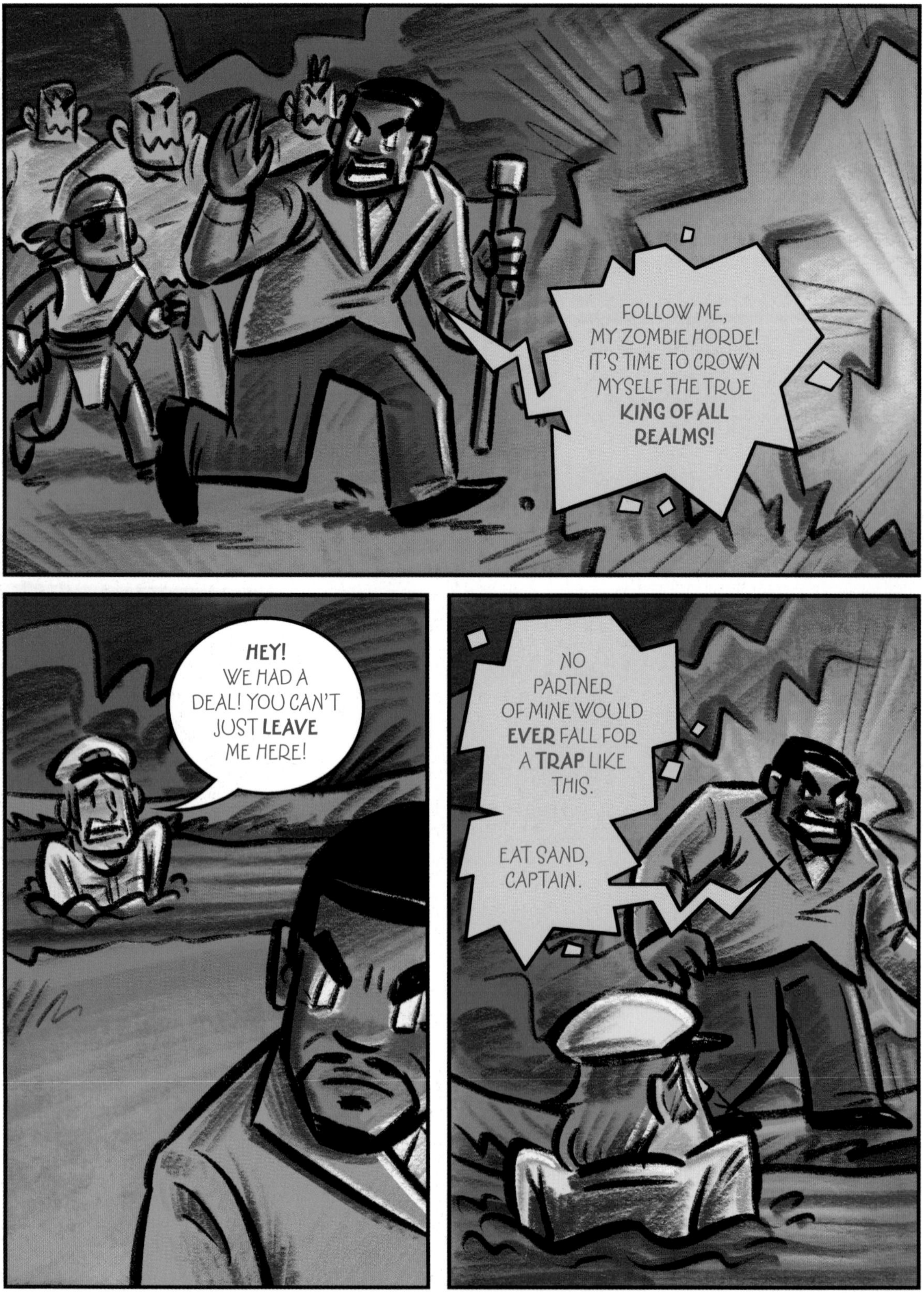
FOLLOW ME, MY ZOMBIE HORDE! IT'S TIME TO CROWN MYSELF THE TRUE **KING OF ALL REALMS!**
HEY! WE HAD A DEAL! YOU CAN'T JUST **LEAVE** ME HERE!
NO PARTNER OF MINE WOULD **EVER** FALL FOR A **TRAP** LIKE THIS.
EAT SAND, CAPTAIN.

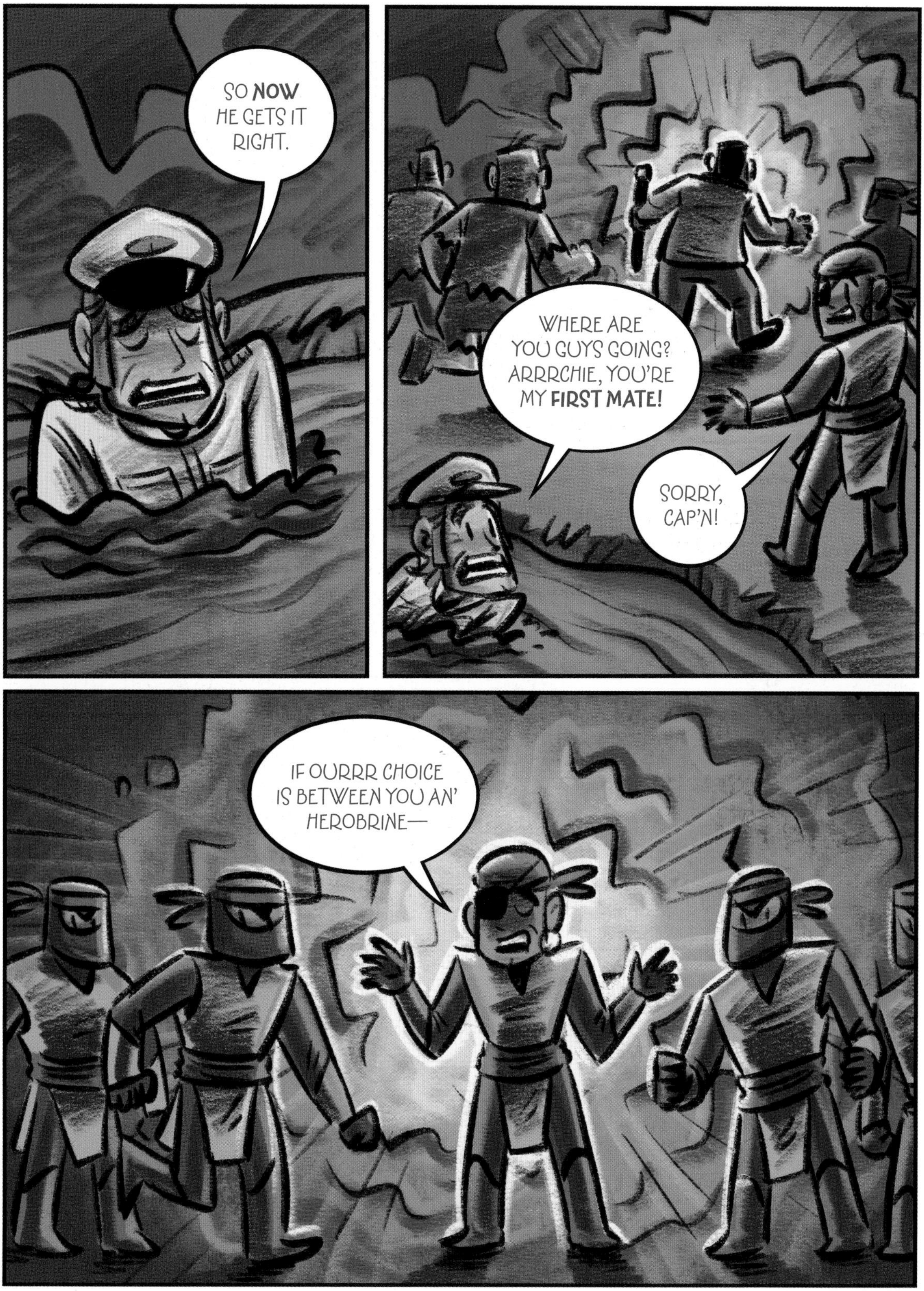
SO NOW HE GETS IT RIGHT.
WHERE ARE YOU GUYS GOING? ARRRCHIE, YOU'RE MY FIRST MATE!
SORRY, CAP'N!
IF OURRR CHOICE IS BETWEEN YOU AN' HEROBRINE—

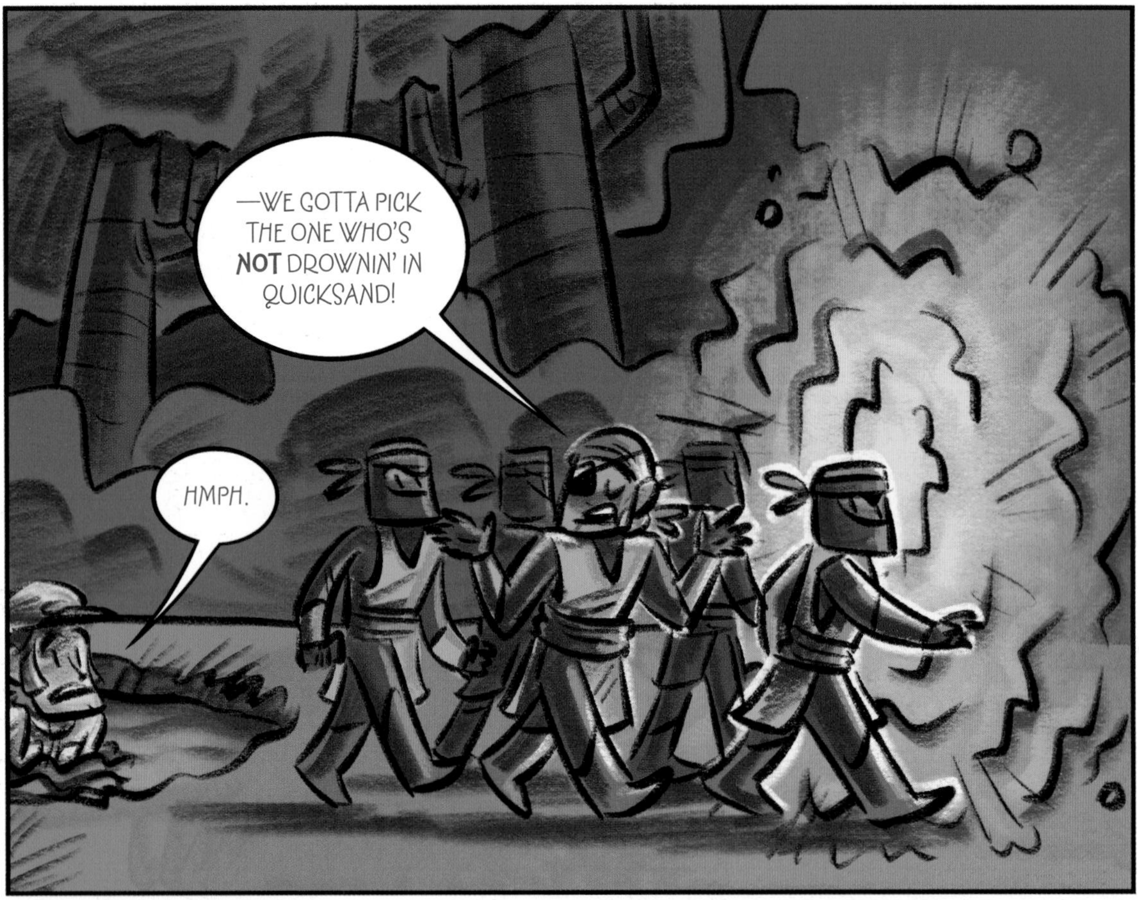
—WE GOTTA PICK THE ONE WHO'S **NOT** DROWNIN' IN QUICKSAND!
HMPH.

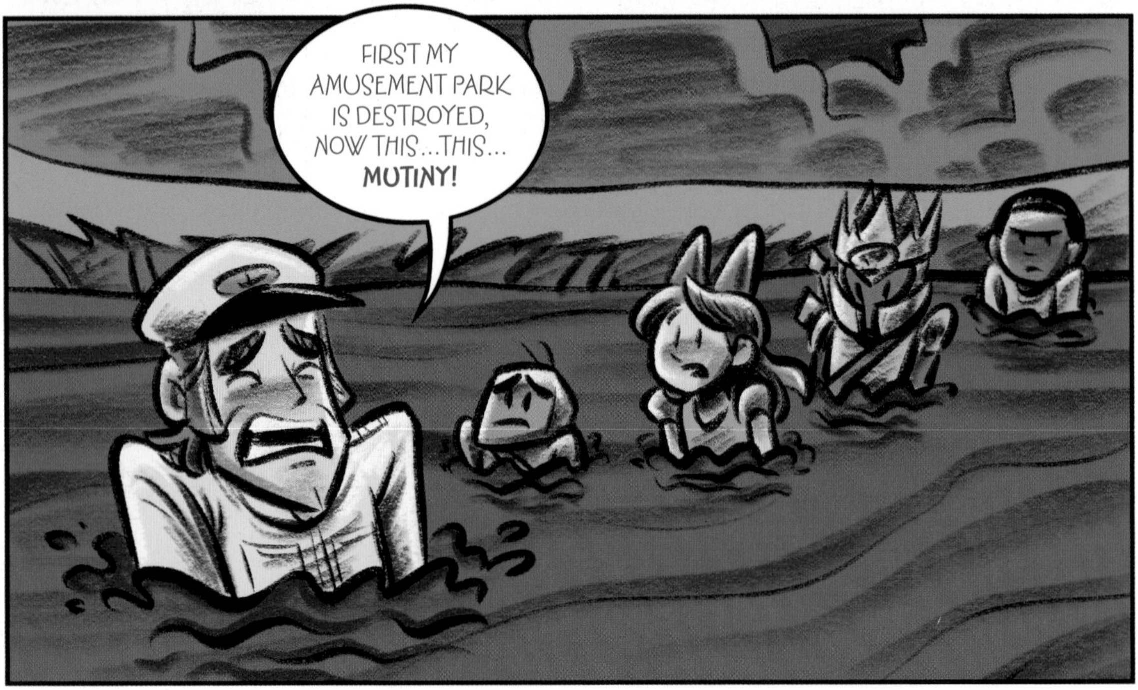
FIRST MY AMUSEMENT PARK IS DESTROYED, NOW THIS...THIS... **MUTINY!**

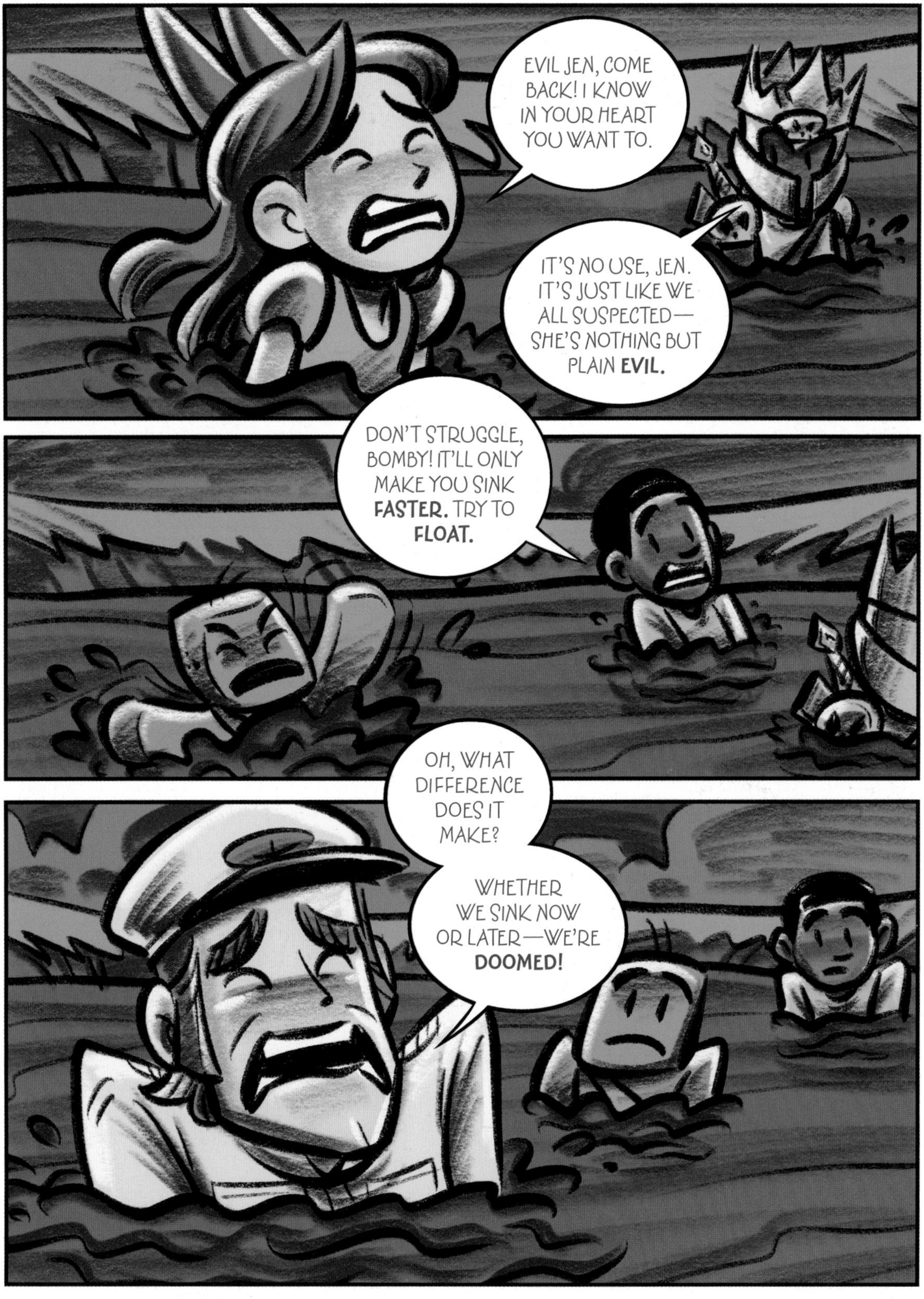

EVIL JEN, COME BACK! I KNOW IN YOUR HEART YOU WANT TO.
IT'S NO USE, JEN. IT'S JUST LIKE WE ALL SUSPECTED—SHE'S NOTHING BUT PLAIN **EVIL.**
DON'T STRUGGLE, BOMBY! IT'LL ONLY MAKE YOU SINK **FASTER.** TRY TO **FLOAT.**
OH, WHAT DIFFERENCE DOES IT MAKE?
WHETHER WE SINK NOW OR LATER—WE'RE **DOOMED!**

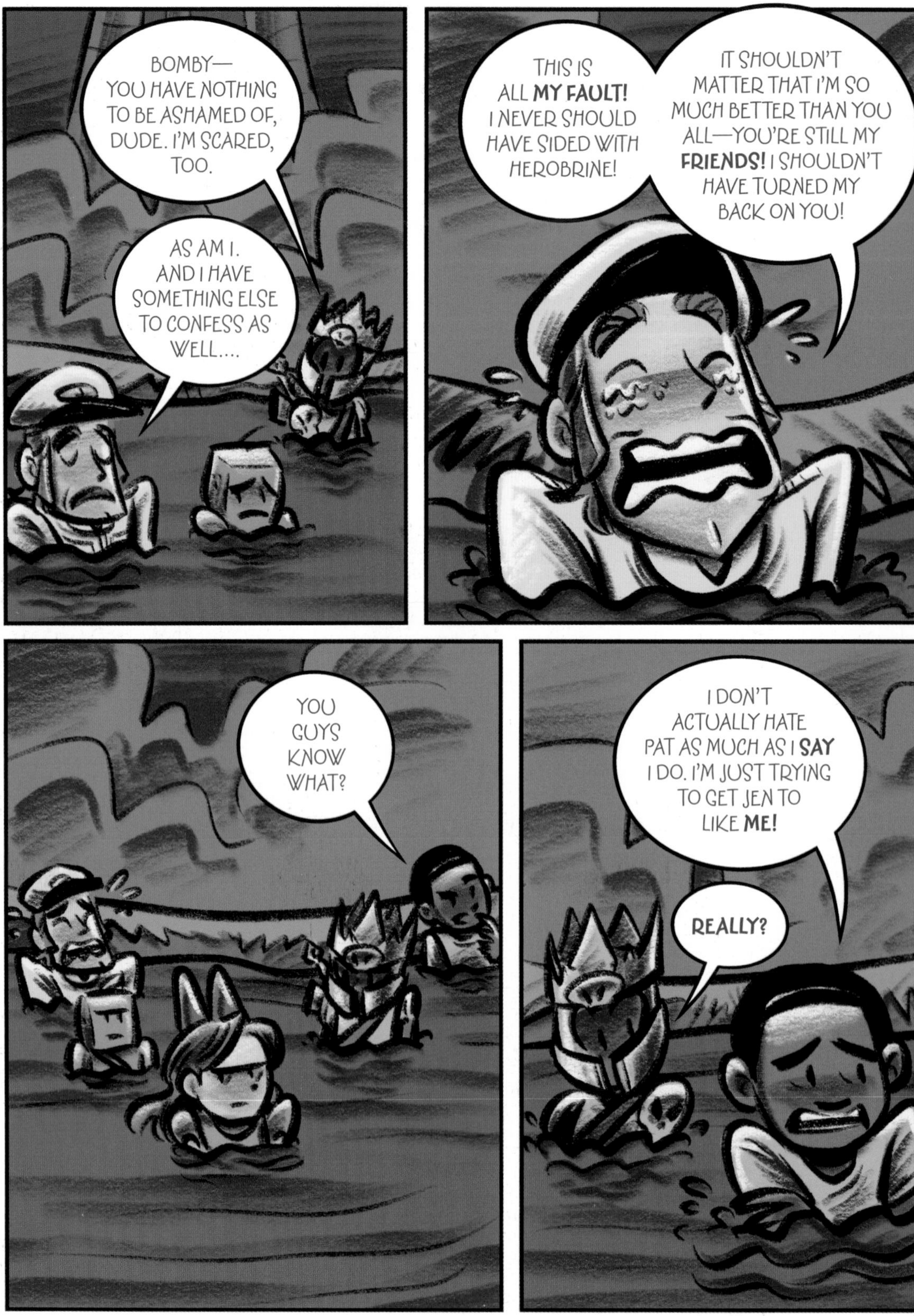
BOMBY—YOU HAVE NOTHING TO BE ASHAMED OF, DUDE. I'M SCARED, TOO.
AS AM I. AND I HAVE SOMETHING ELSE TO CONFESS AS WELL....
THIS IS ALL **MY FAULT!** I NEVER SHOULD HAVE SIDED WITH HEROBRINE!
IT SHOULDN'T MATTER THAT I'M SO MUCH BETTER THAN YOU ALL—YOU'RE STILL MY **FRIENDS!** I SHOULDN'T HAVE TURNED MY BACK ON YOU!
YOU GUYS KNOW WHAT?
I DON'T ACTUALLY HATE PAT AS MUCH AS I **SAY** I DO. I'M JUST TRYING TO GET JEN TO LIKE **ME!**
REALLY?

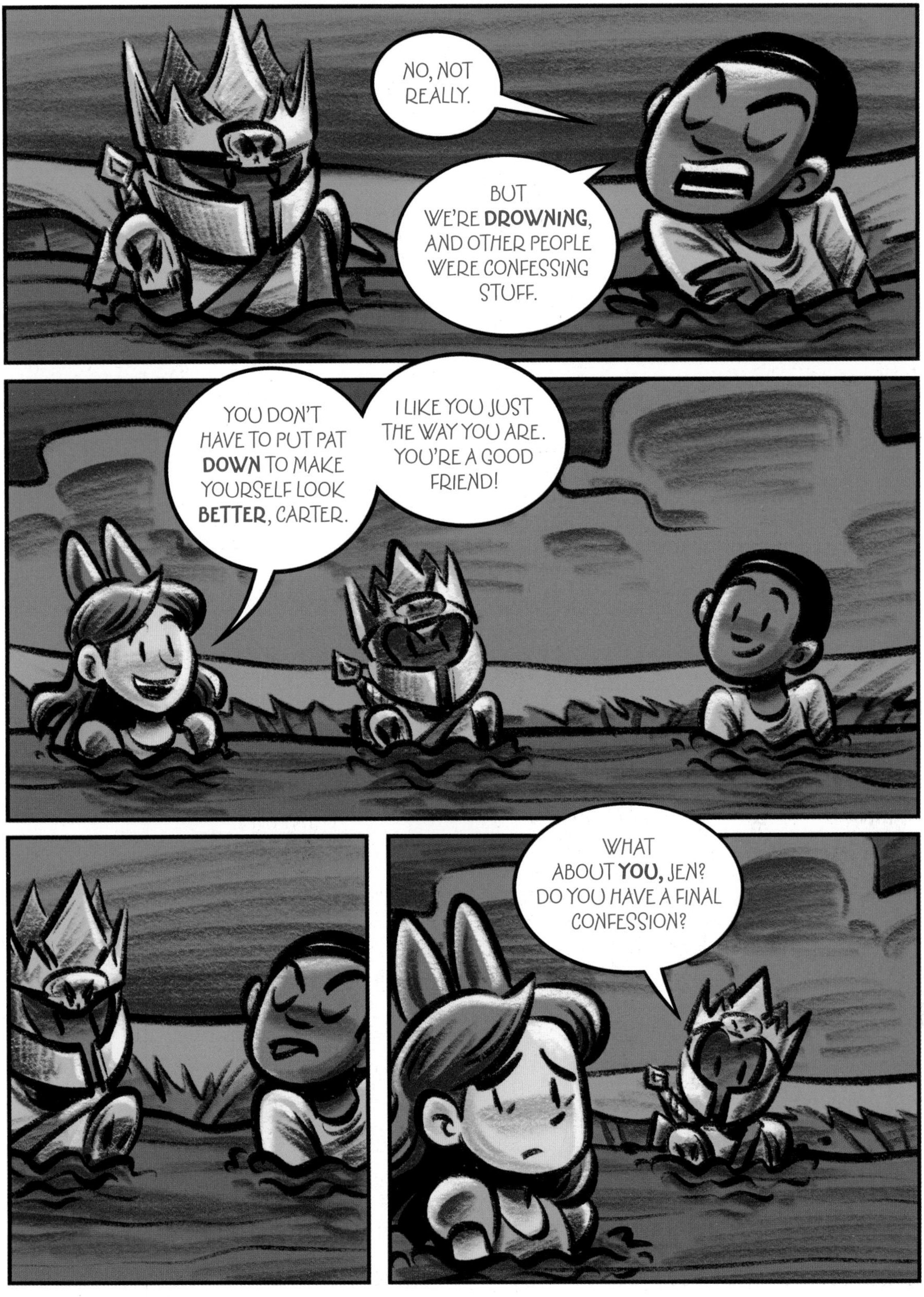
NO, NOT REALLY.
BUT WE'RE **DROWNING**, AND OTHER PEOPLE WERE CONFESSING STUFF.
YOU DON'T HAVE TO PUT PAT **DOWN** TO MAKE YOURSELF LOOK **BETTER**, CARTER.
I LIKE YOU JUST THE WAY YOU ARE. YOU'RE A GOOD FRIEND!
WHAT ABOUT **YOU,** JEN? DO YOU HAVE A FINAL CONFESSION?

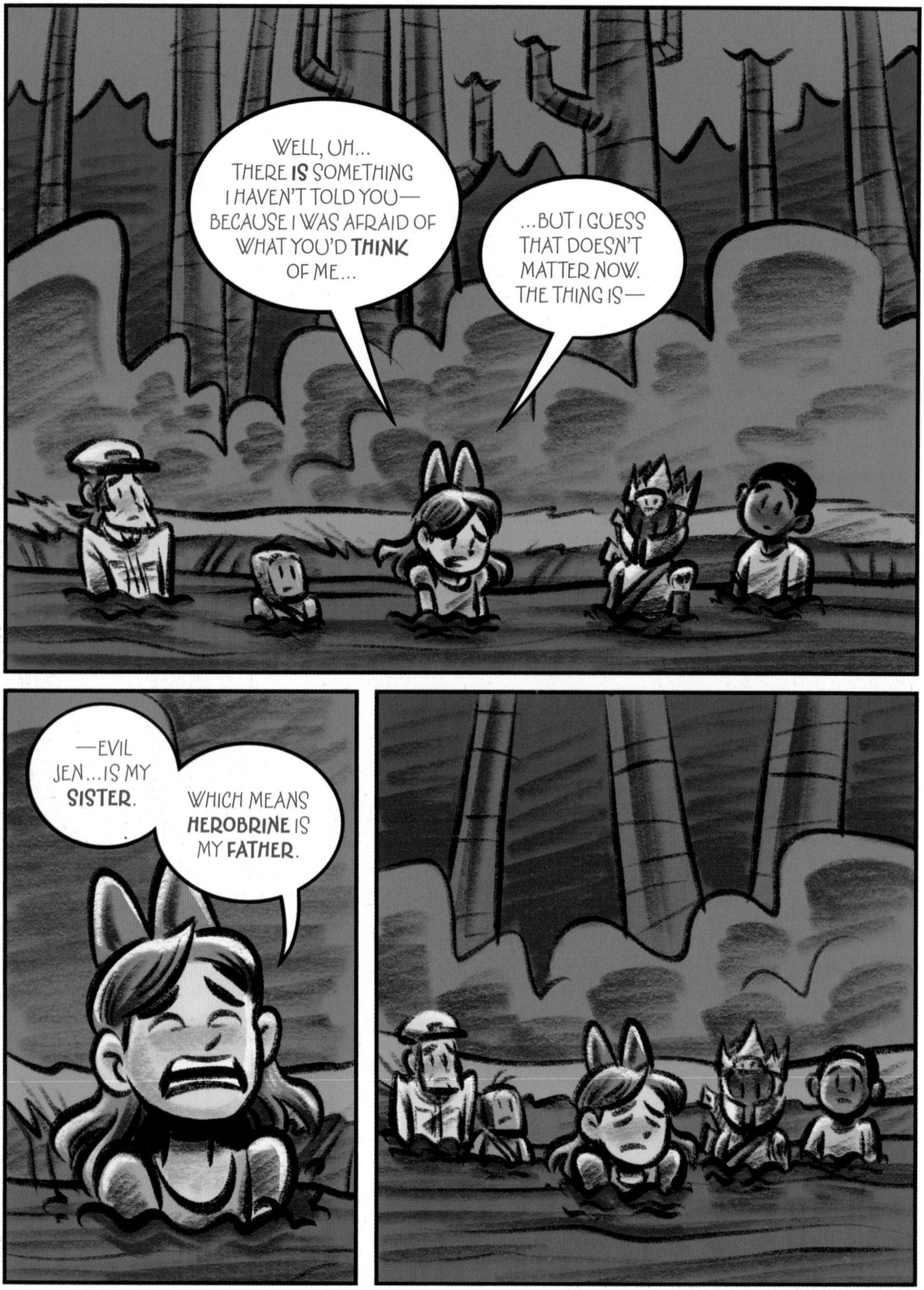
WELL, UH... THERE **IS** SOMETHING I HAVEN'T TOLD YOU— BECAUSE I WAS AFRAID OF WHAT YOU'D **THINK** OF ME...
...BUT I GUESS THAT DOESN'T MATTER NOW. THE THING IS—
—EVIL JEN...IS MY **SISTER**.
WHICH MEANS **HEROBRINE** IS MY **FATHER**.

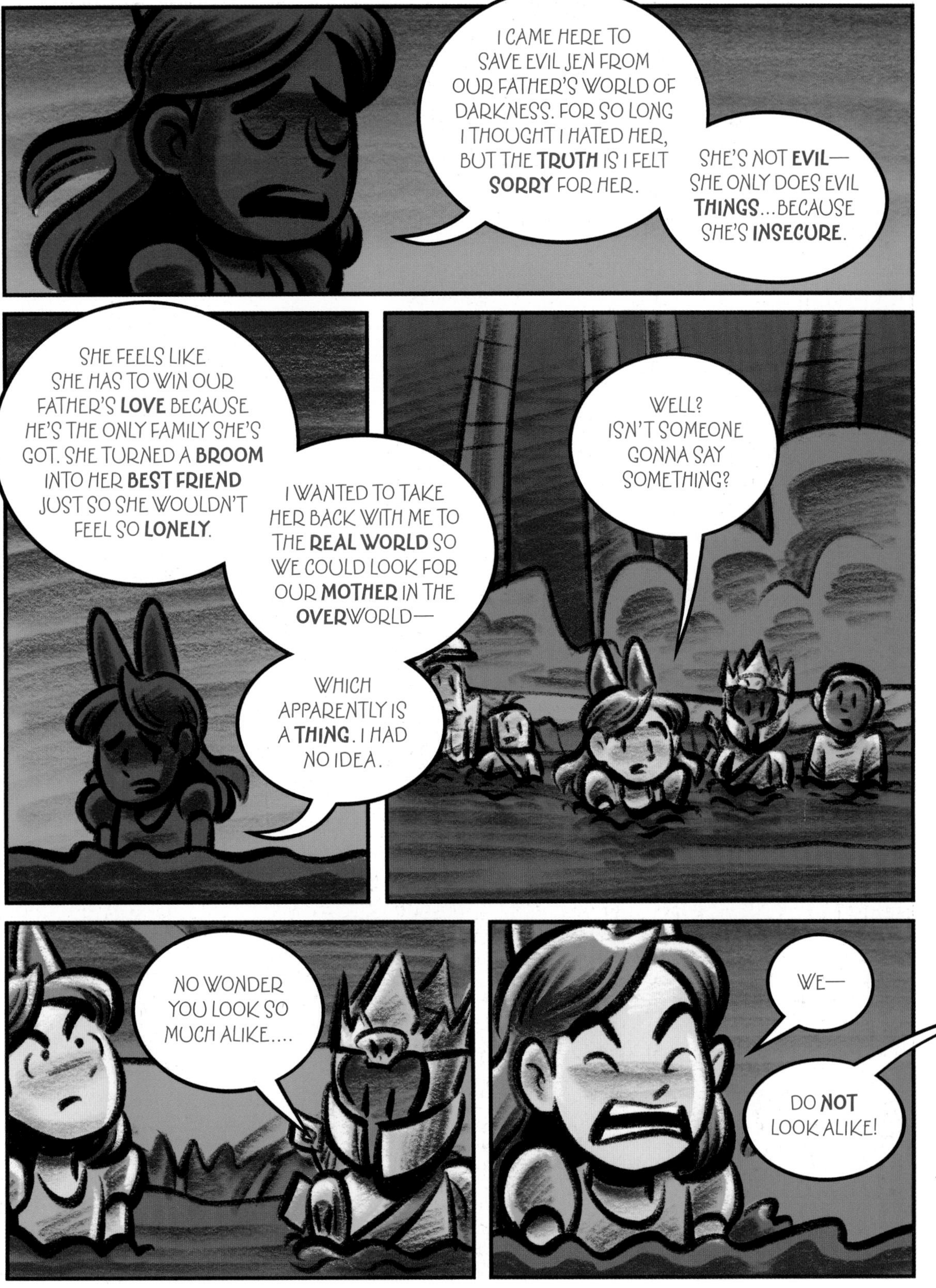

I CAME HERE TO SAVE EVIL JEN FROM OUR FATHER'S WORLD OF DARKNESS. FOR SO LONG I THOUGHT I HATED HER, BUT THE **TRUTH** IS I FELT **SORRY** FOR HER.
SHE'S NOT **EVIL**— SHE ONLY DOES EVIL **THINGS**...BECAUSE SHE'S **INSECURE**.
SHE FEELS LIKE SHE HAS TO WIN OUR FATHER'S **LOVE** BECAUSE HE'S THE ONLY FAMILY SHE'S GOT. SHE TURNED A **BROOM** INTO HER **BEST FRIEND** JUST SO SHE WOULDN'T FEEL SO **LONELY**.
I WANTED TO TAKE HER BACK WITH ME TO THE **REAL WORLD** SO WE COULD LOOK FOR OUR **MOTHER** IN THE **OVER**WORLD—
WHICH APPARENTLY IS A **THING**. I HAD NO IDEA.
WELL? ISN'T SOMEONE GONNA SAY SOMETHING?
NO WONDER YOU LOOK SO MUCH ALIKE....
WE—
DO **NOT** LOOK ALIKE!

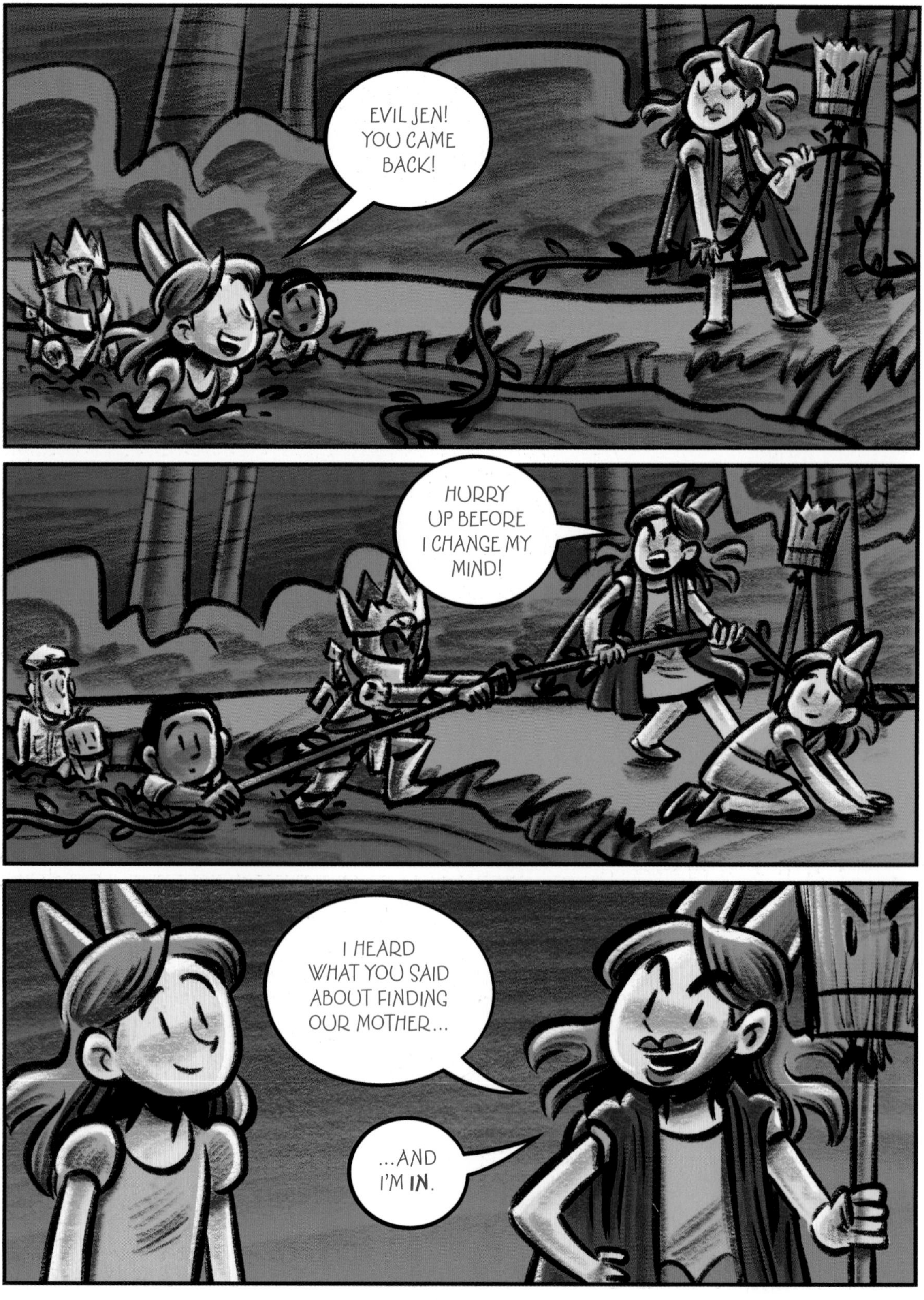
EVIL JEN! YOU CAME BACK!
HURRY UP BEFORE I CHANGE MY MIND!
I HEARD WHAT YOU SAID ABOUT FINDING OUR MOTHER...
...AND I'M **IN**.

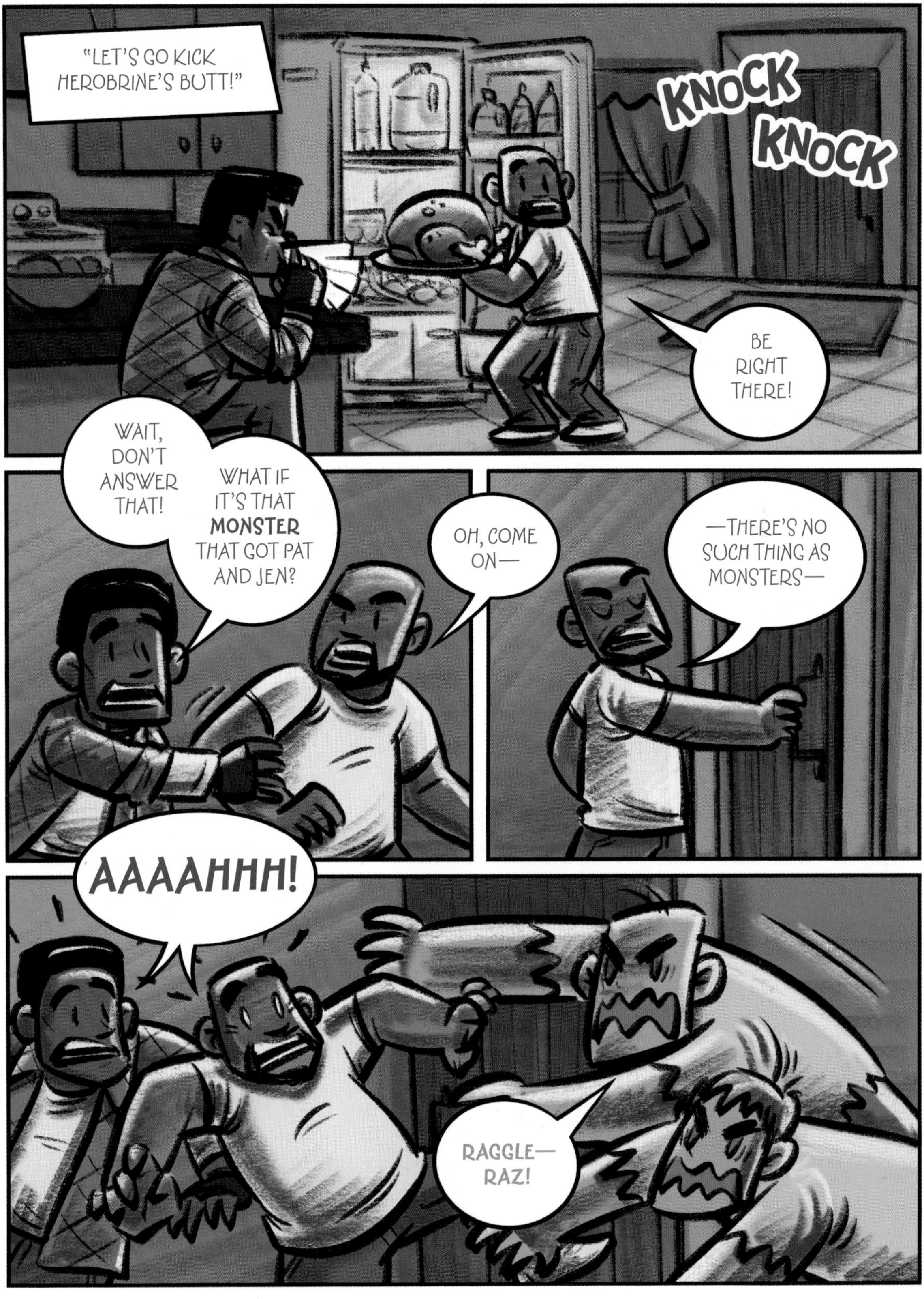
"LET'S GO KICK HEROBRINE'S BUTT!"
KNOCK KNOCK
BE RIGHT THERE!
WAIT, DON'T ANSWER THAT!
WHAT IF IT'S THAT **MONSTER** THAT GOT PAT AND JEN?
OH, COME ON—
—THERE'S NO SUCH THING AS MONSTERS—
AAAAHHH!
RAGGLE—RAZ!

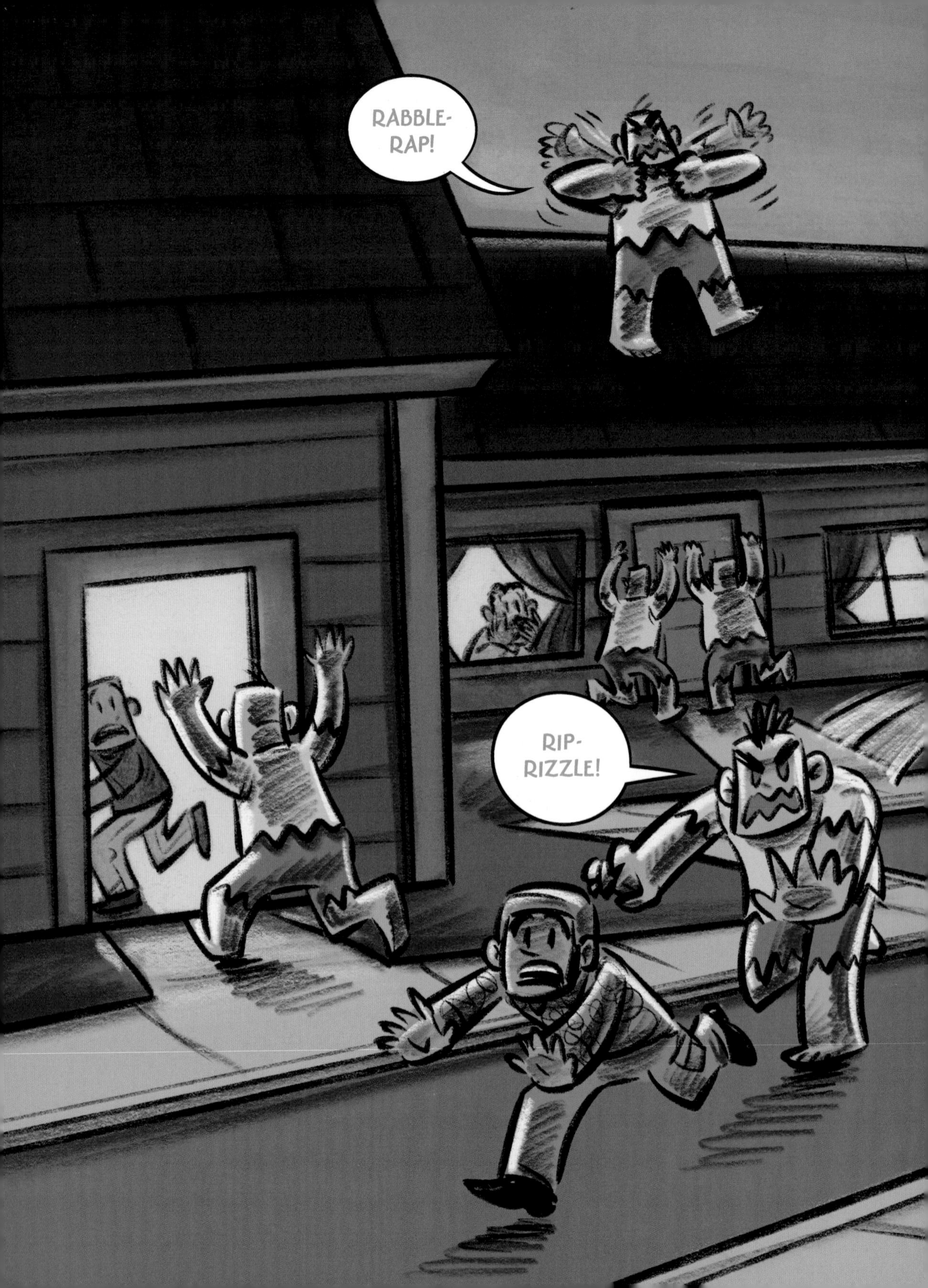
RABBLE-RAP!
RIP-RIZZLE!

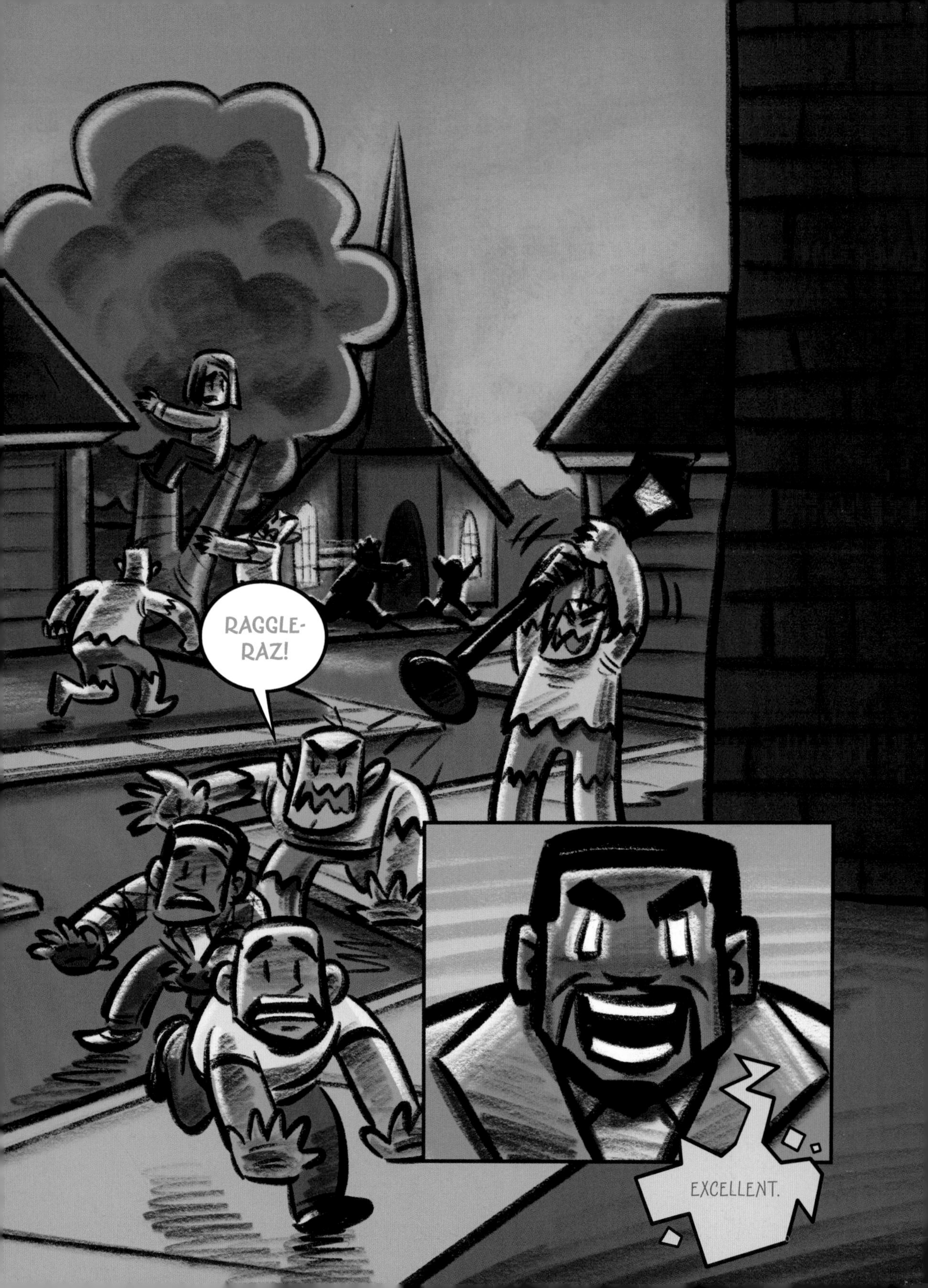
RAGGLE-
RAZ!
EXCELLENT.

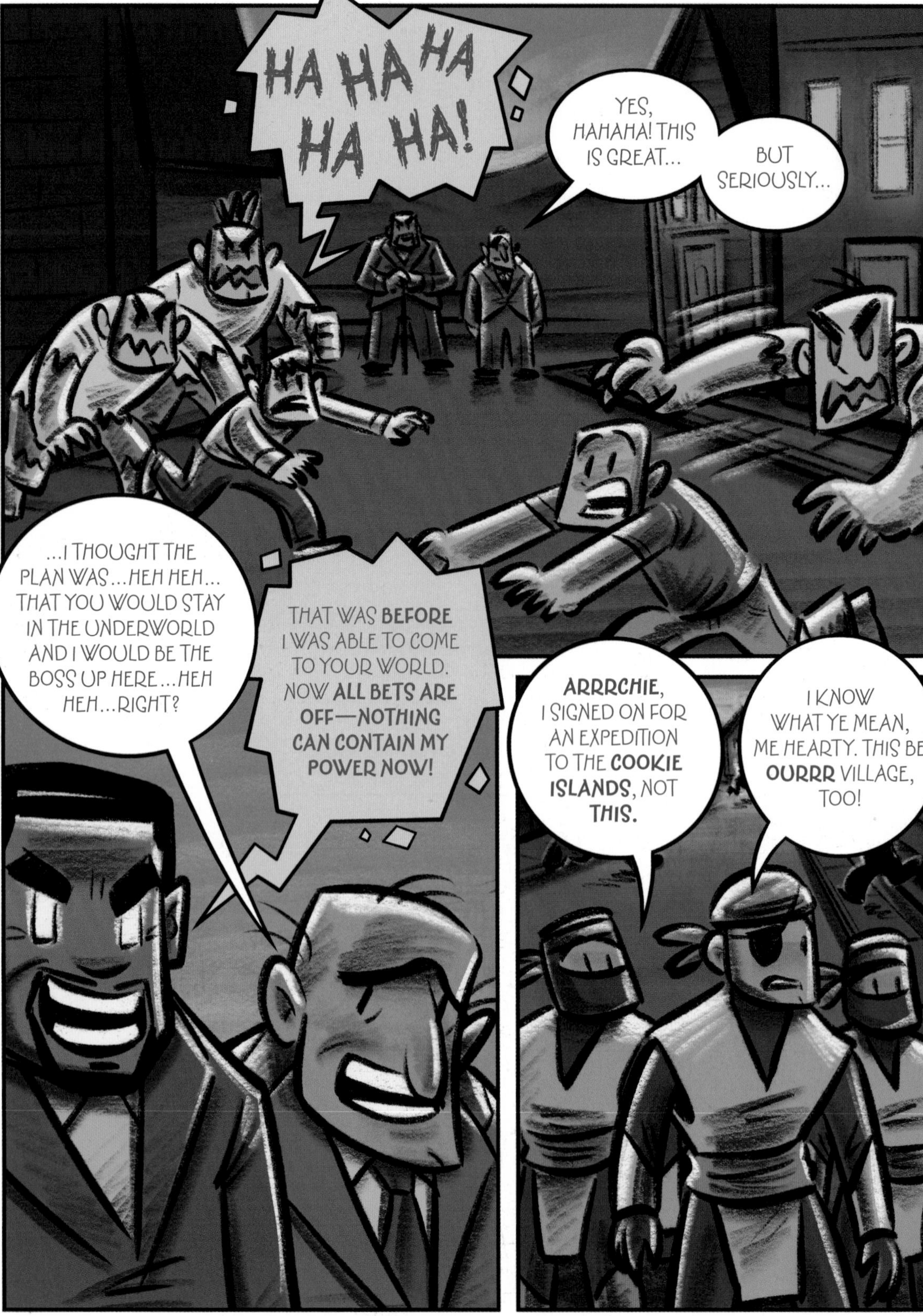

HA HA HA HA HA HA!
YES, HAHAHA! THIS IS GREAT...
BUT SERIOUSLY...
...I THOUGHT THE PLAN WAS...HEH HEH... THAT YOU WOULD STAY IN THE UNDERWORLD AND I WOULD BE THE BOSS UP HERE...HEH HEH...RIGHT?
THAT WAS **BEFORE** I WAS ABLE TO COME TO YOUR WORLD. NOW **ALL BETS ARE OFF—NOTHING CAN CONTAIN MY POWER NOW!**
ARRRCHIE, I SIGNED ON FOR AN EXPEDITION TO THE **COOKIE ISLANDS**, NOT **THIS.**
I KNOW WHAT YE MEAN, ME HEARTY. THIS BE **OURRR** VILLAGE, TOO!

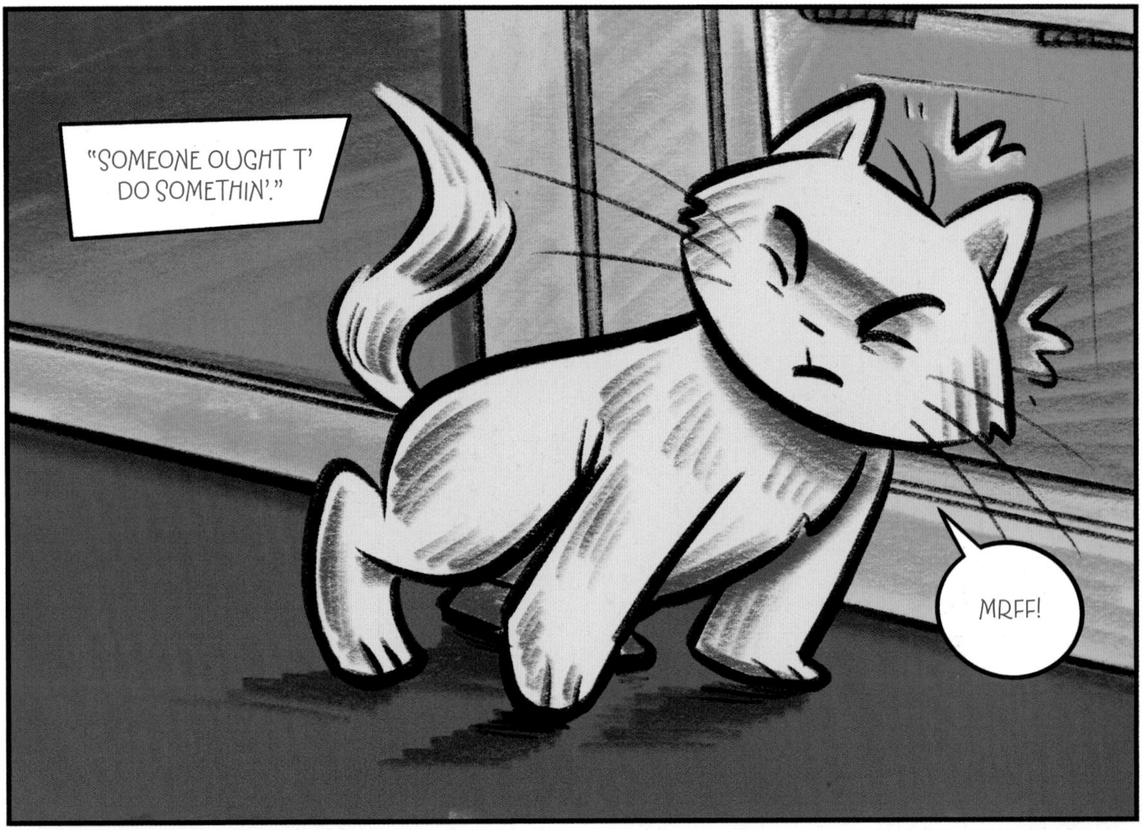
"SOMEONE OUGHT T' DO SOMETHIN'."
MRFF!

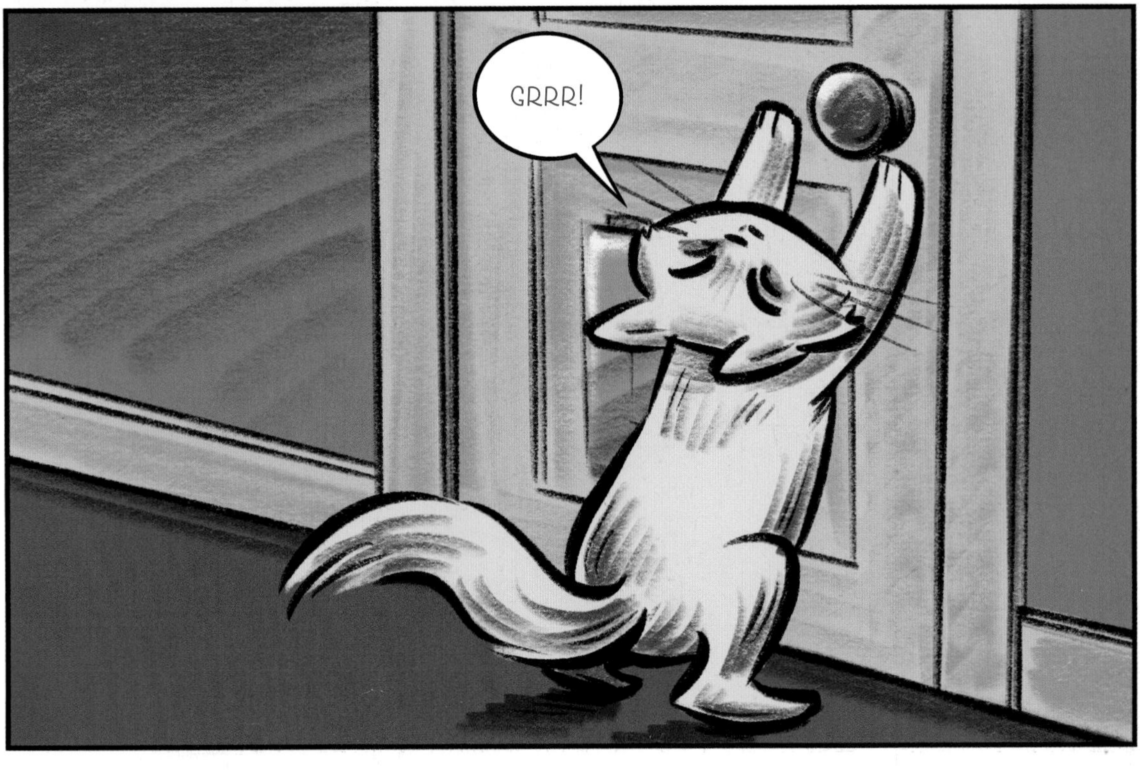
GRRR!

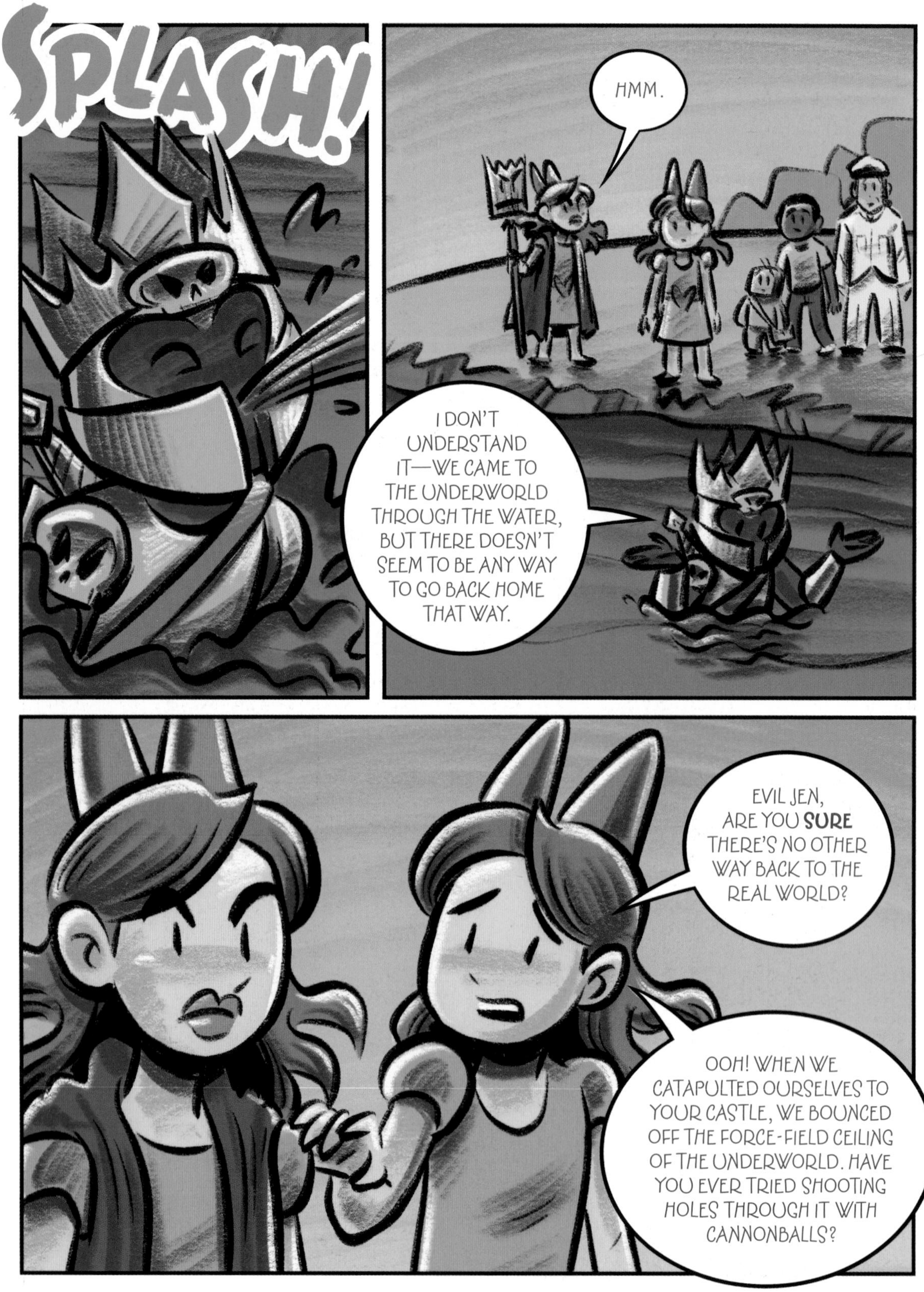
SPLASH!
HMM.
I DON'T UNDERSTAND IT—WE CAME TO THE UNDERWORLD THROUGH THE WATER, BUT THERE DOESN'T SEEM TO BE ANY WAY TO GO BACK HOME THAT WAY.
EVIL JEN, ARE YOU **SURE** THERE'S NO OTHER WAY BACK TO THE REAL WORLD?
OOH! WHEN WE CATAPULTED OURSELVES TO YOUR CASTLE, WE BOUNCED OFF THE FORCE-FIELD CEILING OF THE UNDERWORLD. HAVE YOU EVER TRIED SHOOTING HOLES THROUGH IT WITH CANNONBALLS?

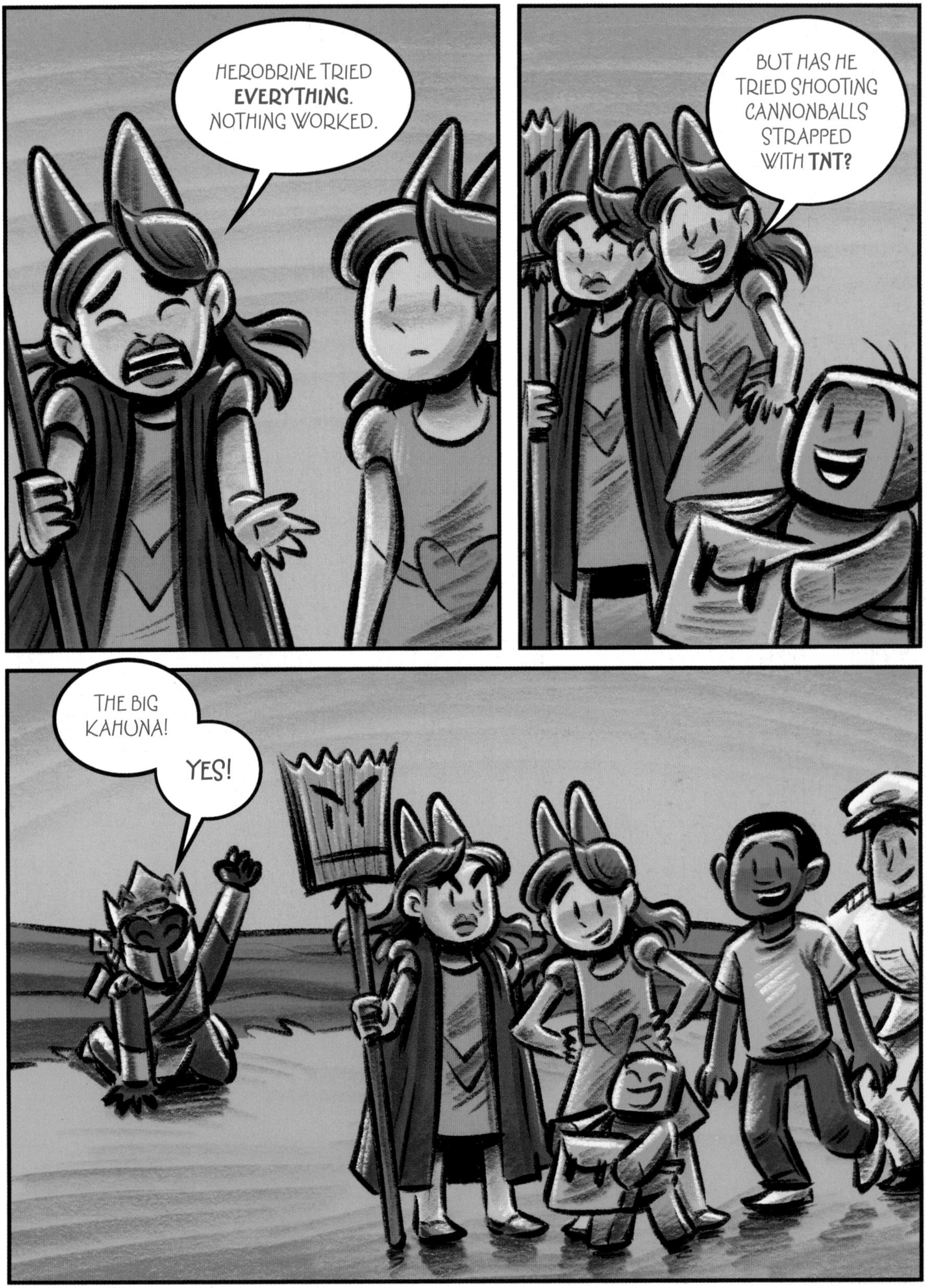
HEROBRINE TRIED **EVERYTHING**. NOTHING WORKED.
BUT HAS HE TRIED SHOOTING CANNONBALLS STRAPPED WITH **TNT?**
THE BIG KAHUNA!
YES!

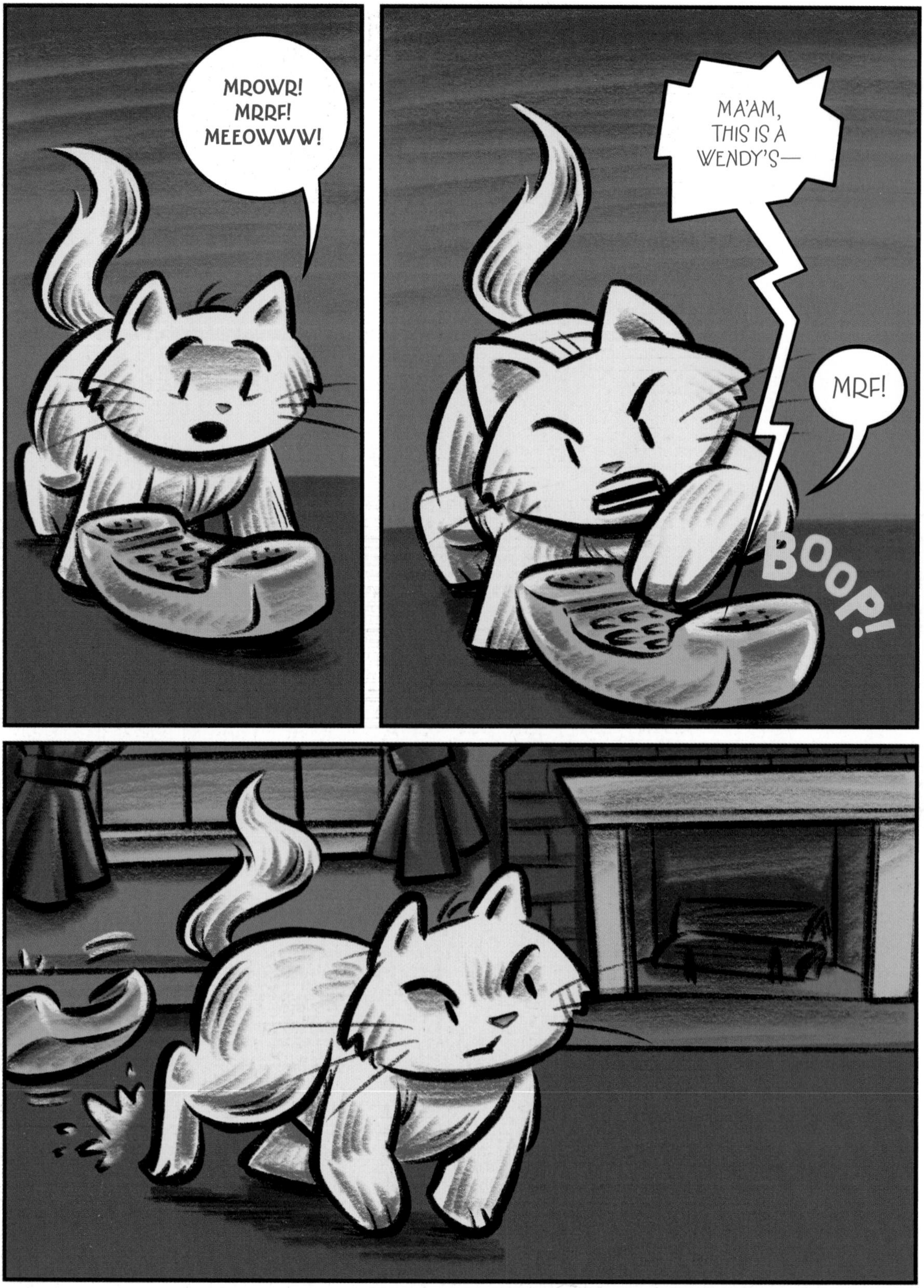
MROWR! MRRF! MEEOWWW!
MA'AM, THIS IS A WENDY'S—
MRF!
BOOP!

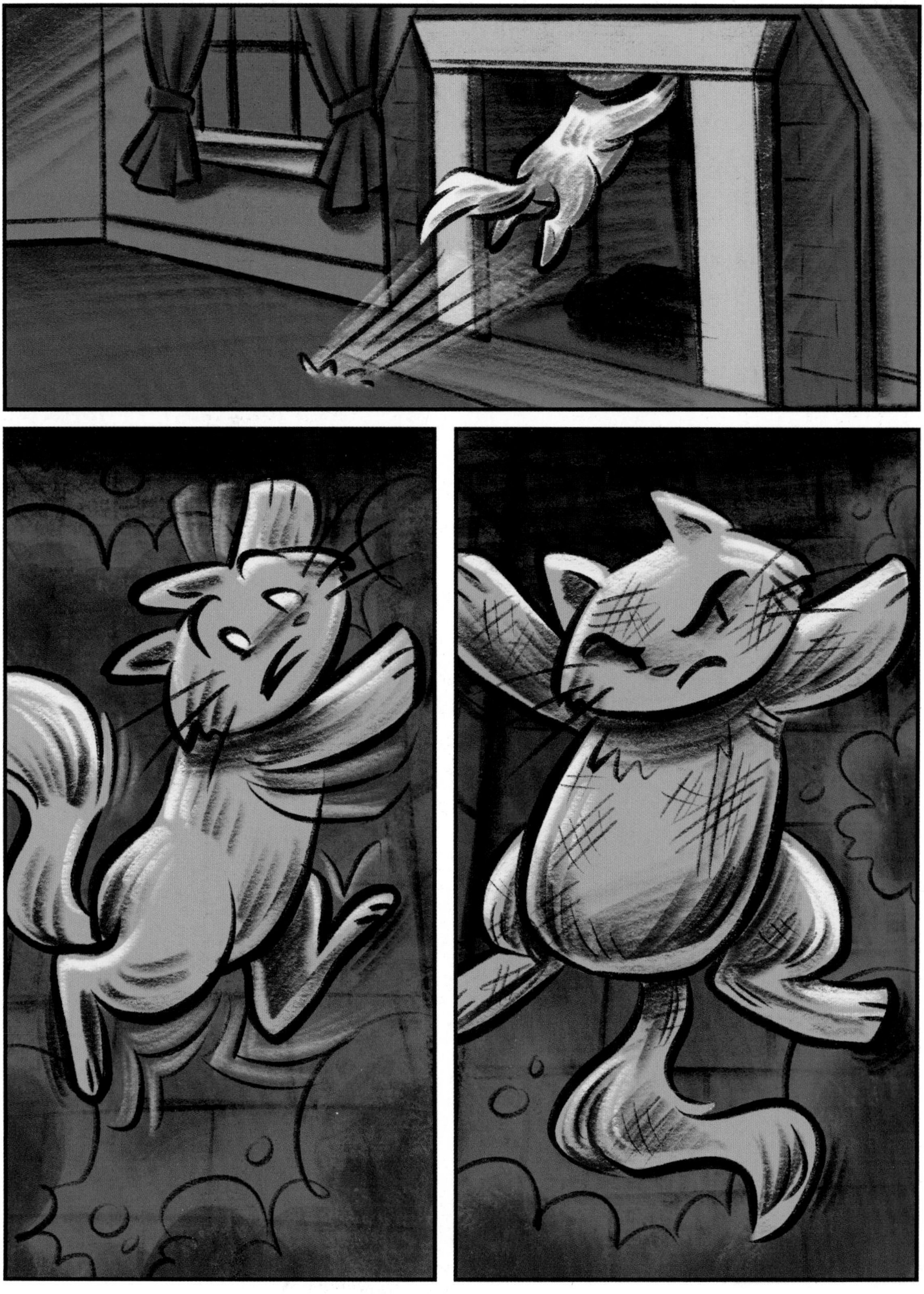

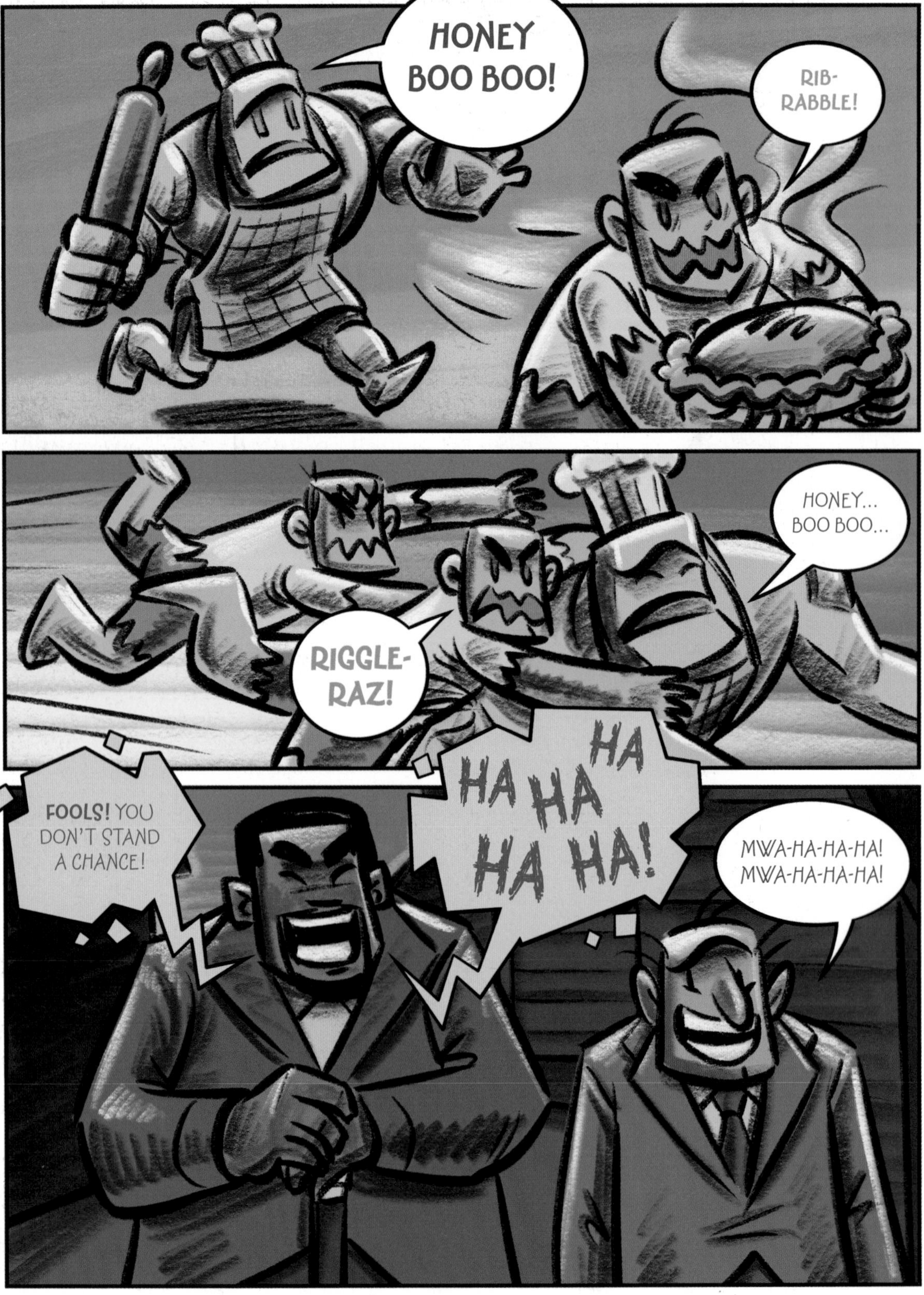
HONEY BOO BOO!
RIB-RABBLE!
HONEY... BOO BOO...
RIGGLE-RAZ!
FOOLS! YOU DON'T STAND A CHANCE!
HA HA HA HA HA!
MWA-HA-HA-HA! MWA-HA-HA-HA!

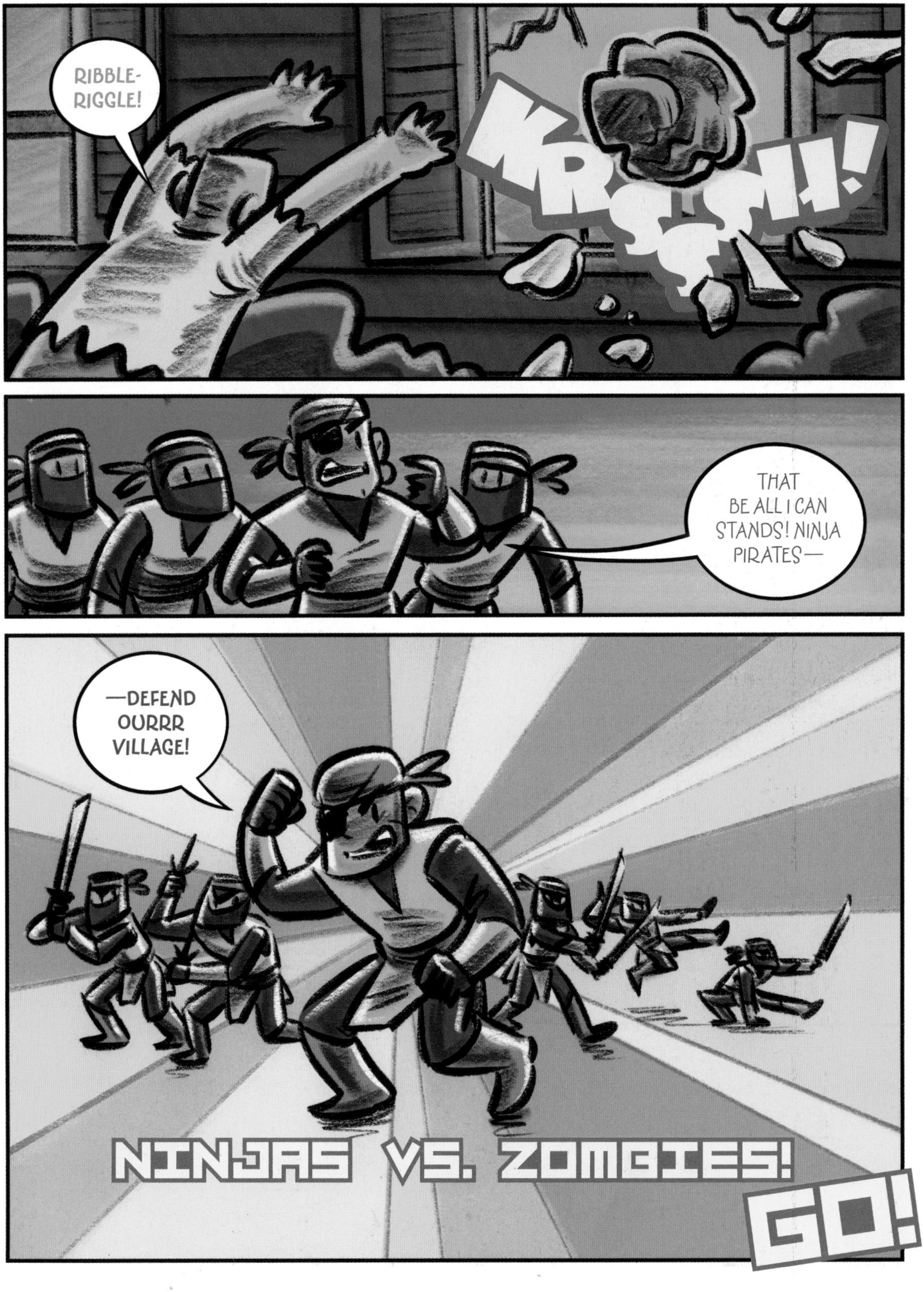
RIBBLE-RIGGLE!
KRSSSH!!
THAT BE ALL I CAN STANDS! NINJA PIRATES—
—DEFEND OURRR VILLAGE!
NINJAS VS. ZOMBIES!
GO!

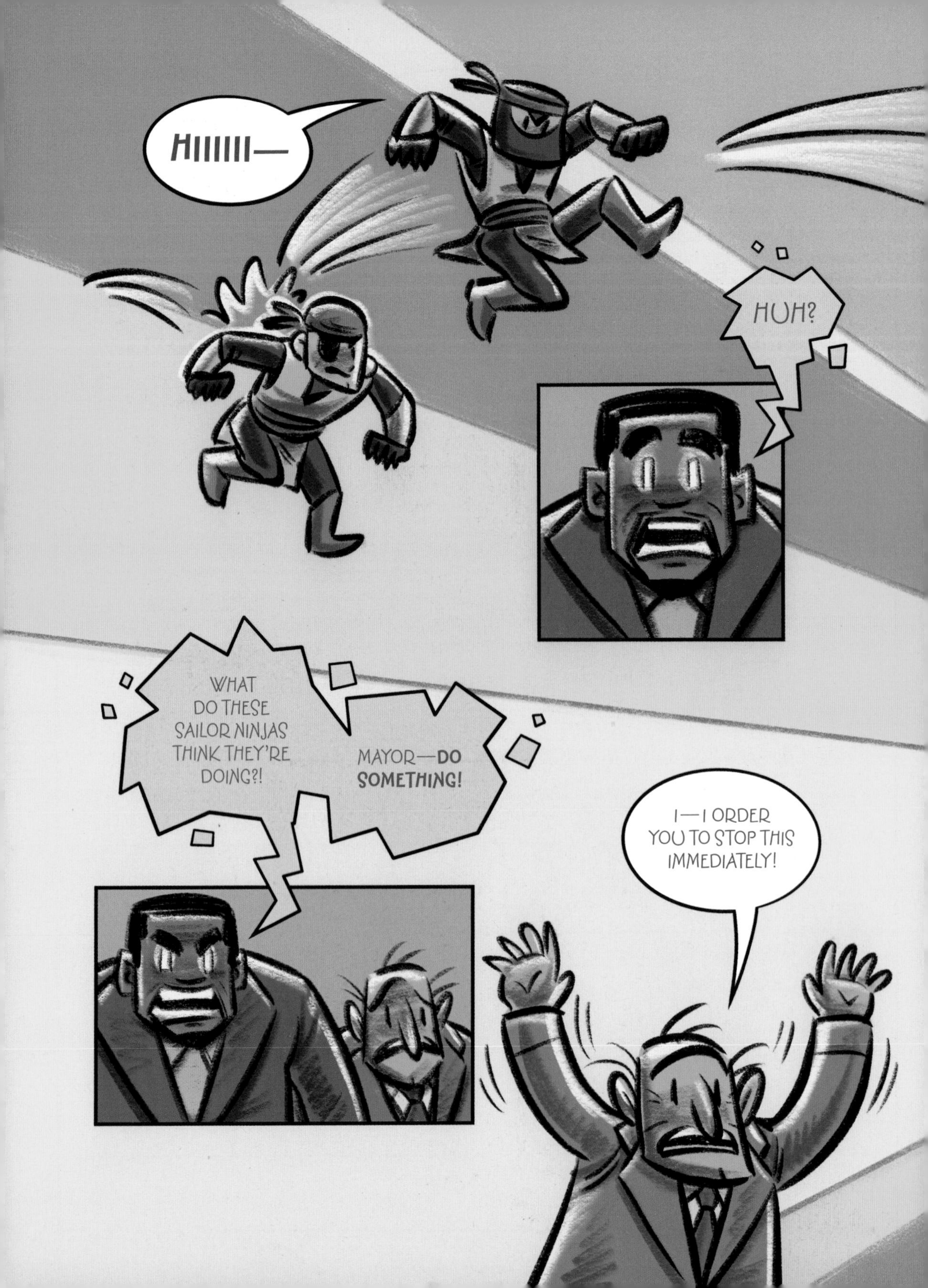
HIIIIII—
HUH?
WHAT DO THESE SAILOR NINJAS THINK THEY'RE DOING?!
MAYOR—**DO SOMETHING!**
I—I ORDER YOU TO STOP THIS IMMEDIATELY!

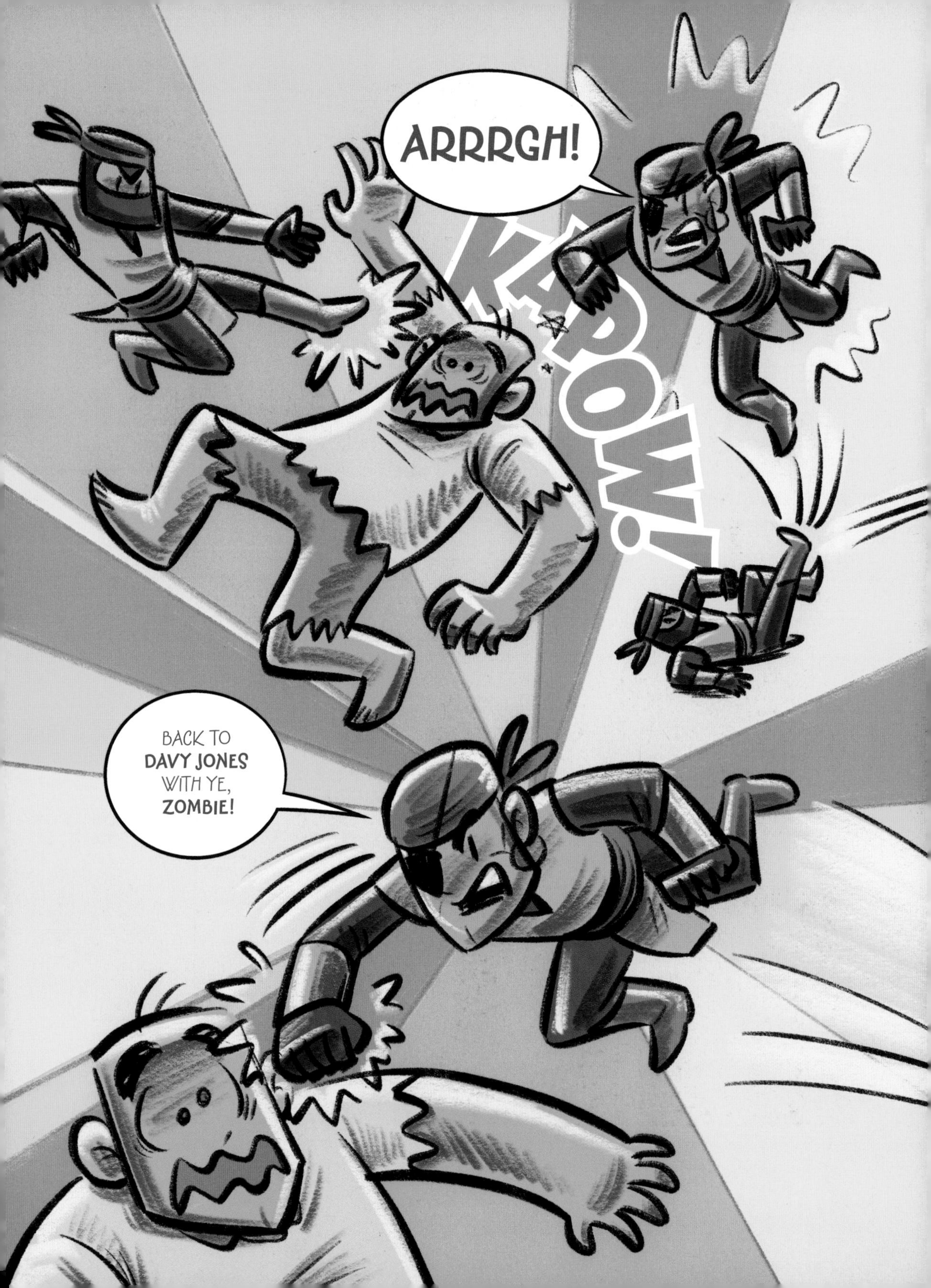
ARRRGH!
KAPOW!
BACK TO DAVY JONES WITH YE, ZOMBIE!

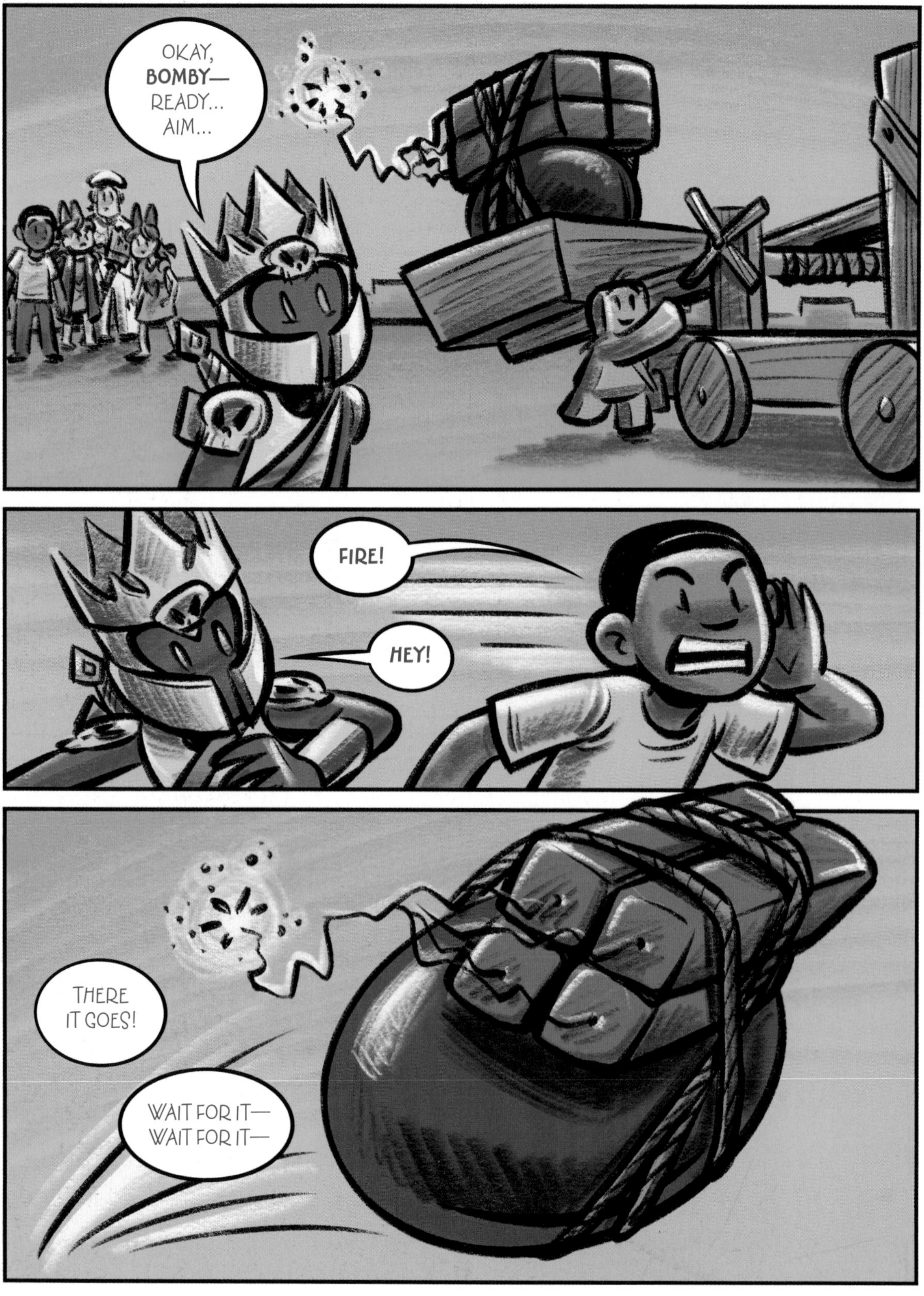
OKAY, **BOMBY—** READY... AIM...
FIRE!
HEY!
THERE IT GOES!
WAIT FOR IT— WAIT FOR IT—

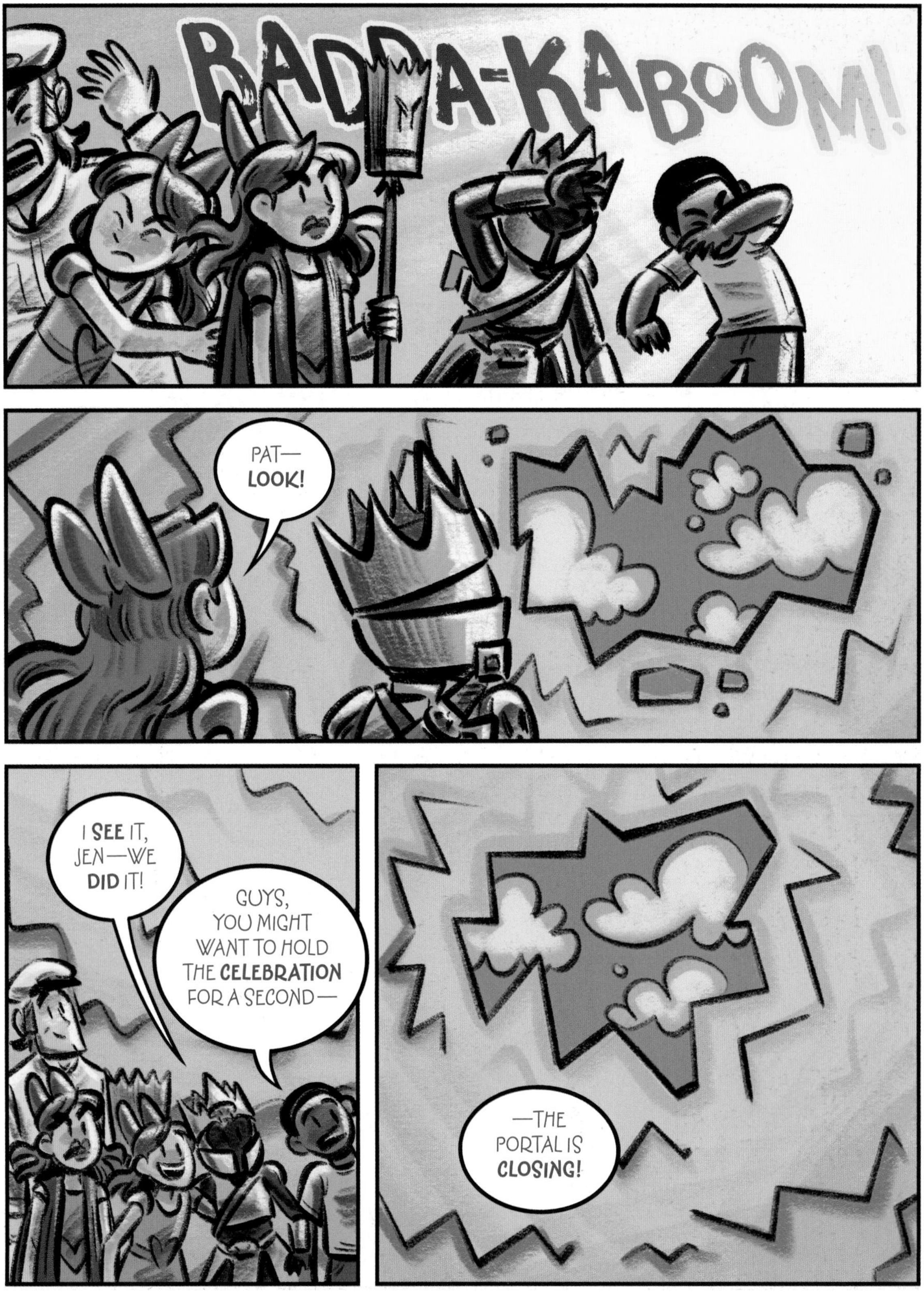
BADDA-KABOOM!
PAT— **LOOK!**
I **SEE** IT, JEN—WE **DID** IT!
GUYS, YOU MIGHT WANT TO HOLD THE **CELEBRATION** FOR A SECOND—
—THE PORTAL IS **CLOSING!**

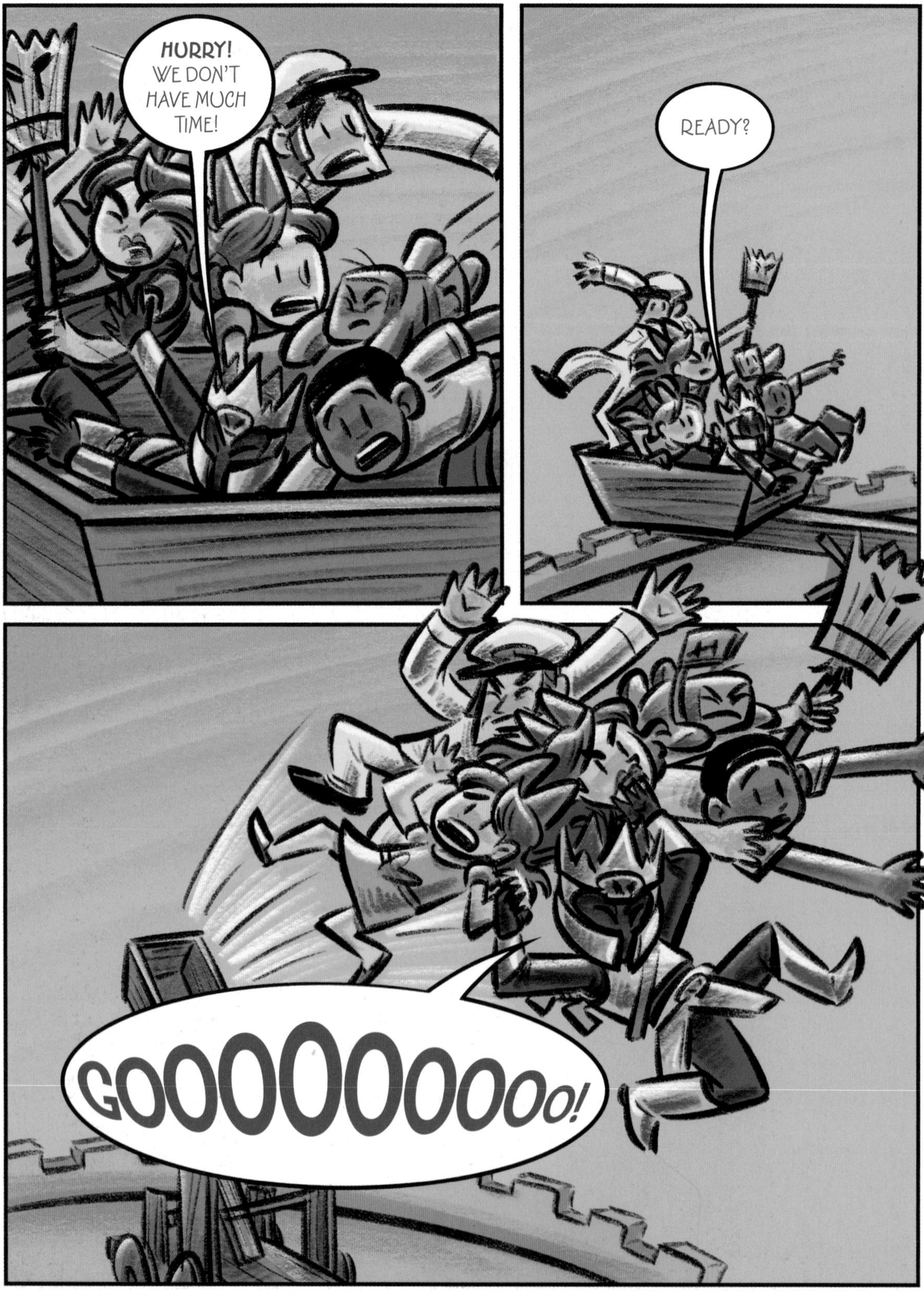
HURRY! WE DON'T HAVE MUCH TIME!
READY?
GOOOOOOOOOo!

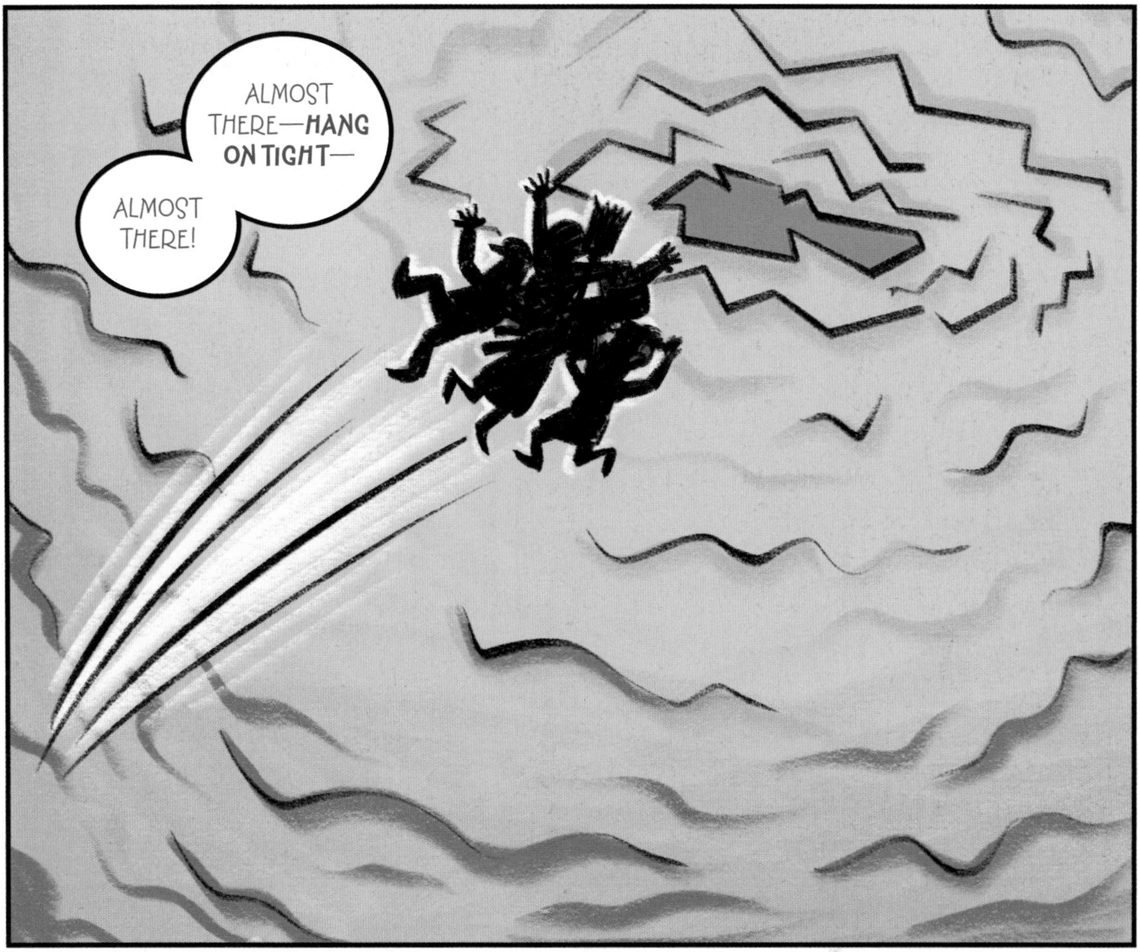
ALMOST THERE—HANG ON TIGHT—
ALMOST THERE!

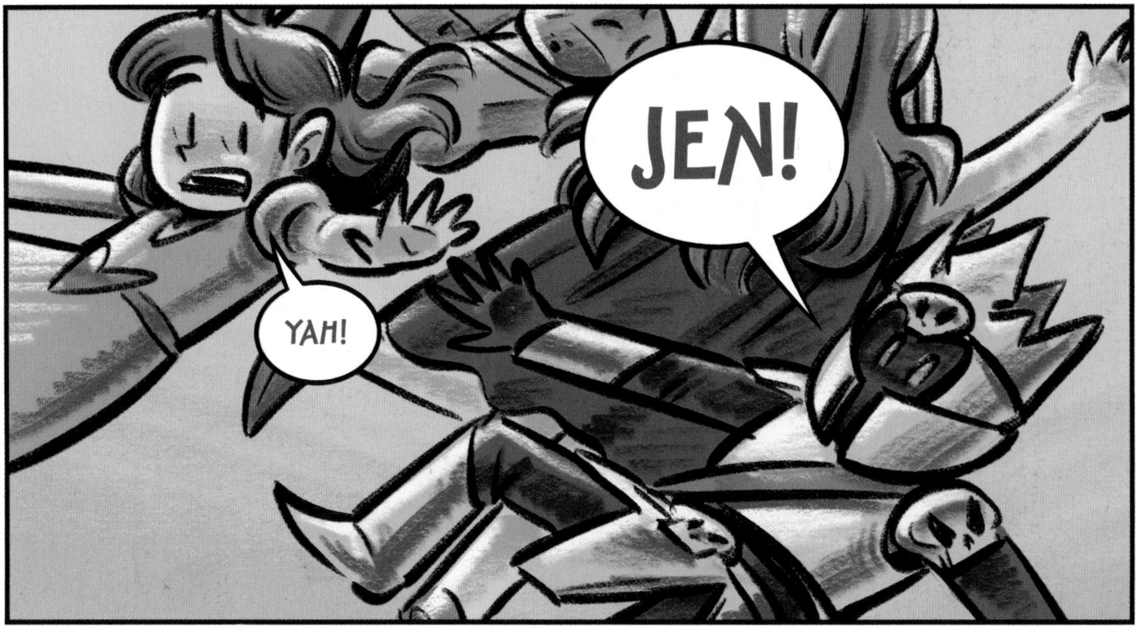
JEN!
YAH!

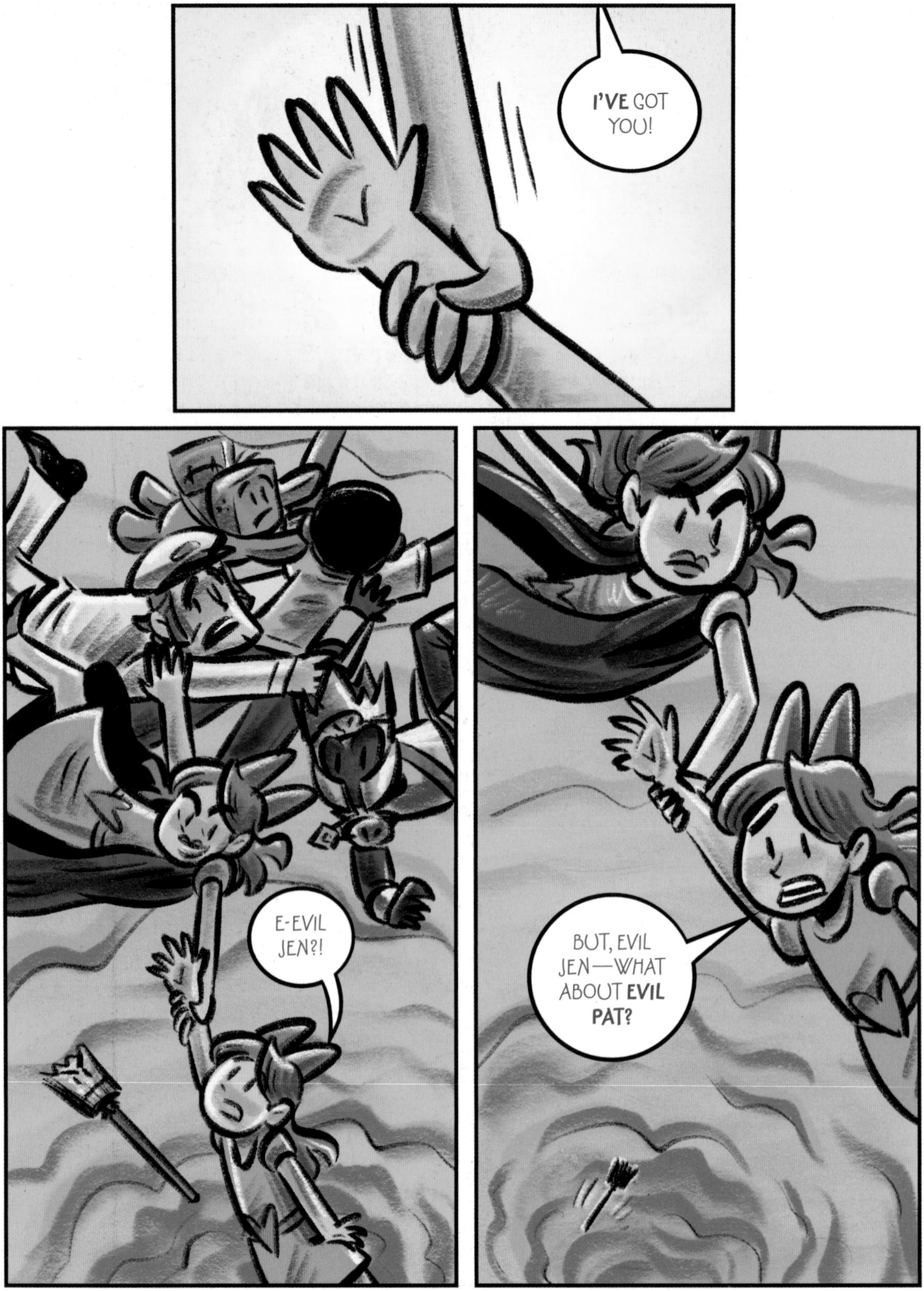
I'VE GOT YOU!
E-EVIL JEN?!
BUT, EVIL JEN—WHAT ABOUT EVIL PAT?

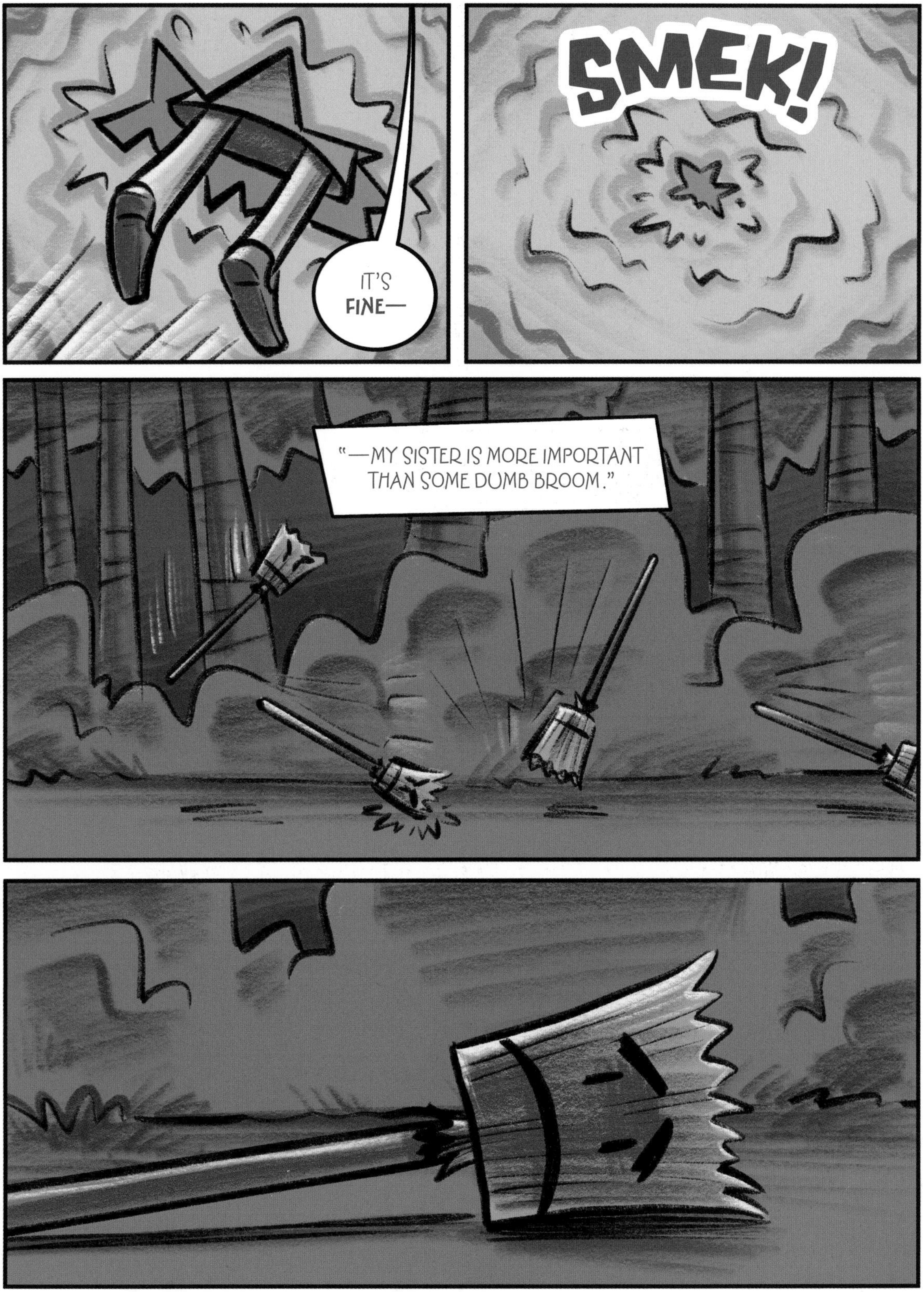
IT'S FINE—
SMEK!
"—MY SISTER IS MORE IMPORTANT THAN SOME DUMB BROOM."

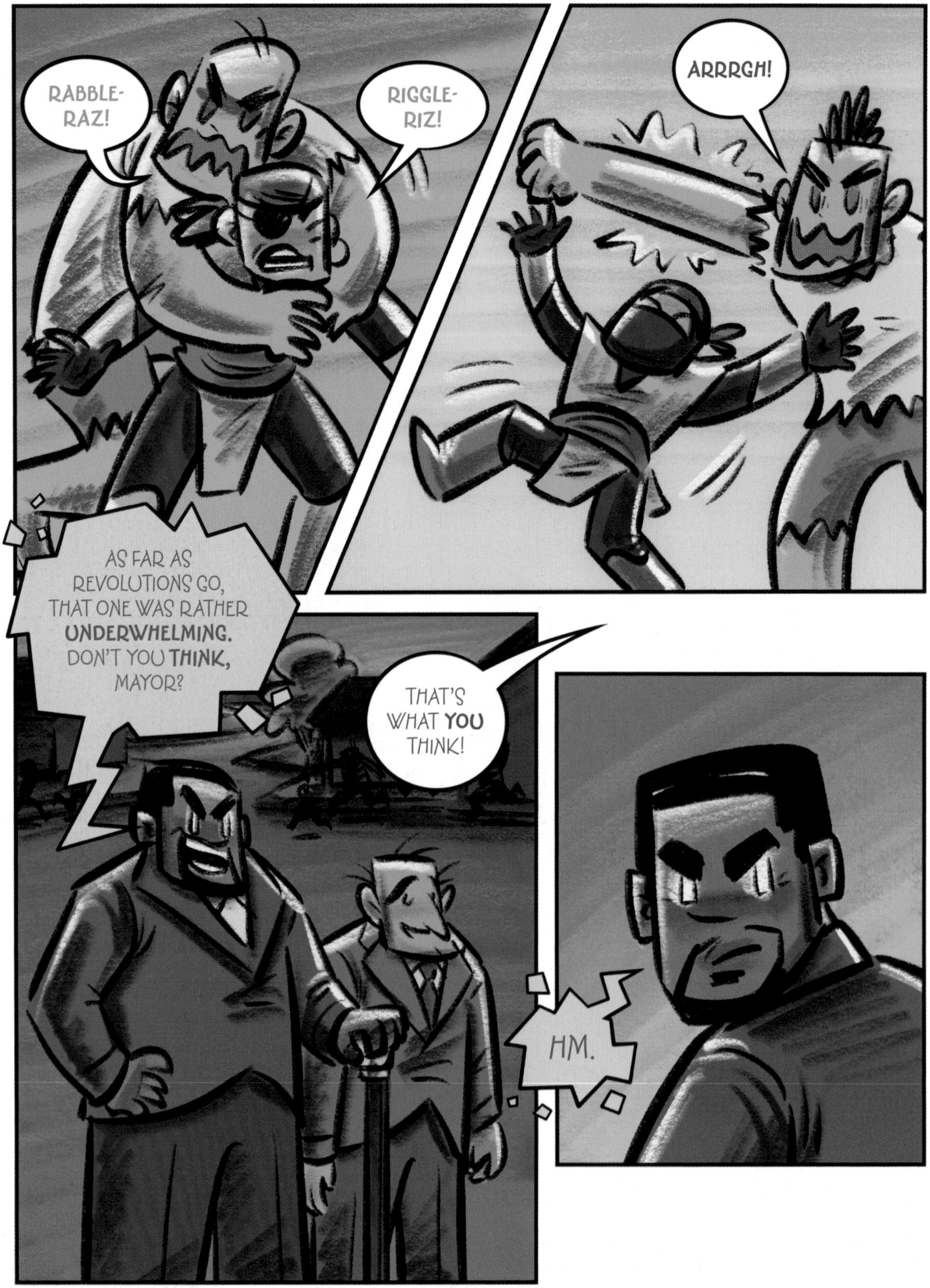
RABBLE-RAZ!
RIGGLE-RIZ!
ARRRGH!
AS FAR AS REVOLUTIONS GO, THAT ONE WAS RATHER **UNDERWHELMING.** DON'T YOU **THINK,** MAYOR?
THAT'S WHAT **YOU** THINK!
HM.

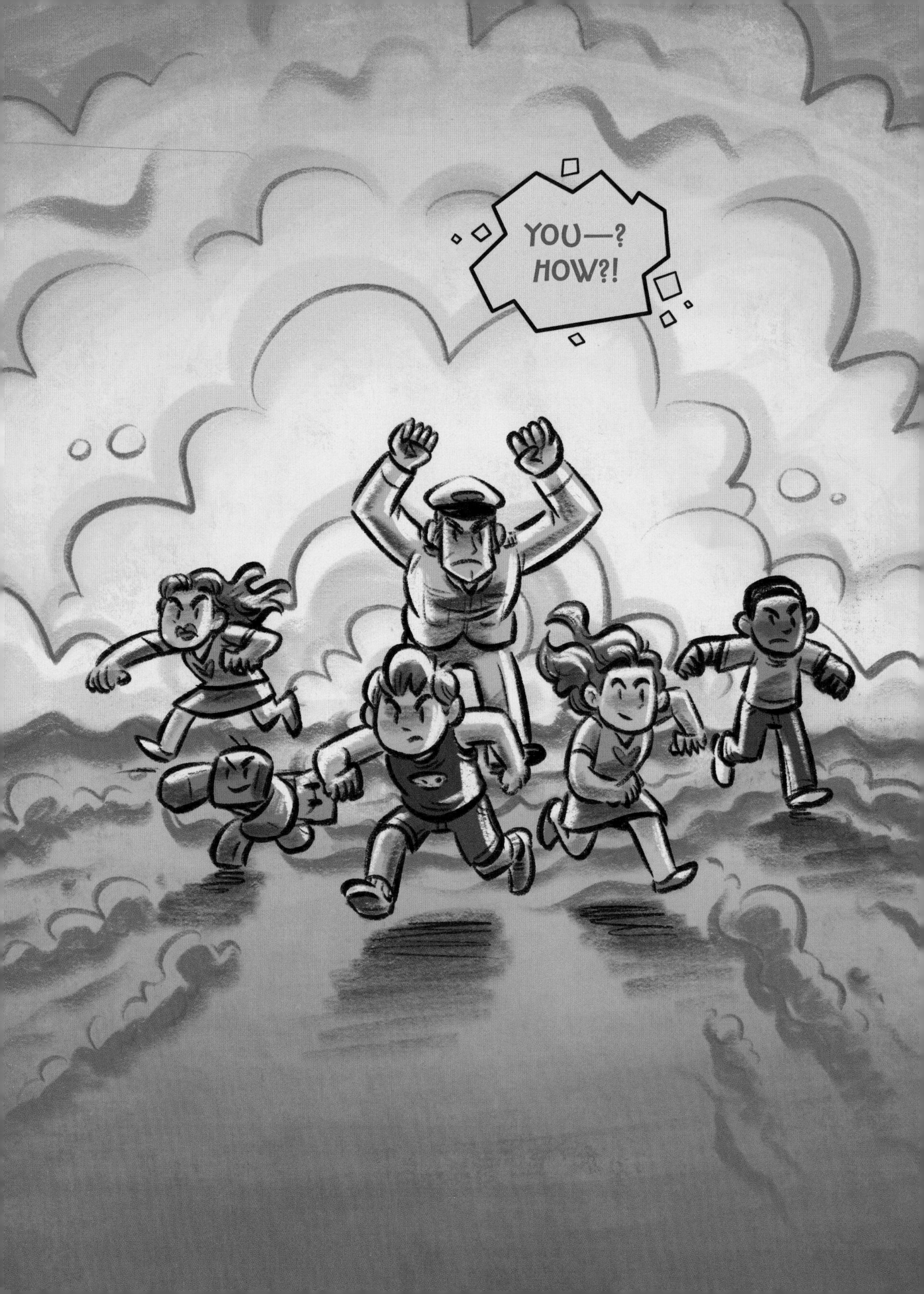
YOU—? HOW?!

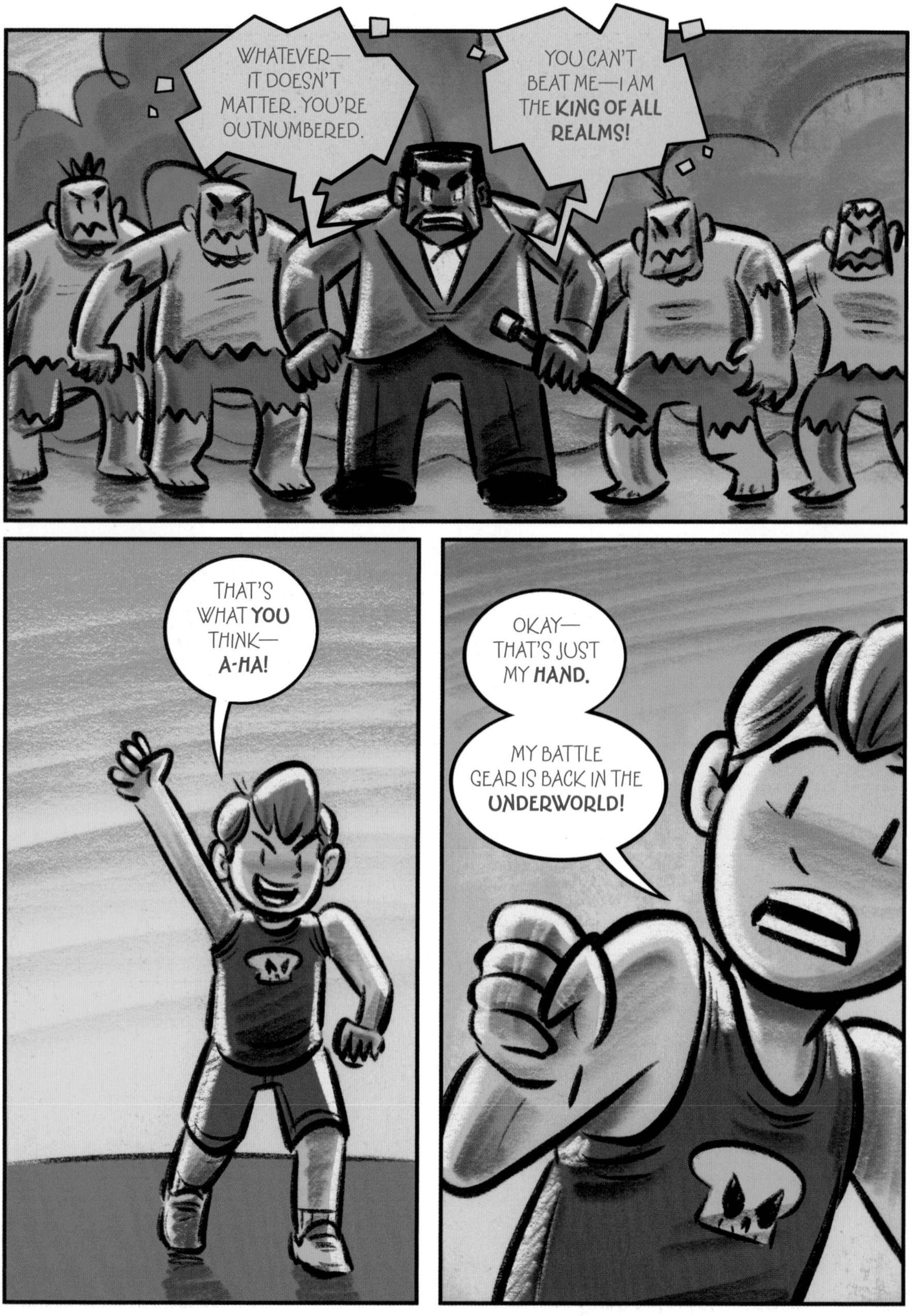
WHATEVER—
IT DOESN'T
MATTER. YOU'RE
OUTNUMBERED.
YOU CAN'T
BEAT ME—I AM
THE **KING OF ALL**
REALMS!
THAT'S
WHAT **YOU**
THINK—
A-HA!
OKAY—
THAT'S JUST
MY **HAND.**
MY BATTLE
GEAR IS BACK IN THE
UNDERWORLD!

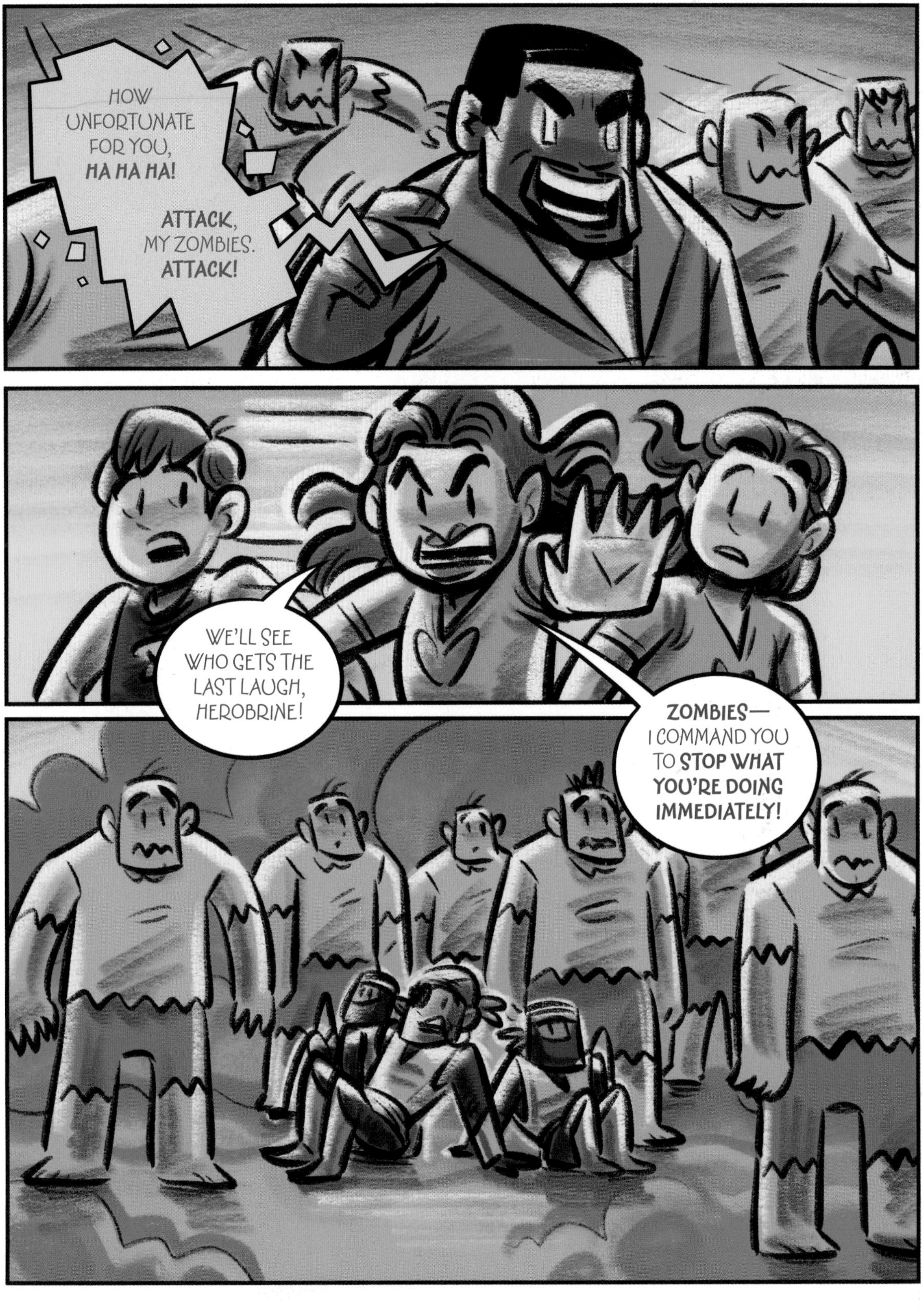
HOW UNFORTUNATE FOR YOU, **HA HA HA!**
ATTACK, MY ZOMBIES. **ATTACK!**
WE'LL SEE WHO GETS THE LAST LAUGH, HEROBRINE!
ZOMBIES— I COMMAND YOU TO **STOP WHAT YOU'RE DOING IMMEDIATELY!**

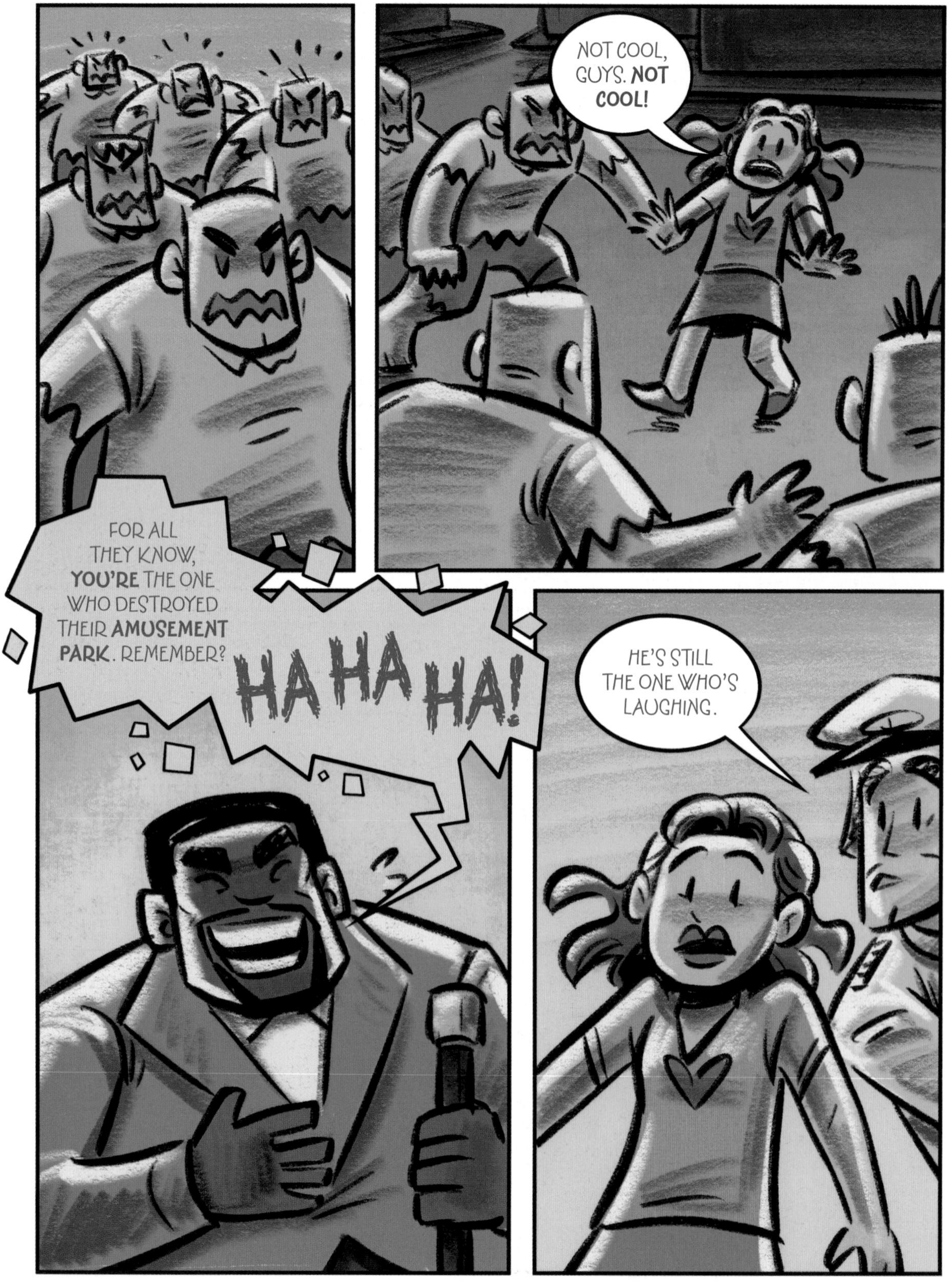
NOT COOL, GUYS. NOT COOL!
FOR ALL THEY KNOW, YOU'RE THE ONE WHO DESTROYED THEIR AMUSEMENT PARK. REMEMBER?
HA HA HA!
HE'S STILL THE ONE WHO'S LAUGHING.

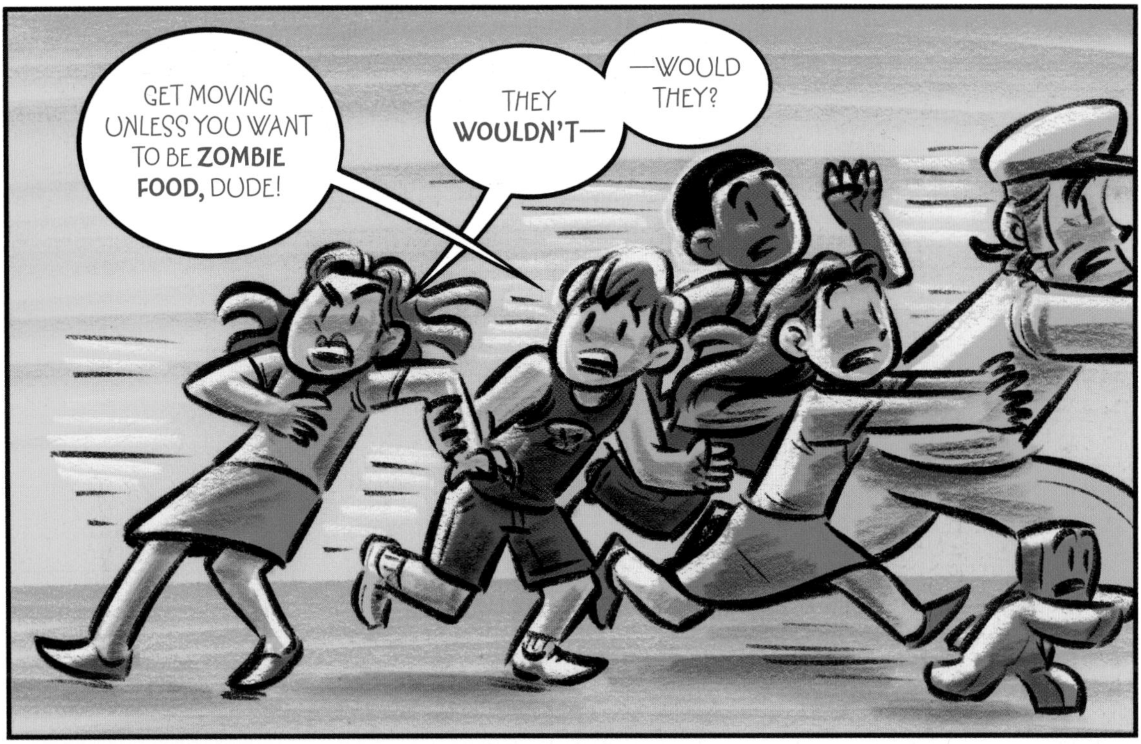
GET MOVING UNLESS YOU WANT TO BE **ZOMBIE FOOD,** DUDE!
THEY **WOULDN'T—**
—WOULD THEY?

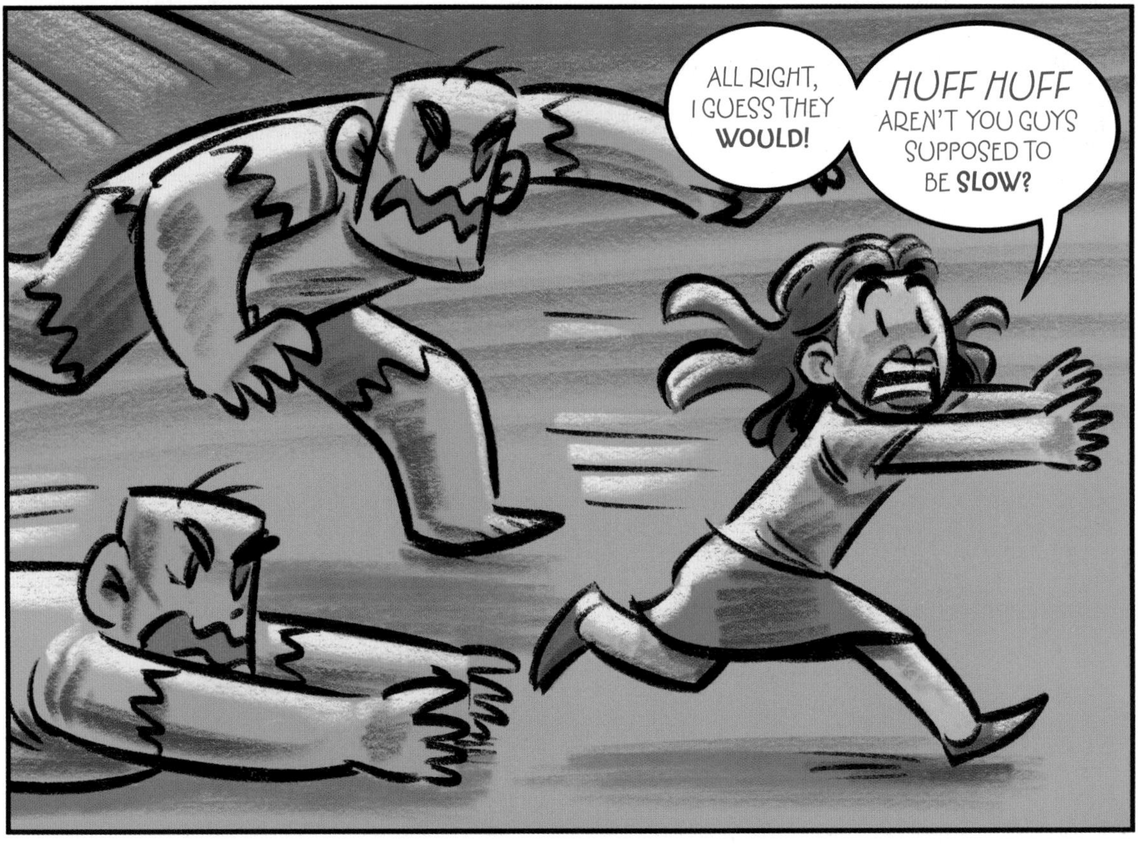
ALL RIGHT, I GUESS THEY **WOULD!**
HUFF HUFF AREN'T YOU GUYS SUPPOSED TO BE **SLOW?**

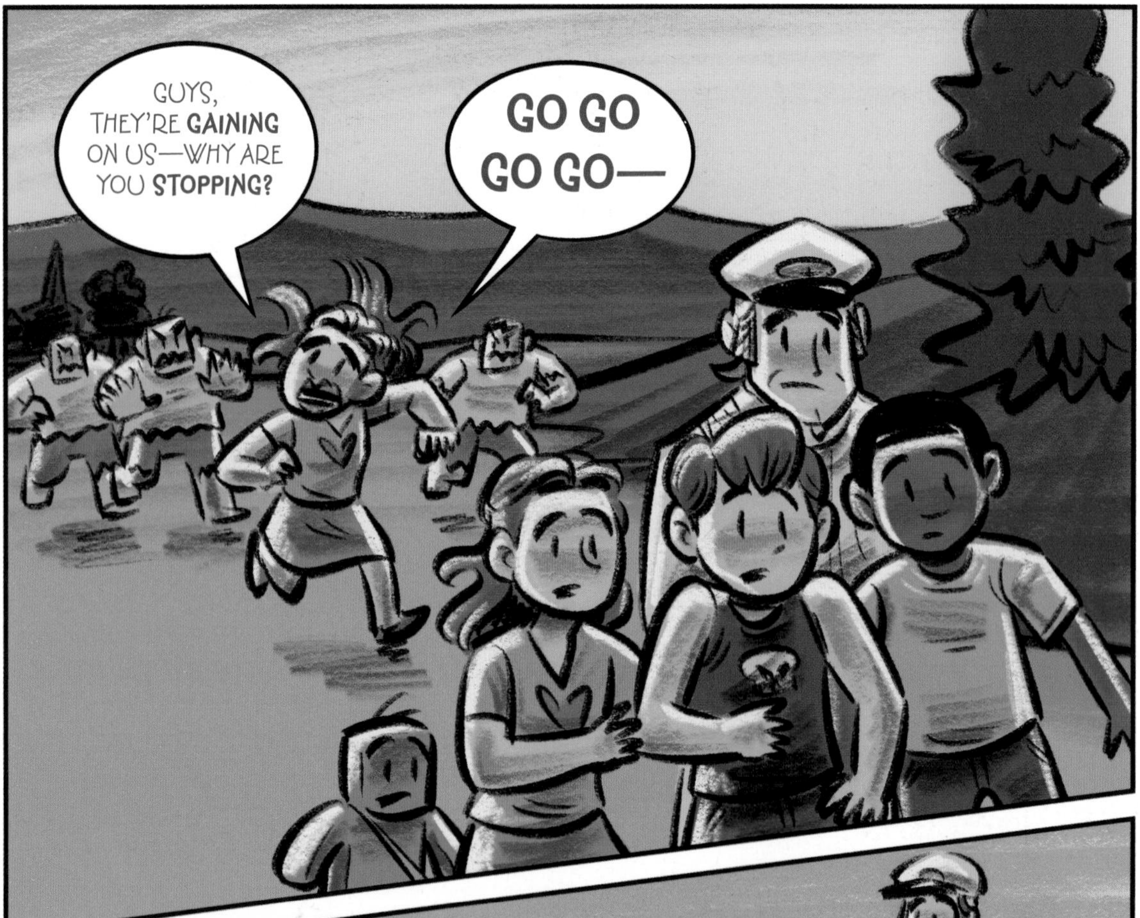
GUYS, THEY'RE **GAINING** ON US—WHY ARE YOU **STOPPING?**
GO GO GO GO—

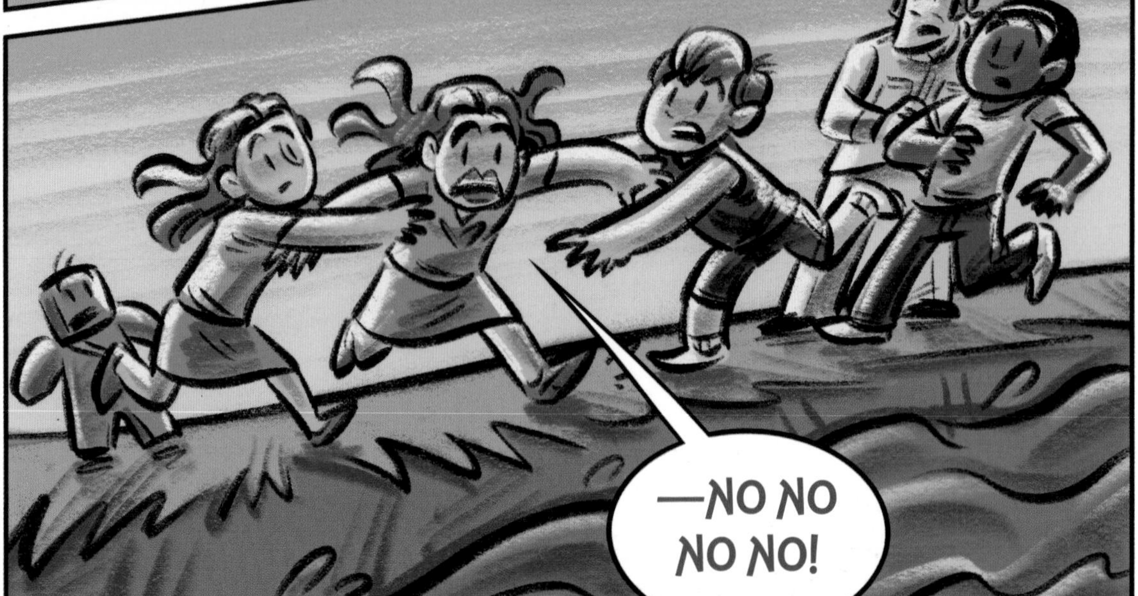
—NO NO NO NO!

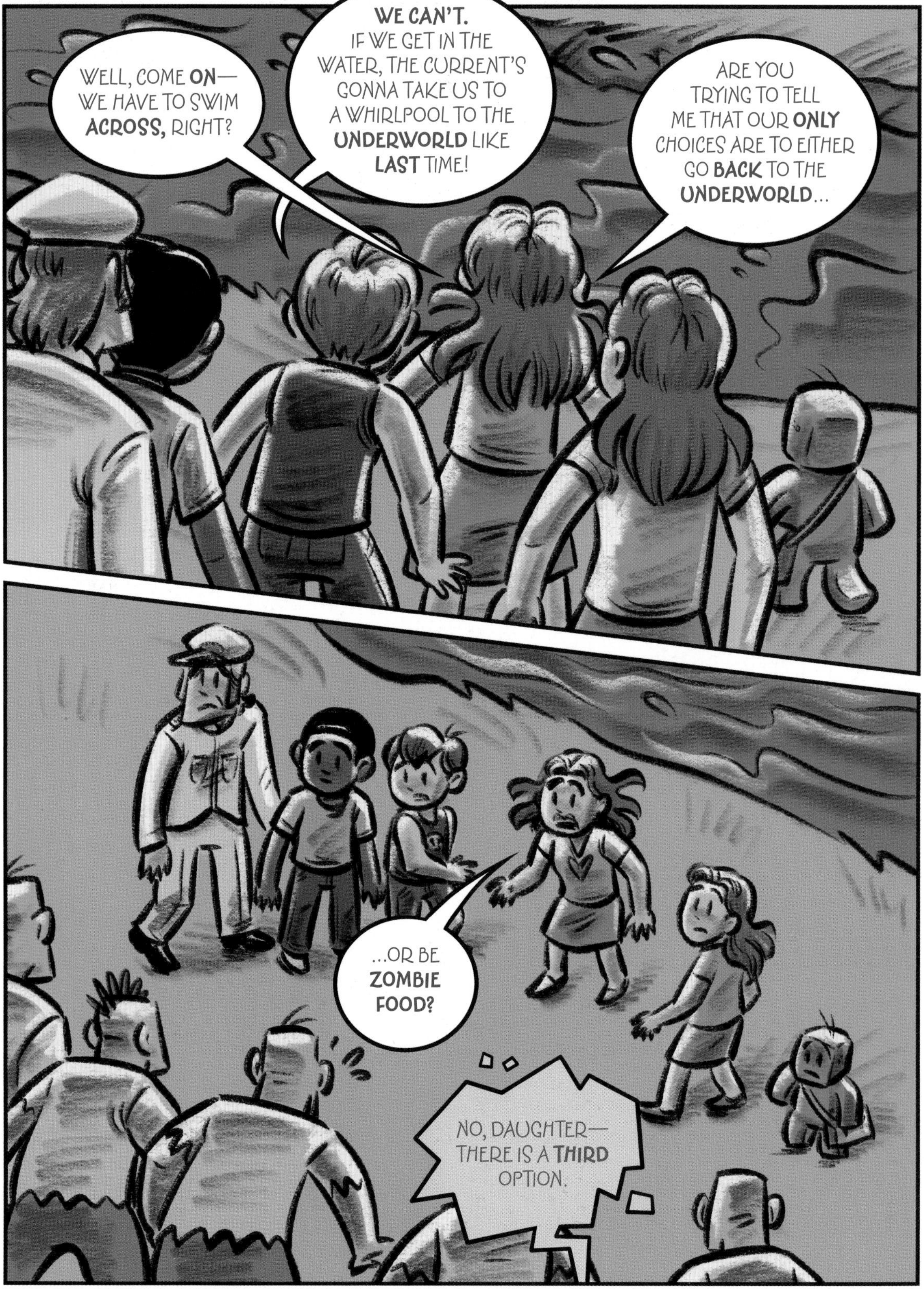
WELL, COME **ON**— WE HAVE TO SWIM **ACROSS,** RIGHT?
WE CAN'T. IF WE GET IN THE WATER, THE CURRENT'S GONNA TAKE US TO A WHIRLPOOL TO THE **UNDERWORLD** LIKE **LAST** TIME!
ARE YOU TRYING TO TELL ME THAT OUR **ONLY** CHOICES ARE TO EITHER GO **BACK** TO THE **UNDERWORLD**...
...OR BE **ZOMBIE FOOD?**
NO, DAUGHTER— THERE IS A **THIRD** OPTION.

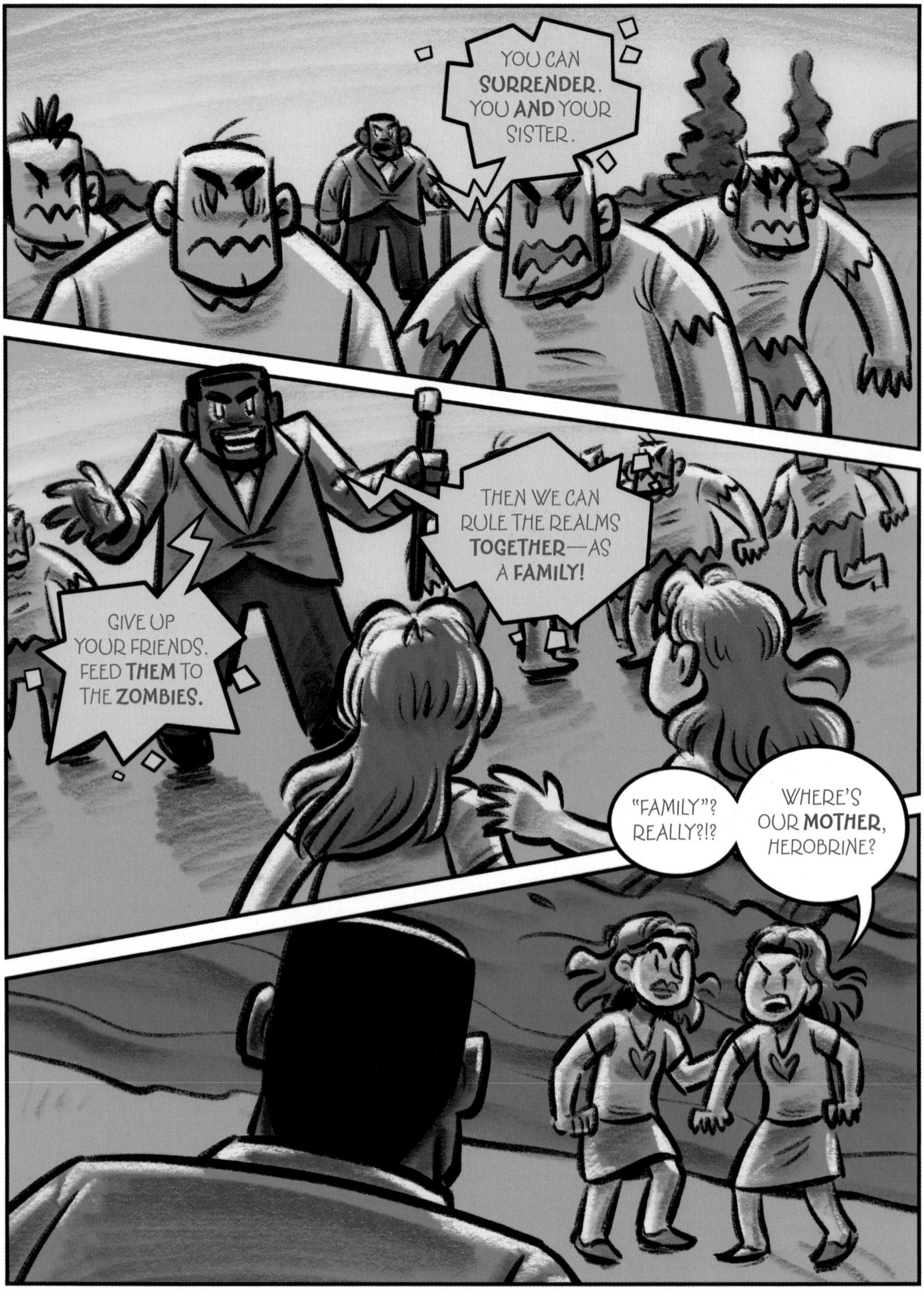
YOU CAN SURRENDER. YOU AND YOUR SISTER.
THEN WE CAN RULE THE REALMS TOGETHER—AS A FAMILY!
GIVE UP YOUR FRIENDS. FEED THEM TO THE ZOMBIES.
"FAMILY"? REALLY?!?
WHERE'S OUR MOTHER, HEROBRINE?

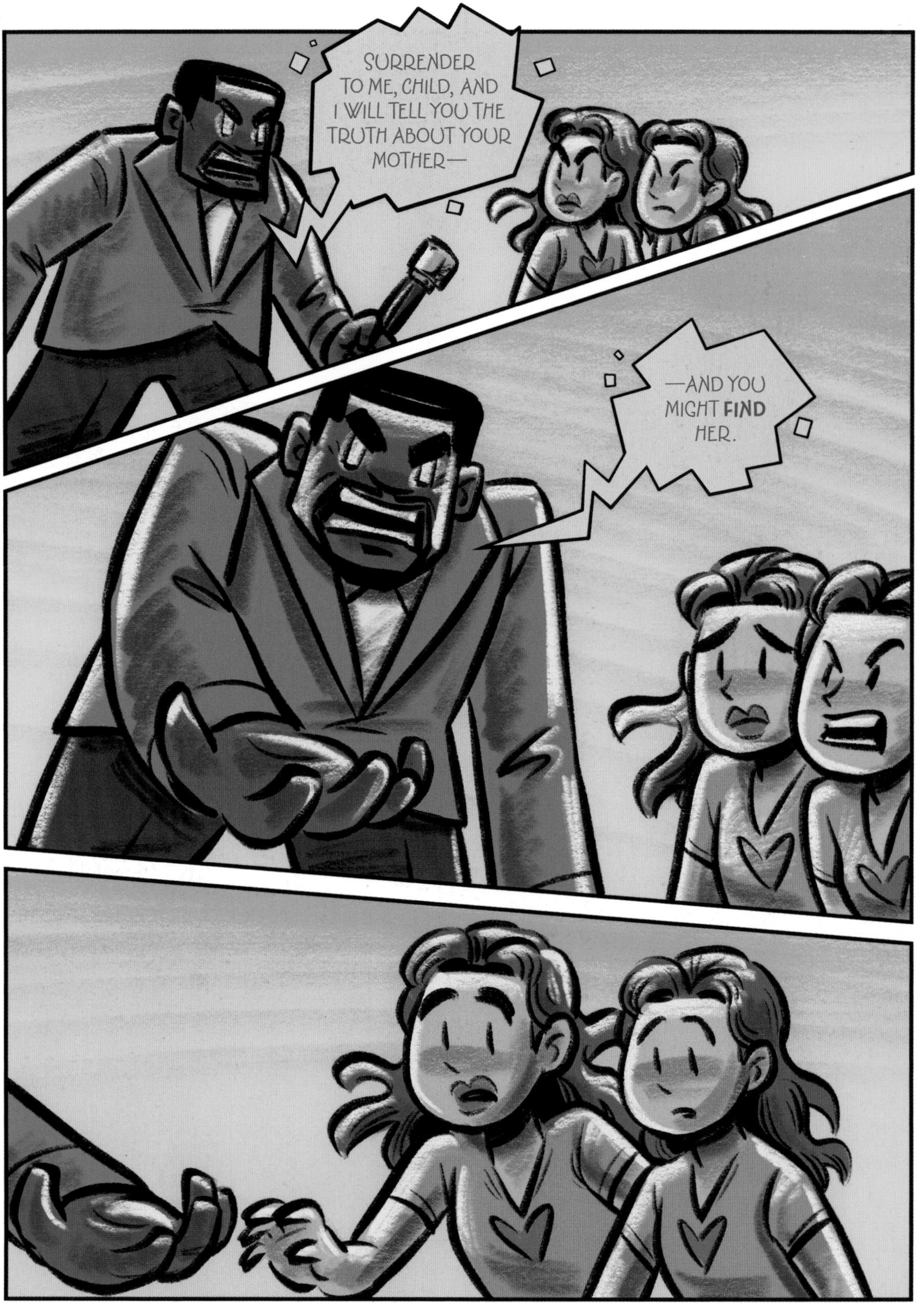
SURRENDER TO ME, CHILD, AND I WILL TELL YOU THE TRUTH ABOUT YOUR MOTHER—
—AND YOU MIGHT **FIND** HER.

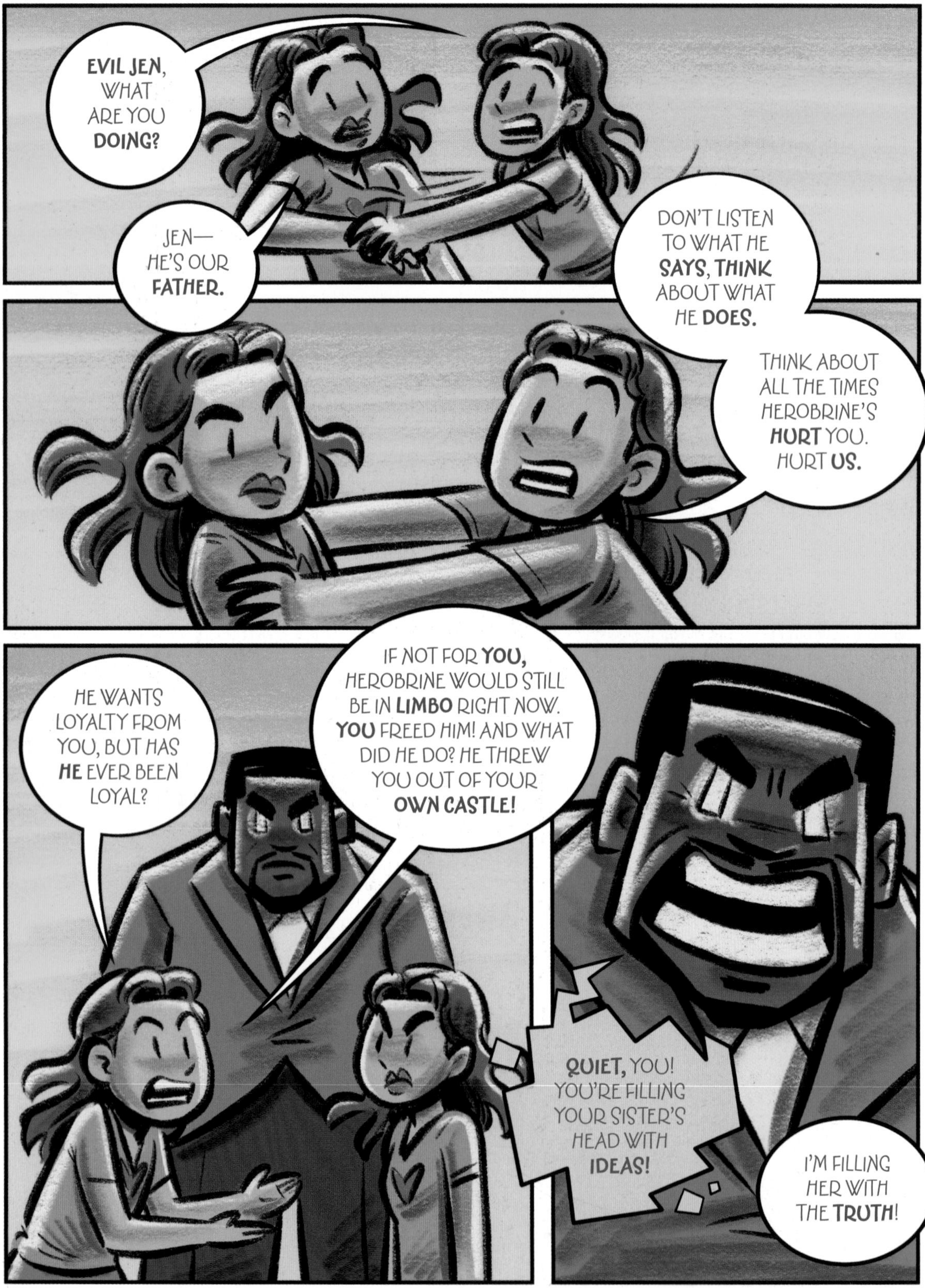
EVIL JEN, WHAT ARE YOU DOING?
JEN— HE'S OUR FATHER.
DON'T LISTEN TO WHAT HE SAYS, THINK ABOUT WHAT HE DOES.
THINK ABOUT ALL THE TIMES HEROBRINE'S HURT YOU. HURT US.
HE WANTS LOYALTY FROM YOU, BUT HAS HE EVER BEEN LOYAL?
IF NOT FOR YOU, HEROBRINE WOULD STILL BE IN LIMBO RIGHT NOW. YOU FREED HIM! AND WHAT DID HE DO? HE THREW YOU OUT OF YOUR OWN CASTLE!
QUIET, YOU! YOU'RE FILLING YOUR SISTER'S HEAD WITH IDEAS!
I'M FILLING HER WITH THE TRUTH!

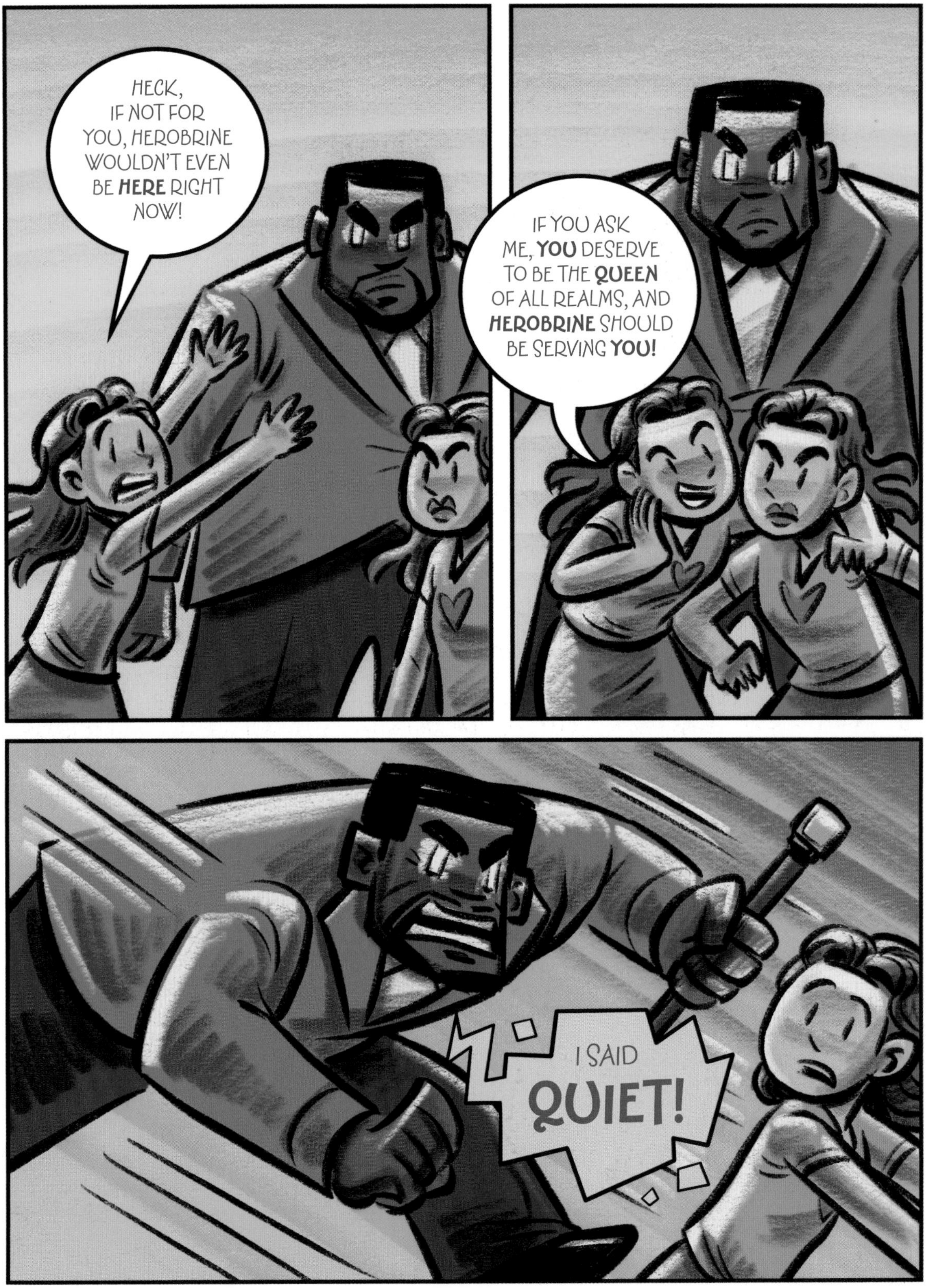
HECK, IF NOT FOR YOU, HEROBRINE WOULDN'T EVEN BE **HERE** RIGHT NOW!
IF YOU ASK ME, **YOU** DESERVE TO BE THE **QUEEN** OF ALL REALMS, AND **HEROBRINE** SHOULD BE SERVING **YOU!**
I SAID **QUIET!**

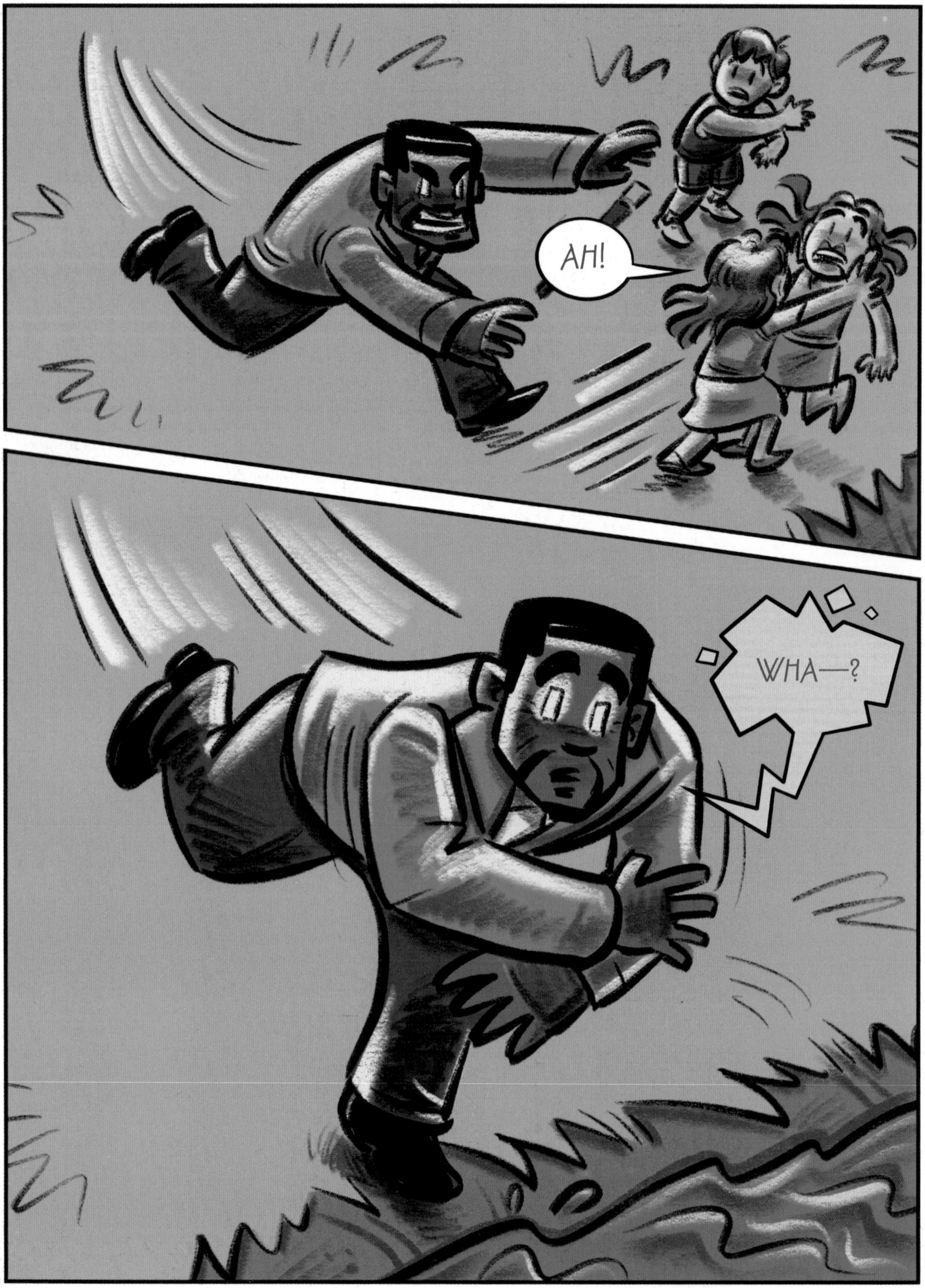
AH!
WHA—?

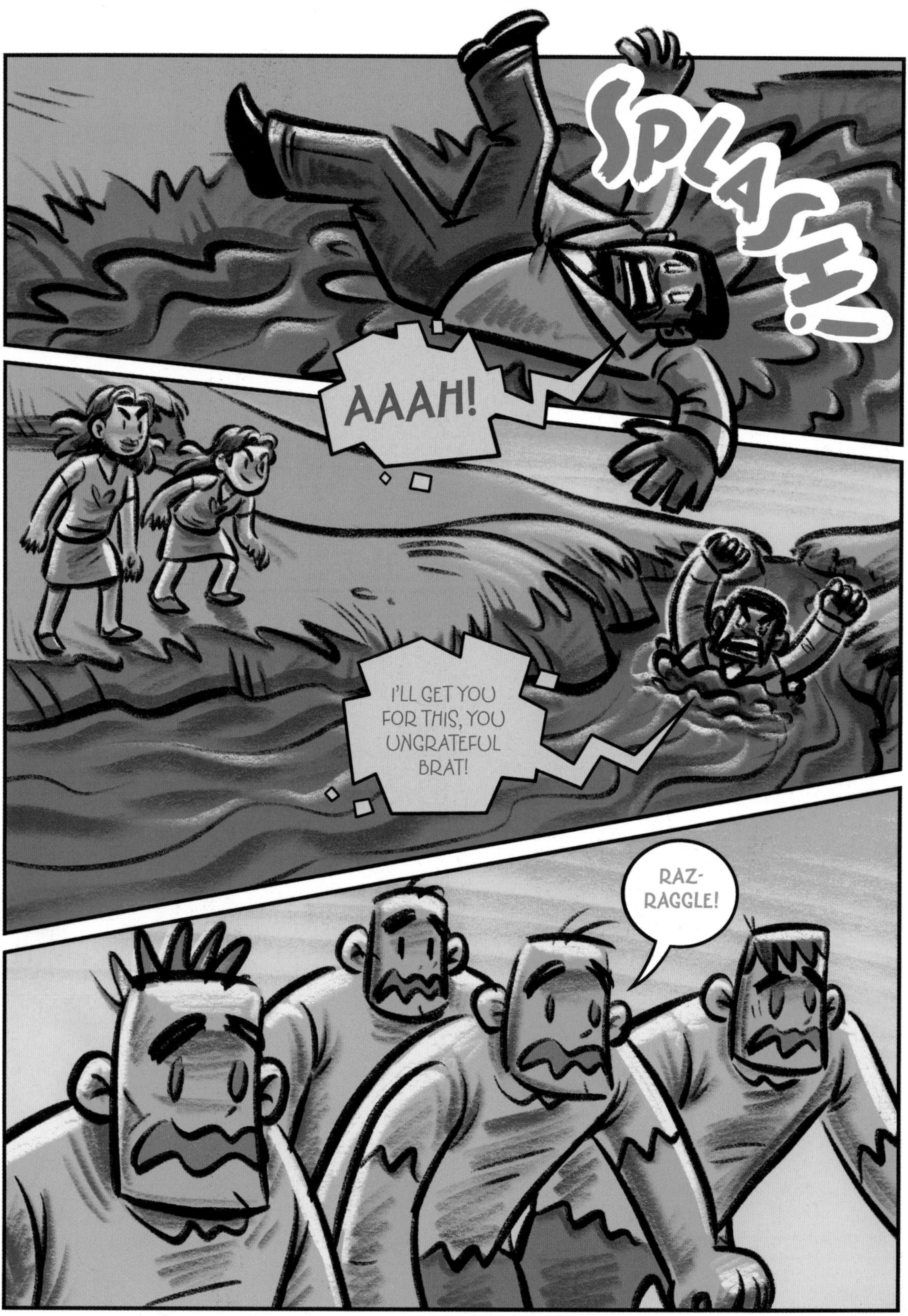
SPLASH!
AAAH!
I'LL GET YOU FOR THIS, YOU UNGRATEFUL BRAT!
RAZ-RAGGLE!

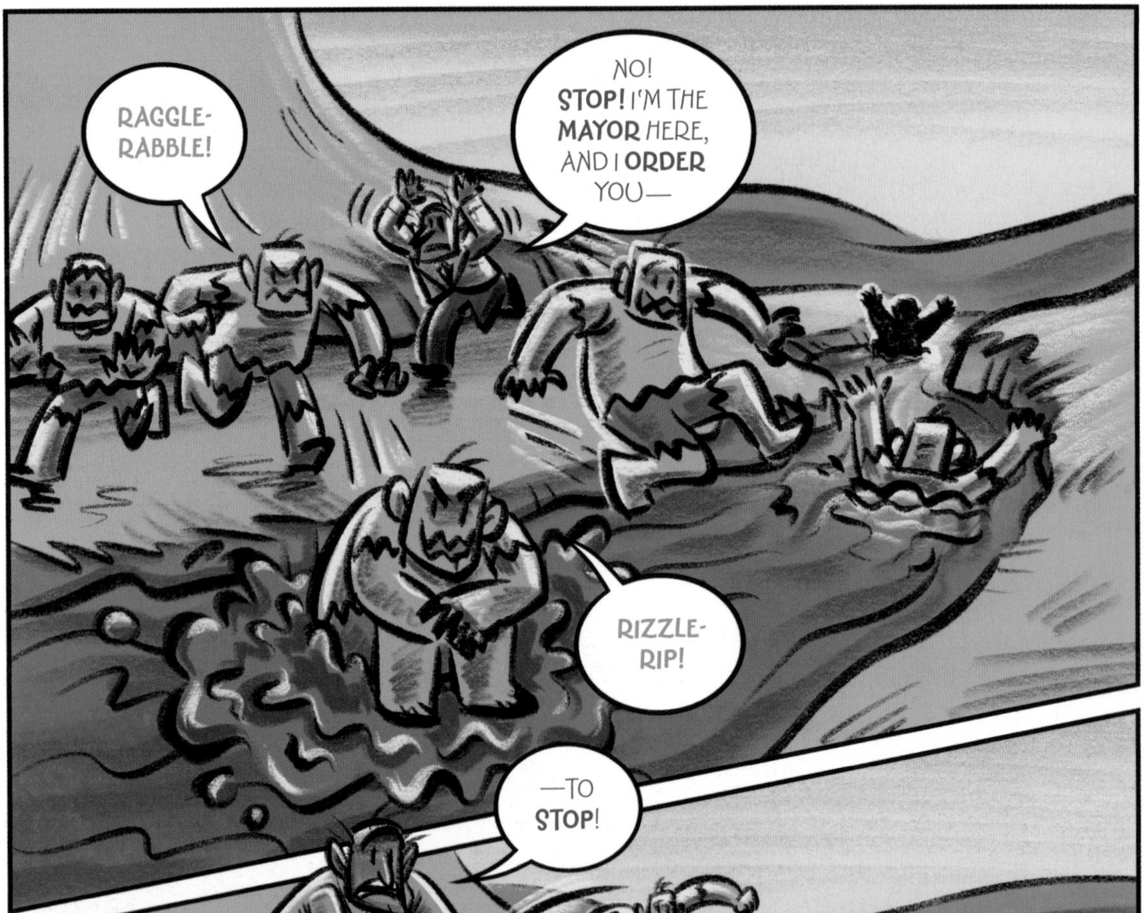
RAGGLE-RABBLE!
NO! STOP! I'M THE MAYOR HERE, AND I ORDER YOU—
RIZZLE-RIP!
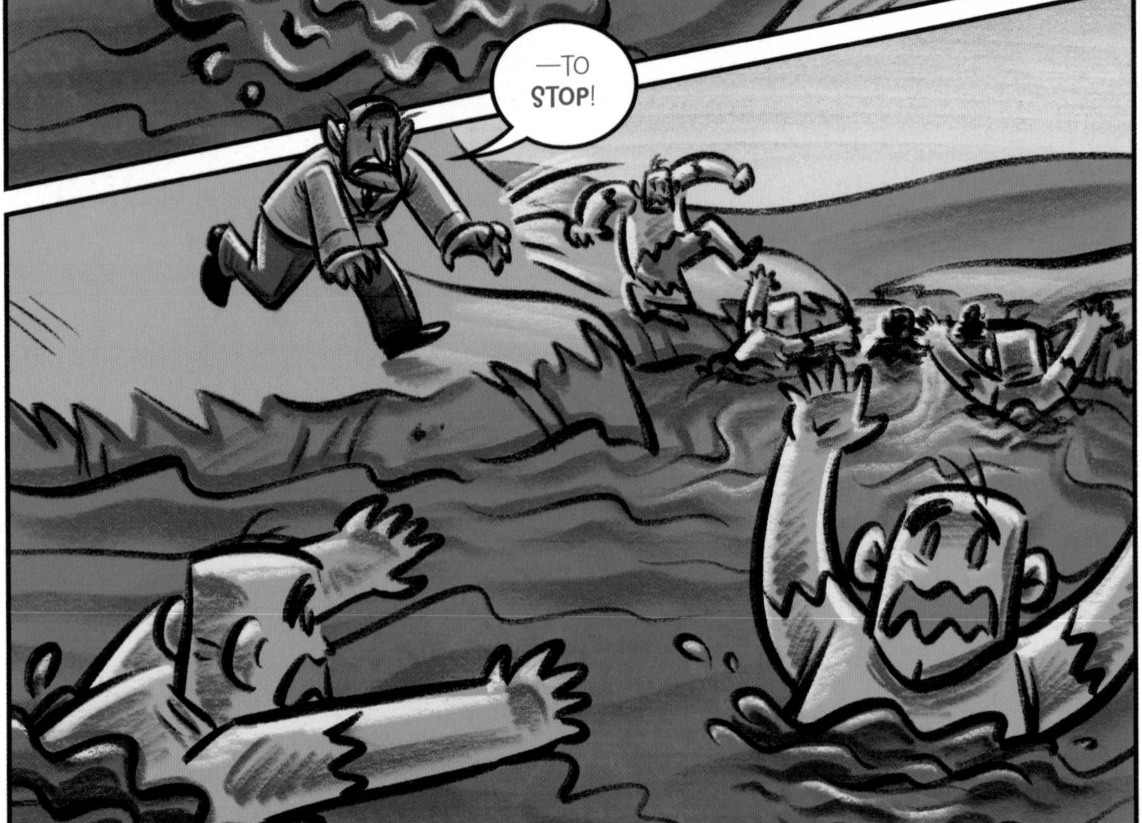
—TO STOP!

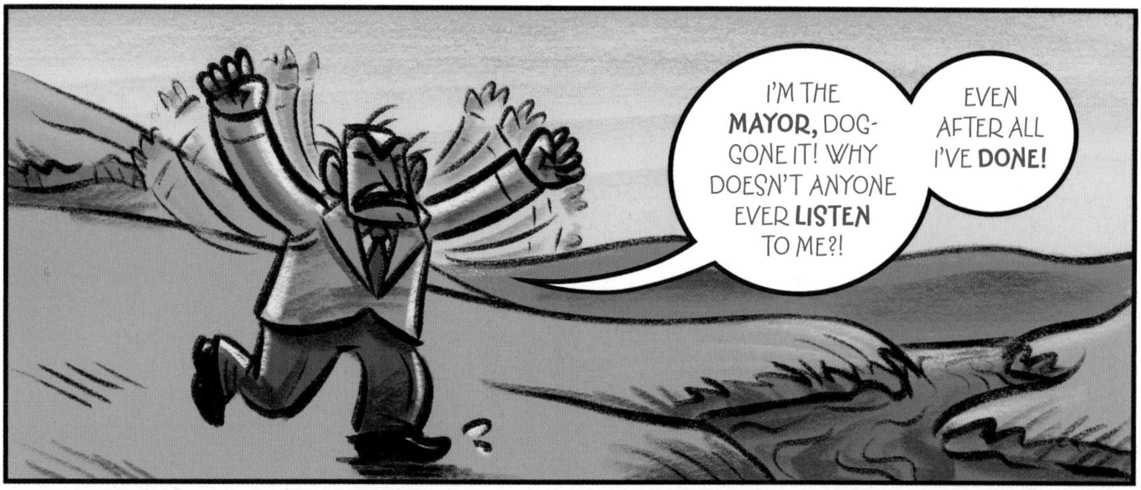
I'M THE **MAYOR,** DOG-GONE IT! WHY DOESN'T ANYONE EVER **LISTEN** TO ME?!
EVEN AFTER ALL I'VE **DONE!**

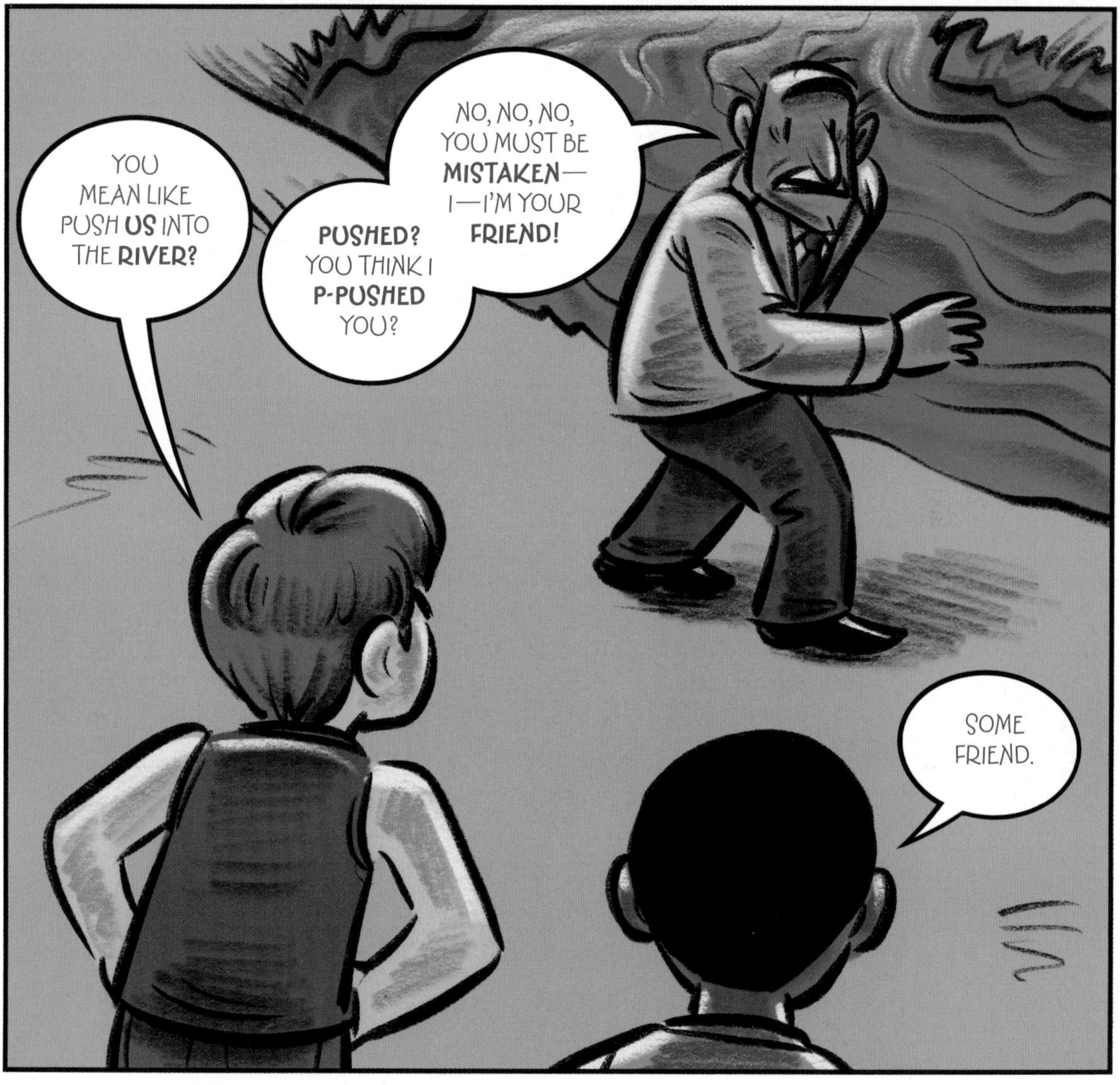
NO, NO, NO, YOU MUST BE **MISTAKEN**— I—I'M YOUR **FRIEND!**
YOU MEAN LIKE PUSH **US** INTO THE **RIVER?**
PUSHED? YOU THINK I **P-PUSHED** YOU?
SOME FRIEND.

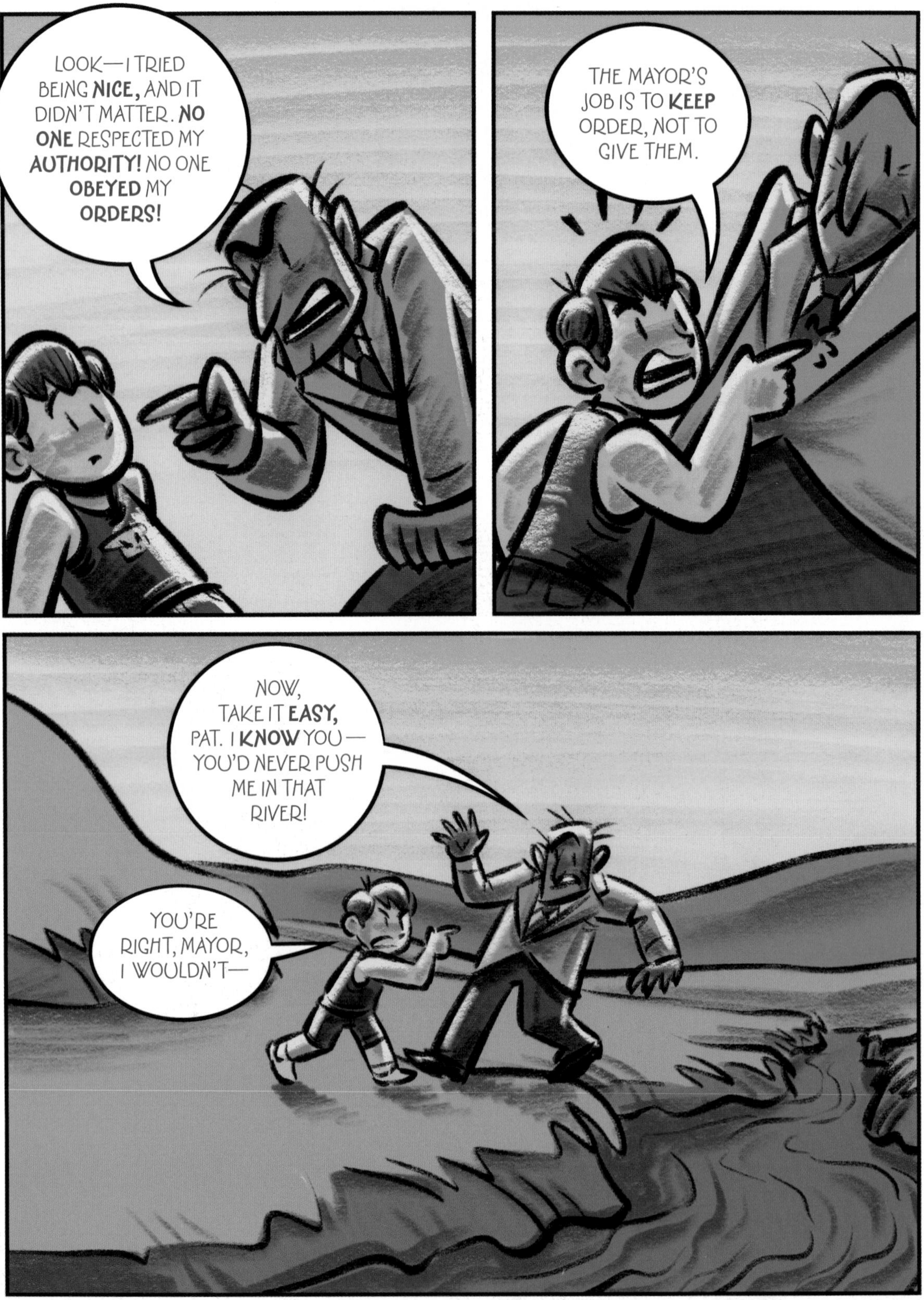
LOOK—I TRIED BEING NICE, AND IT DIDN'T MATTER. NO ONE RESPECTED MY AUTHORITY! NO ONE OBEYED MY ORDERS!
THE MAYOR'S JOB IS TO KEEP ORDER, NOT TO GIVE THEM.
NOW, TAKE IT EASY, PAT. I KNOW YOU— YOU'D NEVER PUSH ME IN THAT RIVER!
YOU'RE RIGHT, MAYOR, I WOULDN'T—

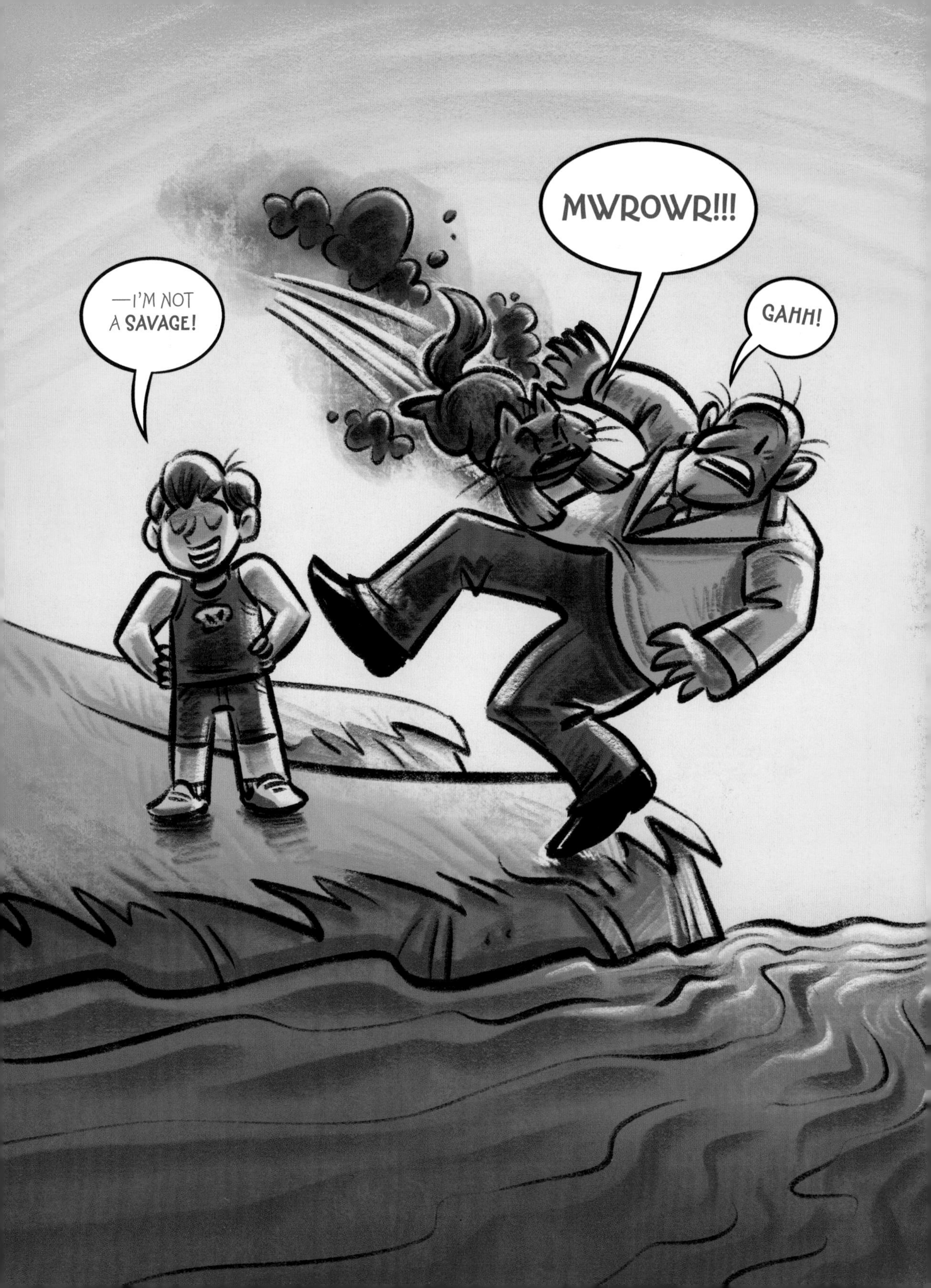
—I'M NOT A SAVAGE!
MWROWR!!!
GAHH!

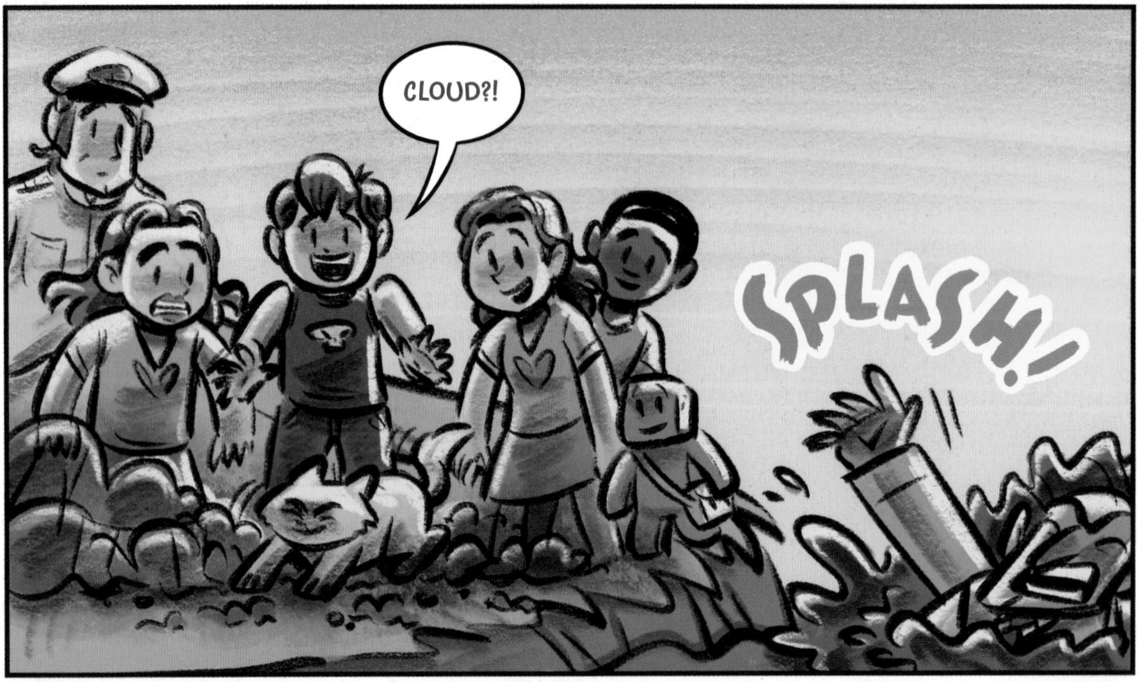
CLOUD?!
SPLASH!

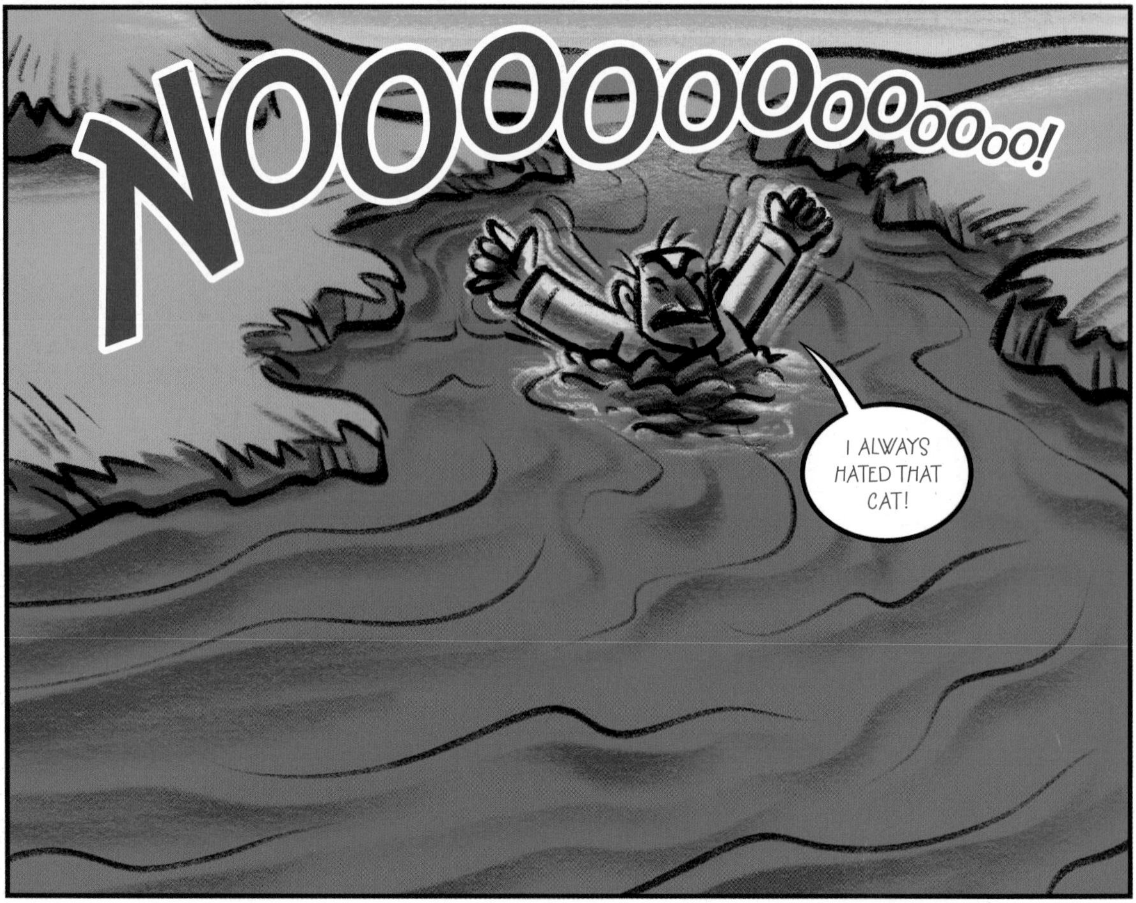
NOOOOOOOOoooo!
I ALWAYS HATED THAT CAT!

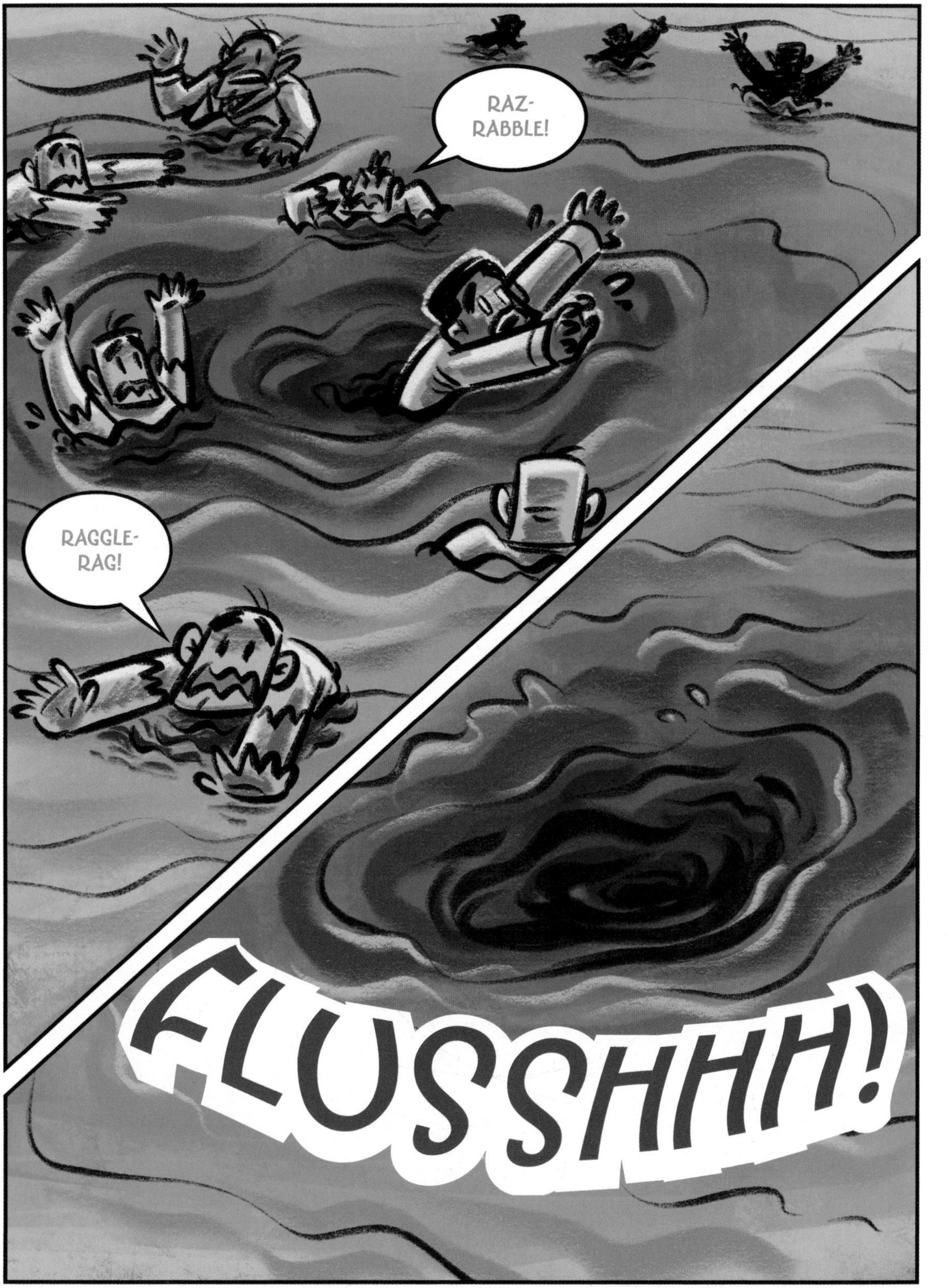
RAZ-RABBLE!
RAGGLE-RAG!
FLUSSHHH!

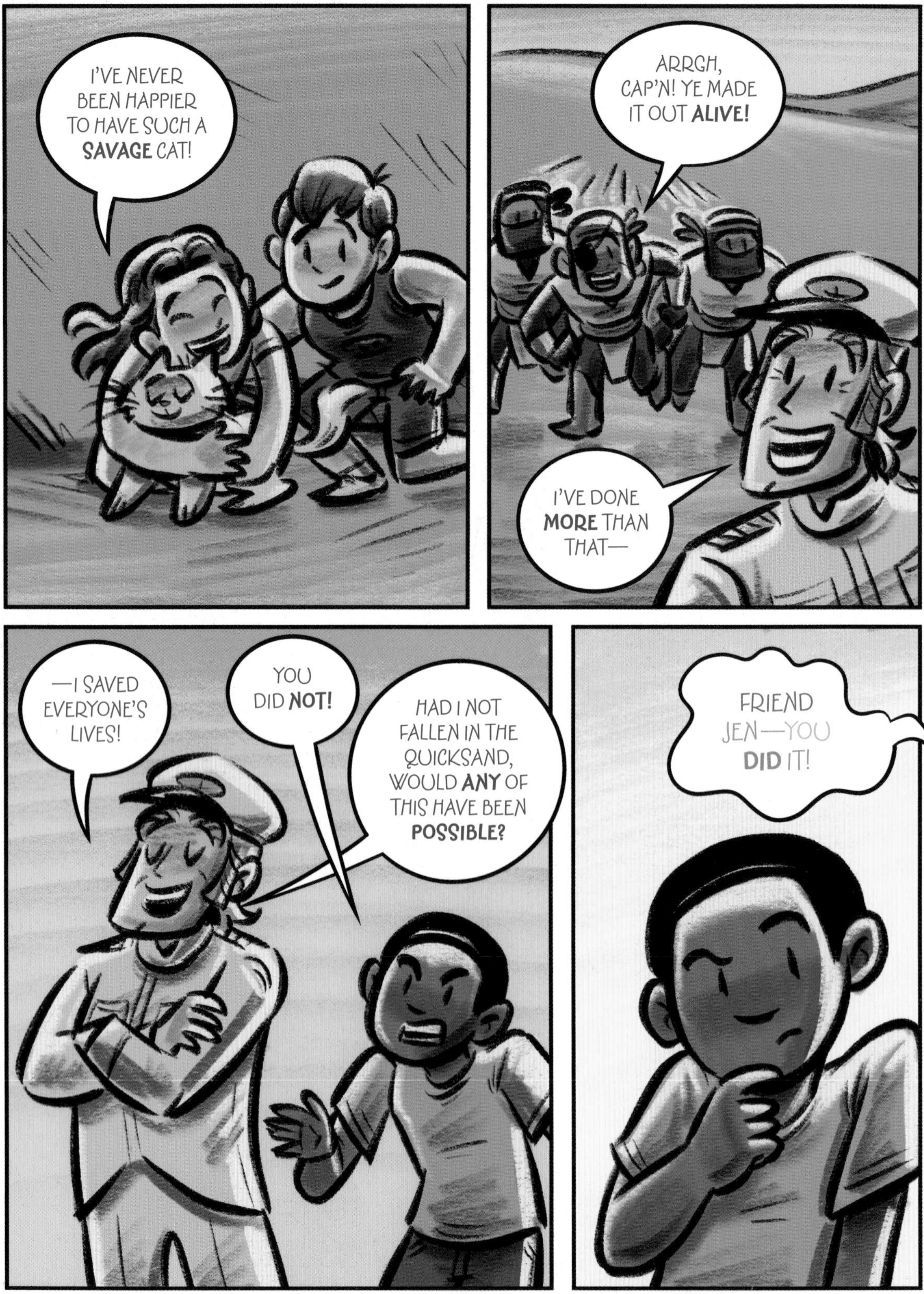
I'VE NEVER BEEN HAPPIER TO HAVE SUCH A **SAVAGE** CAT!
ARRGH, CAP'N! YE MADE IT OUT **ALIVE!**
I'VE DONE **MORE** THAN THAT—
—I SAVED EVERYONE'S LIVES!
YOU DID **NOT!**
HAD I NOT FALLEN IN THE QUICKSAND, WOULD **ANY** OF THIS HAVE BEEN **POSSIBLE?**
FRIEND JEN—YOU **DID** IT!

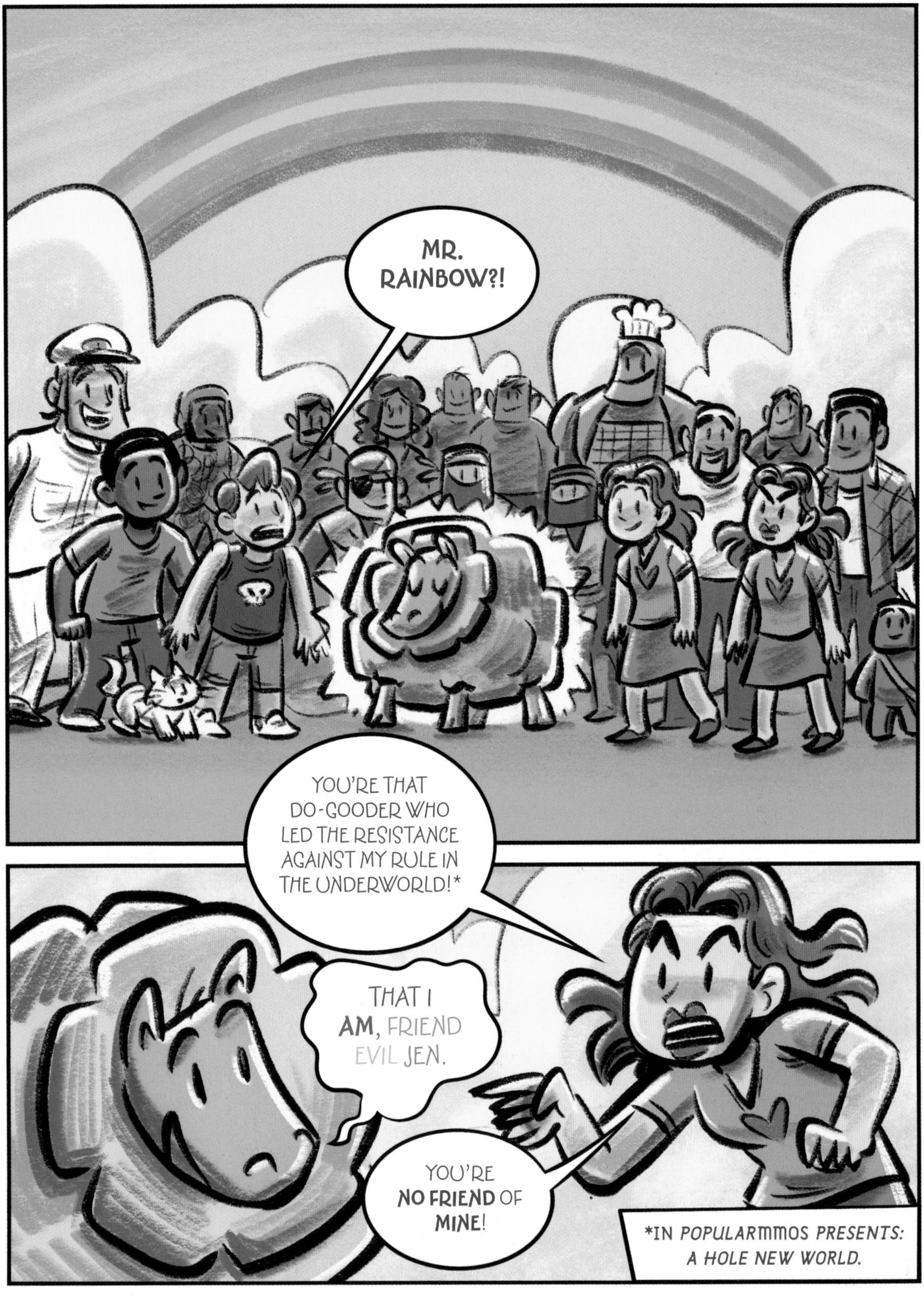
MR. RAINBOW?!
YOU'RE THAT DO-GOODER WHO LED THE RESISTANCE AGAINST MY RULE IN THE UNDERWORLD!*
THAT I AM, FRIEND EVIL JEN.
YOU'RE NO FRIEND OF MINE!
*IN POPULARMMOS PRESENTS: A HOLE NEW WORLD.

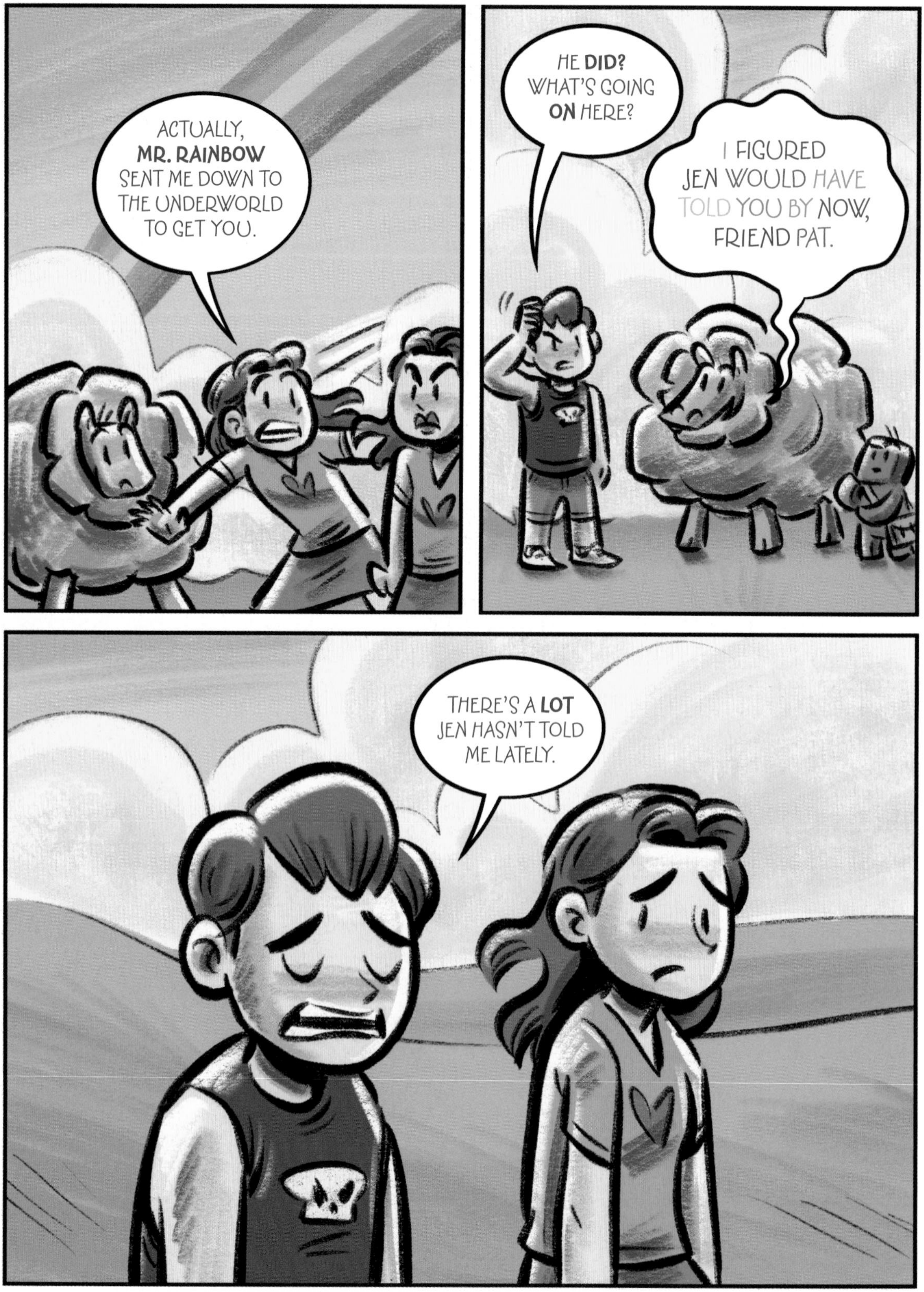
ACTUALLY, MR. RAINBOW SENT ME DOWN TO THE UNDERWORLD TO GET YOU.
HE DID? WHAT'S GOING ON HERE?
I FIGURED JEN WOULD HAVE TOLD YOU BY NOW, FRIEND PAT.
THERE'S A LOT JEN HASN'T TOLD ME LATELY.

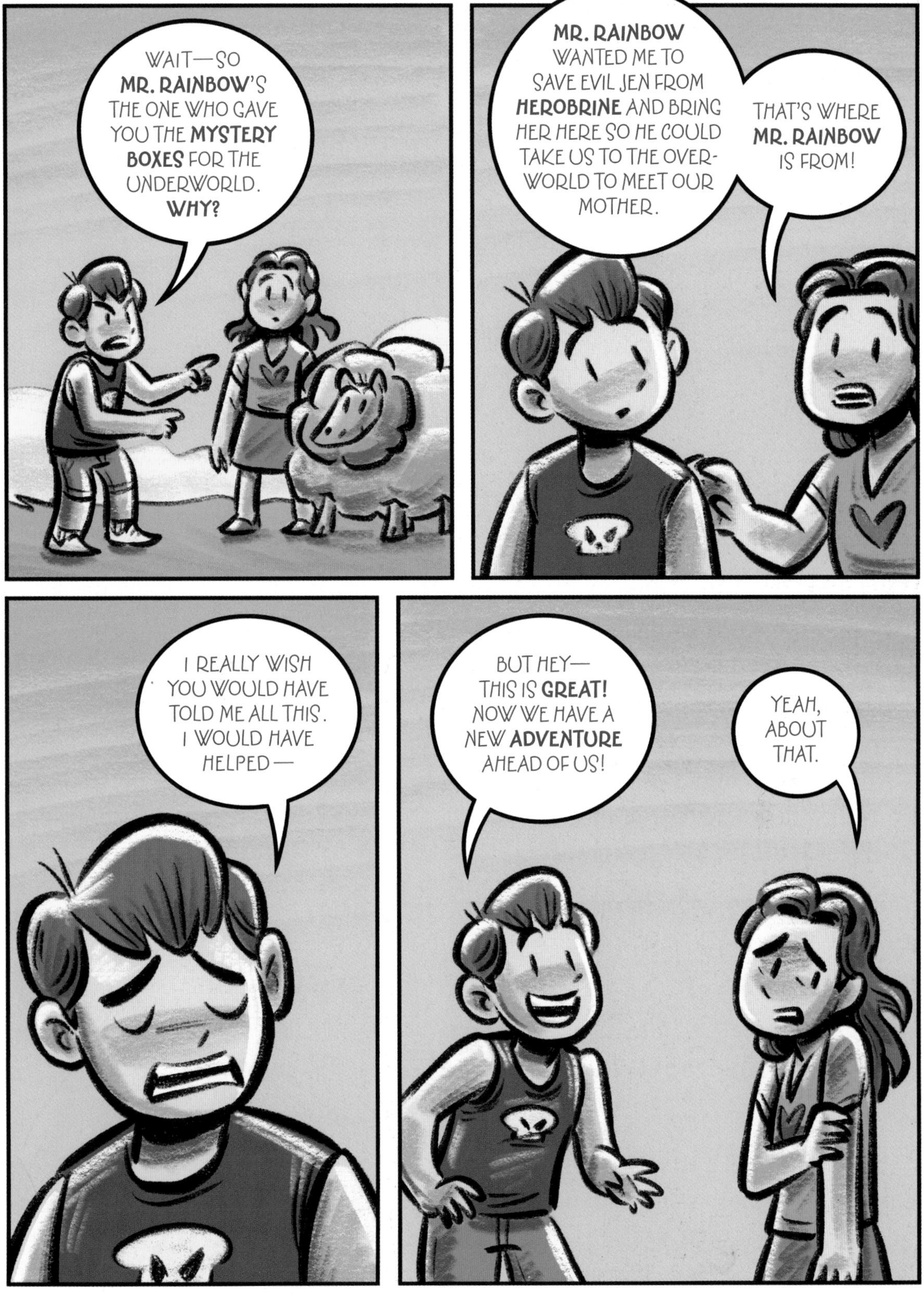

WAIT—SO **MR. RAINBOW**'S THE ONE WHO GAVE YOU THE **MYSTERY BOXES** FOR THE UNDERWORLD. **WHY?**
MR. RAINBOW WANTED ME TO SAVE EVIL JEN FROM **HEROBRINE** AND BRING HER HERE SO HE COULD TAKE US TO THE OVER-WORLD TO MEET OUR MOTHER.
THAT'S WHERE **MR. RAINBOW** IS FROM!
I REALLY WISH YOU WOULD HAVE TOLD ME ALL THIS. I WOULD HAVE HELPED—
BUT HEY—THIS IS **GREAT!** NOW WE HAVE A NEW **ADVENTURE** AHEAD OF US!
YEAH, ABOUT THAT.

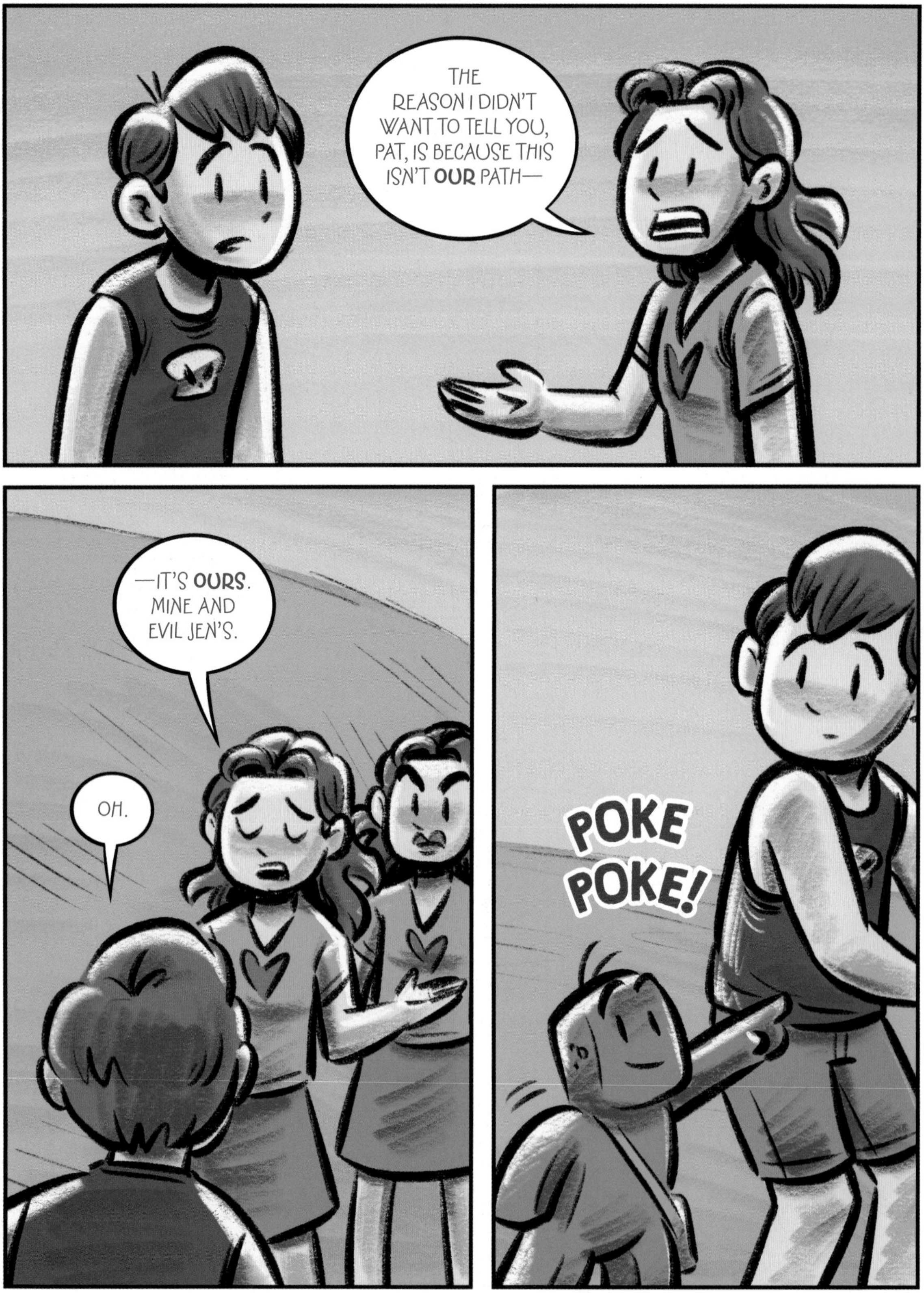
THE REASON I DIDN'T WANT TO TELL YOU, PAT, IS BECAUSE THIS ISN'T **OUR** PATH—
—IT'S **OURS**. MINE AND EVIL JEN'S.
OH.
POKE POKE!

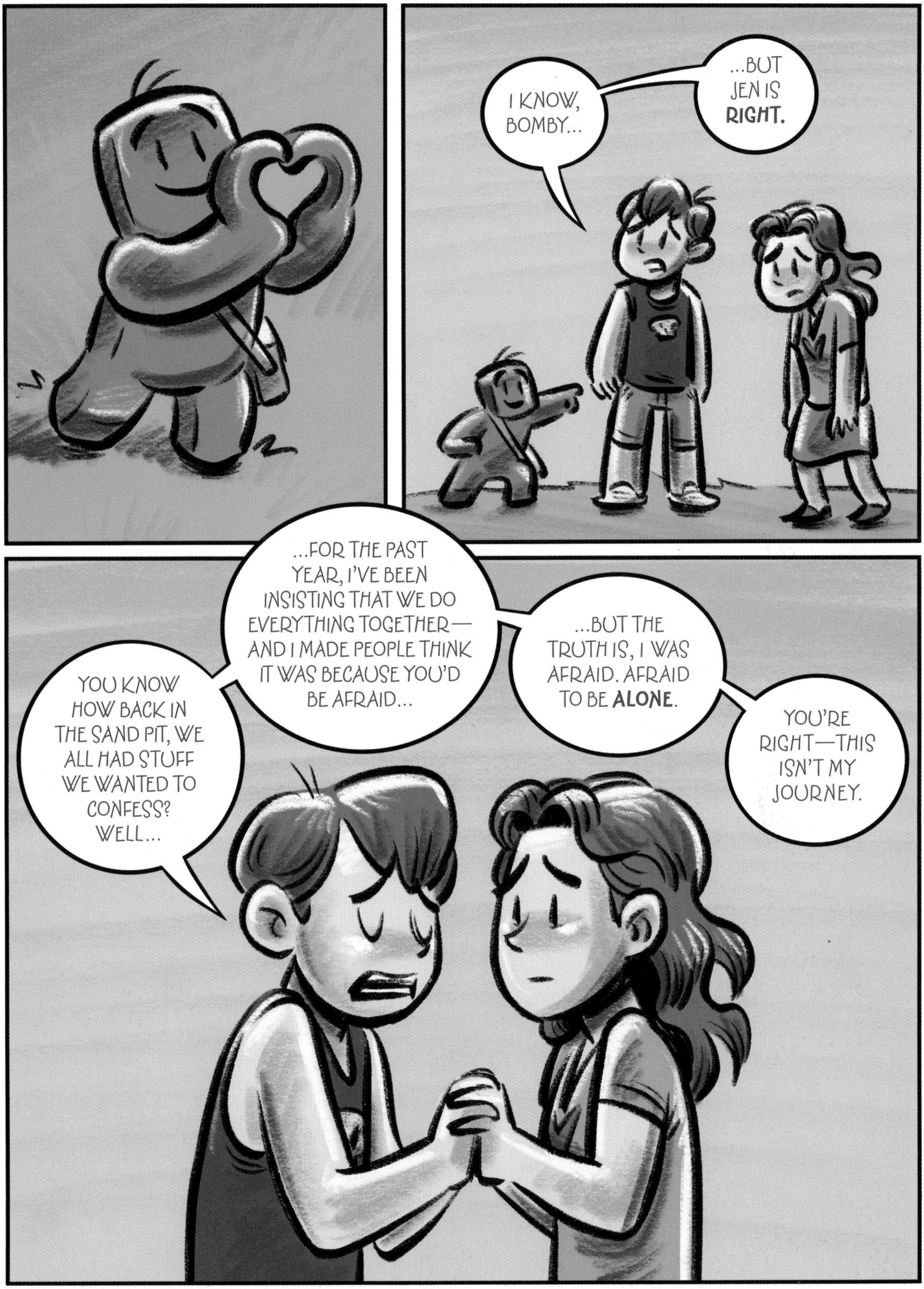
I KNOW, BOMBY...
...BUT JEN IS **RIGHT.**
YOU KNOW HOW BACK IN THE SAND PIT, WE ALL HAD STUFF WE WANTED TO CONFESS? WELL...
...FOR THE PAST YEAR, I'VE BEEN INSISTING THAT WE DO EVERYTHING TOGETHER—AND I MADE PEOPLE THINK IT WAS BECAUSE YOU'D BE AFRAID...
...BUT THE TRUTH IS, I WAS AFRAID. AFRAID TO BE **ALONE**.
YOU'RE RIGHT—THIS ISN'T MY JOURNEY.

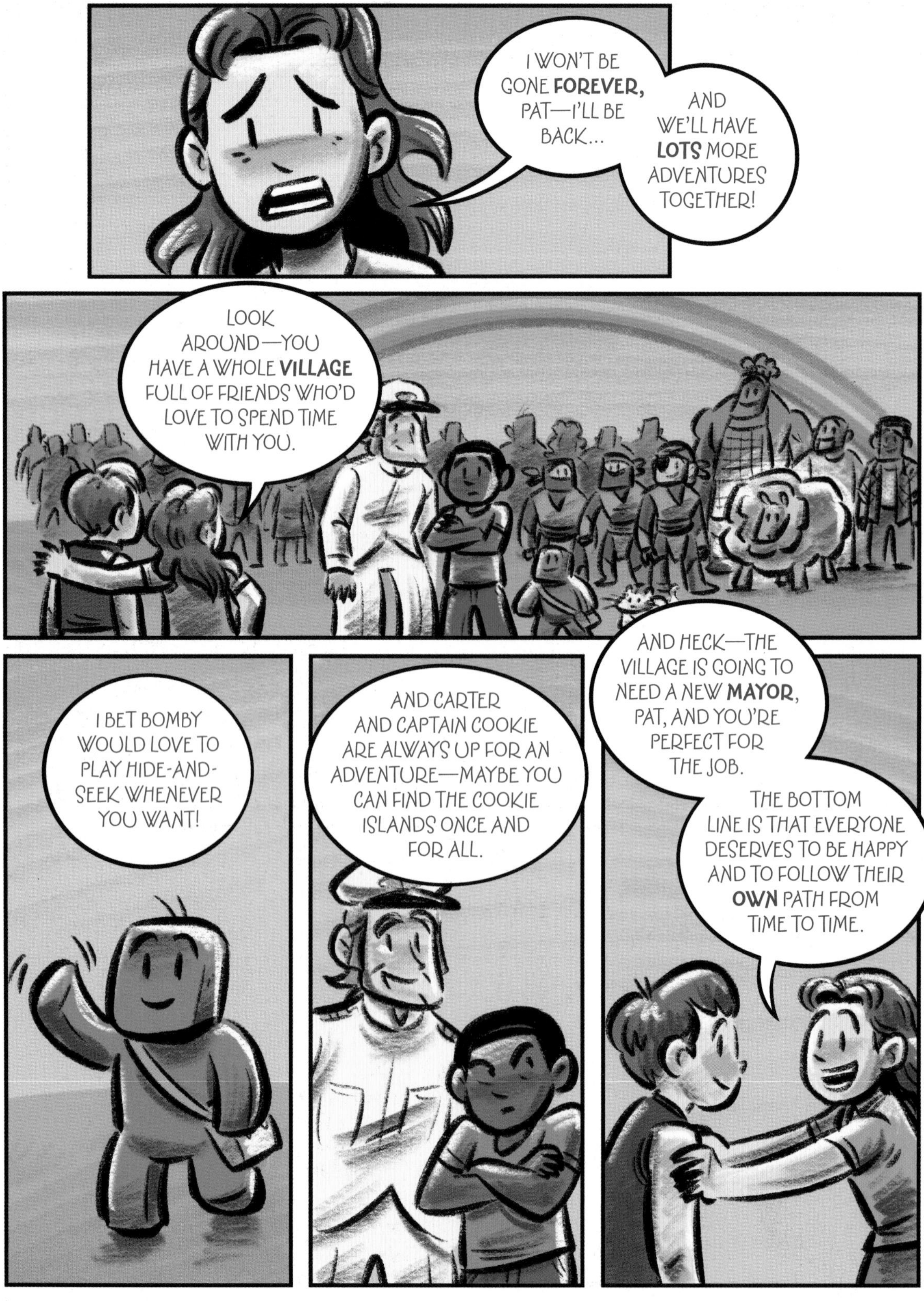
I WON'T BE GONE **FOREVER,** PAT—I'LL BE BACK...
AND WE'LL HAVE **LOTS** MORE ADVENTURES TOGETHER!
LOOK AROUND—YOU HAVE A WHOLE **VILLAGE** FULL OF FRIENDS WHO'D LOVE TO SPEND TIME WITH YOU.
I BET BOMBY WOULD LOVE TO PLAY HIDE-AND-SEEK WHENEVER YOU WANT!
AND CARTER AND CAPTAIN COOKIE ARE ALWAYS UP FOR AN ADVENTURE—MAYBE YOU CAN FIND THE COOKIE ISLANDS ONCE AND FOR ALL.
AND HECK—THE VILLAGE IS GOING TO NEED A NEW **MAYOR**, PAT, AND YOU'RE PERFECT FOR THE JOB.
THE BOTTOM LINE IS THAT EVERYONE DESERVES TO BE HAPPY AND TO FOLLOW THEIR **OWN** PATH FROM TIME TO TIME.

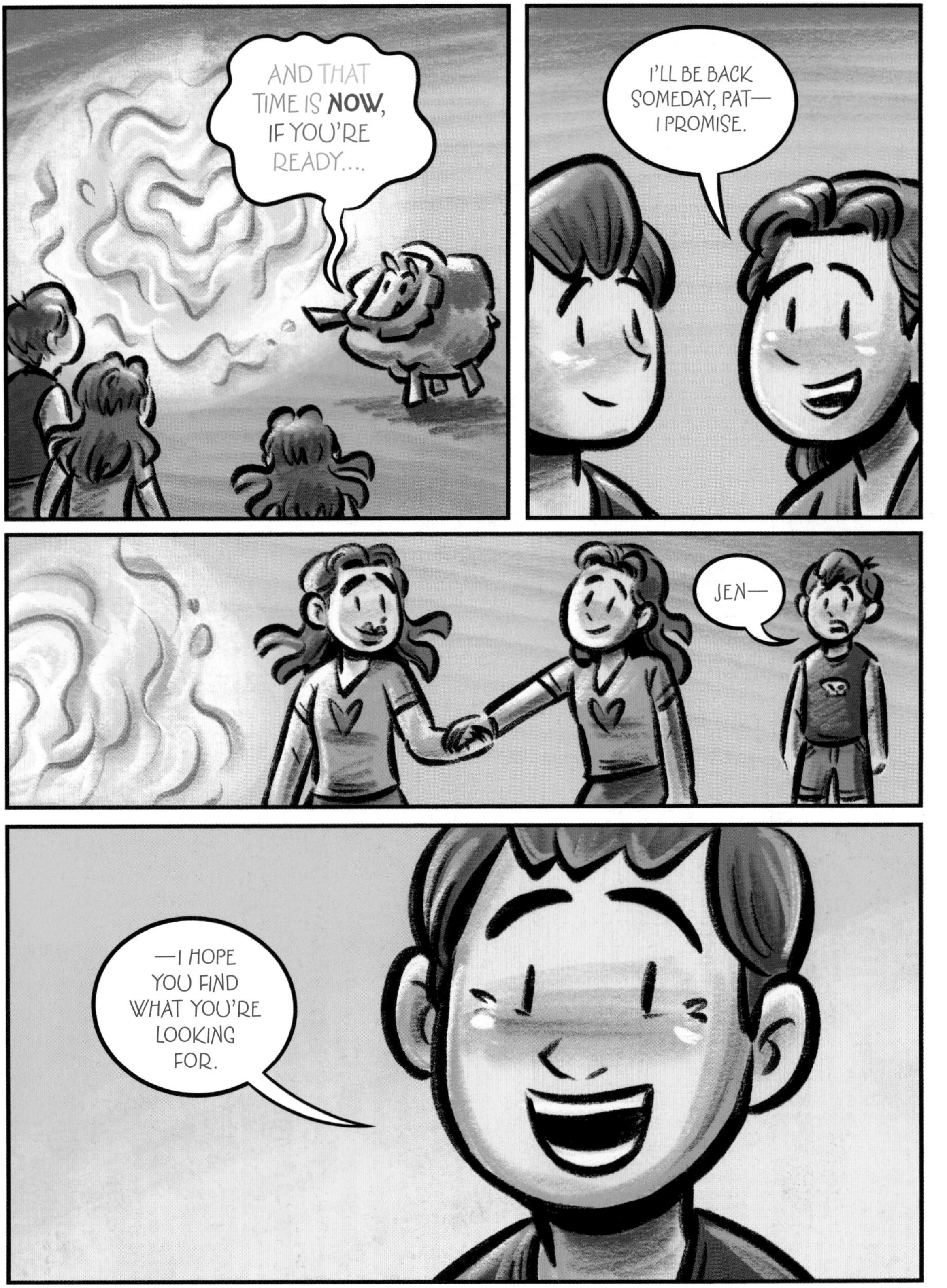
AND THAT TIME IS **NOW**, IF YOU'RE READY....
I'LL BE BACK SOMEDAY, PAT— I PROMISE.
JEN—
—I HOPE YOU FIND WHAT YOU'RE LOOKING FOR.

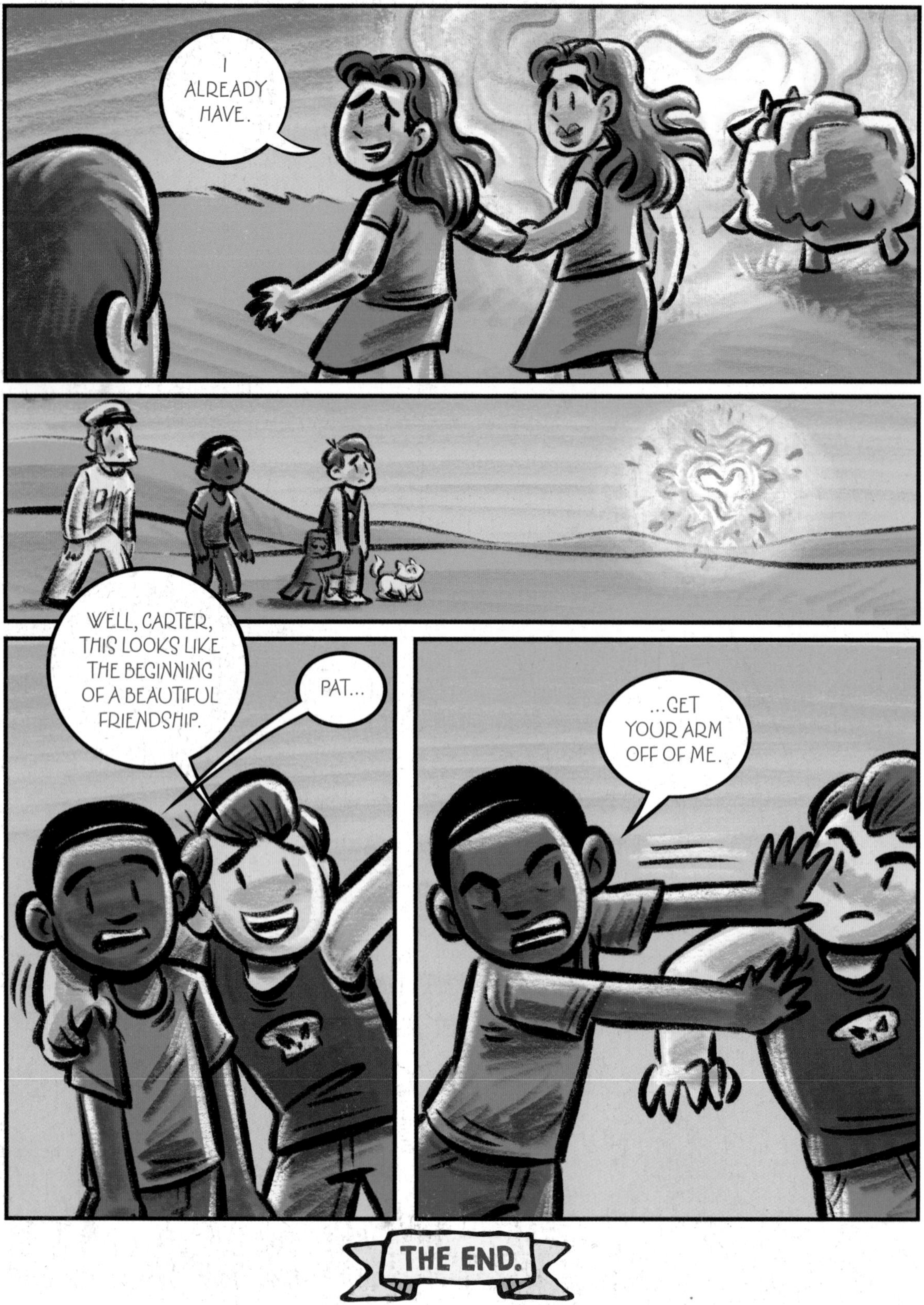
I ALREADY HAVE.
WELL, CARTER, THIS LOOKS LIKE THE BEGINNING OF A BEAUTIFUL FRIENDSHIP.
PAT...
...GET YOUR ARM OFF OF ME.
THE END.